The
Light in
Hidden
Places

SHARON CAMERON's debut novel, *The Dark Unwinding*, was awarded the Society of Children's Book Writers and Illustrators' Sue Alexander Award for Most Promising New Work and the SCB-WI Crystal Kite Award, and was named an ALA Best Fiction for Young Adults selection. Sharon is also the author of its sequel, *A Spark Unseen*; Rook, which was selected as an IndieBound Indie Next Top Ten Pick of the List; *The Forgetting*, a #1 New York Times bestseller and an IndieBound Indie Next List selection; and its companion, *The Knowing*.

She lives with her family in Nashville, Tennessee, and you can follow her on Twitter at @SharonCameronE or visit her website at sharoncameronbooks.com.

Also by Sharon Cameron:

The Forgetting
The Knowing
Rook
The Dark Unwinding
A Spark Unseen

The
Light in
Hidden
Places

A Novel Based on the True Story
of Stefania Podgórska

SHARON CAMERON

EBURY
PRESS

First published in the UK in 2020 by Ebury Press
First published in the US in 2020 by Scholastic Press, an imprint of Scholastic Inc.

1 3 5 7 9 10 8 6 4 2

Ebury Press, an imprint of Ebury Publishing
20 Vauxhall Bridge Road,
London SW1V 2SA

Penguin
Random House
UK

Ebury Press is part of the Penguin Random House group of companies
whose addresses can be found at global.penguinrandomhouse.com

www.penguin.co.uk

A CIP catalogue record for this book is available from the British Library

ISBN 9781529106534

Typeset in 10.22/14.78 pt Bodoni MT Std
by Integra Software Services Pvt. Ltd, Pondicherry

Printed and bound in Great Britain by Clays Ltd, Elcograf S.p.A.

Penguin Random House is committed to a sustainable future for
our business, our readers and our planet. This book is made from
Forest Stewardship Council® certified paper.

MIX
Paper from
responsible sources
FSC® C018179

For Helena, Malgosia, Ed,
Lori, and Mia

IN MEMORY OF
Izaac, Lea, Chaim, Izydor, and Ernestyna Diamant,
and all the Jews and Poles of Przemyśl
who lost their lives to hate

1.

Przemyśl, Poland
November 1942

SOMEONE IS OUT THERE. IN THE DARK.

I open my eyes.

And the dark is the same as always. A blank page. I can smell the cabbage Emilika boiled two floors below us. Feel the sigh beside me that is my sister's sleeping breath. But the dark has also changed. There's an echo inside it. A sound my ears have missed.

Someone is here.

Now I am awake.

I fold back the blanket, quiet, listening, stretching my legs to the floor. A mattress spring pops like a gunshot. My sister breathes, but she doesn't stir.

If someone is here, they are not in this room.

I tiptoe, barefoot, across the boards, and put a finger to the edge of the rug I've nailed over the window. The streetlights glare, hard bits of snow glinting like dust as they fall through the light. But the sidewalk below my building is deserted, the windows across the street rows of dead eyes, dark with curtains and dresses and rugs. Like mine are.

In Przemyśl, light is like a candy poster. And it's not smart to hang signs showing where the sweets are.

I let the rug fall back into place and go to the door, pressing an ear to the wood before I turn the lock. The empty hall outside our room stretches to the other empty rooms of the empty apartment. As it should. Everything is as it should be.

And then a noise shoots through the silence. Louder than a gun. A grenade of fear inside my chest. And I know the sound I have missed.

Someone is knocking on my front door.

They know. They know. They know.

The words beat with my blood.

Another mattress spring pops, and I feel Helena coming up behind me. She doesn't speak. She is six years old and doesn't have to be told that this is not the time for questions.

The knocking comes again, louder, this time with a whisper through the cracks.

"Stefania?"

It's a trick. The Gestapo want me to open the door without a fuss. So they don't have to break it down. So they can give a nice, unblemished apartment to some nice German officer and his law-abiding wife with clean hair and mended stockings.

Maybe this means they will shoot us outside, like Mr. Schwarzer.

The whisper comes again.

"Open the door! Fusia!"

The Gestapo do not know me by that name.

I run for the door, hands out, fingers already searching for the newly repaired lock. I know it isn't him. It can't be him. But I fumble and twist at the lock anyway, then fling open the door. Helena gasps. Or maybe the gasp comes from me. Because the bare bulb hanging in the hallway has shown me that it's not him. It's not who I thought it would be at all.

"Max!" I whisper.

2.

1936

MY LIFE BEFORE PRZEMYŚL WAS FULL OF CHICKENS. AND HORSES. CLEAN air and trees and long brown fields that curved with the hills like patches on a wrinkled blanket. I ran the winding roads to school in the spring and fall, ate rye soup and bread in our steamy kitchen when the snow was too deep. And every Sunday, snow or not, I rode to Mass in the village of Bircza, piled in the back of a hay wagon with brothers and sisters who eventually reached a total of eight. It was a perfect childhood.

And I hated it. The pigsty stank, and so did the outhouse, the refuse pit, and the field workers plowing in the sun. I hated the piles of manure purposely hidden in the grass to spoil my shoes. The redness of my mother's hands after scrubbing the laundry or delivering another woman's baby. And I hated the irritating and incessant *cluck, cluck, cluck* of our chickens. They never stopped. I was sure they never slept. Except for the rooster, who was insane, crowing again and again to the rising moon rather than the sun.

I didn't mind plucking the chickens.

I made my first bid for escape when I was eleven. Mama took me on the mail cart to see two of my grown-up sisters, who had taken jobs in the city. A treat, she'd said, for my birthday, which was the holy week of Easter. We all had our birthdays on Easter,

3

all nine of us, or at least, that's when we celebrated them. Mama didn't have time to remember our real birthdays. Or our real names. I was never Stefania. I was Stefi. Or Stefusia. Or Stefushka. But mostly, just Fusia.

If I had nine children, I wouldn't remember their names, either.

Mama paid the driver of the mail cart, then took my hand in hers. Her skin was rough and scratchy. Mama took good care of me, mostly, and so did my *tata*, when he was alive. They took good care of all of us, but I didn't want to hold her hand.

Sometimes I miss her hands now.

I pulled and squirmed the rest of the way into Przemyśl, and then I forgot all about the embarrassment of hand-holding. Wagons rumbling by on the paving stones, automobile horns bleating like sheep. A train screaming steam into the sky. And the clamor of the farmwives shouting the prices of their goods in the square was so much nicer than chickens. It was music. A brass band. A symphony.

We went shopping in open-air booths and stores with glass-fronted windows. A dress for Mama, shoes for me, and a bonnet for baby Helena. I fingered red silk ribbons and the shiny silver wrapper of a chocolate bar. My sisters gave us an elegant lunch—meaning our meat came from a tin instead of the slaughter shed—on a clean tablecloth in the apartment they shared three stories above the street. Mama was gasping before we got there, but I wanted to run down the stairs just to climb back up them again.

Mama and my sisters sipped tea while I pressed my nose to the window glass, drinking in the comings and goings of the street, and when it was time to go I cried. Begged. Stamped. Threatened and pleaded to be left behind. I would sleep on the floor. I would sleep below the stairs. My sisters wouldn't mind. I would be no

4

trouble. Only I was being nothing but trouble. I was dragged to the mail cart by Mama's rough hands.

It was eighteen months before she let me go back. And this time when I stepped into the noise of Przemyśl, I was nearly thirteen. Older. Wiser. I had outgrown the bust of my dress. And I knew how to play Mama's game. I had a whispered conversation with my sisters, bolstered by the letter I'd sent the month before. I wiped the corners of my mouth after lunch, crossed my legs, drank the tea, and listened while Mama talked. And when it was almost time to catch our cart, I told her I wouldn't be catching it.

Mama begged. She pleaded. She even cried a little. She did not stamp her foot. I told her that Marysia had a job for me. "It's true, Mama," said Marysia. "Mrs. Diamant has been looking for a girl. Just a few blocks away." That Angia had made up a cot behind the sofa. "Two blankets, Mama. And Mass every week," Angia said. I explained how I would give part of my wages to my sisters so they could feed me. How I would send even more back home to the farm so Mama could pay another farmhand. Or buy more chickens. "Wouldn't that be such a help, Mama?" Marysia smiled.

"But, Fusia, what about your education?" dithered my mother. I smoothed my dress. "Przemyśl will be my education, Mama." She got on the mail cart without me.

I skipped to my first day of work at the Diamants' shop, putting the pigeons to flight, peeking in little alleys that tunneled between the buildings, staring in the window of a photography studio, and playing with a wandering cat. The cathedral bells rang across a sky that was a deep, perfect blue.

When I pushed open the door to the shop, a much smaller bell tinkled, and a woman looked up from her perch behind a counter.

The air smelled like fresh bread, apples, parcel paper, and string, and I saw rows and rows of wrapped chocolates living behind glass. The woman looked me up and down while I bounced on my toes. Her bottom hung over both sides of her chair.

"So," she said. "Look at what the sunshine has brought to me. You are the Podgórska girl. What is your name, my *ketzele*?"

"Stefania." I thrilled at the sound of my real name.

"And I am Mrs. Diamant. Do you read, Stefania?"

"Yes, Mrs. Diamant."

"Do you write?"

I nodded. The farm wasn't that far away from the rest of the world.

"Good. Very good. Then you will please make a count of the items on my shelves."

I stowed my coat and my lunch of bread and cheese in a corner behind the counter, and Mrs. Diamant handed me paper clipped to a board, a little stub of a pencil tied to one end. My shoes made a sharp *clip, clip* across the creaking floor, which sounded important and made me smile. I wrote the inventory in big, clear strokes. Mrs. Diamant worked rows of numbers in her book, observing, and when I scooted over a bottle of soda water, there were two brown eyes staring at me from the other side of the shelves.

"Do you always sing while you count?" a voice said. A boy's voice. A deep one.

I clutched my clipboard to my chest and flushed. I had been singing. To myself. Like a little girl.

I was a little girl. I just didn't know it yet.

The eyes crinkled between the water bottles, and then they were gone. And then they were above the shelves, peering over the top. A tall boy, still thin from growing, two dark brows reaching for a mess of black and curling hair. He grinned.

"Don't stop now," he said. "You're my morning entertainment. What's your name?"

"Stefania."

He cocked his head. "Nobody calls you that, do they?"

They didn't.

"So what do they call you? Stefi?"

"Stefushka."

He waited.

"And Stefusia," I added. "And Fusia. But I'd rather be called—"

"Stefi, Stefushka, Stefusia, Fusia." The boy shook his head. "Too late. It's Fusia. Sing me another song, Fusia. *Mame* might start selling tickets …"

"Izio!" shouted Mrs. Diamant from her chair. "Leave the child alone, *bubbala*. It is her first day. *Nemen deyn tukis tsu shule.*"

"*Mame …*"

"Go to school!"

He shrugged and ran off, joining two more boys waiting for him at the shop door. One was taller and one was shorter, but they had the same dark hair. And all three were older than me.

Brothers, I thought. I knew brothers. With brothers, it was best to give as good as you got.

I turned back to my work, made a check mark on my paper, and at full voice, began singing a tango that my mama switched off every time it came on the radio. Which of course meant I listened to it every time I could.

Your words send me into the storm clouds,
Your laughter is a cold and wet spell …

I felt the room go tense with anticipation.

I don't want your windy words. I don't want
your dripping laughter.
I just want you to go to ...

Only I didn't say the next word of the lyrics. I inserted the word "school" instead. Laughter burst out from behind my back, and I held in my smile while arms jostled one another and feet ran out the door, setting the shop bell tinkling. When I snuck a look at Mrs. Diamant, she was shaking her head, but her eyes were crinkly, just like her son's.

And that became our ritual. Every morning, Izydor Diamant, more often known as Izio, would stick his head in the shop and say, "Sing to me, Fusia!" and I would make up a rude song that told him to go away. Within a week, everyone on Mickiewicza Street called me Fusia.

I learned the other brothers' names. Henek, the youngest, who had no time for me, and Max, the next step up from Izio, who had already started an apprenticeship and smiled more often than he talked. There was another brother, Chaim, a physician studying in a town in Italy I'd never heard of; a sister not far away in Lwów; and Mr. Diamant, who stayed at home, recuperating from something that had to do with his blood. I learned that I would not work on Saturdays because the Diamants were Jewish and that Mrs. Diamant made excellent *babka*.

I swept the floors and wrapped parcels and dusted the shelves, and Mrs. Diamant said I was a quick learner. Before long, she was sending me on errands to the market square, where the real business was done, and it was there that I saw my first fight. Two boys pummeling each other into the late summer dirt of the street gutter.

This was not like the match-flare temper of my brothers or the boys at my school in Bircza. This was something ugly.

A policeman squashed his cigarette on the sidewalk, watching, and then a man with dirty pants and a smear of grease on his cheek broke through the circle of observers and pulled the two boys apart by their shirt collars, both of them still hissing and spitting like cats. He shook the one in his right hand until I thought I heard teeth rattle.

"What is wrong with you, Oskar?" the man said. "Why are you fighting in the street like a criminal?"

"He hit me!" Oskar managed.

"Oh, ho, he hit you, did he? He hit you for nothing?" The man looked to the other boy, and so did the crowd.

The boy picked up his hat and wiped the blood from his nose. "He called me a dirty Jew."

The man shook his head, then shook Oskar again. "What is the matter with you? Look at this boy ..." If Oskar could look, it was with his eyes crossed. "He has arms and legs and blood in his veins. What do you care if his family follows Moses? Now, shake this boy's hand. Do it! Before I tell your mama."

The boys shook hands, though they didn't look as if they wanted to, and when they parted ways and the crowd began to melt, I heard a woman behind me mutter, "Dirty Jew."

I got a good bargain on plums for Mrs. Diamant. And when I ran back to the shop, I slipped through the door to the toilet and stood there, looking in the mirror. I touched my face, the skin of my arm, and my brown hair. People hated that boy because he was a Jew. Could the Diamants hate me because I was a Catholic?

That afternoon, I coaxed Mrs. Diamant down from her chair and into the exercises I'd seen the students doing outside the gymnasium. Some of the pretty wrapped chocolates went toppling from the shelves to the floor, and Mrs. Diamant laughed and laughed, mopping between the folds of her neck.

"Sometimes, my *ketzele*"—I had discovered this meant "little kitten"—"the sunshine you bring is hot!" Then she handed me a chocolate, her soft face dimpling as she unwrapped another for herself.

And suddenly I knew that Mrs. Diamant had been lonely before I came to the shop, and that she wasn't lonely anymore. That I had been lonely on the farm, surrounded by brothers and sisters with lives of their own, a mother with too many cares, and a pen full of chickens. And I wasn't lonely anymore, either.

That Sunday, at Mass with Angia, I thanked God for the Diamants. Moses was in my Bible, too, after all, and I felt certain that God had liked him.

My education had begun.

Izio taught me rude songs in Yiddish, and I decided not to bring tinned-ham sandwiches to the shop, even though Mrs. Diamant said she didn't mind. When the winter blew in and the dark came early, I ate my suppers around the corner in the Diamants' apartment, full of mostly grown boys talking medicine and Mr. Diamant asking questions like, "Which is better? A good war or a bad peace?" And we would listen to their arguments while Mr. Diamant sat back and smoked cigarette after cigarette. Izio would walk me home on those nights, in deep, cold snow lit golden by the streetlights.

Mrs. Diamant did her exercises with me every morning. She had to take in her dresses. I had to let mine out. I learned how to smile at a boy so he would buy two chocolates instead of one, and to smile even prettier when he put the second chocolate into my hand. Then, as soon as the shop bell tinkled, I would slip the chocolate back into the display, the coins into the register, and this made Mrs. Diamant chuckle. I pinned my hair into curls and borrowed my sister's lip rouge, humming while the radio blared the news that Germany had invaded Czechoslovakia. And when Angia went to Kraków and Marysia wanted to take an apartment on the far side of the city, Mrs. Diamant just clicked her tongue, crinkled her eyes, and said, "So you will live with us, my *ketzele*."

The Diamants did not have an extra room in their apartment. So they made me one, at the end of the hallway, with a cot and table with a lamp on it, a mirror hung above that, and a maroon curtain strung from wall to wall for privacy. I propped my picture of Christ and the Virgin on one wall and hung my rosary on the bedpost, and Mrs. Diamant kept a secret stash of blintzes under my bed, because Mr. Diamant didn't eat during Yom Kippur. It was a soft red lair in the lamplight.

But there was no window in my lair. And so when the nights were hot, I crept out to the living room, where the window stayed open, letting out the stale smoke. I sat on the sill with the lights switched off, bare feet wedged against the frame, listening to the trains coming and going at the station, a sleepy apartment on one side, a long, dark drop into the city on the other.

I didn't know, then, that fear comes with the dark.

Izio would come to me at the windowsill, sprawling in a chair or hands behind his head on the rug. He whispered about his new university classes, the parts of the world he most wanted to see (Palestine and Turkey), the parts of the world I most wanted to see (America). And he wanted to know my opinion on things, like if I thought Hitler would invade Poland. But wars were not the first, second, or even third thoughts in my mind on those nights. Izio had turned eighteen. He'd filled in. Grown up. And his eyelashes curled like soot smudged against his lids.

Max came to the windowsill, too, sometimes, that very last summer. He was smaller and quieter than his brother, but when he did talk, he made you think long, serious thoughts about your life. Or told jokes so terrible it made your ribs hurt. Izio wrapped his arms around his middle, trying to hold in the laughter so he wouldn't wake his mother.

I loved it when Max made Izio laugh.

But after a while, Max didn't come to the window anymore. It was just Izio and me while the rest of the world slept.

I think Max knew before I did.

Summer cooled to the final autumn, and when the leaves blew yellow past the windowsill and the air smelled like coal smoke, Izio reached out and held my hand in the dark. We promised not to tell a soul. And two weeks after that, the first German bombs fell on Przemyśl.

3.

September 1939

I THOUGHT THE PLANES WERE RUSSIAN AT FIRST, FLYING SO LOW THAT Marysia's dishes rattled. It was the first day of school, and the sidewalks were full of children with books and satchels, on their way home from a half day. I was leaning out the window of my sister's new apartment, on the far side of the river San, waiting for her to come and have lunch with me. I shielded my eyes from the sun. The planes were leaving long black streaks across the sky. And then the hotel on the corner exploded in a cloud of mortar dust and fire.

I screamed. Everyone screamed. The children in the streets ran, and the apartment building shook. I slammed the window shut against the noise and heard more explosions in the distance, a billow of smoke rising up over the city. Something whistled and boomed, and the building quaked, knocking me to my knees. Marysia's picture of the Virgin fell off the wall. I crawled across the floor of the apartment, and when I threw open the door, the smoke was so thick I had to shut it again. The stairs were on fire. And I was on the third floor.

For the first time in years, I wanted my mother.

And then I thought of our farmhouse, and the long banister to one side of the stairs. Of Olga and Angia squealing as they slid down it, racing each other's time to the bottom with *Tata*'s old pocket watch. I snatched a wool blanket from Marysia's bed, wrapped it around me so that it doubled across my front, took a deep breath, and ran straight into the heat of the burning stairs.

I slid down the flaming banister, holding tight with my blanketed elbows and legs, the wool clenched together with my teeth. Third floor to second floor, second floor to first, heat scorching my eyes and my throat, then the first floor to the cool damp of the basement, where I coughed and choked and stomped out the blanket edges that had caught on fire.

A group of people sat huddled in the dim corner. They seemed surprised to see me. I peered at them with streaming eyes.

"Don't you know the building is on fire?" I yelled.

We scattered like rats into the debris-filled street, and I could barely recognize where I was. The air was full of dust, smoke, and panic. People were crying out. For help. From pain. Not just one but dozens of them, from all directions. The building across the street from Marysia's had been sheared down the middle like someone had cut a cake, a bed hanging from one layer, perfectly balanced, and at the very top, a man dangling from a beam, his legs kicking this way and that. A plane rumbled past him, whining overhead, explosions and an ambulance bell ringing in the distance.

And then a hand moved inside the rubble at my feet.

I dug the man out, a gray and bloody ghost beneath fallen bricks. Before I could even ask his name, he staggered away, murmuring something about his wife and the Germans. I ran home. Not to the farm, but to the next best thing, sprinting over the bridge across the river, thinking halfway what a good target a bridge would be for a bomb. I darted through the tunnel alley that ran between the buildings at Mickiewicza 7, into the courtyard, and as soon as my feet crossed the threshold of the Diamants' apartment building, Izio was there, half pulling, half carrying me to the cellar.

Max was already belowground. Mr. and Mrs. Diamant, Henek, as well as Chaim, who was only a month back from Italy, sat beside him in the dirt along with every neighbor we'd ever known. Mrs. Diamant opened her arms, and I went to them, Izio settling in on my other side.

"You're burned," he said, pointing at my wrist. I hadn't noticed. He held my blistered hand in the shadows, where his mother couldn't see.

Tanks shook the streets above our heads, but I felt safe anyway.

Someone had brought a battery-powered radio, and we listened to President Mościcki tell the young men of Poland to rally in Lwów. To never become soldiers of Germany. To go to Russia if they had to. The Diamant men had a whispered conversation. It might have been a conversation they'd had before. Within fifteen minutes, the four boys had kissed their mother and were on the road to Lwów with the clothes on their backs and a little bread in their pockets.

My burned hand still felt warm from Izio's.

Mrs. Diamant put her head in her hands and cried, and I hugged her and stroked her hair. She was mine now. My old lady. My *babcia*.

Mr. Diamant shook his head. *"Di velt iz sheyn nor di mentshn makhn zi mies,"* he said. "The world is beautiful, but people make it ugly."

15

It was a long time before I realized that the Diamant brothers had not run because President Mościcki told them to. They'd run because they were Jews.

We sat in the cellar for a week, listening to the Russians arrive and to the babies cry and to gunfire that went from the rooftops to the streets. Once a day someone risked their life to run upstairs for food and water and kerosene for the lamp. And when the guns fell silent and the tanks went quiet and we dared to come creeping out of our hole, Przemyśl was a divided city. My sister's side of the San was German. Our side was Russian.

Hitler's war had crawled right to our riverbank.

And stopped.

So we buried the dead, shoveled the rubble, replaced the glass, and I scrubbed the dust from the shop. There were holes in the streets now, places where buildings had been, empty like pulled teeth. Russian soldiers patrolled the main roads and the train station, and the Jews of German-held West Przemyśl were expelled across the river. The bridge had been bombed after all, so we watched them come in line after line over the railroad bridge, the smoke of the burning synagogue still rising black behind them.

The Jewish neighborhoods became crowded, and the room that had once belonged to Chaim and Max was assigned by the housing department to Regina and Rosa, two German Jewish women who had already fled Hitler once and were not made sweeter by their second experience. They looked at their new room—a little apartment in itself with a small sink and stove—shut the door, and didn't speak to us. And since our part of Przemyśl was practically in Russia anyway, the Diamant brothers came back from Lwów.

"Have you seen your sister?" asked Mrs. Diamant. "How is my Ernestyna?"

"No one has seen her, *Mame*," said Chaim. "Not since the bombs."

I watched my *babcia*'s round face carefully, but it only fell for a moment. "She has gone somewhere safe then," said Mrs. Diamant. "To my cousins, or your *tate*'s sister in Vienna. We will get a letter when the mail begins to come again." And she went back to stirring a huge pot of soup. Max caught my eye and shook his head. Their sister could not be in Vienna.

I'd heard rumors in the street. Whispers that while we were in the cellar a hundred Jews, old men and little boys, had been run all over Przemyśl, right up Mickiewicza Street, German soldiers beating them if they fell. And when no one could run anymore, they'd been taken to the cemetery and shot.

But I didn't listen to rumors. I didn't believe them. No one would do that. And the bombs had left plenty of fresh graves in the cemetery.

I didn't want to believe, and that made the lying easy.

I worked with Mrs. Diamant in the shop. Mr. Diamant's health improved, and he baked bread two days a week in a cafeteria. Chaim got a job in the city hospital, and during the week, Max traveled four kilometers south to be a dental assistant in the village of Nizankowice. Henek and Izio went back to school.

Izio was the same as he'd always been. Only he was different, too. He came by the shop in the mornings. I sang him questionable songs. He taught me insults in German as well as Yiddish, in case Hitler's armies crossed the river, and at night we danced in front of the open window to the orchestra playing in the restaurant across the street. He told me most things. But not everything. He started smoking. I asked Max once what they had seen on the road to Lwów, and he only said, "Blood." I didn't ask any more after that.

I got a letter from my mother when the mail started running again. She was safe at the farm with my younger brother and sister, while my older siblings were scattered over Poland. Mrs. Diamant did not get a letter, though she looked every day. I bought a pair of heels, went to the cinema, and sat with Izio at night, breathing his smoke while German lights twinkled on the other side of the river.

The spring I turned sixteen, Mrs. Diamant began sending me to the monthly shop owners' meetings. The walk across town was tiring for her, the Russian requirements silly, and I only had to sit near the back, reply "here" when Leah Diamant's name was called, and report anything I heard that might be important. The third time I went to the meeting, I was late. It's possible that I had been stopped in the market by a box of cheap stockings. I was trying not to let the door bang shut behind me when I heard the man on the stage say, "Leah Diamant?"

"Here!" I called, and an auditorium of middle-aged men and one or two women turned as one in their seats. A little titter of conversation began. What a young girl to be running her own business. So ambitious! This Miss Diamant is just what our city needs. Someone clapped, others joined, and the whole room echoed. I sat in the first empty seat I came to, red-faced, deter-mined to look only at the man on the stage, hear what he had to say, and run back home to my little lair behind the curtain.

"Good for you!" whispered a voice in my ear.

I glanced sideways. Beside me was a young man with spots on his chin that must have been difficult to shave around.

"Have you been running your shop for long?"

"No," I muttered. His breath was hot on my cheek.

"Did you inherit from your parents?"

I didn't answer. I stared at the man on the stage like he was the only interesting thing in the world.

"My parents have a butcher shop," the boy breathed. "But it's mine now. Just to run, of course. I employ the butchers. Three of them. No dirty hands here, angel. What's your address?"

I turned my head. "Is your mouth always open, or are you able to shut it?"

He wasn't able. And it didn't take him long to find my address, either, because he was in the shop the next day. So were many people from the meeting, to see the young business-woman, and we sold half our inventory in an afternoon. Mrs. Diamant nodded and smiled when asked if I was her daughter, elbowed me to do the same, and whispered that she wished I could go to a shop owners' meeting twice a week. The spotty young man bought half a kilo of apples and some soda water, said his name was Zbyszek Kurowski, and asked me to eat with him in a restaurant.

I said no. He came back the next day and asked again. I gave him more of the same with extra vinegar. He said he had a row of girls waiting for him, that all he had to do was snap his fingers. I told him that was good, to go snap them and hurry up about it. He left with a storm on his face, and I was glad to be done with him.

But three days later, when the shop was so full that Izio had come to help after classes, I saw Izio grinning at me, eyes crinkled, pointing over a Russian soldier's head toward the door. And there was Zbyszek, this time with an older-looking man and a lady. The lady wore gloves, an orange fur collar turned high around her ears. I finished tying the string on a parcel, and she approached my counter, introduced herself as Mrs. Kurowski, and asked for a dozen cream pastries. I got them, and she requested a bar of chocolate with almonds and two kilos of apples. And while I weighed out the apples and wrapped her packages, she asked me questions. How many hours did I work? How often was I sick? Did I keep a bank account? Where did I buy my clothes?

Zbyszek stood next to his father, hands behind his back, studying the ceiling, and I could see that Mrs. Diamant and Izio had both sidled nearer, listening while pretending not to. I handed the woman her parcels and felt my face growing hot.

"Miss Podgórska," Mrs. Kurowski pronounced. "You seem a good and agile worker and very pleasant to talk to. I think you would make a very nice addition to our home."

For two seconds, I thought the woman was trying to hire me as her maid. But one look at the male Kurowskis corrected my thinking. Most of the store was listening now, and Izio was biting his lip, trying to hide his smile.

"Thank you," I said stiffly, "but I don't think I—"

"And such a good family," she went on, raising her voice. "Catholic farmers. From Bircza. Not too high, and not too low." She leaned in. "What doctor did you see there, Miss Podgórska?"

"Magda," Mr. Kurowski said, tugging on his wife's sleeve. She waved him off.

"Go and be quiet somewhere, Gustov. This is women's talk. You—"

"Excuse me," I interrupted. "But how do you know my family? I have never spoken to your son about—"

"Ah!" Mrs. Kurowski looked around, pleased with her audience. "As soon as my Zbyszek told me he had found a girl he liked, I hired a detective. You should do the same, Miss Podgórska. It's best to have everything honest, don't you agree? But I can tell you right away that my son is a good boy. He does not smoke. He does not drink. He has good prospects and no illnesses. Everything that is good for a marriage. And you should marry soon, Miss Podgórska, before someone unworthy comes along and corrupts you."

I really didn't know what to say.

"But we can discuss everything more over dinner."

I shook my head. "No."

"When do you finish your work?"

"No!"

Mrs. Kurowski looked confused.

"I am not interested in marriage, and I am especially not interested in marriage to your son! Goodbye and ... thank you for coming."

The woman stepped back with her parcels, a hand to her fur collar, and Zbyszek took her place at the counter. He winked.

"No need to be rude," he said. "It's a good offer. Everything my mother said is true. My parents just want to look you over, you know, just in case you—"

"I am not a piece of cloth to be examined before you buy it!" I snapped.

Every customer in the shop had stopped to watch by now. Even the Russian soldier, and he couldn't speak Polish.

"You ..." My gaze took in the three Kurowskis. "You can all just ... *geyn in drerd*!"

21

Half the shop sucked in a breath. I'd just told the Kurowskis to go to the devil. In Yiddish. A skill that was 100 percent Izio's fault.

Mrs. Kurowski turned on a heel and thrust open the door, her husband close behind her, but Zbyszek only grinned.

"You're so arrogant," he said. "I like it. I'll see you soon, angel." And he blew me a kiss before the door shut behind him.

The shop was as silent as I'd ever heard it. Then my *babcia* laughed so hard she nearly fell out of her chair. The whole shop laughed, and after a few minutes, I was laughing with them. Izio laughed, too, but he was thoughtful.

And he was still thoughtful that night at the windowsill, his head on a cushion, feet propped up on his mother's sofa, smoking in the dark. We'd been talking about my dislike of chickens, other than on a plate, the difference between the German *"Nichnut"* and Yiddish *"nudnik"* (there wasn't one), and whether the Russians would ever get that statue put up in the square, or just keep letting children climb on Lenin's head. But it was late now, and Izio was quiet. Thinking. He was like that sometimes. I was thinking the glow of his cigarette made him look mysterious.

Then he said, "Fusia, I have three more years of medical school. And when that's done, Chaim thinks he will be able to get me a job at the hospital. Unless ..."

He meant unless the Germans came. But the Germans weren't coming. Hitler had an agreement with Stalin. "The Germans have lost one war," Mr. Diamant liked saying. "And Russia, she is a big country ..."

"But if the Germans do come," Izio said, blowing smoke, "Chaim and Max and Henek and me, we will have to run again."

"But why?" Running hadn't worked the last time.

Izio sat up. "Haven't you been listening? Or have you closed up your ears? You know what the Nazis are doing to the Jews."

"But those are only stories ..."

"They are true stories, Stefania."

I frowned and looked out the window, stung by the use of my full name. The sharp clap of Russian boots passed and faded on the sidewalk.

Izio went on. "So it could be a long time before I'm able to get my diploma and then a job good enough to support a wife. Three or four years. Maybe five. But I've been wondering, Fusia, if maybe you would wait for that."

I squinted into the darkened living room, but Izio had put out his cigarette and I couldn't see his face. "You want me to wait for your wife?"

"No, you *Dummkopf*." He sighed. "I'm asking you to marry me."

I swung my feet from the sill to the fringes of the rug.

"You're not going to tell me to go to the devil, are you?" he asked. "Or sing me a tango?"

I couldn't even think what a tango sounded like.

"You're not going to fall out the window?"

Actually, I was in danger of falling out the window. I stood, surprised to find my knees were shaky, and Izio got up from the floor. He took both my hands in his.

"Three years," he said. "Probably more. Will you wait for me?"

"But what will your parents say?" I was thinking of the synagogue on Saturday and a cathedral on Sunday. What would mine say?

"You're already one of the family. You know that. But maybe it will be our secret. For now."

Like it always had been. He touched my hair. "Stefania, Stefi, Stefushka, Stefusia, Fusia Podgórska," he whispered. "Will you wait for me?"

And then I kissed Izydor Diamant. I kissed him for a long time. And a month after that, German bombs fell again on Przemyśl.

4.

June 1941

THIS TIME THE EXPLOSIONS CAME DURING THE DEEP SLEEP BEFORE THE dawn. But I knew exactly what they were. I came out from behind my curtain, and Max grabbed my hand and his mother's, pulling us into a stampede of people in nightclothes making their way down the shaking steps to the cellar of the apartment building. Chaim and Henek were behind us, Izio carrying his sick father like a sack of potatoes.

We shivered in our thin clothes, and then the crowded cellar got warm. Stuffy. Full of crying children and dirt shaking down from the bombs above us. Henek complained that I was crowding him, complained again, and I kicked him in the shin. Izio put his arm around me. Mrs. Diamant saw and shook her head, mumbling.

When the sun was halfway across the sky, the bombs and the artillery shells went quiet, and I heard the machine guns come, faint, then closer, jeeps driving fast past our building. Izio looked down at me, and I looked at him, and then we both looked at Max. If the Germans came, they would have to run. But I thought Mr. Diamant could be right. Russia might win.

The fighting came right outside, gunfire and breaking glass, and when the shots finally slowed and stopped, Henek crept up to the street. There were dead German soldiers, he said, propped up in the shop windows like mannequins. A few people in the cellar cheered. Until the guns started up again. I pressed my hands to my ears, trying not to hear the wounded men, and when it finally stopped, and Henek again stole up the stairs, he said there was no one on the streets at all. No wounded, no vehicles. And the dead soldiers posing in the shop windows were Russians now, propped up with broomsticks, their faces painted with swastikas.

"The Germans are coming, *Mame*," said Chaim.

Mrs. Diamant stirred, as if she'd woken from a sleep. "Upstairs," she said. "Quick! All of you!"

We did what we were told, stepping over the miserable crowd and up the stairs.

"Fusia," said Mrs. Diamant, huffing as she climbed. "Get the cashbox from under the bed. Count the money and divide it five ways, yes? Boys, wear your boots and two layers of clothes so you will have room in your bags for food. And on the way you will go to the shop and take all the bread you can carry ..."

By the time I got the money doled out, the boys were dressed and Mrs. Diamant was stuffing empty bottles into knapsacks, because there was no water coming from the pipes. Chaim nodded to me, and Henek looked away; Max smiled once, and Izio kissed my forehead.

"Wait for me," he whispered.

"Take care of our parents," said Max. "Please," he added.

And before I could answer, they were gone.

I hadn't thought this would happen.

Mr. Diamant slumped down in his chair, too stunned to smoke, and I had a great bleeding wound somewhere deep inside my chest. And Mrs. Diamant saw it. Just like she had seen Izio's arm around me and that kiss on the forehead. She took off her glasses, rubbing them on the coat she was wearing over her nightgown. She had dust on her face, a clean ring around each eye, and there was an emotion there that I had never seen directed at me. Anger.

It hit me like a blow to the stomach.

I went to the sink to do the dishes we'd left two days ago, but when I turned on the faucet, nothing happened. I'd forgotten there was no water. Only what was streaming down my face. Then Mrs. Diamant sighed, pulled me into her arms, called me her *ketzele*, and we cried together for her sons while the ambulances went by.

We should have saved our tears for later.

The German Army marched down Mickiewicza Street, row after row with boots that could be heard with the windows closed. Rosa and Regina came out of the cellar, shook their dusty clothes in our hallway until we sneezed, and slammed the door. I thought about how they'd fled from Germany. About Izio, and every story I'd ever heard and refused to believe. The stories that he believed. I looked at Mr. Diamant, weak and thin, at my *babcia*, soft as warm butter with her tear-streaked face. I turned my back to the army marching on the other side of the glass and said, "I think we should run."

It took some convincing, but without her sons, Mrs. Diamant wasn't as hard to persuade as I thought she might be. We'd go east, I said. To Nizankowice. Maybe the Germans wouldn't care so much about Jews in a village. Not like in the city. They'd have to come a long way to find us.

Mrs. Diamant sewed her jewelry into her girdle and our money into her bra while I found water, tidied the kitchen, packed food, and hid the candlesticks. I didn't trust Regina and Rosa not to

27

ransack the apartment while we were gone. We didn't even tell them we were leaving.

There were no trains, so we made our slow way through the city, staying off the main streets as long as we could, finally joining a line of people like ourselves, all trying to escape the Germans in Przemyśl. Mr. and Mrs. Diamant had to stop and rest about every forty-five minutes, even though I was carrying all our supplies in the knapsack, and I had to bite my tongue and force my feet to slow. I stared at the sky, waiting for them to catch up. What was I doing? How could I take care of two people old enough to be my grandparents? Someone else should have been doing this job. Making these decisions.

Only there was no one else. There was only me.

The second part of my education had begun.

It was late in the afternoon, and we were only halfway to Nizankowice, traveling with a group of other old people, some older than Mr. Diamant, women with children, and carts carrying the sick. The slow-moving. Weapons lay scattered along the road, dropped as the Russians fled, free for the taking. We heard single shots, bursts of machine-gun fire in the woods, the whooping of boys right after. We passed three people nursing their own bullet wounds beside the road. I wanted to stop, to do something, but I had my two old people, and no way to help them.

The sun was still hot, Mr. and Mrs. Diamant were exhausted, and there had been no water for a long time, so I led our group down a lane, hoping to find a farmhouse with a well.

Which is exactly what we did find. A house with a sloping red roof and a barn where cows mooed, a sheltered well right in front. I knelt in front of the well, grateful, while the others sighed with relief, pulling up the chain with a full bucket on the end, trying to fill a bottle with a very narrow opening. Mr. and Mrs. Diamant helped each other to the ground to sit, chests heaving.

"What do you think you're doing?"

I looked up to discover a woman with a scarf around her head. And the end of a Russian rifle.

"Sorry," I said. "I should have knocked." I gave her my best buy-me-a-chocolate smile, but it didn't work. Not this time. "My ... my friends are tired, and we've traveled a long—"

"I know who you are," said the woman, pointing the rifle at my ragtag group huddled in her yard. "Swine Jews. Now get out!"

I looked back at the group. Were they Jews? I didn't know. "But ..."

"Get out before I shoot!" she shouted.

Some people didn't like Jews. Of course I knew that. But denying a drink to children and a few ragged old people was something beyond my experience. I helped Mr. Diamant to his feet and watched the group make their slow way to the road, backs bent. I adjusted the heavy knapsack and looked back at the woman with her rifle and her well full of water. And suddenly I was so angry that my vision blurred.

"I hope one day you will be dying of thirst," I told her, "so that, then, someone can deny you water the same way you did to them!"

"Come, *ketzele*," whispered Mrs. Diamant. I turned my back, then jumped as a shot rang out. Something buzzed past my head, and blood pooled from a man's arm just in front of me, a man I didn't even know. He cried out, but he didn't stop moving down the lane. None of us did. Not until we got back to the road. Mrs. Diamant used her scarf to bind the stranger's wound, and I wanted to be sick, but I wasn't.

If I was going to take care of them, if they were my responsibility, if any of us were going to survive, then I had to learn to control my temper. No matter how unfair. No matter how angry I became.

I wasn't sure I could do it.

We hobbled into the village of Nizankowice near midnight, and I knocked on the door of Mrs. Nowak, the Catholic woman who had been boarding Max during the week while he worked with Dr. Schillinger. She was surprised to see us, but she didn't seem sorry. She put us in Max's room, and I think Mr. and Mrs. Diamant fell asleep before their heads were on the pillow.

I looked at Max's room. It was a young man's place. There were dirty shoes in the corner, medical books beside the bed, pictures on the bureau. One of his brothers and sister. One of him in a hat and coat in front of the shop. One of a girl I didn't know. And one of me with his mother, caught by surprise, smiling behind the chocolate display. I found his extra blanket and slept on the floor.

I would miss the shop.

The next afternoon, while the Diamants rested, I slipped out of the house to the village square. We needed food, a job, a more permanent place to stay. I thought there might be a store that needed help. A house that needed cleaning. What I found was three bodies lying in the dirt—dead or unconscious, I wasn't sure—and a village near rioting. Two men were taking turns standing on a crate, shouting over the noise of a raucous crowd. They were unshaven, dressed in boots and coveralls like factory workers. But their haircuts were short. Suspiciously neat. I shrank behind a parked delivery truck.

"This war was started by Jews!" the man on the crate yelled. He was pointing at the people, his face red and sweating. "They bankrupt our country, starve our children. Your families will not be safe, this war will never end, until every … last … Jew … is dead!"

A roar went up from the crowd, some against, some for this speech, and while the people were busy arguing, the man in the dirty coveralls and his companion trotted out of the square and into the woods just beyond. I watched three men follow, and immediately there was gunfire. The crowd scattered, a few heading for the woods with sticks and clubs. There were still three bodies lying in the square. I ran back to the boarding house and locked the door. I was sweating.

"Did you find anything good?" asked Mrs. Diamant. She was reading a magazine, her swollen feet propped up on a cushion. I plastered a smile on my face.

"Not today," I said, and shut myself in the toilet. I could hear that bullet whizzing by my head, the old man's cry when it passed through his arm. The Jews didn't do that. Or drop bombs on my city. What had come over everyone? I splashed cold water on my face.

Mrs. Nowak knocked on the door and then opened it a crack. I straightened over the sink. She was very sorry, but after tonight, we would need to find another place to stay. Someone else had reserved the room. Max's room. With his pictures in it. Mrs. Nowak's mouth was drawn in tight.

"Does someone know you have Jews here?" I asked.

She looked caught. And guilty. "I … I just don't want trouble, that's all."

I patted my face dry, trying to think. I wanted to cry.

"Should we go east?" I whispered.

Mrs. Nowak shook her head. "I do not think they will let you into Russia," she said.

We didn't wait for morning. I got Mr. and Mrs. Diamant up at three thirty, before the house was stirring. Mrs. Diamant left a note, thanking Mrs. Nowak for her hospitality; I shut the door without noise and hurried them down the dark road. I wanted to be far away from Nizankowice before the sun rose.

We made excellent time. Much better than the first trip. Mrs. Diamant kept a good pace, and Mr. Diamant wasn't having as much trouble with his diabetes. Or maybe they were more afraid this time than sad. Not that I told them what had happened in town. But the obedient way they were following me said maybe they had figured it out for themselves.

The woods were quiet, no gunshots, the morning air cool, the rising hills misty, and the only people we saw were a few more refugees going the opposite way. We arrived back in Przemyśl at two in the afternoon with nothing worse than sore feet.

So much for me being in charge, I thought. In the city, at least, our neighbors wouldn't shoot us.

Mrs. Diamant steered us toward the shop before the apartment, to take some inventory home. We were hungry and tired, and the market hadn't reopened. A long, jagged crack ran through the front window of the shop, a dripping yellow Star of David and the word *"Jude"* painted across the glass. And the shelves were empty. Not an apple or a chocolate remained.

I left the Diamants on the sidewalk and walked across the street to the bank. The manager, a man Mrs. Diamant had known since he was in diapers, said that the Diamants no longer had an account there. That no Jew had an account there. I emptied my account instead. Mrs. Diamant didn't say anything. She just took her husband's arm, and we walked slowly back to the apartment.

At least that was the same. Though it looked as if someone had gone through the cupboards and the desk. And someone had beaten their dirty rugs right in the hallway, because my red bedroom curtain was gray with dust. I saw my suspect for both crimes, Rosa, peeking out from her door, though she slammed it shut again when she saw me looking. I think she hoped we weren't coming back.

Mrs. Diamant went with me to the market the next morning to use some of my savings and buy something that could be sold for profit in the shop. Only to discover that Jews were no longer allowed in the market between eight in the morning and six o'clock at night. Which was, of course, when all the food was there. I sent her home and I did the shopping, and all the shopping after that, though there was very little money to do it with.

I also crossed the bridge the Nazis had thrown up to replace the one that was bombed. But my sister was no longer on the other side of Przemyśl, and neither was anyone who knew where she might have gone. I wrote a letter to my mother, giving it to the postman the first day we had mail again. He whispered that it was good we'd come back from Nizankowice when we did, that the road wasn't safe. Others trying to come back to the city had been beaten, robbed, murdered on the way. But it wasn't safe here, either. Mrs. Diamant brought home new German identity papers and white armbands stamped with Jewish stars, and she did it by walking in the gutters, because Jews were not allowed on the sidewalks. We watched boys in their yarmulkes scrubbing the streets beneath the eye of a German machine gun. I didn't get a reply from my mother.

Somehow, the air felt like winter long before the cold came. Oppressive. Dark.

Lonely.

It made me angry.

I splashed home in a cold rain with the little food we could afford, and when I walked through the front door and slipped off my boots, my feet made tracks across the hallway. My curtain, my bed, and even the door to the kitchen were once again covered in dust. I went to Rosa and Regina's door and knocked. When there was no answer, I banged. One eye—Rosa's, I think—appeared in the opening crack.

"Didn't your mother ever teach you to shake a rug outside? You're covering everything in dirt!"

The eye in the door crack narrowed.

"And you're taking it right back into your room every time you come and—" But the door had slammed shut. I went to find the dustpan.

The next morning, my coat, left hanging to dry in the hallway, had been cut into ribbons.

"Never mind," Mrs. Diamant said, running her hands through the shreds. "Sadness can become cruelty. Remember that, *ketzele*. We do not know what happened to them in Germany. We should pity those women."

I wasn't sure I could. But maybe I wouldn't have so much to forgive if I could control my own temper.

Two days later, Regina and Rosa called the new German police, the Gestapo, to the apartment. The first time we met the Gestapo, they'd helped themselves to most of the books, one painting, the silver menorah, and all of Grandmother Adler's china. Now they'd come because Mrs. Pohler had refused to give Regina the key to the attic—where we all took turns hanging our wet linen—until her own linen was dry. Two SS officers with skulls on their caps hammered on Mrs. Pohler's door, called her a stinking Jew, slapped her face, and removed the linen key from her shaking hands. They gave the key to Regina, whom they also called a stinking Jew, and Regina and Rosa disappeared to the attic, I assumed to shred all Mrs. Pohler's clean laundry.

This time Mrs. Diamant did not speak of pity. "I will take care of this," she muttered. She put on her coat, tied her scarf around her head, and hurried out the door.

I made broth for Mr. Diamant, who was ill and in his bed, then sat stewing on the windowsill. Mrs. Diamant couldn't have gone to the market. It was late afternoon. Curfew wasn't until nine o'clock, but even the Polish police, who did what the SS told them, would find any reason to stop a Jew. Rain blew and streaked down the window glass, and when Mrs. Diamant blustered back into the apartment, I hurried to meet her.

"Where have you ..."

She dismissed me with a wave and locked the door behind her. Water dotted the scarf on her head and the white armband on her coat, and she was barefoot, her round, muddy toes sticking out from torn and filthy stockings. I changed my question.

"Where are your boots?"

"Hitler has them," she said. "The Gestapo says their *Führer* has more need of them than an old woman walking in gutters running with the rain."

I remembered Mrs. Pohler's bruised cheek and crossed my arms over my stomach. "And what did you say?"

"That their *Führer* should find work that pays better so he can buy his own boots!"

I looked her over, but I couldn't find any blood. She shook her head.

"They only pushed me down, *ketzele*, and the back of me is too soft for that to hurt so much."

I didn't believe her, since I was fairly sure her mother's jewelry was still sewn into her girdle.

And then there was a knock on the door.

Mrs. Diamant froze, turned, and looked at me. Her smile was gone.

"Did they follow you home?" I whispered. She shook her head and shrugged at the same time, the scarf crumpled tight in her hand. The knocking came again.

"What they've come to do, the door will not stop them, my *ziskeit*," said Mr. Diamant. He was stooped, leaning against the doorway of the living room. He looked one hundred years old.

Mrs. Diamant went slowly to the door. The lock clicked. The hinges creaked. I expected to hear German. Instead I heard Max say, "Were you hoping we wouldn't come back, *Mame*?"

"Oh!" she said. "Oh, oh!" And pulled him inside. Then Chaim came through the door, and Henek, and there was Izio. They were dirty and wet, their sleeves ragged, and their mother kissed each of their unshaven cheeks twice. I kissed them once, making Henek push me away and Max blush, both of which made me laugh.

Izio hugged me, not long, but long enough to let me know he'd missed me. He was thin beneath his shirt. Older beneath his eyes. I wanted to tell him everything that had been happening. And then I didn't want to tell him anything that had been happening at all. I went to make tea while Mr. Diamant smiled and smiled, pumping the hands of his sons.

There was a lot of talk all at once, about the Russian military hospital where they'd all found work, hoping to be evacuated with the army. But the evacuation order never came.

"The border is sealed," said Chaim. "We can't get out."

None of us could.

We had a small feast of the broth with *kasha*, which was more filling than good, the rest of the bread, a pot of marmalade Mrs. Diamant had been saving, and a sack of apples. And even though the stories Chaim told were terrible, of German planes shooting down the refugees on the road and the executions of innocent men, there was more laughter than tears. We laughed at the ugly dishes I'd bought in a secondhand booth to replace the china. Roared when Henek asked why the Germans hadn't taken the jewelry and his mother told him. And Max's impression of Hitler reading Mr. Diamant's copy of *Commentary on the Talmud* while wearing women's boots made me laugh until I hurt. Izio held my hand tight beneath the table.

We didn't know it then, we were all too happy to be together, but this was when the men should have been going to God with their heads beneath the prayer shawls. When I should have been on my knees, calling out to the Virgin and the Christ.

If we had known it, this was the time we should have cried.

5.

April 1942

A FEW DAYS LATER, THERE WERE TWO LETTERS ON THE KITCHEN TABLE
from the housing office. Mrs. Diamant slit a knife down one end
of the first envelope. Whatever it said inside, a grim look of
satisfaction came across her face. She trotted off, and I heard an
argument in the hallway. I drank my tea, wondering what
Regina and Rosa had done now, and slit open the second
envelope.

I read the letter. Twice. And then Mrs. Diamant came back to
the table and tossed the first paper down in triumph. Regina and
Rosa were moving, because the front bedroom had now been reassigned. To me. I had my own room.

I savored this news for about thirty seconds before I gave her the
second letter. This one said all Jews were being reassigned to housing in a ghetto. The Diamants' new apartment would be only a few
blocks away, inside a designated area behind the train station.

I might have my own room. But I would be alone.

Mrs. Diamant's face worked. "We will not go until we have to,"
she said.

Two days after that, Regina and Rosa moved to the ghetto.
Three weeks after that, the posters went up. Any Jew not in the
ghetto by midnight on the following day would be shot.

We did not sleep that night. I moved furniture and packed the ugly dishes while receiving advice in a nonstop stream.

"Remember, you are Catholic," said Mrs. Diamant, as if I might forget. "They will not touch a Catholic. Lock the doors at night and lock your bedroom door at night. But it is only a place to sleep. We will see each other every day, yes? The things in this box, these you can sell when the money runs out …"

She shoved the box into my hands. She'd already given me one quarter of the money, now stuffed into the unused stovepipe in the kitchen.

"… and you will come to us," she went on, mopping her brow, "and bring us the little things we do not have, because you can buy and sell, yes?"

"Why don't I come with you?" I said for the hundredth time. "I can sleep in a hall, like I do now …"

"Don't be stupid, *ketzele*."

I probably was being stupid. I was probably being a *Dummkopf*. But my heart was breaking.

There was a burst of machine-gun fire in the street, shouts, and a woman screamed. Max set down his box, went to the window, and abruptly shut the curtain.

"Don't look outside, *Mame*," he said. "Okay?" He glanced at me, and I didn't need to be told. Leave the curtain shut. And then a fist hammered on the door.

We knew now what it sounded like when the Gestapo came. Like Hitler and Stalin were fighting to see who could break down a door first. Like they were coming in whether you opened it or not. Mrs. Diamant spun and snatched a knapsack out of Izio's hands.

"Quick," she whispered, "all of you! Put your boxes in the front bedroom. Under the bed. Everything in the bedroom. Go! Chaim,

Max! Put the kitchen table in there, too. And four of the chairs. Hurry!"

There was a scramble in the apartment. The fist hammered again. Or it might have been the butt of a club this time. *"Gestapo! Öffne die Tür! Öffne!"*

The table and chairs disappeared into my room. Izio waited for his mother's nod, and he opened the door. Four SS officers crowded into the front hall, then fanned out through the house. One stayed, his cap with the skull grinning down at us. His boots were shiny black mirrors.

"What is happening?" Mrs. Diamant asked.

"Silence!" said the man. "Your *Führer* will allow you to donate what you will not need for the provision of the German Army ..."

The German Army must need our sofa, I thought, because it was already being carried out the door. I ran to the living room. The third officer had come through from the kitchen and was rifling inside a box of Chaim's clothes that hadn't made it to the front bedroom. The room was dim from the closed curtains and the cloud of smoke surrounding Mr. Diamant's chair, cluttered with all the little items from our packing. The officer wrinkled his nose and tucked the box beneath one arm.

"You Jews live like swine," he said, or that's what we thought he said. His Polish wasn't near as good as the other man's. He fished a full packet of cigarettes out of Mr. Diamant's shirt pocket, put it in his own, and slapped him. And then he spit on the floor.

Chaim took a step away from the wall, and I watched Max put out a silent hand to stop him. Henek stood in the doorway of the kitchen with a clenched fist, Izio right behind him.

The room had the whining, whistling anticipation of a falling bomb.

I turned quickly to the spitting man and smiled like I wanted him to buy me a chocolate. He started, looked me over, set the box on the floor at his feet, and pulled out a list from inside his jacket.

"What is your name?" he asked.

"This is Miss Podgórska," said Mrs. Diamant, hurrying through the door with the first SS officer. She went straight to the desk, fumbling through the papers in the drawer. "Like I have said to you, she has been assigned to our bedroom. So the things in there belong to her. Not to Jews." She found the letter from the housing office and held it out. "Not to Jews," she repeated while the man with the shiny boots read. She shot me a look that said very clearly to keep my mouth shut. I shut it.

The second officer checked his list, then shook his head.

"Leave the girl's room!" the first officer barked. "Take the rest."

We watched while they took the last of the furniture, down to Mr. Diamant's chair and the rugs off the floor. A truck stood parked in front of the building, its back end bulging with what had once belonged to the families of our building, and I saw a woman on the other side of it, throwing water over the sidewalk by the bucketful. The gutter ran red.

I dropped the curtain back into place. I'd forgotten I was supposed to leave it closed.

The SS man with the list took one last look around the empty apartment, at the seven of us sitting or standing on the bare floor. Satisfied that he hadn't left anything valuable behind, he turned to go. Then he turned again, came back to me, and pinched my cheek.

"Find some new friends soon, *ja*?"

He smiled and left, and I scrubbed my cheek beneath the faucet in the kitchen sink.

It didn't take much time for the Diamants to gather the things that had been left in my new room. But the table and the chairs, Mrs. Diamant said, were for me. She kissed my forehead, and Mr. Diamant, bent with a pack on his back and a red cheek, patted my arm. Henek ducked his chin at me, and Izio kissed me on the mouth. Max studied the pattern of the cracks in the plaster.

"Wait for me," Izio said.

And when the door was closed, I went to the window and threw it open. There was a line of Jews with arms loaded or pushing carts, making their way down the street past the train station, and I listened to some of the same people who had bought blintzes and soda water and crackers and cheese in the Diamants' shop hurling abuse as they left their home.

"Dogs."

"Vermin."

"Filthy Jews!"

I turned the lock on the front door, went into my new room, locked that door, put a chair beneath the knob, and got into the bed. I cried until the sun went down, until the commotion outside had died. The floors didn't creak with footsteps. No distant call or slam of a door. The building had been Jewish, and now it was as empty as a freshly dug grave. And I was by myself in a corner of it. I saw shadows move. Imagined shiny black boots coming soft down the hall. And there was no one to talk to. No one to tell. I wanted my mother. I wanted Mrs. Diamant. I wanted Izio. I clutched my blanket to my chest, sweating.

I did not like being afraid.

The next morning, I put on Mrs. Diamant's old coat, the one she'd lent me when mine got shredded, and peeked out the door of the echoing apartment. I put a foot over the threshold, then another, and another, until I was hurrying down the stairs, out the front doors, and into the quiet courtyard, where no children played. I darted through the tunnel alley that was Mickiewicza 7, around the corner, and over the little bridge that crossed the train tracks. Beyond the station was the neighborhood that was now the ghetto, and there I had to stop.

A fence had been put up, string after string of barbed wire, and a gate made of fresh planks of wood. A German policeman patrolled back and forth in front of this gate, and when he saw me staring, he yelled and waved his machine gun. I ran back along the train tracks, circling, trying to find an end to the fence, but every street that led into the ghetto had been blocked. The Jews had not been "reassigned." They had been taken prisoner.

I wandered the streets of Przemyśl all day. Looking at the rubble piles where buildings used to be, in the windows of the shops or watching the factory workers—the factories were all German now—go to and from their shifts. I told myself I needed a job, that's why I was wandering like this. That it had nothing to do with being lonely. That it had nothing to do with being afraid to go home.

I investigated a Help Needed sign at a dressmaker's shop and discovered I would not find work anywhere because I didn't have the proper papers. My papers were Polish. They needed to be German. So I went to the labor office in the city hall. My Polish papers would not do, said the little German man from behind the desk, one finger pushing up his wire-rimmed glasses, because I had never provided proof of my birth. I could be a Romany. I could even be a Jew. To get papers, he said, I would need a photo I could not afford and a birth registration that did not exist. No? Then perhaps there was someone who had known me since birth. Someone who could sign an affidavit swearing to my name and nationality and religion. No? Then *auf Wiedersehen*.

I went back to the apartment. I didn't know what else to do. I shut the front door with the softest of clicks, afraid to hear the emptiness of an echo. But then I did hear a door slam. From somewhere downstairs. I listened to my heart beat, faster, faster, as footsteps came one by one up the stairs. Someone knocked on a door, but it was across the hall. Then the footsteps came again, and the knock was on my door.

"Hello?" said a voice outside. Young. Female. I opened the door a little and saw a smile. I opened it the rest of the way and saw a woman in a blue print dress, rocking back and forth on her heels.

"I'm Emilika," she said. "And I've got a room on the first floor, only it's spooky in here, isn't it? All these empty apartments and closed doors. It's quiet, much too quiet, and I wanted you to know I have sugar. Not a lot, but enough, and I thought maybe you would want tea. Or, I mean to say, that you might think this building is too big and want to have tea with me, too. Before the sugar runs out ..."

"Yes!" I said, before she could keep going.

She smiled bigger. "I'll get it." And she disappeared down the stairs.

I hurried into my room and shoved the boxes under the bed and spread the blanket over my rumpled sheets and nightgown, hung the rosary on the bedpost, and straightened up Jesus and Mary on the windowsill. Then I lit the little stove. Emilika came running back with a teapot, two cups, the tea, and a paper parcel of sugar, and it was amazing how this time when the sun went down, my room seemed cozy instead of something from my nightmares.

Emilika was twenty-three, Catholic like me, had brown hair, a freckled nose, and worked in a photography shop. She thought it was terrible, what the Germans had done to Przemyśl. When the trains were running properly and she'd saved up enough money, she would go back to her family in Kraków. Or maybe the Russians would come back. Or maybe the war would be over soon and everything would go back to the way it was. But in the meantime, we were the landlords of the building, weren't we? Queens of the kingdom of apartments. We could have it all our own way, couldn't we?

She brought up a mattress and slept in my room that night, and neither one of us worried about the silence, because there wasn't that much of it. She asked about boys. I told her I had one. But I didn't tell her he was Jewish. I asked her about boys. She said she had several. She slept in my apartment every night.

And in the morning, ten days later, a noise woke me up. The sound of feet on stone pavement, all moving at the same time. I pushed the curtain to one side. The street below was filled with men, Jewish men, walking in lines, one behind the other, German guards with guns marching with them on either side. The men's heads were down, eyes on the ground, but there was one looking up. Staring straight at my window.

Max.

I yanked off my nightgown, threw on a dress, and flew down the stairs without my shoes. Out the front door of the apartment building, through the passage of Mickiewicza 7, around the corner, and behind our block of buildings. A train was coming into the station, and I pushed through the crowd trying to get to it, all of us blocked by the people standing on the sidewalk, watching the Jews go by. I shoved my way along the column of marching men, chose a moment when the guard wasn't looking, and stepped into the moving line beside Max.

"Hi," he said.

"What's happening? Where are you going?"

"To work, or that's what they say. We are all supposed to work."

I had a feeling that pay did not come with it. "Are you all right? How is everyone? Your mother? And Izio?"

He shrugged. He looked like Max, but with an expression I wasn't used to. Tense. Tight.

"*Mame* wants you to sell some things and get us some food. There's no way to buy in the ghetto, and there are eight other families in our apartment. We've already used what we brought."

"How can I get it to you? I tried to come, and there were fences ..."

"We pass this way every morning. Meet me here. I'll bring it in somehow—"

"*Halt!*"

I jumped at the harsh bark. A German guard had spotted me. And now his gun was pointed at my head.

"I just needed to tell my friend something," I said, backing away from the line of moving men. "I'm finished now ..."

I turned and fled, not sure if the man was going to shoot me. He didn't. I climbed the stairs, found Emilika gone, and washed my feet while I thought.

Eight families to an apartment. How could that be? That would have to mean twenty, thirty people. At the least. And they were already out of food, with no way to buy more. So they were hungry now and would stay that way until Max brought food after work tomorrow. Only how could Max carry enough for all of them? And even if he could, would he be allowed? Or would the Germans take that away, too?

I turned a brush through my tangled curls. How was anyone in the ghetto supposed to live? Were the Nazis planning to starve every Jew in Przemyśl? I put my clean feet into some socks and tied my shoes.

Maybe they were. But they weren't going to starve mine.

I went through the box of things to sell and settled on a silk blouse long since too small for Mrs. Diamant and a set of silver candlesticks the SS hadn't found because they'd been so tarnished in the back of a cabinet. I spent half the morning haggling at the market and the secondhand shops and came out with one chicken, a sack of coarse flour, half a kilo of butter, three dozen eggs, and some change to stuff up the stovepipe.

I got my purse and filled it with as many eggs as it could hold, the package of butter on top, where I hoped it wouldn't melt, then wrapped the chicken in brown paper and a long string, the other end of the string tied to my wrist. I did the same with the sack of flour and carefully slid my arms with the strings into Mrs. Diamant's enormous old coat. Now I had a chicken and a flour sack hanging under each arm, hidden beneath the coat. I filled the pockets with the remaining eggs, grabbed a handkerchief, and picked up my purse.

The Germans had taken the mirror, but I didn't need it to know I looked silly.

I crept down the stairs, avoiding the creaks, just in case Emilika was home from work, then out into the empty grass of the courtyard, through the passage, around the corner, and across the bridge that ran over the train tracks. And there was the ghetto with its guarded gate, but I avoided that this time, slipping along the fence line to a narrow alley between two buildings, where there was only a small section of fence. I looked over my shoulder. There was no one around. So I went close.

Two wooden posts had been set into the ground at the corners of the buildings, barbed wire strung thick between them. But the posts weren't put in very well. In fact, if you just wiggled and pulled ...

The post came free. I swung the whole fence out like a door, stepped inside, and put the post back again, scraping my shoe over the fresh dirt. I was inside the ghetto.

I fished the handkerchief from my pocket and tried to tie it around my upper right arm. This was harder than I thought, and in the end, I used my teeth. Then I turned and stepped out from between the buildings, heart hammering in my chest.

And three old men with black coats, white armbands, and side-locks sat on the stoop of the opposite building, staring dispassionately at me from across the street. Then they looked down, muttering among themselves. I heard the clip of boots. A policeman was coming. I crossed the street with my shoulders hunched and my head down. Like everyone else seemed to do. The policeman switched his gun from one hand to the other and passed me by. I lifted my head, watching him go, and smiled.

I wasn't afraid anymore.

Which only goes to show how foolish I was.

"The Diamant family?" I whispered to the old men. "Izaac Diamant, and Leah, his wife? And four sons ..."

"*Gey avek*," said one.

I was being told to go away.

"Go back to where you came from, girl, before you get killed!" whispered the other, in Polish this time. They turned their backs on me, and I moved on down the street.

People hung in clumps around the doorways, children playing on the sidewalks and in the gutters. It looked like a neighborhood on a holiday, when the factories are shut down, but without the fun of a party. And if a policeman walked by, people melted into the corners like shadows in the sun. I did the same. My pretend armband was only going to pass at a glance, not to mention my oddly bulging shape beneath the coat. I asked for the Diamants again and again, until finally a woman whispered, "Reymonta 2." I found the street, and the building was like any other in Przemyśl, though small, only two stories. I pushed open the door.

And the hallway was packed with bodies. In the corners, on the stairs, ducking beneath the laundry strung on ropes from door to door. There were babies squalling, children yelling and fussing, and it smelled like the toilets had overflowed. I passed a little girl on the stairs smacking a child even smaller than herself, telling it to stop crying. Which, of course, made the baby cry more. I paused, ready to pick up the baby and find its mother, but the little girl met my gaze squarely, ready to do battle, clutching the crying baby around its middle. And then I understood. The baby was crying because it was hungry. This little girl was hungry, had maybe been hungry before the ghetto. All these children were hungry, and I had a coat full of food.

Guilt wormed its way through my middle. I should feed them. I wanted to feed them all. But how could I? I walked away from the children, step by step up the stairs, trying to focus my eyes on nothing but the Diamants' door. I found it, knocked, and a stranger answered. A man with a full beard and a gruff voice.

"What do you want?"

"I'm looking for—"

"Fusia?"

And there was my *babcia*, hurrying down the hallway, wisps of gray hair floating beside her cheeks. She hugged me to her soft chest. I sighed, instantly soothed. And then she pushed me away again.

"What are you doing here?"

I blinked.

"Why have you come here?"

"But you said I was to ..."

"Not like this! Do you care nothing for your life? You ..." And then I opened the coat, just a little, and she caught sight of the chicken.

Mrs. Diamant pulled me through the door and shut it, hustling me down a hall to a room that had probably once been a dining room and was now everything the Diamants needed it to be. Mr. Diamant was on the floor, his back cushioned by a rolled-up blanket. He held out both his hands, took mine, and kissed them, and then they were ripped away, because Mrs. Diamant was stripping off my coat.

"Careful of the eggs ..." I whispered, and then I closed my mouth. She was muttering angrily in Polish and Yiddish, untying the strings from my wrists, her eyes darting toward the hall. As if she was afraid someone might come and snatch the food from her hands.

Maybe they would.

"Foolish girl," she said over and over beneath her breath. "Stupid, foolish girl ..."

"But you said I was to come to you!"

"I said to give these things to Max, not paint a target between your shoulders." She turned circles with the flour sack, finally shoving it behind Mr. Diamant's back. "Do you want to be dead? What would I do if you were shot in the street?"

I felt ashamed. Maybe I had been reckless. If I got myself killed, maybe they would starve. I opened my purse, meek, and Mrs. Diamant stared down at the squashed butter and the eggs. Then her face crumpled up, and she took my cheeks in her hands and kissed them.

"You are a good girl, *ketzele*," she whispered. "But you do not understand. How could you, when I did not understand? But you listen to me now." She held my face and looked me in the eyes. "They will kill you. And they will like killing you. Do not give them the chance."

"Fusia!" I looked past her shoulder and saw Henek coming into the room, a girl right behind him, and he was smiling. I wasn't sure whether it was more surprising that he was smiling in the ghetto or smiling at me.

"People said there was someone asking for us in the street. Was it you? You should be careful. Did you bring any—"

"Hush, Henek!" Mrs. Diamant said. She patted my hair and stepped back. "Fusia is going now."

The girl with Henek peeked around his shoulder. She had dark curls around a pale face, though I wasn't sure if that was her usual color or the color of the ghetto. "I've heard all about you," she said in a soft voice. "You're the Gentile of the family, isn't that right?"

My eyebrows went up a little. "This is Henek's girl, Danuta," said Mrs. Diamant quickly. The girl stuck out her hand, and I shook it. Since when did Henek have a girlfriend? Mrs. Diamant started bundling me into the coat.

"Where's Izio?" I asked.

"Working," she said. "At least he will get soup."

"Can I wait? I . . ."

"Are you not listening? No!" She put a hand on my back, and I waved goodbye as she started pushing me down the hall. We stopped in front of the door.

"What else do you need?" I asked.

She thought quickly. "Soap. And a little food each day. You give Max only what he can carry, yes?"

I nodded.

"And you will never come here again. Do you understand?"

I nodded. She adjusted the pretend armband on my sleeve and kissed me on the forehead. Like my mother did when I was two.

"*Sholem aleikhem,*" she said. I thought she might cry. "Go quickly now. Be smart, and be careful, and do what you can to keep your life. Do you promise me that?"

I promised, turned, and made my way around the crying children. Each step down felt heavier and heavier, like I'd grown or gained weight. But the weight was only fear. Because I was afraid.

I was afraid I would never see them again.

6.

June 1942

ON MY WAY OUT OF THE GHETTO, I SAW A GIRL BEATEN TO DEATH WITH THE
butt of a rifle. I couldn't tell how old she was, what she'd done, or
if she'd done anything at all. But the SS man smiled while he did
it, then left her body and her blood on the street. It was all I could
do to come out of the shadows, to make my feet walk down the
sidewalk, to wait for the right moment and lift the fence post out
of its hole. I ran home and I shook.

And that night, for the first time, I understood what I was
facing. Before, it had been easy to imagine that all these terrible things were some kind of mistake. The misguided ideas of
a misguided leader who in turn was misguiding his army and
his people. Hadn't there always been people who were poor
and hungry? People who were hated and despised? Hadn't
there always been wars where the young men fought and the
innocent died? It was horrible, and it was the world. But that
was not what I saw in that officer's face. What I saw was the joy
of hate. The happiness of causing another person's death and
pain.

What I saw was evil.

And every part of me defied it.

The third part of my education in Przemyśl had begun.

The workers, we discovered, were being searched on their way back into the ghetto, and any extra food was being confiscated. So I met Max every morning on his way to shovel coal, not to give him food but to arrange a signal. I did it so often, the guard got used to me, just shaking his head and keeping one eye on me until I went away again. I blew him a kiss. Then, in the evening, Max would whistle or cough, sneeze or sing, letting me know there were no police, and I would pass him food through the weak place in the fence. This was dangerous. But not as dangerous as a non-Jew entering the ghetto, and it didn't break my promise to Mrs. Diamant. Or didn't break it much.

What I brought was not enough. I could see that on Max's thinning frame. But it was better than nothing.

Emilika still slept in my room, though during the week she often stayed late at the photography shop, developing the film, sometimes breezing in only just before curfew. So I was surprised to hear her knocking before the sun had even gone down. Only when I went to the door, it wasn't Emilika.

It was Izio.

I didn't know how he'd gotten there. I didn't ask. And he didn't say anything, not even hello. Just wrapped his arms around me. He was like the ghetto fence post, thin and tough and so easily pulled in my direction. I locked the door behind him.

The sun sank and the evening came down, but it was a long time before I bothered to light the lamp. Oil came cheaper than bulbs, and the flicker of the flame made the dark dance. And I was happy. So happy. Izio pushed the hair from my face and kissed my forehead and my cheeks.

"You know I love you?" he said.

I nodded. I did know.

He rolled onto his side, head propped on his hand, his other arm still holding me tight. "I came to tell you that the Germans are taking a thousand of us away. The younger men. To work in a labor camp."

"Where?"

"Lwów, I think. I don't know how they chose, but Max's name is on the list."

I felt my heart squeeze. People disappeared in Lwów. Like their sister.

"The coal yard has been hard. Men are dropping with their shovels in their hands, and Max doesn't eat enough for the work. I think the camp will be worse." He twined his fingers through mine, his forehead wrinkling in a grimace. He closed his eyes. "We're not all going to live through this, Fusia."

I frowned. "Of course we are. Something will happen ..."

"You mean Russia will come? Didn't do us a lot of good last time, did it? Not in the long run. Not for the Jews."

I wanted to say that Germany would be defeated, that the war would end and everything would go back to the way it was. But I wasn't sure that was true.

I knew it wasn't. Even then. Nothing would ever be the same.

"I want you to know," Izio said, "that I want it to be me who lives. And you. Don't forget that's what I want. More than anything."

I didn't know why he said that. I didn't even think about it. I was too blind with love. Not until the next time I saw Max, going to the coal yards with the other men. I blew a kiss to the guard, who looked in the other direction, and stepped into line, timing my steps to the march. Max looked terrible, a deep purple shadow underneath each eye. He wasn't going to the labor camp in Lwów after all, he said.

Because Izio had taken his place.

The next morning I went to see the German with the wire-rimmed glasses at the city hall. It turned out to be a different man, though the glasses were the same. Only this one looked like the weasel that used to steal our chickens.

He scowled at the question of how a person might find out who was in which labor camp. Poles from Przemyśl were going to Germany and what used to be Czechoslovakia, doing their duty for the glory of the Fatherland, while our city's dirty Jews were earning their keep in Bełżec and at the Janowska work camp in Lwów, he said.

Janowska, then.

I thanked him instead of spitting on him, and when I went back to the apartment, a poster had been pasted at the entrance to Mickiewicza 7.

DEATH PENALTY FOR ALL WHO GIVE AID TO A JEW.

DEATH TO ALL WHO HARBOR A JEW.

DEATH TO ALL WHO FEED A JEW.

DEATH TO ALL WHO PROVIDE TRANSPORTATION TO A JEW.

**DEATH TO ALL WHO TAKE PAYMENT FROM A JEW,
IN MONEY, OR SERVICES, OR VALUABLES.**

I read the poster three times. I'd done most of those things. Some of them that day. And now I needed a train ticket, and it was more money than I had.

I ate nothing but bread for a week to save part of the money and, in desperation, sold a skirt from Mrs. Diamant's box. There was almost nothing left in there now, but I had to know if Izio was okay. If he was strong enough. If he was alive. And the rest of them would want to know that, too.

It was early morning, and the sun hadn't risen high enough to get into the windows yet. When I'd chewed four of my nails to the quick instead of drinking my tea, Emilika got impatient.

"What's got a fly up your nose? Are you fighting with your boy?"

"Not fighting," I replied. The glasses man had told me that Janowska was also for political prisoners as well as Poles, Romanies, and even some Ukrainians. People from all over. Emilika wouldn't have to know Izio was Jewish. "He's been sent to a labor camp in Lwów. I want to go and see him, but the train ticket is expensive, and even when I'd saved enough, they wouldn't give it to me. I need German papers."

"So, switch them for your Polish ones."

"I tried, but I never showed a birth registration, and I need a new photograph."

"And?" urged Emilika.

"I don't have a birth record, and I can't afford the photograph. Not for a while. It took two weeks to save up the train fare ..."

"Is that why you haven't been eating? Oh, for Christ's sake, Fusia."

I winced for God and myself. I hadn't told her she could call me Fusia. But Emilika was a girl of action and didn't notice.

"Stop sulking and put your clothes on," she said. "We have things to do."

I thought she meant the laundry until she tied a scarf around her hair. As soon as I was decent, she led me past the dirty linen and out into the baking sun.

I had to trot to keep up with her. Emilika nodded in a friendly— though not too friendly—way to two German soldiers smoking cigarettes beside a pile of fallen bricks and kept a brisk pace, as if we had business their army would do well not to delay. They didn't question us. We passed the yellow star on the cracked window of what had been the Diamants' shop, and then a booming clang made me start. Cathedral bells. It was Sunday.

Emilika stopped in front of the photography shop, took a stealthy look around, slipped a ring of keys from her pocket, and had us inside, the door shut and locked again, before I even knew what was happening. The shop was dark with the blinds down, but I could see framed portraits, film canisters, and camera parts on the shelves. Emilika lifted a curtain that divided the front of the store from the back.

"Hurry," she said, going to a camera standing ready on a tripod. "Sit there." A stool posed in front of a backdrop painted with shades of swirling gray.

"But ..."

"Sit!" she ordered. "So I can see where to aim the lights."

"But ..."

She flicked a switch and blinded me with the beams. "Sit!" she said again.

"But I can't pay you!"

Emilika raised her head from behind the camera. "Of course you can't, you idiot. That's why we're here on a Sunday! Now, do you want to see your boy or not? Sit!"

I sat. Emilika adjusted the camera, adjusted me, clicked the shutter twice, and shut down the lights.

"That should do it," she said, shoving me to the door. "Mr. Markowski will never notice two extra frames, and I'll sneak the prints into my purse as soon as they're done."

She locked the shop, dropped the keys into her apron pocket, and smiled.

"Thank you," I said.

She took my arm in hers, and we walked down the sidewalk.

I learned three things from Emilika that day: First, walk as if you have important business, and most people will assume you do. Second, always have your hair curled. And third, help can come when it's least expected, and that's good to remember, because it means you're never really alone.

Even when it feels like it.

On Tuesday, I sat again before the little man and his wire-rimmed glasses. His hat was off today, showing a bald spot on the crown of his head.

"What is your birthday, *Fräulein*?"

I said the birthday I'd concocted, with a year that made me sixteen. I was fairly certain that part was right. The man peered at me.

"Registration?"

"Affidavit," I replied. I handed him a paper saying Emilika was my cousin with all the feigned confidence in the world.

He did more peering at me, at the paper, at my photograph, and then at Emilika, standing behind my chair. "And this is your signature, *Fräulein*?" he asked.

"Of course it is." She smiled lazily.

And two hours later, I was on the train to Lwów.

*

It took another four hours to get there, and by the time I found the camp, at the end of a side street right in the center of the city, it was after seven o'clock. A factory stood on a hill to one side, the field below filled with flimsy buildings arranged in a square, fencing and razor wire strung around the perimeter. I couldn't see beyond. I went to the only building with a door and stepped inside.

People waited in a line. Whether they were trying to find friends and family, like I was, or doing business with the Germans, I couldn't tell. I didn't want to know. The woman in front of me was having a long, low conversation with whoever was sitting behind the desk. She turned abruptly and left, giving me a swift view of her face. Whoever she was looking for—friend, brother, sister, parent, or child—wasn't here. Or wasn't here anymore.

Or maybe they just weren't living anymore.

And suddenly, I was terrified. I shuffled up to the desk with concrete feet, to yet another pair of wire-rimmed glasses. Did they sell no other kind in Germany?

"*Nein,*" the man said.

I hadn't even asked him a question.

"*Nein, nein, nein!*" He shouted at the whole room in a broken mix of German and Polish. "There are no visitors. You may not bring food, and I will not tell you the names of any prisoners in this camp!" His chair screeched on its back legs as he stood, stuffing his stack of papers into a folder. "*Heil* Hitler!" he said, and was gone.

We all stared at one another, then filed back outside like obedient sheep. I had two hours before the next train, and the German-run trains, I had noticed, always kept to schedule. I could hear the workers somewhere inside that square of buildings. Shouts and grunts and the sounds of machines, and oddly, an orchestra playing somewhere inside. The summer sun was still hot, and most of the flock of people had gone to stand in the shadow of the building.

And then I wasn't terrified anymore. I was angry. I hadn't lied to the Nazis for nothing. And a train ticket for no reason was food straight out of the Diamants' mouths.

A guard appeared, taking up a position outside the door of the little office. I eyed his uniform. Not the SS. This man was dusty and a little crumpled, machine gun limp in his hands. He looked almost as dejected as the rest of us.

Fear got me nowhere. I knew that. And neither would anger. I wiped them from my face and sidled up to the guard. His eyes darted right and left before fixing on me.

"They've given you door duty," I said. "That's bad luck."

"There's worse luck," he replied.

I was pleased to hear good Polish, even if it was with a German accent. I smiled. "What's the best way to get into the camp?"

"There is no good way into the camp," he said. "You don't want to get into the camp. I would not let my girlfriend within ten kilometers of this camp."

"But ... there is someone inside, a friend ..."

I could see his jaw going stubborn. I lowered my eyes.

"And his wife, my sister, she has had a baby. A little boy ..."

The lies rolled across my tongue like currant wine.

"... and I only want to tell him that he is a father. That his wife and his son are well. Surely that is not so difficult? And don't you think," I went on, "that a man who knows he is a father will work so much harder, will be so careful to obey every rule, so that he can see his wife and son one day? Isn't it a good ... motivation? And look"—I fished a small parcel from my bag, the bread and cheese I'd packed for the journey. Grease stains were beginning to seep through the wrapping—"there's even dinner in it for you."

The guard's mouth twitched. I smiled even bigger. I think he might have blushed.

"What is your brother-in-law's name?" he asked, voice low.

"Izydor Diamant."

"I will bring him. But you must give me something in return. Something that is not your food."

My stomach twisted.

"One kiss," he said. "On the cheek."

I could feel the stares of the other people in the shade, gazes drilling holes in my back like bullets. I held my grin in place, stretched onto my toes, and kissed his Nazi face.

He smiled. "Come with me."

The guard led me back through the door to the now-empty office and through another door behind the desk. There was a plain room behind it, with only a table and one chair, and another door in the opposite wall. It smelled like cigarettes and sweat. "Wait here," he said.

And he locked the door behind him.

I stood alone in that room and decided then and there that I was just as foolish as Mrs. Diamant had said. And very, very naive. These men cared nothing for right or wrong. They were predators, and I had just made myself prey. Mama would have slapped me for not having any sense, and so, I think, would Mrs. Diamant.

The other door was locked when I tried it, and there were no windows. But a floorboard was loose, the nails having missed their targets underneath. A hole in the floor was something. And a board with nails in it might be something else. I was trying to get my fingers underneath it when a key rattled in the door, the one I hadn't come through. It swung open, and a stranger in loose gray clothing shuffled in.

"Ten minutes," said the guard, poking his head around the jamb before he shut and locked the door. The stranger tried to move toward me, but he was slow. His ankles were chained.

"Fusia," he said, and then he wasn't a stranger at all. He was Izio. I ran across the room and threw my arms around his neck.

His head had been shaved, and he was covered in dust, and filth under that. I could feel every bone in his back. He'd aged thirty years in four weeks, and I'd never known a human could smell so bad. But he was still Izio.

"Fusia," he said again, then backed off to look at me. "The man said I was ... a father?"

I could see why he was confused, considering the rules of biology. I waved away my lie and gave him my food instead. We sat in the two chairs, and I watched him wolf down the sandwich without stopping for breath. He was tense. Jumpy. His hands shook a little.

"Do you have water?" he asked. I didn't. And then he whispered, "You have to get me out."

I opened my mouth and closed it. He took my hands.

"You have to get me out of here! I can't stay ... They're going to kill me. Us. Everybody. Do you understand?"

I didn't. He squeezed his eyes closed. The skin stretched thin across his skull.

"Get me out, Fusia. Please. Please."

Something broke inside me. I think it was my heart. But broken hearts wouldn't help us survive any more than my temper. I said, "Tell me what to do."

*

The train ride back to Przemyśl was much shorter than the one that had brought me. At least in my mind. I couldn't stop thinking.

"They're going to kill every Jew," Izio had said. "Every communist. The Romanies. But especially the Jews . . ."

Kill us, kill us, kill us, the train engine chugged. I closed my eyes, trying not to hear.

"They know you're going to die, so they play with you. Like a toy. Beat and starve. Humiliate. Torture. They shoot men in the woods, then crush their bones so they can't be found. They have an orchestra, all prisoners, and they write special songs for every execution, for every beating . . ."

Kill us, said the train wheels.

"It's not random. It's a plan. It's what they want . . ."

Like the SS man with his rifle butt in the ghetto.

Izio had said the guards were often lax. That the prisoners were unchained at night. That if he walked away after the evening work session, he might not be missed until the night ration. He needed street clothes, soap, shoes, a cap, a pair of glasses. A train ticket. I could come to him like I had today. Hide the clothes beneath a bush near the officers' latrines, walk with him away from the camp once he'd changed, then wait with him at the platform until the train came. No one would notice, not once he was out of his prison clothes, not once he was with me. We could disappear into Przemyśl, and maybe even Russia after that.

"Help me, Fusia," he'd said. He had tears running down his face.

I sold everything. What else could I do? I bought in secondhand shops and sold to other secondhand shops for a few coins more. I saved money, and I saved more money. My last two dresses hung loose around my waist. I met Max at the fence and fed the Diamants. Maybe not as well as I had, but I fed them.

I told Max I had seen Izio. That he was alive and working. I did not tell him about his condition.

And I did not tell Max about the plan.

On the day I'd set with Izio, I bought a train ticket, one men's shoe hidden beneath each armpit under a coat that was much too warm for July, a shirt stuffed inside my dress, a cap, pants, and one pair of slightly bent glasses I'd found in the street all rolled into a little package that could pass as my lunch.

I sat sweating on the swaying, jolting train, then went to the hole that was the lavatory and threw up the tea I'd had for breakfast. I felt better for it, went back to my seat, and let the window glass down, concentrating on the air in my face and what would happen when this was over. The war would end. Izio would finish medical school and get his job in the hospital. We'd have a new apartment with pale cream carpets that never got dirty and modern wallpaper with no flowers. Two children, with jackets and ribbons and birthdays written down.

My nerves rattled inside me like the train wheels.

And then the wind in my face slowed. The swaying seat slowed, and the train wheels chugged to a stop. I craned my neck out the window. Far ahead there were tanks crossing the tracks, guns poking out of their turrets, jeeps with swastikas driving along by their side. And then came men, line after line of them.

No one spoke in the train car. There wasn't any point. We just sat, waiting for the German Army to pass.

We waited for five hours.

The train jolted forward. A sigh of relief went up from the passengers. We moved for maybe twenty minutes and stopped again.

For three and a half hours. And when I finally got to Lwów, the moon was up and the camp was shut down.

I'd missed Izio.

7.

July 1942

I FOUND A WOMAN WHO WOULD GIVE ME A ROOM FOR THE NIGHT, THOUGH IT meant I wouldn't have money for food the next day.

I hoped he hadn't waited for me. Surely when he hadn't seen me beside the latrines, he hadn't come. Surely he hadn't done what we'd planned.

The woman would only let me stay in my room until lunchtime, and since there was no lunch, I put on my hot coat and wandered Lwów until it was evening and time for the imprisoned workers to shuffle back into Janowska. They came into the camp in stooped lines, and I took my post near the latrines, tying a bright red scarf around my hair. Waiting. I didn't see Izio, but it was difficult in the crowd of men with their shaved heads and gray cloth. I, on the other hand, was easy to spot. Conspicuous in the twilight.

I waited.

And I waited.

The summer dark came late and reluctant. If Izio didn't appear soon, we would miss the last train. If he didn't come at all, I would have to sleep in some field and do this all over again tomorrow. The guard in the front of the office door changed. And then I heard a "pssst."

I looked around. The new guard was beckoning. I came slowly while he peered at me through the dim. It was the German soldier whose cheek I'd kissed. He shook his head.

"It's you," he said. And he didn't sound happy about it. "I thought it was you. Looking for your 'brother-in-law'?"

I didn't answer. There was something awful about the way he was speaking. He slurred like he was drunk, but I wasn't sure he was. There was a look on his face I didn't understand.

"I knew I shouldn't have let you in. I should never ..." He said words in German that were foreign but ugly and spit on the ground at my feet.

I looked up. "Why are you angry with me?"

"Because you got him killed, didn't you, *Liebchen*? Because one of the officer's wives went to use the latrine, and he thought it was you. Only it wasn't you. He made a plan with you, and you didn't come. That's the way it was, wasn't it?"

There was a noise inside my head. A soft, rumbling roar. It made it hard to concentrate. Hard to hear.

"That's what he said to us, in the end. But he would have said anything in the end, wouldn't he? I never should have ..." The man grimaced, spat again, and muttered, "Damned orchestra."

"You're lying to me."

The man laughed. "You're a Pole, and you say I'm the liar? I grew up in Poland, and I say all Poles are liars." He took a sudden step forward, grabbed me by the hair, and pulled my face to his. And he whispered in my ear all the things they'd done to Izio. I shook my head, cried out that it wasn't true, but he wouldn't stop. And then he shoved me so hard I stumbled back.

"Go away," he said. "Before I call the commandant."

I stood there, panting. Frozen.

Dead. Dead. Izio was dead.

"Get out!" the man yelled.

I took a step back, and another, and then I ran, straight into the field beside the camp. The roaring in my head was the sound of a low-flying plane. It surrounded me. I couldn't hear. I couldn't think. I could barely see. I staggered and tripped my way over the uneven ground, took out Izio's shoes from beneath the coat and threw them in two directions. Then I threw the package with the cap and glasses as hard as I could, yelling as it disappeared into the night. I nearly fell over a pile of stacked stones, bruised my shin, and sat on them instead.

And then I cried. Great, wracking sobs that must have been heard in the streets and maybe even in the camp.

He'd wanted to live. Tried to live, and they hadn't let him. The Nazis had killed him. They had made him suffer.

Something twisted inside me. Burning. Sick.

There was a tugging at my sleeve, and I realized a woman was standing in the dark in front of me, four or five other people-shaped figures behind her. One of them raised a flashlight. I saw my dirty shoes and crumpled dress, my wet coat lying on the dewy grass.

"Are you ill, child?" said the woman.

I put out a hand, steadying myself against the cold stone I was sitting on. The rock was smooth, flat, and now that there was light, I could see writing chiseled on it. I wasn't on rocks. I was sitting on a pile of discarded tombstones. I looked back at the soft and lumpy ground. This was a cemetery.

Maybe Izio was here.

"Have you eaten?"

I realized for the second time that a woman stood beside me, and now she was holding out a cracker. I took it and ate like the child she obviously thought I was.

"You've lost someone?" another voice asked.

I nodded.

"Poor girl."

"Can we take you home?"

Their kindness hurt almost like cruelty, because there had been no kindness for Izio.

"The train station," I whispered.

They bundled me off and got me to the station in a cart, making sure I had a ticket and a whole package of saltines in my hands before they left. I don't know how many there were. I don't even remember what they looked like.

I got to Przemyśl after curfew, but I went home anyway. To my empty grave of an apartment building. And I didn't see one policeman or German patrol on the way. Emilika had left me a note. She'd gone to visit her mother in Kraków. I drank some water and lay down on my bed. Had it really been that long since he was here?

It had. Because that had been a different world.

I got up with the sun, found paper and pen, and wrote a letter to the Diamants. I told them Izydor had died in the camp. That he had been shot, quickly. That he had been buried in Lwów and maybe they could visit the grave after the war.

Lies.

Except that he was dead.

I gave the letter to our mailman, Mr. Dorlich. He tipped his cap. He was Jewish, but he was still allowed to run the mail, as long as he showed up in the ghetto afterward. The SS men waited for him at the gate. I watched him drive his horse and cart and my letter away down the paving stones, then hoisted a packed knapsack onto my back.

I wanted my mother.

I wanted my sisters.

I wanted to go home.

I didn't have any money.

So I started walking.

I walked like a machine. An echoing shell made of metal and mechanical parts. And twenty-five kilometers and one short wagon ride later, I was walking down the lane to our farm.

The sun was low, sending bright orange beams over the hills and curving fields. But there was nobody in them. Oats rippled alone in the wind, branches waving at the edge of the forest, and when I got near the house, I knew something was wrong. There was no sound of chickens. There were no chickens at all, and no cows, either. No *whoosh* and *nicker* from the horses. The barn was empty. And the back door of the house stood open.

I stepped slowly, warily inside.

The kitchen had shrunk since the last time I was in it. The table was lower, the fireplace smaller, and the place was a mess. Chairs overturned, a cabinet door hanging from its hinges, the shelves inside dusty and bare. The air was stale. Unlived in. Unloved.

"Mama?" I whispered. "Stasiu? Is anyone here?"

I went from room to room, asking the same questions, but the house had no answers. Everything of value that could be carried was gone, down to the pillows off the beds. Some of Mama's oldest clothes were still in the closet, and one or two of *Tata*'s jackets, but her jewelry was missing, along with my grandmother's gilded egg that opened like a box.

And then I came to the room that had been mine. The hinges creaked as I pushed on the door. There was different paint on the walls, a pair of faded yellow chintz curtains fluttering at the open window. And in the center of the floor, on a bare mattress where I had once slept, was a brown-haired girl curled up into a ball.

"Helena!" I said. She started to cry.

"Where's Mama?" I asked her for the tenth time, but she only cried, letting me carry her downstairs like a newborn calf. I turned a chair back onto its legs and sat her on it, looking for something, anything, to boil water in. All I could find was an ancient chamber pot that had been the drinking bowl for the cat. There was no electricity. There had never been electricity, but I found matches on the mantel that no one had bothered to take, and there was some firewood still in the pile. I hauled water from the well, boiled it, threw it out the back door, and started again with a clean chamber pot.

All the while, Helena sat, hands folded together, watching me. Her short brown hair was tangled, her dress so torn it was barely decent. The gaps showed me bruises on her arms and the backs of her legs. I fished the one cup I owned out of the knapsack and poured in hot water and a spoonful of sugar from my supplies, plus a sprig of mint from Mama's window box.

I told Helena to blow on it before she drank. She did, and then she drank it in one gulp. I made her another. Her eyes were huge. Was Helena six or seven now? I decided she was six.

"They took them away," she whispered. "The men with the broken cross."

I realized she meant a swastika. I sat down in a chair. "Who did they take?"

"Mama and Stasiu."

But we're Catholic, I thought. "Was anyone else here?" I asked. "Did they take anyone else? Was Marysia here?"

"No. I don't know."

"When was the last time you ate, Hela?"

"This morning. I found raspberries in the woods."

They must have been overripe. "How many raspberries did you find?"

"Four."

"And when was the last time you ate before that?"

"Yesterday morning. I found raspberries."

"And where did you sleep before that?"

"At Mrs. Zielinski's. Mama left me there."

Ah. Now we were getting somewhere. "And you've been here by yourself since yesterday?"

She nodded, tears rolling down her cheeks. "Why did she leave me there, Stefi?"

I didn't know. Because she didn't know what else to do? I felt like crying, too. About everything. Only I couldn't. I smiled for Helena. "Let's have something to eat."

"Do I have to go back to the Zielinskis'?"

I eyed her bruises. Mrs. Zielinski had been a great friend of my mother's, dandling baby Helena on her knee. But ever since the German Army had come, it seemed like anyone was capable of anything.

The Germans. They'd taken both my families. My insides writhed. Hot.

Helena was waiting for my answer. I didn't know what to do with her any more than Mama had, so I only said, "Let's stay here tonight."

I let her eat the rest of the crackers the people in the cemetery had given me while I cut a green stick from the hawthorn bush outside the front door and managed toasted bread and cheese with the food I'd packed. She ate slowly, savoring each bite. I made do with an apple.

Then I banked the fire, locked the doors, and took her back upstairs with a chamber pot of warm water and a lantern I'd found in the barn. I scrubbed her off as best I could, being gentle with her sore places, combed her hair, and let her wrap up in one of Mama's leftover shirts. There were no linens. I lay down beside her on the bare mattress, and she was asleep in seconds.

Every part of me ached. I'd barely eaten, hadn't slept more than a few minutes since Lwów, and I'd walked nearly thirty kilometers in a day. I'd lost Izio, and my mother and Stasiu. Maybe others I didn't even know about. My feet hurt. My head hurt. And in my chest there was a well of grief that felt worse than the sickness.

I watched Helena sleep in the lantern light. She was thin, but her face was still soft, round with childhood. And all I could think was that she was my sister. My family. And she was here. Right now. She needed me. Everyone else was beyond my help.

I pushed Izio into some deep, deep place inside me and built a dam across my sadness. I would deal with it later, when I knew how. I put my arm around Helena and slept.

In the morning, I took the paths through the fields. It's funny, what isn't forgotten. I knew their twists and turns like the streets of Przemyśl. After half a kilometer or so, Helena slid from my nearly numb arms to the ground in front of the Zielinskis' gate. Her face was solemn above her indecent dress, and she held my hand so tight it hurt. I knocked, and an old man, a stranger with a few strands of white and rumpled hair, peered blearily into the sunlight.

"Could I see Mrs. Zielinski, please?"

"No," replied the man. I felt my brows come together.

"Why not?"

"Because she's dead. I'll get my son-in-law."

The door shut again. This was Mrs. Zielinski's father, then. He'd never lived here before. I looked down at Helena. "You didn't tell me Mrs. Zielinski died."

"You didn't ask," replied Helena. She was close to crying again, her hand shaky in mine. I held it tighter. The door opened again, and there was Mr. Zielinski. Helena shrank back.

"Oh, ho. Another Podgórska. What do you want?"

The man was drunk. Before eight o'clock in the morning. And I don't think he'd even noticed Helena. I was remembering why I'd never liked Mr. Zielinski. "I want to know what happened to my mother and my brother."

He shrugged. "Soldiers came, dragged them off. A labor camp in Germany. Working for Hitler now, and the farm going to the devil."

Germany. In a labor camp. Like Izio. The sickness inside me flamed.

"How long ago was that?"

He shrugged. "Six, seven weeks."

While I had been taking care of the Diamants. If I had been here, maybe I could have warned them. Told them what the Germans were like. Hidden them. Made them run.

I shoved this guilt behind the dam inside me. To punish myself with later.

"You've been caring for my little sister," I said.

"Who?"

"My sister, Helena."

He leaned on the doorframe. It helped him stay upright. "That was my Ela's business. But she's gone now."

I didn't know if he meant Helena or his wife.

"So do you think it's your business to beat innocent children and turn them out to starve in the woods, Mr. Zielinski?"

He raised a pointed finger. "Your mama said she would pay, and she hasn't sent one *zloty*. No money, no food. And if the girl won't clean, she'll take the back of my hand."

I stared at his smudges of whiskers, the bags under his eyes, and the fat that had collected at his armpits. He smelled. When he didn't have to. I held Helena behind me and took a step forward.

"God is going to pay you back," I said.

He looked a little startled.

"For every time you hit her, I'm going to pray that a German soldier comes and beats you ten times with a club. And for every day you made her go hungry, I'm going to pray that you go ten days with nothing to eat and especially with nothing to drink. I'm going to pray that you break out in boils. That you're bitten by a rabid dog. That your teeth turn black and your ... your parts fall off ..." I glanced down, and so did he. "And that the nasty vodka you brew in that barn of yours rots you slowly from the inside out!"

Mr. Zielinski opened his mouth. And closed it again.

"And between the two of us, Mr. Zielinski, I think you know whose prayers God is going to answer, you miserable *schmuck*."

I picked up Helena, turned, and marched away from the house, kicking the front gate shut behind me with a bang. The door to the house slammed, and with a glow of satisfaction, I heard the thump of the lock bar coming down. Helena's arms gripped tight around my neck.

"Do you have any shoes or clothes in that house?" I whispered.

"No. They sold them."

"Good." I was hot with rage.

"I don't have to go back?" Helena asked.

"No."

"Never?"

"Never."

She laid her head on my shoulder, her feet dangling around my knees. And then she giggled.

The farther we got from the Zielinskis', the less Helena clung. After a while, she walked beside me. A little longer, and she skipped. Three kilometers later, and I started to think about what I was doing. How was I going to feed a little girl? Clothe her? Was she supposed to be in school? I had no idea how to take care of a child.

But there was only me to do it. And so I would.

If God had any justice, I thought, tromping up and down the hilly road, he would answer my prayers for Mr. Zielinski. And then I prayed a thousand times more agony on the Germans. For the ghetto. For taking my mother and brother. For stopping trains. And for what they had done to Izio.

Helena needed to rest every kilometer or so now. She said her head hurt and her feet hurt, so I carried her on my back, and then I needed to rest. I split the last piece of bread with her, drank from a stream, and we walked on. We didn't see a car or cart all day, and with all the stopping, it took twice the time to retrace my steps, come down through the hills, and see the lights of Przemyśl spreading out on either side of the river.

Only there were very few lights. The city was dim, the windows dark, just a streetlight here and there, half-hidden by the buildings. I didn't have a watch, but it had to be well after midnight. I held Helena's hand, biting my lip. Thinking.

I'd come back to the city after curfew before, once or twice, when there was a better price to be had for Mrs. Diamant's goods in the villages than the city shops. I'd slept in the fields on those nights, waiting for the sun and the right to be on the streets. But it was still a long time until dawn, and I didn't like the look of my sister. She was silent and staring, swaying on her feet, and our sweat had turned chill. She shivered, and I made a decision. There hadn't been any German patrol the last time I went home after curfew. We could stay in the back alleys.

"Come on, Hela. Not far now. We'll have tea and a warm bath, and you can sleep in a bed all night ..."

She nodded like she was dreaming, half-naked in her fraying dress. I bit my lip again. She couldn't go among people like that, even if they were already in their beds. I steered her behind a tree, pulled my own dress over my head and threw it over hers. She woke up a little, putting her arms in the huge sleeves while I cinched the belt tight. The extra material bulged over the tightened belt, but at least she wouldn't trip. I got my coat out of the knapsack and put it on over my slip.

"See," I told her, "no one will know. But you have to be very quiet, walk fast, and do exactly what I tell you, yes? It's like a game. We're going to see if we can get to the door of my house without anybody seeing ..."

I started off at a trot, Helena stumbling along beside me, and we slipped into Przemyśl. We ducked behind the first buildings, staying out of the light, pausing to listen and look around each corner. The city was as silent as I'd ever heard it, only the rumble of a train in the distance. Then we came up on Mickiewicza Street. This was a main road, and there was little cover.

"Hurry, Hela!" I whispered, dragging her along by the hand. We skirted the yellow circles around the bottoms of the streetlights, running past the steps of shops and apartment buildings.

"Stefi ..." Helena panted. "I can't ..."

"Come on!" I whispered.

"I can't ... breathe ..." Helena made a choking sound that was much too loud in the quiet. And then her hand went limp, and she fell face-first onto the sidewalk.

She didn't get up. She didn't move.

I dropped to my knees and flipped her over. She'd scraped her forehead, and the blood looked bright against her white, white face. Her cheeks were cold. Her hands were cold. I couldn't see her chest move. I couldn't find her heartbeat.

And suddenly the dam inside me burst, and grief gushed out in a torrent. I was going to lose them all. Every single person I loved. And it was always my fault.

My fault. My fault. My fault ...

I looked down at Helena's still face, and I screamed.

8.

July 1942

I SCREAMED AGAIN. I SCREAMED HER NAME, BUT HELENA WAS STILL. EVEN when I shook her.

And then she opened her mouth and sighed.

I gasped, hand to my chest, and a voice in the darkness said, *"Halt! Wer ist da?"*

Beams of light played across my face, blinding me. A pistol cocked.

Helena wasn't dead. But I had just killed us. I slowly raised my hands.

"Please," I said, squinting. "My sister, she's sick. I need a doctor ..."

I could see boots and the little tunnel of the pistol coming down the sidewalk. A dog barked.

"A doctor!" I said. "Please!"

The boots stopped, and a German toe prodded Helena's side. She coughed, and the boots leapt back. There was muttering behind the lights.

Then the voice that had spoken before gave another order in terrible Polish that might have been "pick her up" and "come with us."

I scooped Helena into my arms, staggering to my feet. She was heavier when she was unconscious, and I was shaking, but I managed it. A German policeman walked behind me, his gun pointed at my back while I followed the rest of the patrol down the sidewalk in a slow parade.

We were being arrested, and I knew what would happen. They would beat me, torture me. Find out I had been feeding Jews. That I had tried to help a Jew escape. That I had false information on my papers.

That looking at them made my stomach sick and my blood run hot and every bone in my body burn.

Telling them that part might actually feel good. But only, I suspected, for a minute or two.

We got to the police station but used a back entrance instead of the front. I laid Helena on a bench in an austere hallway bright with electric light, and two of the policemen searched my knapsack. I saw them pull out the cup and the matches and half a piece of bread. Half a piece of bread. That was Helena's share. From the stream. I glanced down at my sister's still face. Why hadn't she eaten her bread?

One of the policemen came and searched my pockets, then tried to take off my coat. I slapped his hands away. I was wearing nothing but a slip, and all the money I had in this world was tucked inside my bra. And I had no idea what they would make of that. I slapped the man's hands away again, and the other policeman laughed. They talked a little, probably about me, and left the way we'd come in.

One German with a pistol stayed with me. He didn't speak. He didn't even look at me. Probably he knew what was coming. I was less afraid than I thought I'd be.

Probably much less afraid than I should have been.

I sat down beside Helena. She was breathing, but she hadn't opened her eyes. I stroked her hair, wondering what would happen to her.

A door opened at the end of the hallway, and a man stuck his head through it. He looked at us both, then beckoned for me to come. I glanced at the guard, but he gave me no sign. It was time, then. I bent to pick up Helena.

"*Nein*, no. Let me," said the man. He came down the hall and scooped her up himself. He was in a German officer's uniform, but his Polish was very good, only a trace of an accent. I followed him into the room behind the door, which was not full of police and SS and guns and clubs. Instead it had a desk, some shelves, and an examining table, where he laid Helena.

"I am Dr. Becker," he said, pulling a stethoscope out of his pocket. "This is your sister?"

I nodded, numb with surprise.

"Tell me what has happened to her."

I told him while he undid Helena's ridiculously large dress and looked her over. I was afraid to have him touch her, but I was also afraid not to have help. He asked questions about what we had eaten and when, and what her behavior had been before she fainted. He examined her bruises. Helena began to stir a little and opened her eyes.

"Lie still," Dr. Becker told her. Then to me, "Please. Sit down. Would you like to hang up your coat?"

I sat and shook my head, holding the coat closed.

"Wait here, please," he said, and left the room.

And this is where the police come, I thought. They'll take me away, and I'll never see Helena again. I broke out in a sweat.

The door opened again, and the doctor came back. With two cups of tea. He handed one to me and took one to Helena, sitting her up and holding the cup so she could sip.

"Your sister is undernourished and exhausted," the doctor said. "Mostly she needs rest and good food." He pulled a package of biscuits from his pocket, helped Helena stand up, and gave one to her. "Drink," he said to me. "It's full of sugar and a little milk. You look as if you need it."

I did what he said, watching him intently over the cup. Waiting for the trick.

"She does have a small fever, and I do hear something in her lungs," he said. "So I will give you a course of antibiotics and some aspirin. You will give it to her? You will not sell it?"

I looked at Helena, eating biscuits much faster than was polite, and shook my head. "I'll give it to her."

"Good. I will come and see her tomorrow, to make sure all is well. What is your address?"

I was so stunned, I gave it to him. Then he called two policemen, who escorted us home so we would not be bothered by the patrol. I locked the door and washed Helena's face and hands, gave her one of the antibiotics and an aspirin, and tucked her into my bed. Emilika wasn't there. I hoped her visit to her mother had turned out differently than mine.

I fell asleep in a chair, waiting for the Gestapo to bang on the door.

When someone did knock the next morning, it was Dr. Becker. Just as he had said. Helena was sitting up in bed, hair combed and in my clean nightgown, and he chucked her chin and listened to her lungs and said she was a mouse and a little fairy. Then he told me I should keep taking good care of her with no more long journeys and left behind a sack of meal and a bottle of vitamins.

And I never saw him again.

On that day, I began the fourth part of my education in Przemyśl. It was wrong to paint all men the same color. Whether they be Jewish or Polish.

Or even German.

I stayed with Helena the next day, keeping her in bed and using the last of my food supplies. The morning after that I watched at the window, glass blurred by a drizzling rain, and when I saw the guarded lines of men coming down the street, I ran out to meet Max. I started to step into line beside him, water dripping from my hair, but he shook his head and looked back over his shoulder. This was not the usual guard. This was an SS man. I backed away, and Max held up seven fingers. He would meet me at the fence at seven in the evening. Then he put his head down and faced front, so as not to attract attention.

I watched him walk away, rain dripping off hair as dark as Izio's.

He had the saddest eyes I'd ever seen.

I thought he must have gotten my letter.

I walked down the street, thinking, then stood on a street corner, turned my back to the road, and reached surreptitiously for the money in my bra. I still had the *zloty* from Izio's train ticket. If I was careful, I would have enough to feed Helena and the Diamants for another week. At the most. And Helena needed a dress, shoes, underclothes, a nightgown, and probably other things I hadn't thought of yet.

I straightened myself up in the glass of a shop window and went to the dressmaker's, where I had asked about work before, but that position had been filled long ago. Then I stopped in every shop between Mickiewicza and the market square. Either there was no work, or I wasn't suited to the work, or there was just no shop at all, because it had been owned by a Jew. I gave up, went to the market, and got a decent bargain, since not many people were out in the rain, even managing a skirt for Helena that might be a little large. If I could get some thread, maybe I could tighten the waist and make her torn dress into a blouse.

When I came down the sidewalk, the sky was clearing and two trucks were blocking the road in front of my building, furniture piled in the backs like a house had been turned upside down. We were getting neighbors. I climbed the stairs, negotiating around people and boxes, and when I got to my room, I found a neighbor already there. Emilika had Helena in her lap, combing her hair, and Helena did not look pleased.

"I've met your sister," Emilika said, pulling Helena's hair straight back from her face. "She's been telling me all about your trip home, haven't you?" This last was to Helena, and Emilika didn't seem to notice when my sister didn't answer. I set down my packages, dropping my coat on top. If Emilika saw how much food I'd bought, she would ask questions. She talked on and on. About her mother, even though I didn't have mine. About a boy she'd met, even though I didn't have mine.

It wasn't fair. She didn't know. But I wanted to toss her out the window.

"So, Fusia, been biting pickles?" Emilika asked pleasantly. I think this meant I had a sour look on my face. So I told her about my search for work.

"Oh, but there are plenty of factory jobs," she said, "if you're willing to work for the Germans. There was a long line at the labor office yesterday just to put in applications. All the way down the street."

Which meant I was too late. I rubbed at my temple.

"There, there, Fusia, there's always a way," Emilika said. She'd tied back Helena's hair with a string. It was too tight. "A small gift might do the trick. Something to help the Germans put your name at the top of the list."

"What do you mean? What kind of gift?"

"About three hundred fifty *zloty*. That's what I've heard."

Three hundred fifty. How could I ever raise that much money? The box was nearly empty. I didn't have anything left to bargain with.

None of these thoughts sweetened my mood, and Helena's was no better. As soon as Emilika left, she sat down on the bed, arms crossed, refusing to come to the table for the bread and butter I'd cut. I told her she had to eat. She said she didn't. I told her Dr. Becker said so. She said no, he didn't. I ordered her to eat. She said she didn't take orders.

She was my sister, but she was also a child, and I didn't know what to do with her. I told her I had to go on an errand. Really, I just needed to walk. To think.

"I want to go with you," Helena said.

I must have already had the word "no" on my face, because she screwed up hers, arms tightening across her chest.

"I want to come."

"No!"

"Then take me home."

I didn't know what to do with that, either. I wasn't her mother. I wasn't anyone's mother. "I'm not taking you back to the farm, Hela."

"You don't want me here!"

"That's not true!"

But something guilty squirmed inside me when she said it. Something quickly squashed by the relief that my sister was alive. I sat beside her on the bed.

She wiped her eyes and said, "I heard you last night."

"Heard me what?"

"Crying. You wish I wasn't here."

I let out a long breath. And then I thought about Helena alone in the farmhouse, alone before that with a man who had beaten and neglected her. Of Helena sick in a strange room in an unfamiliar city. Of what it must have been like to wake up this morning and find me gone, only to have a stranger waltz in and ruin her hair. I thought about that leftover piece of bread.

I would not have my sister thinking she needed to starve to stay with me.

I pulled on the string, freeing her bangs. "I am not Mama," I said. "I won't try to be. But I am your sister. If we all can't be at home, then I'd rather have you with me than anywhere else in the world. So now we're a team. I'm going to need you to do what I ask, even if sometimes you don't understand, and in return I'm going to promise that I will tell you the truth. Always. Even if it's bad."

She frowned at the bed.

"And I'll start right now. Last night I was crying because someone died whom I wish hadn't. Okay? Nothing about you."

"Was it somebody I know?"

I shook my head. Her bare feet bumped against the bed rail.

"I'm not a baby," she said. "I can stay by myself. I went to the farm by myself every day. Only . . . nobody ever came back again."

"Well, I will come back again. That's another promise." I hoped I wasn't lying. "I will come back, Helena."

She didn't look convinced.

"Here. Come with me."

I took her to the front door and showed her how the lock worked, then showed her how a chair could be propped beneath the knob so it wouldn't turn. We made up a special knock so she would know it was me. Then we looked at all the empty rooms of the apartment, locked the bedroom door, and put a chair underneath that one, too. Helena smiled, then smiled bigger when I gave her the skirt. She sat on one of our two remaining chairs and chewed her bread.

"She called you Fusia," Helena said with her mouth full. "And Michal did, too." She was talking about our older brother. "I can't remember what I call you. For fun."

I supposed she couldn't. She had been a baby when I left home.

"Can I call you Fusia?" she asked.

Everyone else did. But I only said, "Call me whatever you want."

Helena thought hard, then she shrugged. "I'll call you Stefi."

Later that evening, when I shut the front door, the Diamants' food packages tucked inside my coat, I listened to the lock tumble into place behind me, the scrape of a chair on the other side.

Part of me wanted to lock my sister in the apartment until the war was over.

Part of me wanted to lock myself in with her.

I got to the fence a little before seven. The sun was low behind the buildings, but it was still warm, making my heavy coat a strange choice. I waited around the corner, tapping a nervous toe, a new DEATH TO THOSE WHO AID A JEW poster pasted above my head. I didn't like it there. It was as if the Germans knew someone standing in this spot needed the warning. Then I heard a tango being whistled from the alley. From the other side of the fence.

I ducked around the corner into the narrow passage with the fence post. Max was waiting, but instead of taking the packages, he lifted the fence post out of its hole and pulled me inside.

"Shhh," he said when I protested. "Do you have a handkerchief?" He found it in my pocket without waiting for my answer and tied it around my upper right arm. Then he took me to a door and opened it. There was an abandoned warehouse inside, a dark, dank sort of place where rats scuttled. He leaned close to my ear.

"There will be an *Aktion* in the ghetto."

"What is a ..."

"Everyone without a work card will be taken to a labor camp."

I didn't trust the words "labor camp." "Why are you whispering?"

"Because anyone will denounce anyone to the Germans. Even Jews, if they think it will save their life."

"Do you have a work card?"

I felt his nod in the dark. "And Chaim, and Henek and his girlfriend. Our parents do not."

"They're going?"

I felt his nod again.

"When?"

"In the next few days. So we're giving this to them ..." He held up the food packages. "Or as much as they can carry."

This was all happening so quickly it was hard to register the emotions. I would deal with them later.

"Can you bring more," he said, "for after?"

"Do you have anything to sell?" And then I told him quickly about Helena, and the lack of work, except for German jobs that required money to get.

"Okay. I'll ask. And, Fusia ..." I think he was rubbing his fingers over his head. "I wanted to know ..."

We both stopped to listen. There were boots going down the alley at a sharp clip. They passed our door, the barbed wire rattled, and then they passed by again, fading out of hearing.

"I think they know about the fence," I whispered.

"I think you are right. Meet me here tomorrow, inside, and after that, we'll find a new place." He rubbed his head again. "I have to ask you. About your letter."

Something inside me seized. Max's words could barely be heard.

"It was a lie, wasn't it? About it being ... quick."

It felt impossible to speak. If I had gotten there on time, maybe none of it would have happened. Maybe Izio would be with us now. But if anyone understood this pain, it was Max. Izio had taken his place. I gritted my teeth, and I nodded.

"Okay," Max said. "Okay." We stood for a few minutes in the dripping dark, and then he listened at the door. "I think the alley is empty. Be careful, and ..." He caught my hand and kissed it. "Thank you for lying to *Mame*."

I slipped through the fence as quick as I could, and when I rounded the corner with the poster, there was no one there. And there was no one there the next night, either, when Max handed me two shirts, a watch, and a brooch that had been stowed safely inside Mrs. Diamant's girdle.

"Use it to get work," Max said. "We'll be hungry now, but we'll eat for longer if you have regular pay."

I put the treasures under my coat, but this time, as I set the fence post back in its hole, I heard the sharp bark of a German order from the street in front of the empty warehouse. And then Max was talking, telling them he wasn't doing anything, only looking for an uncle, who ...

I made it around the corner and stood beneath the poster, breathing hard, closing my eyes to the sound of fists hitting flesh.

Please, God, don't let them kill Max.

I couldn't sleep that night.

But in the morning, right on time, there was Max, looking up at my window as he was marched to the coal yards. He had a bruise on his face and a swollen lip, but he was whole. I spent the day making bargains, and the next day, I had 340 *zloty.*

I had to hope it was enough.

I was in line at the labor department early.

Chuztpah. Mrs. Diamant always said I had it. And today, it was what I needed.

I shifted from foot to foot in the line, arms across my grumbling middle, hair neat and mouth smeared just the tiniest bit red. By midmorning, I'd made it inside the building. By midafternoon, it was my turn. I straightened my back and walked briskly to the desk, smiling as if the German sitting behind it were the only person in the world I'd ever wanted to sell something to.

This man did not have wire-rimmed glasses. He had a mole on his chin.

"Hello," I said. "I hope you're well today."

The man glanced from my overbright face to the line behind me. He almost faltered. "Papers," he said wearily. I sat myself in a chair.

"I was hoping to get work," I said. "And I was hoping to get it quickly. You see ..." I leaned forward. "I have a little sister. She's six years old, and she's without her mother. Our mother and brother are away at the moment, working hard for the Fatherland, like you are ..."

The man sighed and wiped his nose on his uniform sleeve. I could have been spreading on this jam a little thick.

"And while they're away, I will need to feed her ..."

"Papers," he said again, holding out his hand.

"So I was hoping," I went on, "that you would be understanding and put my name at the top of your list." I gave him my papers, watching his face as he unfolded them. Trying to read his expression when he saw the money tucked between the pages. There was a little silence.

"I'm a very good worker," I said quickly. "I've had a job since I was twelve. I'm always on time."

The man opened a desk drawer, tilted my papers, and let the *zloty* drop neatly inside before slamming it shut again. He handed back my papers, then slid a form and pencil across the desk. "Fill this out, *Fräulein*."

I did, my stomach twisting into knots. The money was gone. But I smiled at the man again when I'd finished the form.

"And the job?"

"You will receive a letter."

"But ..."

"You will be contacted, *Fräulein*."

"But ..."

"Next!"

I clutched my papers and walked away from the desk. The watch. The brooch. They were sacrifices, and I'd just gambled them away to a Nazi. For nothing.

It made me sick to think about it.

I woke up in the night. Worrying about Max and the failure of my *chutzpah*. And then I realized what had woken me. A scream. A woman's scream in the distance.

And I knew that voice.

The mattress creaked and popped as I kicked back the covers, left Helena sleeping, and ran out of the bedroom and through the empty apartment to Mr. and Mrs. Diamant's old room. I threw up the window sash and leaned out as far into the cool night as I dared.

And I saw lights in the ghetto, spotlights blazing, leaving the other places inky in the dark. Train cars were lined up, people thronging so thick it was impossible to make out individual bodies. But I could hear them. Sharp shouts, children crying. Dogs barked. Gunfire popped, sometimes pistols, sometimes the spurt of a machine gun, and then, at the end of the line, I saw that people were being pushed onto the trains. One by one into cars that were too high to step into. Going in on their stomachs, their backs. Sometimes they fell. Sometimes the dogs pulled them down. The din made me want to cover my ears. I wanted to cover my eyes.

But above it all, I heard the voice again. A woman's cry.

It was my *babcia*. I knew it. Mrs. Diamant was being put on one of those trains.

I stood at the window until the crowd was mostly gone and the trains had started moving, steam billowing up from their stacks.

And I was waiting for Max as he was marched to work the next morning, barely able to stand still on the sidewalk. The usual guard glared at me, but when his glare didn't work, he gave up. I stepped into line beside Max. But I didn't speak. Max was pale. His dark eyes shadowed. He marched in time, step by step, and he looked ready to fight. To explode. And then he started talking, slow. Measured.

Henek and his girlfriend, Danuta, were gone. But only to a farm, to work the fields until the harvest. But his parents. He'd begged them to hide. Pleaded. They had said that it was only a work camp. A work camp might be all right. If they hid and they were found, it meant death. But then the trains had come, and the SS officer had laughed when Max tried to bring his parents tea. His parents did not need tea, the man said. His parents would never need tea. Because the trains were going to place called Bełżec, and Bełżec was not a work camp, you stupid Jew.

Bełżec was one great killing machine.

Max stopped talking, staring straight ahead, and I stepped out of line and stood in the traffic of the sidewalk. We were nearly to the coal yard.

Mr. and Mrs. Diamant. They were dead. All those men, women, and children I had seen being put on the trains. They were dead.

We were still living. But we must have been living in hell.

9.

August 1942

THEY MADE THE GHETTO SMALLER AFTER THAT FIRST *AKTION*, DRAWING in the fences like a noose. My loose post wasn't even along the border anymore. I arranged a new meeting place with Max, though if the right policeman was on duty, we could just meet near the gate and trade through the fence. Like everyone else was doing. The Jews inside were selling anything and everything for food, and for those of us outside, there was a bargain to be had, German laws or not. Sometimes I had to find Max through a crowd. Other times the SS were on duty and the only noise at the ghetto gate was the rustle of a newspaper blowing down the street to stick against the barbed wire.

Max and Chaim had to go to a different apartment in the smaller ghetto, sharing a former kitchen with Dr. Schillinger, the dentist Max had assisted in Nizankowice; his young daughter, Dziusia; and another older man, a Dr. Hirsch, and his grown son, Siunek. They began pooling resources, and Max brought me four gold buttons, some earrings, and two coats to sell.

I didn't think he should trust me with these things. I'd lost what he had brought me last time. And one of his brothers. But this kind of guilt was not new to Max. I saw it in his eyes every time we talked about his parents, who were dead when he was not. And Izio, dead in his place. We understood each other, Max and I. Blame wouldn't bring them back. And neither would starving. And so I did what Max did, and set the guilt and the grief to one side. I became an expert at trading and reselling at the secondhand shops. One thing for another, another for another. Selling and selling and selling again until, somehow, I fed us.

It was like a game. Stay alive. Spite the Nazis.

I also managed to find shoes and a coat for Helena and a cast-off rug for our feet. Helena played on the stairs and in the street with the children who had moved into our building, and we saw Emilika most days, though she had stopped sleeping in my room. The building didn't seem as full of ghosts as it had.

Except in the Diamants' apartment. Those rooms were still empty, and sometimes, when I listened close, I thought I could hear Yiddish in the hallway. Smell blintzes and stale cigarettes. And if I sat quiet on the windowsill, I could almost see the shadow of Izio lying on the floor, hands behind his head, his feet propped up on the sofa.

Only none of it was really there.

I was like a gourd. Empty and rattling on the inside.

I came back to the apartment after a full day of running back and forth in the markets, and the best I'd been able to get for our money was *kasha*. A five-kilo sack of it. Too large to carry concealed beneath my coat. So I tied tight strings around the wristbands of my dress, another around my waist, and then Helena, laughing at the silliness of it, stood on a chair and carefully emptied the *kasha* sack into my sleeves and the upper part of my dress. I squirmed. All the little grains felt itchy and terrible, and I bulged in strange places, though it wasn't so bad with my big coat on. But it also meant I couldn't meet Max at the fence. I would have to go inside the ghetto.

Helena locked the front door behind me, and the chair scraped into place. She knew I helped get food for other people, but she'd never questioned who or why. It was just something I did. She believed me when I said I would be back.

So did I. It wouldn't be that hard to get in and out. The rules had relaxed with less of a ghetto to control. The past few days the ghetto had been left to the Ordners, the Jewish police established by the *Judenrat*, Jews appointed to govern other Jews on behalf of Hitler. But if the policeman on patrol was Polish, he might just look the other way.

I stepped onto the sidewalk. The sun was gone, and the wind blew cool, bringing the first hint of the smell of autumn. But the atmosphere felt tense. Heads were down, collars up, everyone hurrying though it was only just past six. And no one was talking. No one was looking at one another. It made me feel cautious. I said good evening to Mr. Szymczak, our new neighbor downstairs, buying a German newspaper on the corner, and he just shook his head.

"Is something wrong, Mr. Szymczak?"

He took a quick glance around the street. "Gestapo," he whispered. "Didn't you hear? They searched every apartment and shop on Na Bramie Square."

I hadn't heard. Na Bramie was only a block or so from my little room, but my windows faced the other way. "What were they looking for?"

"Jews, of course. Hiding from ... you know what."

He meant the *Aktion*.

"And what did they find?" I asked, as if I didn't care.

But Mr. Szymczak was out of information. I went slowly to the ghetto and stood in the shadow of a doorway, watching our deserted section of fence for a long time before approaching it. There was nobody there. But the barbed wire was loose—because Max had made it loose—giving just enough space to crawl beneath.

Sliding under was tricky with a shirt full of *kasha*, but I managed it, and when I did, nothing happened. No shouts or flying bullets. Relief lightened my feet. I slid my false armband—now inked with a neat Jewish star—up and over my bulging sleeve and darted into the ghetto like a bird.

I found the apartment with ease, on a main road not far from the gate. They were surprised to see me. Even more surprised when I took off my coat, stood on a blanket, untied my belt and sleeve strings, and let the *kasha* come spilling out. Siunek Hirsch laughed harder than Helena had, and little Dziusia, her long black curls frizzing down her back, was given the task of picking up every grain I'd spilled. Which made me wish I'd done things more carefully.

"We've gotten a letter," Chaim said while I was shaking out my sleeves. Chaim was a shadow of himself, trying to heal starving people in the ghetto's hospital with no food and no medicine. Max said that mostly, he helped them die. "Henek says he doesn't know how much longer they will stay on the farm."

"Let the boy stay!" said old Mr. Hirsch from his spot on the floor. "It's better than sitting here, waiting for death."

I exchanged a look with Max. We'd already discussed what might happen when the harvest was over. When Henek and Danuta were no longer needed.

"He also says he's asked Danuta to marry him," said Chaim, frowning. "It's a strange thing to do. Now. Of all times."

98

"It's not strange," I snapped. "Henek should be happy in any way he can. For as long as he can." I jabbed an arm into my coat, poking around behind me with the other arm, but I couldn't find my sleeve.

Old Mr. Hirsch waved a hand. "Let the boy be married! Why should he wait for death, wanting to be married?"

Dr. Schillinger went to distract Mr. Hirsch while Chaim shook his head, a move I thought might topple him over. Max came and held up my coat so I could get it on. He knew exactly why Chaim's words had made me mad.

"There are rumors," Max said quietly, "of another *Aktion* in the ghetto."

I turned around. "That can't be true."

But I looked closer at his face and thought it could be.

"Is there a list?"

"Maybe." He shrugged. "Or maybe it's by street. No one knows. It's not official."

"What are you going to do?"

"I won't be sitting and waiting, I can say that to you."

Max had the biggest brown eyes. They reminded me of his brother's. But there was something different from his brother in them. A look of no nonsense I'd never seen in Izio's.

Maybe I'd never had the opportunity.

Max straightened the lapel of his mother's old coat. "It won't be like last time. We know now. We can prepare. Don't worry ..."

But I did worry. His words were exactly what made me worry, as I wandered the ghetto beneath moonlight instead of streetlights because the electricity was out, back to the loose place in the barbed wire fence.

Only I was worrying about the wrong things. I had just lifted the wire, ready to slide back to the other side, when I felt cold metal against my neck. I jumped and tried to turn my head, but I'd already caught a glimpse out of the corner of my eye. The long, gleaming barrel of a rifle.

I froze and slowly held up my hands. A flashlight clicked, and a yellow circle with the shadow of my body inside it appeared on the other side of the fence. Footsteps crunched on bits of gravel and glass, and another gun touched the back of my head. A pistol, I thought, because this body was close, close enough to jerk the handkerchief with its star off my arm. It had been sagging, loose on my emptied sleeve.

A low conversation began in German. I stayed on my knees, hands in the air, and considered dying. Being shot like this might not be so bad. I would never know it had happened. But what about Max? Chaim, and the rest? And Helena.

I should have listened. Paid attention. Done anything but what I had done.

My knees hurt, my heart hurt, and my arms ached. I prayed to God, Christ, and Mary. The German conversation stopped. I closed my eyes. Tried to be calm. And waited through the longest minute that had ever gone by in the history of Przemyśl.

And then I realized there were no guns beside my head. The circle of light with my shadow was changing shape, lengthening while footsteps backed away down the sidewalk.

I didn't turn. I didn't move. I didn't breathe.

The light switched off. And was gone.

I waited on my knees in the alley. And waited. And when I finally looked over my shoulder, the street was empty. I slid under the barbed wire and ran. I ran and ran, past the station, over the bridge, through a small square and up a hilly road of rough cobblestones, until I found an alley behind an apartment block and leaned against its wall, panting beside a rubbish heap. Sweating. Shaking. One of my knees was bleeding.

I couldn't think why I was alive.

I limped slowly back toward the apartment, coat pulled tight around my neck, trying to smooth away the fear from my face before I had to see Helena. New posters had been slapped next to the now-familiar Death to Those Who Aid a Jew warnings, some of them pasted around the posts of the streetlights. The design was simple, the word *"Jude"* at the top and "Vermin" at the bottom, a detailed drawing of what must have been a flea in between. I turned the corner, and it took me longer than it should have to realize there was a commotion in the street.

A small crowd had gathered just a few doors down from the passage at Mickiewicza 7. I heard the sound of blows, shouting, a child crying out. And there was a little girl running as hard as she could down the sidewalk, straight to me. It was Helena.

"What are you doing out of—"

She threw her arms around my middle, and the people thronging the street stepped back enough to show me what was happening. Two SS men were beating a child with clubs, a girl smaller than Helena, and then an older man with a beard came tumbling out the doorway of a warehouse like he'd been thrown. I think he had been thrown. He was followed by an elderly woman and a young girl about my age but smaller. She had lovely blue eyes. I looked again at the bearded man. Mr. Schwarzer. He'd been a friend of Mr. Diamant's. I looked at the three of them.

They were Jews.

And they were not in the ghetto.

And then came a Polish family out of the warehouse. A man and wife and two more children, and another two SS officers behind them. The woman tried to tear the men with clubs away from her little girl, who was no longer moving, and so they hit her instead.

One of the SS came forward, and the noise of the people watching went silent.

"Death to Jews and all who aid them!" he said.

He drew his pistol.

I peeled Helena from my middle, took her hand, and ran her hard down the street in the opposite direction.

"Death to Jews!" he shouted. He sounded insane. Possessed. And then the gunshots began.

One. Two.

People screamed. Scattered. They ran around us, some toward the sound of the shooting, others away from it.

Three. I flinched. Four.

"What's happening?" asked Helena, tugging on my hand.

Our neighbors had been hiding Mr. Schwarzer.

Five. Flinch.

"Stefi, what's happening?"

They had helped three Jews. And now the Gestapo were shooting their children.

Six. Flinch. Seven. Flinch.

I'd promised to tell Helena the truth, even when it was bad. But I couldn't tell her this.

Eight.

We turned the corner, ran another half block, and I turned again without thinking. Helena trotted beside me. I hurried down a set of stone steps into a quiet sunken courtyard and pushed open a carved oak door.

It was empty inside the cathedral. Silent. We were half-below street level here, and the stained glass was a dim muddle of colors. Candles glowed above the altar, the cross with the effigy of the dying Christ above that. We dipped our fingers in holy water, knelt, crossed ourselves like we'd done a thousand times, and I led Helena to a pew. It creaked in the silence.

We sat, smelling the incense. I wanted my rosary. I wanted different words to march like an army through my head.

They shot the children. They shot the children. They shot the children . . .

"Those men knocked on our door," said Helena. "Only it wasn't the right knock, so I didn't let them in . . ."

Fear shot through me like a bullet.

"Then they broke the door and came in anyway," Helena went on. "But we didn't have what they were looking for."

I breathed in and out. Helena squeezed my hand tight.

"Stefi, what is a Jew?"

I looked up at the image of the Christ and wondered what to say to her. And then I remembered the man in the market. When I first came to Przemyśl. Back when I was a little girl myself, full of hope. I stretched out our held hands, straightening both our arms.

"Look at our skin, Hela," I whispered. "Yours is a little browner than mine, but it's still skin, isn't it? It's skin over blood over bones, just like any person. A Jew is a person with blood and skin and a family, some of them good, some of them bad, just like everyone. Only they choose Moses as their leader instead of Jesus. But remember, Jesus was a Jew, too. One God for both, Hela. Our mama said that."

I wasn't sure our mama had meant it the way I did. She'd sounded confused and possibly disappointed. But Helena didn't need to know that. I watched my sister think.

"Is it wrong to help a Jew?" she asked.

"No," I said. "No, it is not."

I didn't know how she could understand. I didn't understand anything. But she nodded, and we waited to go home until it was nearly curfew, though I took her into the little hidden courtyard of our building through the farthest entrance, away from the violence that had been on the street.

The apartment door hung open, as did the door to our bedroom, both the locks splintered from the wood. A chair was turned over, the bed blankets disturbed, but other than the fright they'd given my sister, everything seemed in order. We were lucky not to have been robbed.

I asked Mr. Szymczak if he would help me reattach my locks, and he did, somberly, while I made Helena a late dinner from our portion of the *kasha*. She sang and talked to herself, playing and pretending while she ate, and I couldn't tell how much she understood about what had just happened. Mr. Szymczak left me his hammer and a handful of nails. He said I was bound to need them.

I think he felt sorry for us.

When Helena was asleep, I wandered into the empty living room and turned on the lights. It was dirty and bare and alien, though the scratches on the mantel were familiar, where the clock had scraped back and forth when it was wound, and so was the tear in the wallpaper that Mrs. Diamant was forever pasting back into place. It occurred to me that she was never going to get that wallpaper to stick right there. Because she was dead. Because she was a Jew.

Why did any of this have to happen?

I sat on the windowsill, wiping my eyes, propping my bare feet against the jamb. It was late, the streets empty except for the German patrol. There were no dead bodies down there. But I looked at the moon instead. Just in case. Because the moon, at least, was still beautiful.

I heard a pop and a tinkle of glass. And just above my head, I discovered a hole had appeared in the windowpane, little cracks splaying out from it like the web of a spider. The hole was small. Perfectly round.

A bullet hole.

I dropped off the windowsill like I'd been shoved, crawled across the floorboards, and switched off the main light.

Laughter floated up from the street, German voices joking back and forth as the patrol moved on to somewhere else. I heard another bang, another shattering of glass.

I went back into the dark bedroom, locked the door, pulled a chair up to one of the two windows, and nailed our new rug over it. The next day I bought another rug, very ugly, for next to nothing, then nailed it over the other window.

They would not win, I thought. I wouldn't let them. Not against me.

But there was no need to advertise.

One by one, the windows across the street went dark, and so did Mr. Szymczak's. I wondered if this was why he'd left me the nails.

I didn't tell Max about any of it. And he didn't tell me what he planned to do about the *Aktion*. There wasn't time. The Jewish Ordners were not as understanding as you'd think, being under the thumb of the Gestapo, and even the Polish police were watching closely. I passed him bread and eggs quickly through the fence.

Something was coming.

And it came with the winter cold of November, beneath a canopy of clouds heavy with unfallen snow. Noise in the ghetto. Familiar noise. This time I walked to the railroad bridge, and I saw the cattle cars, the throngs of people, the dogs. And I could hear the shooting. Volleys of it. Firing squads. Panic swirled around me like the mist.

Evil, I thought. This is what evil looks like.

I had to turn away.

Stand up, Max, I thought. Chaim. Dr. Schillinger and Dziusia. Old Hirsch and young. Or hide. Do what you have to. Just don't let them stamp you out.

I listened to the train whistles scream as they pulled out of Przemyśl, and again I broke my promise to Helena.

Because how could I tell her that this was her world?

I didn't know how much food to buy that day. Or the next. Or the next. The ghetto was guarded and silent. The outer fences were being taken down. Moved inward. Hemming in the remaining Jews like animals in a trap. I walked the new fence line. There was no sign of Max. I knew he was dead. But I could not accept it.

Maybe I just didn't want to be defeated.

I washed our clothes. Showed Helena how to sing while she threaded string around her fingers, making patterns that matched the song. We treated ourselves to hot tea and sugar and went to bed.

And I listened to the dark.

How had the Gestapo known that Mr. Schwarzer was hiding in that warehouse? Had he been seen? Recognized? Or were the SS just searching everywhere, breaking down doors until they found something wrong?

Or had one of us, one of his neighbors, gone to the Gestapo and sold eight lives?

If they had, I couldn't think of one reason why they wouldn't do it to me.

I tried to remember if I'd ever been careless. Mentioned how much food I was buying. If anyone had ever commented on my comings and goings. Had Helena said something to a friend on the stairs?

What if those two Germans who had put guns to my head knew who I was? What if they'd followed me home, hoping to catch me at something worse than feeding Jews? What if they had let me go because they wanted my little sister, too?

Fear comes with the dark when you're lying still, waiting for the knock on the door. And fear is not always reasonable.

I sat up in the blackness.

Przemyśl had given me an education since that cart ride when I was twelve. It had taught me that people like to divvy up one another with names. Jew. Catholic. German. Pole. But these were the wrong names. They were the wrong dividing lines. Kindness. Cruelty. Love and hate. These were the borders that mattered.

Przemyśl had shown me my place on the map.

And the road ran straight and dark before me.

I laid my head on the pillow, next to Helena's sighing breath. Listening. Thinking. Trying to let myself sleep.

Until I opened my eyes to the echo in the dark.

To the knock on the door.

Until I ran into the hallway and did not find the Gestapo.

Did not find Izio.

Until the night I found Max Diamant standing at my door.

10.

November 1942

MAX!"

He stands blinking at me, the bulb above him flickering like it wants to go out. Both his eyes are blacked, skin missing from the side of his face. His shirt hangs ripped and streaked with browning blood. He has an arm across his middle. The other holds him upright against the doorjamb.

"Fusia?" he whispers.

I pull him into the apartment, and he nearly falls, stumbling as I get the door shut and locked behind him. He slides down the wall to the floor.

"I need . . . a night. Just one night . . ."

I kneel beside him. He's shaking with cold.

"Hela," I say. My sister's eyes are wide. "Go and see if there's any warm water in the pot on the stove. If there isn't, get more. But don't switch on the lights. I'll light an oil lamp. We don't want to wake anybody up. Can you do that?"

She nods, stares another second at Max, and flits away in her nightgown. I touch Max's scabbed face. Most of his blood is dry. His eyes are closed.

"Did anyone see you come up here?" I whisper. His head lolls against the bare wall. "Max, answer me! Did anyone see?"

He shakes his head, wincing.

"Are you alone?"

His face contorts. And then he says, "I jumped."

"You jumped?"

"Off the train."

"You jumped off a moving train?"

His eyes open slowly. Deep, dark brown. Heavy-lidded. "I need ... one night. Please, Fusia."

Okay, I think. Okay. What are you going to do, Stefania Stefi Stefusia Podgórska? What are you going to do?

Get him warm. Get him clean. Get him fed.

"Come with me," I say. He doesn't respond. "Up," I tell him. "Just a little farther ..."

He groans as I help him to his feet, and we stagger together into the bedroom. Helena comes through the door holding out our soup pot like it's full of holy water. She sets it carefully on top of the heater while I grab the towel we use for bathing and spread it on the bed. Max is filthy. I light the lamp and start unlacing his boots.

"There was a little bit of hot water left," Helena says, "so I poured it in the cup."

"Do you know how to make tea?"

"Yes." Her eyes are on Max.

"Then make it. Please. And put in two spoonfuls of sugar. And you can throw a lump of coal in the fire, too."

Now she stares at me. These are extravagances. But she doesn't say anything. Just puts coal in the stove and makes the tea.

Max is either asleep sitting upright or almost unconscious. I unbutton his shirt and realize the ripped cloth is stiff with blood and sticking. Peeling it off wakes him up a little, and he hisses with pain. He's missing a good bit of his skin down one side, not deep, but over a large area, and in the center of his chest is the worst bruise I've ever seen. A red, green, and purple flower, blooming from arm to arm and all the way down his stomach. I'd bet a week of bread that some of his ribs are broken.

I'm just glad he isn't shot.

The water on the stove isn't warm, but it's not cold anymore, either, so I try to sponge away the dried blood and dirt from Max's side and face. Here and there, it starts him bleeding again. Helena is standing still behind me, and when the cup rattles, I realize she has the tea but is afraid to come closer. She gives it to me instead.

"Here," I tell him. "Drink."

He tries, but his hands are stiff with scabbed skin, and he's still shaking. I help him hold it, and he drains the cup. I set it aside and go on sponging, trying not to hurt him. And then I see that Max is crying. Tears coursing from beneath his closed eyes, down his unshaven face.

Oh, Max.

I want to know what's happened to him. I want to know where everyone else is.

But not in front of my sister.

When I've got him as clean as he can be, I grab my dress from the corner and throw it over my head, get one, then two arms out of my nightgown and into the dress, letting the nightgown fall to the floor while I pull the dress down. Then I pull the nightgown over Max's head, helping him get his sore hands through the sleeves. I'd rather get the nightgown bloody than the sheets. It isn't a wonderful nightgown.

"Take your pants off," I tell him, "and we'll lay you down."

He does, laying his head on the pillow gingerly—I know his side and his chest must hurt—slowly sliding his feet beneath the blanket. I cover him to his neck. He shivers for a minute or two, and then he's asleep.

Helena has been sitting on the floor beside the stove, legs crossed, feet tucked under her knees. Watching. "Stefi," she says. "Who is he?"

"His name is Max. He used to live here." That seems like a long time ago.

"Is he your friend? He called you Fusia."

I watch Max shudder as he lets out a deep breath. "Yes, he's my friend. His family ... they all called me that here."

"Is he a Jew?"

I turn to look at her. "Why do you ask that?"

"Because he's hurt."

Because in this place where my sister lives, Jews get hurt. She can't remember another way. I go and kneel in front of her in the lantern light so she can look in my eyes.

"Max is a secret," I say. "A big one. One that we can't tell to anyone else. Not Emilika, or any of your friends downstairs. If we did, Max could get hurt. Even more hurt," I correct. "Do you understand?"

She nods, very serious, and I think she does understand until she says, "Does he get the bed?"

"Yes. He gets the bed."

She sighs, resigned. Her eyelids are heavy.

I make Helena a nest on the floor beside the stove with my coat, her skirt rolled up for a pillow, and prop the chair beneath the front doorknob. She's asleep when I come back, and the street below us is brooding. Empty. I put a chair beneath the bedroom doorknob, too, turn down the lamp, and bring another to the bed to sit beside Max.

I look at his bruised, torn face. He's alive. Breathing. Bleeding. Alive. And then I think maybe I don't want to know what has happened, because knowing, I think, is going to hurt.

And suddenly, I'm waking up. When I didn't know I was asleep. I slide back upright in the chair, rubbing my eyes. Helena is still, peaceful, curled up in the coat. But Max is having a dream.

No. He's having a nightmare.

His head thrashes from side to side on the pillow, one of his hurt hands coming up to shield his closed eyes. *"Mame,"* he murmurs.

"Shhhh," I say, hand on his chest. He murmurs again, and I lean closer to hear, but I can't understand what he's saying. It might be "Ernestyna," or something else. Until he says, "Jump."

"Jump!" Max yells, his eyes flying open. I get a hand over his mouth, and for a second, I think he's going to fight me. Then his eyes focus, and he goes still. I let go of his mouth and shake my head.

He nods, still panting.

I wait another minute, letting him calm. "Can you eat?"

He nods again. I give him a slice of bread, the rest of the butter, and a cup of water. He sits up enough to get it all down, and I perch on the edge of the bed beside him, trying not to move things that would hurt. And then I can't stand it anymore. I have to know.

"Max."

He goes still.

"Where's Chaim?"

113

He doesn't look at me. He lies back down, blinking, staring into the darkest corner of the room. "Is that your sister?" he asks.

"Yes."

I wait another minute.

"Max, where is Chaim?"

"Gone," he whispers. "He didn't jump. He told me he would jump, and then he didn't."

"What happened?"

He blinks again, looking at nothing, and I think he isn't going to answer, but then he says, "We built a bunker. A hiding place in a basement. There was a door to the cellar, and we built a wall over it so you couldn't see, and we put bags of sand and straw in the cellar windows. And when the *Aktion* started there were fifty, maybe sixty of us in there, waiting in the dark ..."

I remember how that felt, after the bombings. "What about the Hirsches? And the Schillingers?"

He shakes his head. "They weren't on the list. The Gestapo, they were going from apartment to apartment, and if you were on the list and you weren't at the collection point, they shot you right there. We could hear. Shot after shot. Over and over. Maybe it would have been better, maybe ..."

"Were you on the list?"

"Yes. And Chaim. So we hid. All day, and I looked through a hole between the sandbags, just a tiny hole, but I could see ..." His eyes squeeze shut. "I could see what they did ... I could see ... the babies. Why, Fusia? Why?"

I don't know. I give him my hand, and he grips it hard.

"We were silent all day, even the children, and the *Aktion* was almost over, and then a rifle poked through some of the straw and sandbags and let in some light. It was an Ordner, and he said if anyone was in there, to come out, or he would throw in a grenade. And I waved a hand, telling them all to stay quiet. He didn't know we were there. He was going to move on. They wouldn't find us. But there was a mother near the window, and she lost her head and tore away the sandbags before I could stop her, and she pushed her little girl out, telling her to run, to save her life, and the Ordner, the stupid Ordner, he took the girl to the Gestapo, and they beat her until she showed them the way in ..."

I put my other hand over his. He talks faster and faster.

"And the Gestapo came and pulled us out of the basement, and they were hitting us with rifles, and if you fell down, you were shot. And the rest of us, they lined us up, and Chaim told me ... he told me to turn and aim my chest at the guns, because they would not shoot us twice. But an SS man came and said there was room on the train, that they needed fat Jews ... for soap. I didn't want to be soap, Fusia."

I shake my head.

"There were so many people on the train, I couldn't move my arms, I couldn't breathe, and a man, he hung himself with his own belt, and I thought ..." Tears were rolling down his face again. "I thought it would be better to die before they could kill me. And I still had my dental pliers hidden in my pants, and I cut the wires from the window, and Chaim promised ... he promised to jump right after me, so we would both die, and the people, they lifted me, and they pushed me out the window. Only it was headfirst, and it's so stupid, but I couldn't go headfirst, because I would be crushed by the train. Even though I wanted to die. And I made them pull me in again and push me feetfirst through the window. The train took a curve and I hung there, by one arm, and then I went down the embankment and hit a fence post, and when I woke up, the train was nearly gone, and I wasn't dead. I looked, but I couldn't find my brother, and I said to God, why is this happening?"

Because you are supposed to be alive, Max, I think, holding his hand with both of mine. You are supposed to be alive right now. But I can't say this. Being alive is no comfort when your family is dead.

"I found two others who jumped after me. A broken hand, a broken collarbone, and one of them said that Chaim, he didn't jump, because he saw me not moving and thought I was dead already and that he could not help me anymore ... He wanted his blood on German hands, instead of his own ..."

He stops here, because he has to cry. I am crying with him. Chaim, who only ever wanted to heal.

"And so we found shelter with my friend, who runs the coffee shop, where we used to ski ..."

I remember Izio talking about the man at the coffee shop.

"... and he gave me a place to sleep, but I couldn't stay, because his wife was afraid, and so he smuggled me into the city in a wagon, beneath a blanket, under his feet, and I didn't know where to go. I didn't know where to go ..."

He didn't know where to go, and so he came home. To his old apartment. Max is shivering now like he's been plunged into a cold bath. Except he's also sweating. I put a hand on his damp forehead, where the skin is whole. He's too hot.

"Shhh," I tell him. "Don't talk any more. You need to sleep ..."

What he needs is a doctor. Medicine. More food than there is and a safe place to hide. What he's going to get is the two aspirin I saved from Dr. Becker, the rest of the *kasha*, and me.

I get him water and the aspirin, and when he finally calms enough to sleep, I perch in the chair beside the bed. And I cry for all of them. Izio. Mr. Diamant and my lovely *babcia*. Chaim. And especially Max, who now has to live without them. If he can live.

He has to live.

The sun lightens the world behind the window rug. I blow out the lamp. Helena stirs, sighing in her sleep.

I have to make some decisions.

The first thing I do is watch the street. No extra patrols, no eyes down like the night Mr. Schwarzer died. Then I go up to the attic and cut down one of the ropes for the laundry, bring it into the apartment, and tie it to the heater in Mr. and Mrs. Diamant's empty bedroom. There's enough rope to go out the window, nearly to the ground. If the Gestapo come again, Helena can go down the rope, if she's brave enough. I think she would be brave enough.

When I go back into our bedroom, I find Helena awake, in my spot in the chair, watching Max sleep. She turns to look at me, her eyes large, hand across her mouth. Then I realize she's giggling.

"He's wearing a nightgown!" she says through her fingers.

"Maybe you thought I was your sister," Max murmurs from the bed, his swollen eyes barely opening. "I am a surprise."

Helena laughs, and in a world where death is a shadow at the edge of every light, I discover that I have to smile.

11.

November 1942

I GIVE THE SPECIAL KNOCK WHEN I COME BACK FROM THE MARKET, AND when the chair scrapes away and Helena opens the door, she's bouncing on her toes. I lock the door again before I let her speak, and then the words burst out of her.

"Did Emilika see you going up the stairs?"

"I don't think so. What happened?" My stomach twists into a knot. "Did she come up here?"

"She knocked on the door, and I said you couldn't come, and she asked why, and I said because you were sick, and she wanted to come in anyway, in case you needed help, and I said she couldn't, because you said your germs were catching."

Helena says this in one long breath. I wish she'd just told her I was out and to come back later, but Emilika might have tried to come in anyway. Emilika is going to be a problem, until we can ...

Do whatever it is we're going to do.

I look at Helena, waiting for my verdict, and kiss her on the head. "I'll make sure I'm sick."

She really is a smart little girl.

Max is sitting up in the bed when I come in, and from the empty cup, I see Helena has made him tea. He looks terrible, but at least he seems less feverish.

"Fusia," he says, eyes on the bed, "I need to ask you a favor."

I set the parcels on the table. If we're careful and eat only two small meals a day, there's enough here for three days. After that, I don't know what we're going to do. If we haven't been shot first.

I'm wondering what more Max could possibly want from me.

"My brother," he says. "Henek. He doesn't know ..."

His last brother. And Henek doesn't know who's alive and who isn't.

"I don't know what he can do," Max says, "but he should not go back to the ghetto. He should escape, if he has the chance. He doesn't know ... how it's been. He didn't see our parents go. And what could I write him?"

He couldn't. The Germans would read the letter, and Henek would pay. I sigh.

"I'll go today," I tell him. "I'm supposed to be sick anyway."

The farm being worked by the Jews of the Przemyśl ghetto once belonged to a Jew. Now it belongs to the Germans, confiscated for their Fatherland. It's an eleven-kilometer walk from the city. I take the road past the castle, a fairy-tale place of turrets and etched stone where my sisters used to eat picnics, but those memories are like old photographs faded by the sun. The air is gray today, the wind spitting ice, and it's hard to remember a time when I wasn't afraid of death.

Leaving Helena alone to hide a Jew in our apartment is probably the worst thing I've ever done.

I walk faster. The land here is flat and open, not even a hill to hide behind, and when I see the barn roofs rising up from the bare fields in the distance, they're farther away than I think. I trot, out of breath by the time I reach the guard.

The man is Polish, smoking cigarettes, with a pink nose and his collar turned up around his ears, his gun leaning against the farm gate. If I looked hard enough, I'd probably find a bottle of vodka nearby. I ask for Henek, but the guard isn't much bothered whether I talk to the prisoners or not. He's not very bothered to watch them, either. There's nowhere for them to go.

I find Henek and Danuta in a section of the barn that has been fitted with wooden beds stacked on top of one another, ladders going up their sides. Some of them are occupied, while other prisoners gather around a fire giving more smoke than warmth. I can smell cows.

Henek jumps to his feet and kisses both my cheeks, which is a surprise. Danuta shakes my hand. It's cold and dirty in the barn, and they both look thin, but not ghetto thin. And they don't have the same look as the people in the ghetto, either. There's something missing from their expressions.

They're not afraid.

Henek takes me to sit on a cut log near the barn door, and I tell him what I've come to say. That Chaim is gone, and Max is hurt but alive and hidden with me. He frowns and rubs a hand along his head. Exactly like Max does. I've never noticed that before.

"But we don't know Chaim is dead, do we?" says Henek. "Max didn't see ..."

"He didn't jump, Henek. He stayed on the train."

"That's what I mean," he says. "It's like *Mame* and *Tate*."

"So what is Max going to do now?" Danuta asks, cutting in.

"We don't know, but ..." I lean close. I don't see any guards, but I can see other prisoners trying to listen, and who knows which of them might decide that extra food or privileges are worth a betrayal to the Germans. "He says not to go back to the ghetto.

Not if you can help it. And"—I glance around—"you could leave here easily enough. I think you could ..."

"Leave here?" says Henek. "It can't be as bad as all that. Max is overreacting. The worst is probably over."

I feel my eyes widening. "Henek, they will kill you in the ghetto. Max says they want every Jew dead ..."

"And what does he want us to do? Live in the woods and starve? We have food here, and shelter, and the ghetto must be nearly empty now. We'd probably have an apartment to ourselves."

I sit on my log, too stunned to speak. How could Henek say that after what I've just told him? After his parents, two of his brothers, and probably his sister, too?

Danuta takes my arm. "I'm glad you came, Fusia. I'll walk with you as far as the guardhouse."

As soon as we're out of the barn and away from the door, she turns to me. "Don't be mad. He's pretending. It's the only way he can ..." She bites a lip. "He didn't see his mother and father go, and the things he did see, he pretends he didn't. It's easier for him like that."

I don't understand. But I nod like I do.

"Tell Max I'll talk to Henek. We're supposed to be sent back in three days, but maybe we can find a way to work here. Find something that needs doing ..."

"Danuta!" Henek calls from the barn.

Danuta jumps. "I have to go," she says. "What's your address, so I can write and tell you where we are?"

I give it to her, and a little wave as I walk past the guard and back through the gate. Danuta has a nice smile, an upturned nose, and curls that could use a brush. She doesn't seem like a stupid girl. So I wonder what she could be doing with a *Dummkopf* like Henek.

A man with a donkey and a cart offers me a ride on the way back to the city, but he's going too slow. Every unlikely way the Gestapo could have found Max and my sister in the apartment is running through my head like a cinema film I'd never want to see. I cover the eleven kilometers back to the apartment like I've got a train to catch, and when I turn the lock on the front door, it's silent. So completely silent my heart leaps in my chest, then falls straight down to my stomach.

There's no one here.

They've been taken.

They're gone.

I run into the bedroom.

And there are Helena and Max, side by side, peaceful, Helena with her arms around his bruised neck. They're asleep.

If the Gestapo knocked on the door right now, I'd fight the Nazis with my fingernails just to let them stay that way.

But three days later, it's not the Gestapo that knocks. It's Danuta.

"I've run away," she says. "From Henek!"

She looks as surprised about it as I am.

"I think Max is right," she says. "The ghetto is just a place to be killed. And ..." She takes a shaky breath. "And my parents died, too, you know."

I open the door a little wider and let her walk through it.

I don't know what I'm supposed to do with her.

One bedroom is a small place for four people, and it takes exactly three days for someone to lose their temper. Helena kicks a table leg when I say she can't go play with the children in the street, because how can we trust what she might say? And in retaliation, she eats all the butter. By the spoonful. By itself. And then I lose my temper. Max sits up stiff in the bed, shirtless until we can get him another one. He's black and blue with angry red scabs that have a tendency to break open and bleed. But there's no fever.

"Come sit beside me, Hela," he says. "I'll tell you a story ..."

"I'm tired of stories!" she yells.

Max has told her every story known to Poland at least twice. For the past day or so, he's just been making them up. Some more successfully than others.

"Do you know what I think?" asks Danuta. Since no one ever knows what Danuta thinks, this is interesting. "I think Hela knows how to keep a secret. Don't you, Hela?"

I shake my head. This secret is too much to ask of a six-year-old. Our lives are at stake. But Helena's face has brightened. Danuta holds out her arms, and Helena climbs into her lap.

"Now, what would you say if some person asks who lives in your apartment?" asks Danuta.

"I'd say my sister," Helena replies.

"Anyone else?"

She shakes her head.

"And what if someone says, 'But I have heard voices in your apartment, little girl ...'" Danuta's voice has taken on a ridiculous German accent, very accusing, which makes Helena giggle. I raise a brow. "'Your sister, little *Fräulein*, does she have a man up there?' What would you say to that?"

"I'd say my sister tells good stories, and sometimes she does the man's voice, and it's funny."

I catch Max's eye, and he lifts a shoulder. I have to admit, that was a good one. Danuta smiles.

"And what if someone asks to come up to your apartment, just to see? What would you tell them, then, Hela?"

"I'd say my sister has germs, and she's catching. And then I'd tell them that I have germs, too, and try to give them a hug."

Danuta laughs, and Helena grins at me in triumph.

"Oh, go and play, then." I sigh. "We'll try one hour, and if everything is good, we'll try again tomorrow. Do you agree?"

But Helena is already running down the hallway and opening the front door. I steady my breath. The fear has set in, like I knew it would. The breakfast dishes rattle when I stack them up.

I hate being afraid.

"Stefi?"

We freeze, Danuta in the act of shaking out the bed blanket over Max. That voice came from my front door. The door no one locked after Helena left.

"Fusia!" the voice calls again. There are footsteps coming down the hall.

Max dives for the floor, rolls underneath the bed, and the bedroom door opens.

"Hello," says Emilika. "I saw Hela go down the stairs, so I thought you must be well. Finally."

I close my open mouth. Danuta is still holding the blanket in the air. Emilika looks back and forth between the two of us. "Who's this?" she asks.

Danuta unfreezes and spreads the blanket over the bed, leaving it long on the front side to cover Max. Emilika looks at me expectantly.

"This is my cousin," I say quickly. "Danuta."

"Oh," says Emilika, "your real cousin." She winks. "Is there some reason you're both hiding up here? Because you don't look very sick."

Emilika is looking at me, but I can see Danuta over her shoulder, and she is the one who looks sick. I smile, set down the dishes, and close the door behind Emilika.

"I should have known I can't keep anything from you," I say, sighing. "Yes, there's a reason we're hiding. But you can't tell anyone, Emilika. Please."

Emilika shakes her head. Her eyes are eager. I think Danuta might actually vomit on the floor.

"Danuta is hiding because she's ..."

I watch Danuta take a breath.

"Because she's pregnant, and she can't let her parents find out."

Danuta sits hard in the chair beside the bed.

Coming up with quick lies must run in the family.

"Oh," says Emilika, turning to Danuta. "Oh! Sad little mouse! You do look sick ..."

Emilika goes and sits on the bed, patting Danuta's hand. "Do you need ..." She eyes me again, then Danuta. "Do you need some ... advice?"

I look at Danuta. She looks at me. We all look at one another.

"Because if you need advice," Emilika says, "I can tell you exactly what to do."

"I think we would love your advice," I say, and as soon as Emilika's eyes are off me, I wave a hand at Danuta, telling her to participate. Danuta gives Emilika a nod and a weak smile.

"You need a pot," says Emilika. "A big pot, and we're going to fill it with water as hot as you can take, okay? And you're going to sit in this pot for thirty minutes ..."

Oh, poor Max, I think.

"... and after thirty minutes, you're going to run up and down the stairs, just as hard as you can. All three flights, until you're really sweating, and then we'll sit you in the pot again ..."

Danuta is nodding.

"We should start right now. I have a pot downstairs," Emilika says. "Fusia doesn't have anything near big enough." She pats Danuta's knee. "I'll be right back!"

And she dashes out the door.

Danuta jumps to her feet and turns on me. "What do you think you're—"

"She's saving your life," says Max, his head sticking out from under the bed.

"You," I whisper, "turn to the wall and close your eyes. And don't sneeze. Or stretch, or stick your feet out. Don't even breathe. And don't listen!"

Max disappears beneath the bed.

"I may kill you," Danuta whispers as footsteps come running back up the stairs.

"Or maybe the Gestapo will beat you to it," I reply.

She closes her mouth.

After two bouts of Danuta boiling her lower regions in a pot and one vigorous run up and down the stairs, I ask Emilika what time she's supposed to be at the photography shop. Emilika says, "Oh!" then kisses both our cheeks, says to keep going, and runs out the door. Danuta struggles upright, and I hand her a towel. She dries off, pink with heat, exercise, and embarrassment.

"Do you think this would really work?" she asks, getting her dress adjusted.

I shrug. My mother was a midwife, and I think she would have laughed. I give Danuta a raised brow.

"Why, do you need it?"

"Please!" says Max's voice, muffled under the bed.

Danuta smacks my arm once and smiles.

Then Helena comes bounding up the stairs, also with her cheeks blushing, because the air is brisk. She's breathless and happy.

"I didn't say anything," she says as I lock the door behind her. "I told you I wouldn't. Where's Max?"

She lifts up the blanket and crawls under the bed.

Emilika knocks at the door three more times in the next two days, asking if her advice has solved Danuta's problem. We tell her it has. And it's a little bit true. Thanks to Emilika, everyone in the building now thinks Danuta is my corrupt cousin from Bircza. And while I can't send her to the shops, she can at least hang the laundry in the attic without fear and doesn't have to scramble beneath the bed every time a neighbor knocks for the linen key.

So Danuta is standing in the hall right behind me the next time I answer the door. Only it's not one of our neighbors. Or even Emilika. This is a man. A stranger in a threadbare coat, and he doesn't say hello or ask a question. He just points over my shoulder and says, "That's the Jew I'm looking for."

I lean against the door, watching the stranger like he's a devil I've just locked myself in with. The man fidgets, twisting a hat in his hands while Danuta sits at the table, reading the letter he's brought. He doesn't look like the secret police. But that could be the point, couldn't it? I settle on Emilika's laundry pot as the best weapon in the room. Then Danuta sniffs and sets down the letter.

"Henek," she says. "He's back in the ghetto, and he wants me with him. He met this man at the fence and said he'd pay him to bring me back. He's waiting there now. Oh, he really does love me. What should I do?"

What she can do, I think, is go to Henek and kick him as hard as she can. What was he thinking, giving some stranger at the fence my address and telling him there are Jews in my apartment? And then he writes it all down in a letter for this man to carry around on the streets.

He's going to get us killed.

Or I'm going to kill him first.

"If I won't go back now," Danuta says, "he wants me to sign, to show I read his letter. Should I go back now, Fusia? What should I—"

"You can't go to the ghetto now," I snap. "We'd have to plan, make sure there's a safe way in ..."

"But this man won't leave without me or a signature."

The stranger clears his throat. "The Jewish boy said he'd pay me more if I brought it back signed, and that's what I'm going to do."

I don't know what else this man could need for the Gestapo.

"I'm no killer," he says. "I just want my money."

I give Danuta my only pen, so angry that it slaps a little against her palm. The man snatches the letter as soon as she's signed it.

"I'm no killer," he says again, turns the lock, and darts out the door.

Max's head pops out from under the bed. "Maybe Henek is right, and the man just wants to get paid."

And we, I think, have no way of knowing that.

"What a *yutz*," Max says from the floor. He means his brother. I couldn't agree more.

Max and Danuta have a long talk in the empty living room of the Diamant apartment, and when they come back, Max says that he asked me for one night. I gave him two weeks. And in return, they're endangering my life and my sister's. I've done enough. They're going back to the ghetto.

I don't want Max to go back. He has nightmares almost every night. And I'm so frightened that none of them will ever come back out again that it leaves me sick. Part of me is relieved that Helena will be safe. And another small part of me just feels lost. Empty. The rattling gourd.

They're ready as soon as the sun is down, and Helena is crying because Max is going away. Max kisses her head and says that when the war is over, he's going to take her to a beach, where she can feel the sand and play in the wide and salty ocean. There must have been a story told about a beach sometime, while I was out or at the market, because Helena's face lights up like a lamp.

"Do you promise, Max?"

He smiles. "I promise."

I wish Max wouldn't make promises. Especially when his face is barely healed.

We lock Helena inside, and I go partway down the stairs, making sure there are no neighbors to see a man coming out of my apartment. The longer I think about this decision, the worse it seems. Max won't have a ration in the ghetto, because the Germans think he's dead. And what will happen to him if they find out he isn't? Danuta tries to reassure me that he will stay out of the Nazis' way. And the Ordners'. And the Poles'. That she has a little money to share.

But this feeling is terrible. Like the last time I saw my *babcia*. Like seeing the look on the German soldier's face when I came walking up to the labor camp at Janowska.

It makes me doubt everything.

This fear, I think, is Hitler's best weapon.

We each take Max by an arm and walk down the street.

12.

December 1942

WE MAKE SMALL TALK AS WE GO, AND MAX NODS AND SMILES, WEARING A hat and coat I found in a trash heap and washed four times. It passes well enough in the dark, and he keeps his head down, but we slip into the side streets at the first opportunity, across the tracks, skirting the lights until we come to that section of fence where Max loosened the barbed wire all those weeks ago. Where the Germans decided not to shoot me.

Henek is waiting there, all smiles when he sees us coming around the corner with Danuta. There's not a gun or a uniform to be seen. But I remember the feel of metal against my neck, the certainty that I'm about to be shot. Sweat breaks out on my forehead.

I see Max looking at me.

Danuta scrambles under the fence, gets to her feet, and hits Henek as hard she can in the stomach.

I really did not think Danuta had that in her.

"Coward!" she whispers. "Giving Fusia's address to a stranger! You could've come yourself if you'd had any guts ..."

Henek has an arm around his middle. "But they said ... They told me he's reliable! He does business at the fence!"

131

"And how do you know he doesn't do business with the Gestapo?"

Max turns to me. "This should be a good time." He tries to smile, but he can't quite do it. "Thank you, Fusia." He kisses my cheek, holding his own cheek there for just a moment, and then he slips under the fence, waving a hand. Telling me to run away.

And only when he held his cheek to mine did I realize that I'm not the only one scared for him to go back into the ghetto. He's scared. Of course he is. After everything that happened there.

I don't want him to go. But at least Helena will be safe now. And the cupboard shelf is nearly bare.

Maybe I've done all one person can.

I'm the empty gourd.

The next morning, I take Helena with me and go out looking for work. I find nothing, except for more girls like me, or women, or men, searching for the same thing. I even cross the train tracks, to the neighborhoods that used to be inside the ghetto, where new people are moving in, where there might be new shops that want help. But I find nothing.

I wish I had the 340 *zloty* back.

"Is that where Max lives?" Helena asks, pointing as we turn the corner. The gate to the ghetto is just down the street, a German policeman walking back and forth in front of it. People mill in a little crowd on the other side, waiting, but there will be no buying or selling today. I don't think any of them is Max. And then I hear a shout.

A boy, or a young man, I can't tell from this distance, has dropped to his knees inside the fence, and a policeman is raising his rifle butt. I start to turn Helena around. And then I don't. I let her see. When the butt of the gun hits the boy, he drops without a sound. No one on either side of the fence makes a move or lifts a hand. The guard doesn't even break his stride.

"Stefi?" Helena asks, though I don't think she knows her real question.

"Yes," I say quietly, "that is where Max lives, and that is why we helped him. And it's why he—and Danuta—will always be our secret." Helena looks up at me. "The biggest, deepest secret we can ever have, even now that he's gone. It would be dangerous for us if anyone knew. Just like the boy."

She nods and looks back to the gate. "Does it mean that we can't help Max anymore?"

I don't want to tell her the answer is yes. I don't want that to be the answer. Helena takes my hand, and we walk away.

I buy two end-of-day discounted rolls from the bakery for our supper, and two weeks after that, I have to decide between bread for our stomachs and coal for the stove. I choose bread, and on cue, the temperature drops, the air turns bitter, and the wind whips down ice from the hills.

We wear our coats to bed, huddling together beneath the blanket while the wind moans, drinking hot water for breakfast because there is no tea. I have nothing to sell, no money to buy something to resell, and we can't even go to Emilika, because she's with her mother in Kraków. And Helena is losing weight again. The skirt I sized down for her is loose around the waist, and when she sleeps, there's a rattle in her chest.

On the third night of this, I borrow a saw from Mr. Szymczak and cut our table in half. It makes my arm ache and a mess on the floor, but the table is still usable, if propped just right against the wall, and now there's wood in the stove. We use it sparingly, and Helena sweeps up the dust to burn.

We climb into bed, and I keep Helena warm until she falls asleep. Then I consider our options. If we barely eat, we have two days of food left—at best—no money, and half a table. I haven't seen Max or Danuta since they went back to the ghetto, and they're sure to be worse off than we are. I can go out and try to find work again tomorrow. Or would anyone in our building pay me to do laundry? Even if they did, I haven't got any soap. We could go back to the farm, but we couldn't heat that big house, and I don't know how we would eat. Not in winter. Not with everything taken.

I put a hand on Helena's hair and think of my mother's friends in Bircza, anyone who might take Helena in. When Mama had the choice, she left her with the Zielinskis, but even the thought of taking Helena back there is a betrayal. But I can't let my sister starve. I lay my head beside hers on the pillow.

If I can't find work tomorrow, then something must be done.

I do not find work when the sun rises. I don't find it when the sun sets. And I still don't know what the "something to be done" should be. I only know I have failed my sister. In every way.

I save my share of food for the next day.

And then I remember that it's Christmas Eve, and I give it to Helena and hope she doesn't remember what day it is.

The temperature is not as low as the night before, so we decide not to burn the rest of the table. We just shiver, my stomach grumbling, and as soon as Helena is asleep, I let myself cry. Hard. For everyone who's gone. The boy hit with the rifle, the blue-eyed girl shot in the street, and Ernestyna Diamant, whom I never even met. I cry for Max and Danuta, and for Henek, because grief takes all forms. But the truth is, I'm mostly crying for myself. Because I'm sad, frustrated, hungry, and defeated. Because failure is something I don't know how to do.

And in the middle of my tears, a calm steals over me. A warmth in the cold. Like an arm coming around my middle. A cheek pressing next to mine. It reminds me of Izio and the night he told me he wanted to live. I think of rude tangos and how he used to walk me to Marysia's apartment in the snow. How we laughed, trying to get out the front door without Regina and Rosa knowing, creeping up the attic stairs so Mrs. Pohler wouldn't hear, our arms full of . . .

I open my eyes. And sit straight up in bed. I must have been asleep. Dreaming. But I was dreaming of real things. The mattress springs protest as I slide out of bed, but Helena doesn't stir. I tuck the blanket in tight around her, wiggle my feet into my icy shoes—I already have my coat on—and reach up to the high shelf of the mantelpiece to find the linen key. The empty apartment is silent as I tiptoe out of the bedroom and close the front door behind me.

I still don't want the neighbors to hear.

The stairs to the attic are an ink puddle in shadows, but I know exactly how to avoid the creaks. I unlock the attic door. The moon is out, shining through the window at one end, silvering the laundry ropes, making ghost gray shapes on the dusty floor. The roof slopes down on one side to a brick chimney, and that is where I kneel, at the eaves, where the rafters meet the floor.

I remember kneeling here with Izio, all those months ago. We'd taken too long because we were kissing instead of doing our task, and Mrs. Diamant had fussed when we got back. I think she knew. But we did do what she'd asked of us. "No one would think to look here," Izio had said that day, his breath in my ear. "Not even you ..."

Because it doesn't look like there's a hole. But the shadows are deceptive. The eaves go on for a long way, and if you get on your stomach and reach all the way to the end ...

I grit my teeth and stick my hand into the hole, and now there's sweat breaking on my forehead in the cold. The Diamant boys used to tell me stories about the attic, when I was young and teasable, about the dead bodies hidden in the eaves by the previous landlord. I don't really think I'm about to touch a dead body. I think I'm about to touch a mouse. Or a rat. Or get bitten. Or hear something scurry. But when I do touch fur, it's cold, and it doesn't move. I pull it out.

Mr. Diamant's fox fur hat. And Mrs. Diamant's fur collar and cuffs. And there's more in the next eave. The lining of a jacket. A stole in the next. An armful of furs I'd forgotten existed. Until I dreamed of them again.

Or until Izio came back and reminded me that he wanted me to live.

Helena laughs when she wakes up because she's warm and cozy, covered in furs. She stays in bed a long time, listening while I explain what I need to do next.

I have a cousin, a real one. In Lezajsk. I don't know him well, but maybe well enough to get a bed for one night and do some business. And he lives fifty kilometers away, far enough from a city that buying furs might be difficult. A luxury. And I need as much money as I can possibly get for our assets. Helena snuggles deeper, the stole wrapped around her neck.

"Are you sure you have to sell them, Stefi?"

I smile. "You help me decide. Do you like furs best or a full stomach?"

She chooses her stomach. Because she really is a smart little girl.

I will need her to be smart. Emilika is still gone, so Helena will have to be on her own, feeding herself, keeping the doors locked, and staying warm without burning down the apartment building.

"So you won't go out, not even to play, not until I get back? You understand how important that is?"

She nods.

"And if there's an emergency, you'll go downstairs to Mr. Szymczak, yes?"

"Don't worry, Stefi. I can take care of myself."

And the silly thing is, I believe her. I leave her two days of food, the little bit of table wood we have left, and some old magazines I found in a rubbish heap that she can cut up with scissors to make a collage. She promises it will be beautiful when I get back, and when the winter sun rises, I'm five kilometers down the road from Przemyśl.

I get lucky and catch a ride on a farmer's wagon for more than twenty kilometers. I'm half-frozen when I get off, but the forests are beautiful, sparkling like diamond dust, mist lifting off the fields and the hills. Walking the rest of the way warms me up.

My cousin's wife answers the door in Lezajsk, surprised and a little suspicious, but within thirty minutes I've made double what I could have gotten at the secondhand shops in Przemyśl. And traded for more food than I can carry. My cousin's wife asks what I'm going to do with so much food, and when I tell her "sell it again," she laughs and promises to bring the rest on the train next week, because she's traveling to visit her sister anyway and can stop on the way.

I sleep that night on their sofa, and by the next night, I'm back in the apartment, warming my fingers and soaking my cold, sore feet. Helena squeals with excitement at the bounty in my knapsack. We have eggs, buttered toast, and a glass of milk each for dinner; there's a small sack of coal in the corner, and magazine cuttings pinned all over the wall. I have no idea where she got the pins, but it doesn't matter. If we're careful, we can eat for four, maybe five weeks, and feed Max and Henek and Danuta.

I don't know what we'll do after that. But for now, it feels like the first night Emilika came. Like I'm the queen of my own little kingdom.

When I go to sleep, I dream of Izio. But he's far, far away from me.

My cousin visits us a week later with two crates of potatoes, more butter and eggs, beets, dried apples, turnips, and three braids of onions, and four weeks after that, I'm tying the strings in my coat sleeves and filling my purse and pockets with the last of the supplies for the ghetto. It's more than I can pass to Max through the fence, because I need it to last. I've been trading, collecting things to sell in the secondhand shops and sometimes in the rubbish bins outside the nicer houses, washing and sewing and repairing what I find. Now that the food is running low, I'm going to have to walk again, to get the best price. Two, maybe even four days.

And I can't have them starving in the meantime.

I fish out my white armband from where I have it hidden in a little slit in the mattress, and tell Helena she can play in the field down the street until she's too cold or until I get back. The sun is warm for the last day of February, like the world is remembering spring, and when I get to the ghetto gate, it's the Polish rather than the German police on patrol. A few people are trying their luck selling food at the fence, but I take the back alleys to our spot, where the loose barbed wire will let me into the ghetto.

And out of nowhere, my light mood evaporates. My heart slams against my rib cage. I hear German voices, and I can feel the end of a gun barrel press against my neck. It's hard to breathe. It's hard to think. I put a hand to my neck, to push away the cold metal.

I know the gun is not there.

But I can't make my eyes open. I'm afraid to look at the fence. I'm afraid of what might be standing on the other side.

And then I wonder if I'm actually going to let Max and Danuta and Henek go hungry because I'm scared of a fence.

I open my eyes. And all I see is barbed wire and an old tomato tin, blown by the wind. I scoot beneath the sticking barbs, stand up, brush myself off, and pull the armband up over my right sleeve. And start walking.

There are eyes on me in the ghetto. Stares that run away rather than meet my gaze. Different from the last time I was here. I'm not sure where Max is living now, if it's the same place or a different one, or if it's safe to say his name. I'm also scared to knock on the wrong door. So I ask for Henek instead, and the woman who gives me the direction has a sharp jaw and collarbones jutting out on either side of her neck. It's so quiet when she slips away, I can hear her footsteps, soft shuffles on the pavement. There's a cough from a doorway. No one is talking, not even among themselves.

I don't see any children.

The address is the same as before, on Kopernika in the center of the ghetto, and it's Danuta who answers my knock. She kisses my cheeks, scolding me for taking such a risk, leading me into the old kitchen where they live. She doesn't scold anymore when she sees the food. Dr. Schillinger, a stern man, kisses my hand, and Dziusia waves from the bed, where she's using one of her father's shirts for a blanket. I'm glad to see them. I wasn't sure they were alive.

I wish I'd brought a little more food.

"Where's Max?" I ask.

"Out with Siunek. He can't stand to stay indoors." Danuta's brows come down. "Waiting for the boots on the stairs."

I understand. Too well. "And Old Mr. Hirsch?"

"Alive."

And grumpy about it, based on Danuta's wrinkled nose.

"And Henek?" I ask.

"He's fine." And then Danuta blushes so red I know she's forgiven him. Probably thoroughly. I wonder how often she has to forgive Henek. Then I look at her rosy face and little nose and hope she has to forgive Henek many, many times in the future.

Danuta hustles me out the door as soon as she has the food hidden, giving me plenty of advice about keeping my head down and not starting conversations. About never drawing the attention of the police. She smiles when she hugs me, but her eyes are shadowed. Anxious.

I go quickly down the steps, a rat scrambling out of my way, thinking how good it would feel to drive a tank through the ghetto fence.

On the street, I can feel the eyes again. Thin as I am, I think I'm too healthy. I still have a coat and a purse. My hair is clean.

Backs turn just a little as I pass, and I realize that I might as well be walking down the ghetto street with a bright gold crown on my head. I hear a yell.

"You. You there!"

It's Polish. Native Polish. I keep walking.

"Stop!"

I don't stop until a hand pulls me to a halt, and I look up into the face of a policeman. A handsome policeman with a chiseled chin and blue eyes. If I hadn't heard it in his voice, I can see from his uniform that he's not German, and it makes me mad. Or maybe it's Danuta's anxious eyes that have me angry, or Max's fear, or the man lying in the gutter behind this policeman's feet, a man who may or may not be dead. A man who is Polish as well as a Jew. I jerk my arm away.

"What do you want?"

The policeman looks surprised. Not surprisingly.

"I want to know what you are doing." He eyes my armband and frowns. "You don't belong in here, do you?"

I don't answer.

"Where are your papers?"

I don't move.

"Give me your papers!"

I hand them over. Reluctantly. And watch him read. My papers do not have the word *"Jude"* on them.

"You should be ashamed," he says, handing them back. "A pretty girl like you, wandering through the ghetto."

He's the one who should be ashamed, and he must see this in my face, because the heavy blond brows beneath his cap drop down into a scowl.

"Tell me what you're doing, or I'll arrest you."

"I sold some food. What of it?"

"Supporting Jews is against the law."

"I'm not supporting Jews. The Jews are supporting me. They need food, I need money. Now how can there be a law against that?"

For one second, I think my insolence is going to make this policeman smile. But I'm wrong.

"I'm supposed to arrest you," he says. "Do you know that? Any policeman should arrest you and take you to the Gestapo. This is a dangerous place."

He doesn't have to tell me that.

"And the Gestapo, they won't be kind to you because you're a pretty girl. In fact, I don't think a girl like you would leave their office at all."

He's trying to scare me, and it doesn't work. And not because I'm brave or because I don't believe him. I'm just already as full of fear as a person can be.

And I'm still mad.

I give him a long glare. His mouth twitches.

"Okay," he says. "Have it your way. I'm arresting you. Come with me." And the policeman takes off at a fast clip down the sidewalk.

I trot behind him. I don't even know why. He doesn't have his gun out. He isn't touching me. He glances back, giving me a glimpse of blue eyes, and speeds up. I slow down, and he speeds up more.

It's a very strange arrest.

I reach a corner and stop. The policeman doesn't slow. He's half a block ahead. I wait, then take one giant step sideways. Now I'm on a different street, out of sight. I don't hear a shout. Not even a whistle. And so I run. As hard as I can down the sidewalk and around the next corner, leaning flat against the building. And when I get one eye at the edge of the bricks to see if I'm being followed, I catch a flash of a policeman's dark blue hat with the gold around its brim. Peeking around the opposite corner.

It's taken me this long to realize he's trying to let me go.

I take a circuitous route through the ghetto, and when I can't see a Jew or a German or a Pole, I slide beneath the barbed wire, get the armband off my coat, run across the bridge, take a turn through an alley, and come out on Mickiewicza Street. And three blocks behind me, bobbing through the people on the sidewalk, is the police hat.

He's not letting me go. He's following me.

I walk quickly, threading my way to the most crowded place I can find. The market. But even that's not as crowded as it used to be. I try to mix with the bodies and the smoke of fires and the women shouting prices over the din, and then I duck behind a booth, threading my way around the rubbish that litters the back of the market stalls. I watch for a long time from behind a pile of rubble still left from a German bomb, but I don't see the policeman. I hurry away, double back again, slip through the passage at Mickiewicza 7, skirt the overgrown courtyard, and pass through the front door of my apartment building.

Helena is home, her face red with cold and play. She wants to know what took me so long. I lift the edge of the window rug with a finger and draw in a breath. There is my policeman. In the courtyard, talking to Mrs. Wojcik and her little dog. He's managed to follow me after all. And then I remember that I'm an idiot.

My papers have my address on them.

"Who is that man?" Helena asks, looking out from beneath my elbow.

"No one."

The policeman and Mrs. Wojcik both turn their heads to my window, and I drop my finger, letting the rug fall back into place.

"I'm hungry," Helena says. "Stefi? Aren't you hungry?"

"Be right back, Hela."

I hear her sigh of frustration as I run out the door and down the stairs, waiting until I see the policeman leaving. He's smiling. He has a dimple in his cheek. When he's gone, I dart out the door and up to Mrs. Wojcik. She's letting the dog do his business in the weeds. I cross my arms against the cold. I've forgotten my coat.

"So it's you, Miss Podgórska," she says. "What have you been doing to the police?"

"Nothing," I say, checking to make sure the man hasn't reappeared. "What did you tell him?"

"That you live up there with your sister. No parents coming to see you, only that cousin. That you're in and out a lot, you don't have work, and that you spend most of your time selling in the market and the shops."

I had no idea that Mrs. Wojcik observed me that closely. I tighten my arms and shiver.

"Now don't look like that," she says. "I know men. And the last thing that man has on his mind is police business."

"You don't think I'm in trouble?"

"He's not the Pope, girl. He'll be back. And the only trouble you'll be in will come nine months after you let that one through the door."

She chuckles loudly, and I discover just how much I dislike Mrs. Wojcik. I leave her to her dog and its business and hurry back inside. And now I have a nervous squirm in my stomach that won't go away.

When Helena lets me back in, I pretend I'm cheerful. "Let's clean the room," I say. "Get everything put away."

"But I'm hungry!"

"It won't take long."

Helena grumbles, grabbing the broom while I put the extra food in the cupboards, out of sight, and stuff my armband into the hole in the mattress, looking for anything else a policeman shouldn't see.

I'm gathering up the magazine cuttings when I find two envelopes underneath the paper pieces. "What's this?" I ask.

"Oh! It's the mail Mr. Dorlich brought while you were gone. I forgot . . ."

I snatch up one of the envelopes and tear it open. It's from Salzburg, Germany. From our mother. She doesn't say much, except that she's working in a factory, that she and my brother Stasiu are together, and to please go see Helena to make sure she's all right and to tell her that her mama loves and misses her. Helena and I read this part together three more times. Then I tear open the second envelope, read the letter inside, and lay it on the table.

It's from the labor department. I have a job. A good job. Starting the day after tomorrow.

My hard-won bribe has finally done its work.

We celebrate with a can of tinned ham on toast, and Helena falls asleep early. I sit by the stove drinking tea, thinking about my new work, about Izio and Max and, every now and then, a very handsome policeman. And just when I've drained my cold tea and laid out my nightgown, there's a knock on the door.

It's long after curfew. I think it's after midnight. But maybe a policeman doesn't have to be concerned about a curfew. The squirm in my stomach comes back. I smooth my hair without meaning to, and when I open the door, I've decided definitely, most certainly, that it would be wrong to let him in.

Only it isn't him.

"Fusia," Max says, breathing hard. "I've just tried to kill a policeman."

13.

March 1943

WHO SAW YOU COME UP?" I WHISPER, SHUTTING THE DOOR AND TURNING the lock.

"No one, I swear it. I was careful. I waited in the basement ..."

"Max!" says Helena, opening her arms. She's woken up, rumpled in her nightgown. He picks her up, letting her hug him, but he's looking at me. Asking if he can stay.

I give him bread and tea, and he tells Helena stories until she falls asleep again. We sit in front of the stove, and I wait. It takes a long time for him to talk. Finally, Max tells me he's been leaving the ghetto. For no reason. That watching the people from inside the fence makes him feel like an animal in a cage. Like a specimen in a zoo.

He'd rather be shot.

I shift my position on the chilly floor, cupping the warmth from the hot water I've poured over the dregs of my tea, thinking of how close Max came to suicide on the train. But tonight, he says, he lost track of the time. He thought it was a few minutes past eight. It was a few minutes past nine. And a policeman stopped him on his way back to the fence.

"I told him that I work in the salvage factory," Max says. "That my shift had run late, that was all. I told him he could go back with me, that anyone there would vouch for who I was, but he knew I was lying. I didn't look like I'd come from a factory. I wasn't dressed for it. What I looked like was a filthy, starving Jew from the ghetto."

I look up sharply.

"And so he asked me for my papers."

Max's papers say *"Jude"* in big black letters right over his picture.

"I said I forgot them, and he told me I was a spy."

"A spy?" I ask. "For who?"

"I don't know. But he pulled out his gun, arrested me, and said he was taking me to the Gestapo."

I set down my tea.

"I didn't think he would really take me there. I told myself he was trying to scare me, that he would teach me a lesson and let me go. Until I could see the lights in the windows of the police station. And then I asked him why he would do this. He's Polish, I'm Polish. But he wouldn't answer. And I was so angry and scared, and there was no one on the street, and so I hit him in the face as hard as I could. The man dropped before he could even think of shooting ..."

I watch Max's face.

"And when he was down, I hit him again. And again. I could have gotten away, but I just ... I got my hands around his neck ... and he begged me, he was begging me not to kill him."

Max stares at his hands like they don't belong to him. His knuckles are bruised.

"And what happened next?" I whisper.

He shrugs. "Nothing. I ran away. I left him in a gutter, and I ran away."

To me.

He stretches out on the floor in front of the stove, hands behind his head. "You should put me out the door, Fusia," he says, his eyes closing. "You shouldn't let me stay here ..."

I think he is going to say it is because he is Jew. Because he is a danger to me.

But he only says, "Because I'm not any better than they are."

He's so tired, I catch the moment he falls asleep. Max needs a shave and a bath and a month of meals, but he doesn't look like a starving Jew to me.

He looks like a survivor.

I put the cups on the table, lay Mrs. Diamant's old coat over Max, and crawl into bed with Helena. But I can't sleep. I can't stop thinking about what Max said. Because what he said is wrong. So wrong.

He chose life.

And that makes him nothing like them at all.

Helena wakes Max early, wanting to show him the string game I taught her, before he goes back to the ghetto. She teaches Max to sing the song while I slice the bread and boil the eggs. And then someone knocks on the front door.

Max and Helena's song stops like the radio was switched off, and when I turn around, there is no Max, only Helena with her hand over her mouth, pointing at the dark space beneath the bed. I motion for her to pull the blanket farther down, and she pushes the potato sack in front of Max before she does it. For good measure. I put a finger to my lips, she nods, and I run on my toes down the hall.

The knock comes again. Not the harsh clamor of the Gestapo, and it's not Emilika, either. This is sharp. Official. I hesitate in front of the door and finally call, "Yes?"

"Miss Podgórska?"

And I know exactly who is on the other side of my door.

"Miss Podgórska, may I speak with you, please?"

I unlock the door and open it a crack. It's the blond policeman. He tucks his cap under his arm and smiles.

"Hello, again," he says.

This time my nervousness has nothing to do with blue eyes and a dimple.

"May I come in?"

I tighten my grip on the knob. "I don't think that would be a good idea."

"You are right, of course. That's why I have brought a friend with me."

Another policeman, also Polish and also all smiles, steps into view. My stomach drops into my shoes.

"May I?"

The blond policeman steps forward, palm on the door, leaving me with the choice to either let him in or smash his arm. I let him in, his friend following, and we stand awkwardly in the empty hall. Neither one of them has a bruise on his cheek or a black eye, so hopefully Max did not attack them. Mr. Blond Policeman wanders to the open door of my room.

"Is this where you live?" he asks. And then, "And who is this?"

I dash up behind him, but it's only Helena looking back at us through the doorway, her eyes wide. She doesn't trust policemen. She doesn't like them. He saunters into the room, and she backs away, sticks out her lip, and sits on the bed, hard. Defiant. Like she will defend that bed to the death.

"This is my sister, Helena," I say quickly. "Hela, this is ... a man I met yesterday."

"What do you want with my sister?" says Helena. The other man chuckles, following me through the door while Mr. Blond Policeman goes to Helena and squats down in front of her. His feet must be inches from Max's face.

"I only want to talk to your sister," he says. "Tell her some things. We don't want her getting into trouble ..."

Mrs. Wojcik's words come unfortunately to my mind.

"You won't mind if I try to help your sister, will you?"

Helena bites her lip, screws up her face, and I have no idea what is about to come out of her mouth.

Do something, Fusia. Do something right now.

"Why don't you sit down," I say, smiling and pulling out a chair. Mr. Blond Policeman does, and he seems pleased about it. I'm pleased he's no longer close enough to hear Max breathe. "Can I make you some tea? Some bread?"

"No, thank you." He is all teeth and dimple, this man. He nods toward the bed. "Where are your parents?"

"My father is dead, and my mother is in a labor camp in Salzburg." I glance at her letter still sitting on the table in the bread crumbs, and he picks it up. I wait, patient, demure, watching his eyes rove all over the contents of my letter. But I am boiling inside. Who does he think he is, coming to my house, telling me what I should and shouldn't do? Helena, I can see, is not feeling much better. And then I hope that she swept under the bed like she was supposed to, and that Max will not sneeze. Mr. Blond Policeman tosses down the letter.

"Miss Podgórska ... or may I call you Stefania?"

If you do, I think, you'll be the only one.

I smile at him. "Don't you think that would be unfair?"

"Unfair?"

"Because you know two of my names and I don't know even one of yours."

This pleases him even more. I think he knows that dimple is handsome.

"My apologies. I am Officer Berdecki. But you should call me Markus." He drums his fingers on the table while the other policeman examines Helena's magazine cuttings on the wall beside the bed. Then he says, "You ran away from me yesterday, Stefania."

"I thought you ran away from me."

"We'll say we got separated, then." He looks around my room. "It must be difficult to make money in your circumstance. I can understand why you would need to be ... creative and earn money how you can. Why you would risk, maybe, doing things that are not right."

Suddenly I wonder if this man thinks I am a prostitute.

"But I came to tell you seriously that you should not go back to the ghetto. And since your parents are not here, I feel it's my duty to say that anything could happen to you in there. It is not a place for young girls."

"The ghetto is not a place for anyone," I say sweetly. "Even you."

Markus shares an amused glance with his fellow policeman.

"Do you need help? With money? Do you need to find work? I could help you find work that pays, so you would not need to go into the ghetto anymore."

"I have work."

His brows rise over blue eyes.

"In the Minerwa building. I start tomorrow."

"That is a relief to me."

Though I'm not sure how relieved he really is.

"Maybe you would not object to my coming by another day and seeing if your work is going well?" He dimples.

"I don't think that would be a good idea," I say, smiling right back. "My neighbors are all eyes, and men coming in and out of my apartment ... Well, you can see how that would look."

"Then perhaps you would like to meet me sometime, after your work. In a café."

"Perhaps you would like me to bring my little sister with me. She loves a café."

I stand up, waiting for him to do the same. It takes him a few seconds to take the hint. The other policeman is red in the face, and I can't tell if he's embarrassed for his friend or trying not to laugh.

"We shall see each other soon, then. Good luck with your work, Stefania."

"Goodbye, Officer Berdecki."

I shuffle them both out the door, and when I come back into the bedroom, Helena is curled up on the bed, her knees to her chest. Shaking.

"Everything is okay now," I tell her. I sit beside her and pull her to my chest. "Really, it's okay ..." Max sticks his head out from under the bed. He has a cobweb threading his dark hair.

"Do you always have policemen coming first thing in the morning to flirt with you?"

"Why don't you go back under the bed," I tell him.

Relief is making me snappish.

Max stays longer than he had intended, in case Officer Berdecki or his friend is watching the house. I send Helena out into the courtyard to play, hoping her friends will help her forget her fright, and take a walk around the block. I see nothing. No policemen, and no one approaches me, so I tell Max it's time. But he stays still, sitting on the edge of the bed, elbows on his knees.

He says, "You didn't tell me about your job, Fusia."

I hadn't had a chance.

"I was thinking, under the bed. I've been thinking for a while. You'll have an income now. You could apply for more rooms."

"You mean the rest of your apartment?" This place would always belong to Max in my mind.

"No. You don't understand . . ."

I watch him struggle. With memory, or indecision, or something inside himself, I don't know. But I don't like it when he looks like that. I sit down beside him. He rubs a hand through his hair.

"I don't know how it will come. The Gestapo. Typhus. Dogs or starvation or the trains, I don't know. But they will not stop until there are no Jews left. Henek doesn't believe it. But I have heard them. I've seen what they do. They will use us for goulash. They will use us for soap. They will use us for shoe leather . . ."

I don't want to hear this.

"And we just sit and sit in our cage, and we wait for it. And I can't sit anymore. So for a long time, I have thought, who could I ask? Who would help me, now that I am nothing . . ."

"You are not nothing!"

Max shakes his head. "When you watch little children being murdered while you hide in a hole in the ground, too afraid to come out, you know that you are nothing. When whole countries want you dead, when thousands cheer for speeches about your destruction, when the dogs of the guards are treated better than you are, then it's not a question, Stefania. You know you are nothing."

My eyes dart toward the door, because his voice is far too loud. He grimaces. "I'm sorry, Fusia. But I'm looking death in the face, and I don't like what I see."

I want to tell him to stop it. That it's not true. Not to talk that way. That the war will end. Something will change. And then I remember after the first bombing, how I didn't believe the stories of the Jews shot in the cemetery. I didn't believe it because I didn't want to. Maybe I'm not so different from Henek after all.

Max says, "So I've thought, who could I go to? My old boss, maybe. A boy I knew once in school, but he has a wife and child now. I thought of Elzbeta, or her mother ..."

"Who is Elzbeta?"

He looks up. "Elzbeta. My girlfriend in Nizankowice."

"Your girlfriend? You never said anything."

He shrugs.

"Is she Jewish?"

"No."

I wonder what my *babcia* would have thought of that. Both Max and Izio with Gentiles. I wonder what I think of it. And then I study Max. He must be twenty-three, twenty-four now? About the same age as Officer Berdecki. Funny that I don't really know. It is easy to forget he was grown even before the war, that he had another life, outside Przemyśl. Then again, I think I turned seventeen last year, and I hadn't noticed that, either.

"I thought of her," Max goes on, "but I haven't heard from her once since the ghetto. I don't think I will. She'd never risk it, not like ..." His hand goes rubbing through his hair again. "I have no right to ask. But I am asking. Not for one night. I am asking you to hide me, and my brother, and Danuta, and the Hirsches and the Schillingers. Seven of us, until we die or the war ends."

He takes my hand.

"I know what I am asking. It isn't fair, and you have Hela to think of. I will understand if you say no."

I don't know how to answer him. The question feels too big.

"It would mean looking for an apartment where we could make a hiding place. Old Hirsch still has some money. He's willing to finance. That's why he's in, but even then, it will be hard to feed nine on what he has and your pay. It would be easier, maybe, for two. If there were two together, with work. To buy food."

I look up.

"I was thinking maybe your friend. Emilika."

"Emilika? I don't know ..."

"Do you think she knew Danuta was a Jew? Because I think maybe she did. That she spread those rumors to protect her. And she has work that pays well."

I am not sure about this.

"Do you think it would be safe to ask her? To see what she says?"

I don't know. I don't know about any of it. He squeezes my hand.

"Do you want me to go back under the bed?"

I shake my head.

"I could spend the war there."

I bite my lip.

"Maybe you need seven beds."

And that comment gets him what he wants. I smile. Max has one eyebrow that tips up just a little farther than the other. A little quirk of a point that tells me when he's joking. He was joking just then. But only a little.

"I need time to think," I say.

"I know it."

We go to the ghetto arm in arm, chatting like there are no cares in the dark, dark world. Max is careful of policemen, since there is one who will not forget his face. I'm careful of policemen because of Officer Berdecki. We circle around the ghetto fence to a new place, near a small basement window. When there's no one near, Max kisses my cheek, then scoots under the barbed wire and straight into the unlocked window.

I have to think.

I watch Helena sleeping that night, but what I see is the pistol of the demented SS man, pointing at Mr. Schwarzer. Pointing at the blue-eyed girl who was not much different from me. Pointing at the children. I see the blaze of fire coming out its end.

And I don't know what to do. I don't know how to balance Max's life—and six others—against the life of my sister.

I ask God.

But the sky is silent above me.

14.

March 1943

AT FIVE-THIRTY THE NEXT MORNING, I WALK TO MY NEW WORK IN THE DEEP, glowing blue of a late-winter dark. The world has forgotten about spring. But I barely notice the snow or the streets or the empty windows of what used to be Jewish shops. I'm worrying about Helena and how she will get along by herself all day. Worrying about doing a job in a factory that I know nothing about. And worrying about Max.

I don't know how to do what he's asked of me.

I don't know how not to do it, either.

I see the haze before I see the building. Smokestacks belching smog that can be tasted on the tongue. I cross an iron bridge over a ravine of railroad tracks, find the brick walls rising stories above me, go through a set of double doors, and then I am inside the factory.

When I first came to Przemyśl, this place made mechanical toys. Windup cars and clowns and little dogs. I'd always thought of it as happy. Now the little office I'm standing in is dingy and smells of hot metal. There are fifteen or sixteen others with me, men and women looking as lost as I am, gathered around a desk with the inevitable German and the inevitable stack of folders and forms. I unwind the wool scarf from around my head, folding it to hide its ragged ends, and hand my papers to him. He checks me off his list.

And I have begun my life as a factory worker.

The Minerwa factory, says Herr Braun, our director, sweating in his suit while standing on a crate, is a system of rules and regulations, where we, the workers, will be valued. As long as we do not interfere with the system or a rule or a regulation. We are lucky to have been given this work. We are lucky because this work will keep us from starving. We are easily replaced, and those who are late, inefficient, tired, or stupid will be replaced. Immediately.

Clear and to the point.

My job is to operate six machines that make screws. The mechanic shows me how to do it, because while the work is mostly easy, the machines are delicate and prone to breaking down, and he can't be coming across the floor every few minutes to help me. So he says. My quota is thirty thousand screws every shift, the difference to be taken from my pay.

The room is loud. Unbelievably loud, with engines and pulleys running up and along the ceiling. My machines are hot, fast, and dangerous if I don't get my fingers out of the way. I feed them stick after stick of metal, running back and forth, and by the middle of the day, I've learned how to repair a water pump. On my break, a young man smiles at me from behind his cigarette. He is yellow-haired and blue-eyed, though nothing like Berdecki the policeman. He's still a boy. And I ignore him. I've had enough of smiles. A girl named Januka gives me a bite of her sandwich.

When I walk home, feet and shoulders aching, ears ringing from the noise, the sun has already come and gone. Now the blue-black cold feels crisp and clean, soothing after the smoke. When I step into the apartment building, Emilika pokes her head out of her door.

"There you are! I've just had Hela in here. I gave her some tea. You look like you could use tea."

I open my mouth to say no, I'm too tired, but Emilika holds up her sugar bowl.

"Do you have sugar?"

I shake my head.

"Then you'd better come inside."

Emilika pours water that is already hot into a teapot and sits me at her kitchen table, talking nonstop about her boyfriend— not the old one, a new one, more handsome! And the German SS that come into the photography shop to have their pictures made. So vain!

I look around me. She's only one girl by herself, but she has a whole apartment, with a sofa and a lamp, a separate bedroom, and matching dishes. Heavy curtains hang over her windows instead of rugs, blocking the dangerous light.

"And one comes in to get his prints," Emilika is saying, "and the portraits are good, but he won't pay because he says his nose is too wide. Not his whole face. Only his nose. Tell me, Fusia, how the camera can change the shape of a man's nose? And now Mr. Markowski blames me for giving away portraits, only Mr. Markowski wouldn't say no to an SS officer, either, would he? If he wants me to take on the Gestapo, he should provide the ammunition, that's what I say."

She sets down her cup and sighs.

"You know what I miss? Music. Remember how that little band at the restaurant across the street used to play outside in the summer? And when there were weddings at the club? We used to dance all night ..."

For one moment, I am upstairs, dancing with Izio before the open window in a dark apartment while the orchestra plays. Then I look at Emilika curiously. "Did you live here before? I don't remember seeing you."

"Oh, no. I lived in Kraków. But I visited in the summer, with my grandmama's sister. She lived in this apartment. But she's gone now. To some camp somewhere. She married a Jew."

In all her talk, Emilika has never once mentioned this to me. I wonder if she understands that "some camp" probably means her grandmother's sister is dead.

"It's terrible," I say carefully, "what the Nazis are doing."

"I know. I don't think Przemyśl will ever be the same. They disgust me, the Nazis."

I lean forward. "Have you ever thought about getting a new apartment, Emilika?"

"A new apartment? Why?"

"A bigger place. Maybe to share with some ... others."

Emilika tilts her head at me. "What sort of plan do you have in your head, Fusia?"

I bite my lip, trying to decide how to say what I want to. To sway a girl like Emilika. "Do you remember the boy I wanted to see? When you took my picture?"

She nods.

"He asked me to marry him. And they killed him. In the work camp at Lwów. He was Jewish."

Emilika's eyebrows go up and back down. Then she reaches across the table and pats my hand. "I thought it must be something like that. Oh, I'm sorry. Really."

"And now, his brothers ..." The words come slow and difficult, like the secret wants to stay in my mouth. "Now his brothers are in the same danger. In the ghetto. And I'd ... I'm thinking of doing something about it."

"Doing something? Doing what?"

"I want to get a bigger apartment with someone ... someone like you, maybe, and ... I want to hide them."

I take a deep breath. There. I said it.

Emilika sits back in her chair, her red lips open. She stares at me for a long, long minute.

"What are you talking about," she says slowly, "you stupid, stupid little girl? Do you want to die? Do you think you've lived long enough? Well, I haven't. I plan to be around years from now, and I won't throw my life away for some Jew I've never even heard of! You might as well ask me to jump out your window. And you can jump out of it, too. It might be quicker than being shot."

There's a clock somewhere in Emilika's nice kitchen. *Tick, tick, tick.* My hands are shaking. I trusted her. I just put my life in her hands.

Maybe I've just killed us.

I push back my chair, and Emilika says, "Wait. Fusia, wait."

She blows out a breath and lowers her voice.

"The secret police are everywhere. You know that, don't you? Pretending to be beggars, shopkeepers, workers, anyone. They offer help to Jews, or to help someone else help Jews, and when that person says yes, they arrest them and the Jews they were trying to help. You can't trust anyone ..."

"Do you think I'm spying for the Germans?"

Emilika smiles. She almost laughs. "No, Stefania Podgórska, I do not think you are a spy for the Germans. But how do you know that I am not?"

I suppose I don't. "Are you?"

"No. Which means you are very lucky." She leans forward. "What you're suggesting is a one in a million chance, and that means there are nine hundred and ninety-nine thousand other chances to die."

"But it's not zero," I say.

"What?"

"Not zero in a million. It could work."

"It's suicide. And what about Hela?"

I don't have an answer for that.

"These people, Fusia. It's awful. It's sad. But you didn't make these things happen, and it's not something you can fix. They're not your responsibility. Hela is your responsibility. If you won't think of yourself, think of her."

This time she lets me scoot my chair back. I leave my cup half-full on the table. "I'm sorry. It was a silly idea."

She waves a hand and smiles. "You're sad about your boy, that's all. I understand."

"I hope you won't mention this ... our conversation to anyone?"

"What? What conversation? I don't even know what you're talking about. I must have amnesia ..."

I trudge slowly up the stairs while Emilika's door clicks shut behind me. I feel sore inside. And the soreness, I realize, is disappointment.

Not her responsibility, and not mine. Whose responsibility is it then, Emilika?

Helena hugs me and hugs me, and brings me some toast with butter. I fall into bed while I'm still chewing the last bite, and she tugs off my shoes and snuggles in beside me. And before I even know I'm asleep, I'm dreaming.

Of a dark forest, where the trees are as tall as buildings. The moss and leaves are hard like cement beneath my feet, the moon hanging big and low, beams streaming down like searchlights. I push my way through limbs that scratch my face like broken glass, faster and faster, because I can hear screaming. A man, a grandmother, a baby, so many people, hundreds of them, a gibberish of different words that are all the same because they all mean the same thing. Mercy. Mercy.

And then the shots begin. I run and run, let the branches cut my face, because I have to stop the shooting. But the faster I run, the fainter the noise, the slower the shots, until there is no more sound and no more people and no more trees, and I am running in blackness, a void that feels like death ...

I open my eyes, panting, sucking in air like I really have been running. But I am only in bed with Helena, still in my dress, the stove making little ticking sounds as it cools. Like Emilika's clock. Helena pats my hand.

"Someone was shooting in the street," she whispers sleepily. "But they're done now ..."

I close my eyes, and Max is in the forest with me.

"Go," he says. "Run!" But he's not talking to me, he's talking to Henek and Danuta. He takes them each by the hand, forcing them to go when they don't want to, dragging them in a zigzag path through trees that are now made of brick and stone. Planes whine like birds above our heads. I chase after them, a sharp pain in my side, and there are other people with us, little shadows darting on my right and my left and up ahead. They stumble and they fall and they do not get up, and when I look down, the pain in my side is not from running. Blood spurts through my fingers.

"I'm shot," I say. Max slows and turns. Danuta's eyes go wide. The shadows are flitting by, leaving us behind. "Hurry!" I yell. "Save yourselves!"

Only it's Izio's voice that comes out of my mouth. Not my own. Max starts walking, but it's the wrong way. He's left Henek and Danuta. He's walking toward me.

And then Helena is shaking me, telling me that the cathedral bells have rung. It's after five o'clock.

On the way to the factory, I see two bodies hanging stiff and frozen from the ghetto fence. Killed, says the sign, for doing business with the Jews. I go to work and make 28,208 screws. The inspector, who is Polish, writes down 30,208. I go to the market on the way home, buy what they have left, and sleep. And have nightmares. I have nightmares every night that week.

"Max came today," Helena says on Friday night. "He gave the special knock, so I let him in. He wanted to know if you had anything to tell him, but I didn't know. I gave him the rest of the bread. Then that policeman came, but I didn't let him in. I told him to go away ..."

"The one who came before?"

Helena nods.

"Did he come when Max was here?"

She shakes her head.

But what if he had? I imagine Max and Officer Berdecki, both standing at my door, and my stomach feels sick. Max shouldn't be out of the ghetto. He has to stop taking risks. The other policeman, the one he choked, might find him. Or one of the neighbors. Or Emilika.

Or maybe Max never made it back to the ghetto at all. Maybe Max is already dead.

Maybe I don't have a decision to make at all.

"Fusia, what's wrong?" says Helena, tugging at my skirt.

I try to smile at her, to cover up my fear, but I'm in a sweat. And then I say, "You called me Fusia."

"I know," Helena says. "I gave up."

By Saturday morning, my eyes are bleary, and I am so stupid from lack of sleep, I forget to ignore the boy at work. I smile absentmindedly when he tells me hello, and I stumble through my shift, barely paying attention, which is a good way to lose a hand.

"Stefania! Stefi!"

I look up, startled to hear my name in the noise. It's the mechanic, and smoke is drifting up from the knives in my machine. The water pump has stopped working.

"What is wrong with you!" the mechanic shouts. He shuts down the machine. "Your head is in the clouds today! Are you sick or in love?"

If this man knew my loves, he'd run a hundred kilometers in the other direction.

"I don't know what to do," I say, and then remember who I'm talking to. "I mean ... I don't feel well. I'm dizzy ..."

"Why didn't you say so?" the man says. He looks me over. "Okay, come with me."

He leads me to the repair area, where a large wooden table is covered with tools and parts and metal bits and oil stains. He points underneath, and when I bend down to look, the table has a shelf, person-sized, just a few inches from the floor. Someone has left a pillow on it.

"Get under there and have a nap," he says. "I'll fix your machines and wake you up in half an hour."

I believe I thank the man, but I'm so tired I'm not sure I've actually said the words. I crawl onto the shelf and settle my head on the pillow.

And in the noise of the factory, I dream.

We're in the forest again, only now the trees are square, the branches growing out between windows in the trunks. Max is running hand in hand with Henek and Danuta, and I have Helena on one side of me and Dziusia Schillinger on the other. The leaves we kick aside clatter like tin cans.

And I know there is something behind us. Closer and closer. I can feel it creeping like the tiger I saw in one of my *tata*'s books when I was small.

"We're almost there," Max says. And then I see what we're running for. A hole in the ground. An underground bunker. A shelter from the Nazis.

They won't find us there.

"Go, Dziusia," I whisper, letting go of her hand, pushing her toward the hole. She slides in after Max and Henek and Danuta, then Helena tugs on my arm. I turn around, and two soldiers are behind us, skulls grinning on their hats. The skulls have tiny little mustaches, and so do the men.

"Vu zenen zey gegangen?" says one of the skulls, and I think how strange it is that an SS hat would speak Yiddish. Then it says, "Where did they go?" in Polish.

Ah, I think. That's better.

"Where did they go?" the skull demands. "Where are the Jews?" And now I am afraid. Helena raises her arm and points. In the opposite direction.

"They're right there," she says.

"Yes," I say, "except it's over there." I point the other way, just a little to our left, away from the underground shelter. The skulls look confused, I'm not sure how. But the men underneath do not look confused. I see one of the mustaches twitch. They know I'm lying.

They know I'm lying, they know I'm lying, they know I'm lying ...

The one closest to me raises his hand. His hand is a gun. He points it at me and then lowers it down, down. He's going to shoot into the hole. He's going to shoot Max.

And I scream.

And then I am awake in the tool factory, and I know I have just screamed, but no one has heard me in the racket. I curl beneath the table until the mechanic comes back and tells me nicely that I'm useless but he won't tell, and I should go home.

I don't go straight home. I wander through Przemyśl until my feet find the cathedral. I push open the heavy doors, cross myself, light a candle, and sit in a pew, the dying Christ rising high above my head.

Death really isn't so terrible, I think. It's losing the chance to live that's sad. Like I did with Izio. Izio died because I didn't come in time to save him. But what if I had never tried to come?

If I live through this war, can I live with having done nothing, or will my life be poisoned with regret?

How will I tell Helena when we find out Max is dead?

How will I tell my mother that my choices have killed Helena?

I'd never have the chance. Because I would be dead, too.

But who else is there to save them but me?

Oh Great God. Lady Mary. Give me the answer.

The air is silent above me.

I meander out of the cathedral, and now my feet take me to what was once a Jewish street, not that far from ours. The buildings stand empty, row after row of them, the windows broken, the doors gone—probably burned for firewood—and when I poke my head inside, even the floors have been ripped out and salvaged. These apartments would have been much like mine. Typical. With everyone knowing their layout. Everyone knowing how many rooms they'd have, and what size. You could never make a place to hide Jews in an apartment like these. Like mine. The difference would be spotted right away.

I'd have to put seven people under the bed.

The sun is almost down, the sky orange and fiery on one side, luminous and blue on the other. My shoes tap along the paving stones, the wind moaning through the missing windows. The emptiness is unsettling. Spooky. I hold my coat closed tight against the cold and think that this is what the ghetto will sound like someday. Echoes and wind. I stop walking and just stand. I close my eyes.

And there is the silence. Like I'm the only person in Przemyśl.

Only the quiet isn't empty.

I feel a little push against my back.

I open my eyes and stumble, nearly losing my balance. Two women have come around the corner, brooms in their hands. Cleaning the abandoned sidewalk.

Maybe they know of an empty apartment. Ask them.

The other part of my mind says that's a ridiculous thing to do. Why would they know of an empty apartment?

It doesn't hurt to ask.

I should go to the housing department.

Ask them!

My feet move, and the two women look up from the pile of refuse they've been collecting. They watch me approach.

"Excuse me," I say, "but do either of you know of any empty apartments?"

"Eh?" says one of them, squinting at me.

"Do you know of any apartments that might be open?"

I shift my weight to the other foot. I feel silly.

"I know of one," says the other woman, leaning on her broom. She is weathered and lined, her nose red either from cold or vodka, gray hair frizzling from underneath her scarf. "There's an empty place at Tatarska 3. Not an apartment, though. It's a house, almost ..."

"A cottage," says the other.

I look at their dirty, wrinkled faces and ask, "Where is Tatarska Street?"

15.

March 1943

I WALK AROUND THE OUTSIDE OF THE APARTMENT AT TATARSKA 3. THE women were right. They're more like cottages sharing walls than apartments, two stories with steep, peaked roofs made of tin. And it's a short stretch of street, up a hill with very few houses. An empty college building stands directly across the street, a gated convent at the crest of the hill, and I can see the tops of two cathedral steeples and other lights sloping down toward the market square. The building pushes out into an L shape, and the empty section is the dark one around the back, in a patch of frozen dirt. There's a well to one side and a long stinking shack that can only be toilets to the other.

I haven't seen people, but I can smell them.

It almost makes me homesick for the farm.

I go to the side and knock on the door the street cleaner described. It creaks open immediately. Someone has been watching from behind a curtain.

"Yes," says a woman, squinting at the dark.

"Are you the custodian for Tatarska 3? Is it still empty?"

The woman nods on both counts.

"Could I see it? Would right now be all right?"

She grunts and nods, disappears inside for a moment, and comes back with a set of keys and a lit lantern.

"It's nothing fancy," she says. She's a short, squat woman with neat hair and an apron that looks like it has beet stains. She leads me to a wooden door not far from the toilets and puts her key to the lock. It takes a little doing, but it opens, and she steps in first with the lantern.

We're in a small combined kitchen and sitting room, a later addition to the cottage, with wood walls and a rough planked floor, a stove, a sink with a drain but no faucets, and a bucket for the well hanging from a nail. No electricity. There are two other doors. The first opens into a bedroom, with another bedroom directly behind that. The next door, opposite the sink and the stove, leads to a small hallway with a dirt floor and a ladder.

"What's up there?" I ask.

"Attic," says the woman.

I walk back and stand in the kitchen, turning a big circle while the woman watches me.

"It's nothing fancy," she says again. As if I've accused her of something. But I can only smile. I smile like I haven't smiled in a week.

"It's not fancy," I reply. "It's perfect."

The custodian's name is Mrs. Krajewska, and she warms to me as soon as she realizes I'm not put off by water buckets and outdoor toilets. She tells me to go to the housing department to fill out an application, and how much she would like to have a nice young girl as her neighbor. How nice it will be for her two little boys to have my sister to play with. I run back to the apartment like I'm skating on ice, like I've got the wings of a fighter plane, bursting through the door so quickly that Helena gives a little scream. Max is there.

He stands up. "What's happened?"

"I think I found an apartment."

"You've found a place to hide Max?" Helena asks. "I knew you would."

She knew I would. I didn't know I would. And I hadn't mentioned anything to Helena about hiding Max at all. "How did you know?" I ask.

"Because I asked God. Mama always said that's what you do when you want something. So I did."

Yes, Mama did say that. "But how did you know I wanted to hide Max?"

"Because you always hide Max!"

She has a point. "And that's what you want? That's what you asked God for?"

She tilts her head and looks at me funny. "Of course! Didn't you?"

Max is just standing there, listening to us talk. I raise my eyes to meet his gaze. I already know he is looking at me.

"Yes," I say.

He blinks.

"Yes, Hela. That's what I asked for." But I'm still looking at Max.

He doesn't speak. We just look at each other for another long minute, and then Max nods. It's like we've signed a contract.

"What time is it?" he whispers.

"I don't know ..." I look around like my room will have sprouted a clock. "Not seven," I say.

"Then let's go see it."

"Right now?"

He smiles. "Yes. Right now."

We walk arm in arm down the street, like a couple out for a stroll, Max with my old wool scarf wrapped half across his face, as if he's cold. Helena was disappointed to be left behind. I didn't know if we could even get the apartment yet, I told her. I thought she was going to stamp her foot. And, I added, we didn't want to bring any extra attention to Max. She gave in.

Right now, I'm not even afraid.

"Where is Tatarska?" Max whispers through the scarf. "I don't know the street."

"It's across from the college, the one they shut down. There's no other reason to know it. There isn't much there."

"That's good. That's very good ..."

"Alley," I say, steering Max abruptly to the left. A German policeman has turned onto the street, on patrol, walking straight toward us. We scoot quickly down the little passage between the buildings before he passes, circle around the back, wait, and come right back onto the street behind the German's back like we never stopped walking. Max grins and puts his arm around me.

He enjoys fooling the Nazis more than I realized.

When we reach Tatarska, Max looks carefully to the right, left, and across the street, craning his neck up at the roof while we walk around the courtyard.

"Stay here," I say, leaving him beside the door of number 3. I knock again on Mrs. Krajewska's door.

"Oh," she says, opening the door fully. "You're back?"

"Mrs. Krajewska, I'm sorry to bother you, but you were kind earlier, and my older brother is here. He wants to see the house before I put in the application. You wouldn't mind opening it up one more time, would you?"

She sighs. "I'll get a light."

When we come back to Max, still standing in the cold beside the door, she raises the light and looks him over in a way that would be frightening if she hadn't done the same to me an hour ago.

"Hello," Max says. His hands are tucked into his pockets, and suddenly I wonder if he's got a weapon in there.

Mrs. Krajewska grunts and unlocks the door.

"It's not fancy," she says as we walk in. I let Max explore. He takes the light and goes into the bedrooms, climbs the ladder to the attic, and even steps outside to examine the toilets.

"You mentioned a sister," says Mrs. Krajewska. "Will your brother be staying with you, too?"

"Oh, no, he lives in Kraków," I lie. "He just worries for me, maybe a little too much. But he's a good brother ..."

Max comes back inside and sticks his head in the stove, trying to look up the chimney. Mrs. Krajewska's face goes soft like melting chocolate.

"Well, isn't that nice," she says. "Why don't I leave the light and let you two talk it over, and just bring it back when you're done, yes?"

"Thank you, Mrs. Krajewska."

When she shuts the door, Max comes close to me. We whisper, in case Mrs. Krajewska is listening.

"I'm worried about the neighbors," Max says. "The bedroom walls are not very thick, and there's another cottage on the other side. And all of them will have to walk right past the back window and door to get to the toilets. It will be hard to keep quiet ..."

"Maybe you thought I could find an apartment in a desert? Or the Himalayas?"

"Don't be smart, Fusia." But he's grinning at me. "The place was made for us. There's dirt just an inch or two under the floor. We can dig a bunker, maybe, beneath the boards, for when someone comes to the door."

We look around at the room again, and suddenly I'm seeing the cleaning that needs to be done. The water to be carried. The food that will need to be bought and hauled up that hill. My doubled walk to work. Nine people in three rooms and the lack of privacy.

Max says, "Are you sure?"

I nod. "Yes. I am sure."

We walk back to Helena arm in arm again, posing as a couple. It's been a long time since I've seen Max look this alive.

Max stays at the apartment because it's too close to curfew to make it safely back to the fence. Not that the fence is safe. There are two more men hanging on it, killed for leaving the ghetto to buy from the outside.

It bothers me that Max knows this and came anyway.

He's pulling on his shoes the next morning when there's a knock at the door. Sharp. Official.

We freeze, and then Max drops to the floor and slides beneath the bed, taking his shoes with him. Helena goes to move his teacup, but I shake my head, a finger to my lips. I tiptoe to the hall and wait. The knock comes three more times, and I'm sweating before I hear the telltale creak of a board that means someone has just set foot on the second stair. Going down the steps. I creep back into our room, finger to my lips again, and get an eye around the edge of the rug nailed over the window, careful not to move it.

And there comes Officer Berdecki, glancing up at my window before he walks away down the street.

"You can come out," I say, but Max is already grunting his way from under the bed.

"Is it that policeman?" he asks.

"What makes you think that?"

"What? You have other boyfriends knocking at your door at six thirty in the morning?"

"No," I reply sweetly. "Mostly I just let them sleep over." I see the little point of his eyebrow rise, his smile coming out into the open. He doesn't mind being teased, because he's happy. He's happy because we found Tatarska Street.

"But, Fusia, nobody stays here except Max!" says Helena. "And aren't you late for work?"

"I have to go to the housing department," I say. "I paid the Szymczak boy to take a note to Minerwa." Which they are not going to like. But the hours of the housing department and my shift are almost the same.

"I need to go, too," Max says, his cheerfulness gone. "Before the day soldiers get there. While the night ones are still tired."

"Max," I say, and now I am serious, too. "You shouldn't come back here again. You should stay in the ghetto until . . ."

Until it's time to risk leaving it forever.

"I'll need to know if you get Tatarska," he says. "I don't want to tell Henek or Danuta or any of them until I know how things will be. And we will need time to prepare."

"Is the mail still being read?"

"What comes of it, yes."

We think about this for a minute. Then Helena says, "I can bring you a letter, Max."

We both turn to the table, where Helena is stacking the dishes to wash. Her job now that I am working.

"I can bring a letter to the fence," she says.

I pull my coat on. "No, Hela."

"But I can do it! I've played there before, and the guards don't pay any attention to the children. Even when we go right up to the fence."

"When were you at the fence?"

"Last week. Looking for Max."

"She's right," Max says. "They don't bother the children."

"We'll think of something else," I say. "Hela, do the dishes, and be careful. And the same for you," I say to Max. "Except for the dishes."

"Come on," I hear Max say as I'm hurrying down the hall. "I'll help you dry before I go ..."

There are no wire-rimmed glasses in the housing office. Instead there is a nice Polish secretary who brings me the right papers to fill out for Tatarska 3. Her eyebrows rise when I don't leave, watching as I retreat to a corner to fill them out, chewing on the end of the pen. I give them back to her.

"How long?" I ask.

"Two days," she says.

"And you are certain it's still empty? That no one else has applied?"

The woman smiles. "I don't think so, little butterfly. You will get a letter."

I run out the door, all the way across Przemyśl to the factory, and when I hurry onto the floor, Herr Braun is waiting. He stops the engines and yells at me in German and Polish. Notes are insufficient, and so are excuses. I am a stupid, lazy girl who will never consider coming late to work again. I will arrive five minutes early. I will exceed my quotas. If I do not exceed my quotas, I will be grateful and glad to keep on working until I do.

Sometimes it's best just to nod.

I work through my break, and when I glance up, the blond boy is standing on the other side of my machines. Lubek is his name, or so says Januka, the girl who occasionally shares her sandwich.

"Let me know if you need help," he says, and saunters away.

The next day I do need help, and Lubek brings me more metal stock to feed into the machines, so I don't lose the time going to get them. I exceed my quota. Just. And as soon as I exceed it the next day, I hurry from the factory floor, getting my arms in my coat as I run across the iron bridge, scarf in my hand instead of on my head, because I don't want to wait for a letter. I have twenty-three minutes until the housing department closes.

I burst through the door. The little waiting area is full of people, and the room smells stuffy, hot and sweaty after my run through the clean cold. The secretary looks up from her desk. Her eyebrows rise. Then she picks up a stack of papers and shakes them at me.

"I've got it?" I call through the bodies.

She nods.

I push my way through the crowd, grab the secretary's face, and give her a smacking kiss on the cheek.

"Stop that," she says, laughing, and hands me the papers. And a set of keys.

"If I give you a kiss, do I get an apartment, too?" some man shouts.

"Kiss me!" says another. Now the whole room is laughing.

I stroll back to the apartment under a sky thick with stars, and when I tell Helena the news, she jumps up and down. I go to sleep that night, thinking about how to move a bed.

And I do not dream at all.

The next morning, I leave early and walk by the fence, just in case I can see Max. I don't want to be able to see Max, because I'm afraid of what might happen if he draws the attention of the Germans. Or the Polish police. But I need to see Max, to tell him about Tatarska. The area behind the fence, usually full of desperate, milling people, is empty. Nothing but the *tap, tap, tap* of the patrolling SS man's boots. I circle around to the place where the barbed wire is loose, only it isn't loose anymore. Wooden planks have been nailed across the opening, and when I go to the basement window where Max scooted in last time, there's no one there, either. Now I have to run to work. Only to discover that thanks to Herr Braun, I am now on the night shift. I'm not due at work for another twelve hours.

When I come back through the door, I scare Helena almost to tears, because she thinks I've lost my job. She's at the sink in the kitchen, my apron around her middle, washing the dishes in water she's warmed on the stove. I kiss her head and help her finish.

"Look what I found," she says. She pulls the old wooden crate Mrs. Diamant once gave me from its nook behind the bed. It's where she puts her things now, the extra magazines to cut and the string and marbles and buttons and whatever else she finds on the street. Now she pulls out a deflated ball.

"Mr. Szymczak told me yesterday that he has a pump to put air in tires and that he could put air in my ball," she says.

"Don't you think it probably has a hole in it somewhere, and that's why it doesn't have any air in the first place?"

"It's okay. It doesn't need to be full of air for very long. Just long enough for me to kick it to the ghetto fence."

I sit back on my heels. "What do you mean?"

"I mean, I'll go near the fence and play a game with my ball, and I'll call out things like, "Maxi! Maxi! Fusia letter!" And the guard won't know what that means, but Max will, and he'll come out, and I'll kick the ball under the fence when the guard isn't looking, and Max will give it back, and when he does, I'll give him the letter. I've played ball with the guards twice to see if it works, and it does, so it's easy."

I look at my little sister. Who plays ball with the SS.

"I can do it," she says.

We make a deal. She can try, but I'm going with her, watching from around the corner. If Max doesn't come in five minutes, she will stop. If anything even looks like it's going wrong, I will make it stop. I take my place behind a little stand near the train tracks, where they used to sell ice cream, while Helena starts bouncing the ball Mr. Szymczak has put air in. She has a scrap of paper in her coat pocket that says, "We have it. Window. Two days." Meaning we got Tatarska, and Max is to meet me at the basement window—which seems the safest spot—in two days.

My chest is thumping so hard I think I might be sick.

Because I'm the worst sister that ever was.

Helena kicks the ball against the wall of a building, catching it on the bounce. "Maxi! Fusia letter!" she calls. She kicks it again and calls. Like it's a game. I see the SS man watch her for a moment as he walks the length of the fence. Then she turns and kicks it toward him. He bends down and catches the ball, throwing it to her. She laughs and kicks it back.

Oh. Helena is good at this.

The SS man smiles and throws the ball to her again, pointing toward the brick wall of the building. Helena calls, kicks the ball to the wall, and catches. Calls and kicks and catches.

And there is Max, appearing like a shadow in the doorway of a building inside the fence.

I don't think Helena sees him. She kicks the ball while Max sidles nearer, and then when the SS man has his back to her, a few feet from his turn at the far end, Helena kicks the ball hard at the fence.

It rolls right under. Max chases the ball while Helena waits, her nose poking through, and when he rolls the ball beneath the wire, I see the crumpled paper slip from her hand to his. And in the other hand, a piece of paper goes from his to hers.

I hadn't expected that.

It's over in seconds. Max melts away, and Helena throws the ball back toward the wall and chases it. The guard turns and begins his walk down the length of the fence. She plays for a minute or two more, then runs around the corner. Grinning.

"Here," she says, giving me the paper. I take her hand, and we walk fast, until we're two streets away and standing in the line starting to form at the bakery.

"Are we getting rolls?" asks Helena.

"You can have a cookie," I say. "Because you are the smartest girl I know."

I think her smile is going to split her face. And then I open the paper from Max.

Typhus. Food and medicine.

And I wonder who is dying.

Whoever it is, they will have to wait for my first wages tomorrow.

I take Helena to Tatarska Street next, one of us carrying a broom, the other a mop and a ruined dish towel. Helena runs from room to room, slamming the doors, climbing the ladder, turning circles with her arms outstretched in the kitchen.

"It's so big!" she calls.

It must feel like forever to her, since the farmhouse.

I start a fire in the stove with some lumber scraps we find behind the ladder in the little hallway. And we get to work, brushing down the walls and scrubbing the floor, disturbing more mice than I want to see. Helena learns to work the pump and pull water from the well, filling bucket after bucket, fending off the two Krajewska boys at the same time, and in the end, we are dirtier than Tatarska 3.

I hurry home in the long twilight, get cleaned up, and hurry out again to work, arriving just before my time. There's no one there I know, and no one to help me make my quota. I'm short, but the inspector looks at my tired face and takes pity. And when I'm leaving, the German at the desk gives me an envelope with my name on it. My wages. I turn around and tuck it in my bra.

And I run to the shops in the dawn light, stepping into the druggist's the second he opens the door. The aspirin costs half my wages, which is frightening. I comfort myself with the thought of more wages to come and go to the market. The farmer's wife I usually deal with is just setting up her booth and complains that I have been going elsewhere. I tell her no, it's just that I have a job now and have been early to work. I buy eggs, cheese, butter, and half a chicken. Sickness needs protein. Or that's what Mama always said about birthing mothers, and I think it must be close to the same thing.

I stumble through the door of the apartment, tell Helena she can have a slice of bread and an egg, sleep for three hours, and then pack up the food for Max. It hasn't been two days, but I didn't know about the typhus, then. I'm hoping he will guess this. I make a bundle out of brown paper and my apron, then take the back way around the ghetto fence to the basement window, avoiding the guarded gate.

The narrow alley is empty except for some piles of refuse and the icy stains of someone's dirty dishwater. The windows above me feel like eyes. I stay back, leaning against a building, the bundle tight in my hands. It's cold. Deep cold. If I were Gestapo, I think, I'd have a man in some of these apartments, watching the fence, unseen from above. The thought makes me shiver. When nothing happens for a long time, I toss a pebble at the basement window.

And I miss. I toss another and manage some noise. Another few seconds, and the window pushes open, and Max's head comes out. And then I hear footsteps, loud, coming along the fence. Max disappears, the window shuts without a sound, and I duck into the deep doorway of an abandoned shop. I watch the opening to the fence through the store glass, and a policeman walks by, Polish, his cap pulled low.

I wish I knew how often the patrol passes.

I creep back toward the fence, and Max has his head out again, beckoning. I hurry forward, kneel down, and push the bundle through the barbed wire. He pulls it into the window.

"Who's sick?" I whisper.

"Henek and Dr. Schillinger."

Please don't let Max lose another brother. "There's aspirin," I say.

"I've told them about the house," Max says. "I have a plan to—"

The footsteps are back. Max disappears, the window shuts, and I get to my feet. Boots are crunching in the gravel between the paving stones, coming at a trot. I dart across the alley, but there's no time to disappear into a doorway. I lean against the wall, as if I'm bored.

A flash of blue, and a Polish policeman runs by. And then he stops, backs up, and stares into the alley.

It's Officer Berdecki.

His blue eyes blink, and we look at each other. His cheeks are flushed.

He really is handsome. Like someone in a magazine.

I look like I'm hanging around, waiting for someone at the ghetto fence.

He ought to arrest me.

But he walks away. Shaking his head.

I wonder what I could have done to make this man like me enough to let me go. Again.

Or how I will pay for it later. He knows where I live.

I run home, burst through the apartment door, and say, "Hela, let's move. Today."

It takes three hours to pack up everything we own, and that's only because I spend an hour finding someone who will rent me a cart. Two of the boxes we carry to Tatarska ourselves, and I leave Helena with them while I go back to load the dishes and the bed frame and the mattress. I want to be quick about it so I can be gone before Officer Berdecki ends his shift and before Emilika comes home. I'm afraid if she looks at my face, she'll know what I'm doing. Better to leave her wondering.

I slide the mattress awkwardly down the stairs, balance it on top of the loaded cart, pay the Szymczak boy to watch it for me, then run back up to make sure I've left nothing behind.

I look at the empty room, dirt and dust I would have sworn didn't exist littering the bare floor, then walk through every inch of the echoing apartment. The memory of what was and the sight of what is clash together in my mind like tangos in two different keys. I should have swept, I think. Mrs. Diamant would have wanted that. She always kept her floors clean, especially in the shop.

And then I think not. My *babcia* would have wanted me to save her sons.

I leave the key on the mantel, close the door, and push the precarious cart all the way across Przemyśl to Tatarska 3.

16.

March 1943

I'M SO TIRED THAT NIGHT AT WORK I'M LUCKY TO MAKE IT TO MIDNIGHT WITH all my fingers. The night mechanic comes and taps me on the shoulder, jerking his head toward the repair table. I sleep for an hour, then work again.

When I come home to Tatarska Street, Helena is on the floor on the bare mattress, shivering in her sleep because the weather is still bitter and she knows she's not allowed to start a fire. But she's hung our clothes on the hooks in the bedroom, put the ugly rugs that were over our windows on the floor, and stacked the dishes on the shelf beside the sink. I spread my coat over her, start the fire, and put the bed back together. There are two eggs and half a cup of milk left for breakfast. I have to go to the market. And I have to get a message to Max. If he goes looking for us at the apartment, there will be no one there to hide him.

I write three words on a torn piece of brown butcher paper. *Moved. Sick? When?* And as soon as Helena's eyes are open, I say, "Did you pack your ball?"

In one hour, Helena stands at the gate to the ghetto, playing with her ball, the note in her pocket, and I am at my post beside the old ice cream shack. Only this time she's going to wait and play more after she's passed the note to Max, to see if she can get a reply. I'm hoping he will tell me who's alive, who's still sick, and when they can come to Tatarska. Helena kicks the ball, bouncing it against the blank brick wall of an apartment building.

"Maxi! Maxi! Fusia letter!" she calls.

There are other children hanging around the fence today. Some try to play with Helena, but she ignores them. Next to the dry fountain in the disused square, a group of four boys, young teen-agers with fuzz on their lips, stand in a tight circle, passing around a cigarette. Helena tosses the ball toward the guard—an SS man, though not the same one—and he barks at her, yelling something unfriendly, though it's hard to hear because a car is honking. She plays her game and calls but stays away from the guard.

Good girl, Hela.

And then I see Max walking by on the other side of the fence, well back from the wire. Helena throws the ball hard, misses her kick, and lets it roll underneath the fence. The guard has his back turned. Max stops the ball and trots up quickly to give it to her. But I can't see if Helena has given him the note.

"Stefania Podgórska, what are you doing standing in the street?"

I jump like I've been pinched. Mrs. Wojcik is standing beside me, holding her little dog. I try to put a smile on my face.

"Just waiting for someone."

"Who?" she asks.

I really don't like this woman. And what is she doing on this side of the railroad tracks anyway? I glance at Helena. She's play-ing very near the fence. I can't see Max.

"Is it your policeman?" asks Mrs. Wojcik. "It is, isn't it? He's been trouble already, hasn't he? You can't fool me. I was married for thirty-two years, raised two sons, and expect to soon have a husband again." She pauses here, obviously hoping I'll ask. "So, you can't argue with me. Because I know men."

I am much too tired for this. "Mrs. Wojcik, I have only one thing to say to that." She leans in, expectant. "And the thing I have to say is *geyn in drerd*!"

I'm sure Mrs. Wojcik has no idea she's just been told to go to the devil in Yiddish, but from the look on her face, I think my sentiment is clear.

The dog yips as Mrs. Wojcik huffs and marches away, and when I turn back around, the children are playing and the guard is standing in front of the gate, talking to one of the boys with the cigarette. Helena's ball is still rolling along the fence.

But Helena isn't there.

I step out from the shack.

"Hela?" I call. "Helena?"

I walk out into the empty space of pavement. "Helena!" I yell, turning in a circle. And then I see Max behind the fence, pointing with fast jabs to my right. The SS guard stops his conversation to look at me. I point and mouth the words, "This way?"

The guard raises his gun, but at Max's nod I sprint in the direction he showed me before the guard can even bark.

"Helena!"

People turn and stare as I run to the next street corner, skidding to a stop to look both ways. I can't see her. The train tracks mean there's only one way to turn. But which block?

"Did you see a little girl run by?" I ask a man leaning against the post of a streetlight. He grunts and points left. I run that way, along the ghetto fence and into a neighborhood of apartments. There are some girls drawing squares for hopscotch on the sidewalk.

"Did you see a little girl run this way?" I ask them, panting for breath. One with pigtails squints up at me and shakes her head.

"But some boys did," she says. "And a soldier."

I think of the boys sharing the cigarette. The one talking to the guard. Oh no.

No, no, no.

What did Max give her?

"Which way did they go?" I say. My voice is rising with panic. "Which way? What kind of soldier?"

But the girl doesn't know.

I look down the sidewalk. I can see at least four cross streets where Helena could have turned. But if you wanted to get to the footbridge over the train tracks, if you wanted to lose a pack of boys and a member of the Gestapo and get back to Tatarska Street, then down this lane, where there are lots of little alleys, would not be a bad way to go.

I run along the lane, all the ways I think Helena could have gone, but I see nothing, no one. I turn toward home, flying over the bridge, across the market, and up, up the hills until my feet hit the frozen dirt of the courtyard of Tatarska 3. I unlock the door. Maybe she came through the window.

"Hela?" I yell. I even call up the ladder to the attic. But I can feel no one's there. I run straight back out into the courtyard. "Helena!"

Mrs. Krajewska sticks her head out her door. "What's the trouble?"

"Have you seen my sister?"

"Isn't she right behind you?"

I turn on my heel, and there is Helena, coming over the hill from the backyards instead of the street. Her lip is bleeding, tears streaming down her face.

"Sorry to bother you!" I call over my shoulder to Mrs. Krajewska and get Helena inside. As soon as the door is shut, I drop to my knees and hug her hard. Her back is rising, falling with sharp sobs.

"The boys ..." she says. "They were watching. They were ... trying to catch people who help Jews, and they saw ... one of them saw ... Max ... give me the note."

I look Helena in the face, wiping the blood from her lip with a sleeve, trying not to show her how scared I am. Because I've already felt her coat pockets. They're empty, and I can't see a note in her hand.

We might need to run. Now.

"The big one ..." Helena sobs, "he said to give him what that Jew gave me, and when I ran away, he called the soldier with the black cap, and they chased me. For a long time, and I couldn't ... barely ... run, and then they caught me ..."

I glance out the window, but the street is still empty. "Hela, what did the note say?"

"I don't know! I didn't look! I don't know all the words ..."

If Max used our name, or our address, anything that could give us away, then there's no safe place for them now. Or us. "What did the boys do when they took it?"

Helena crinkles her forehead at me.

"Who took the note, the boys or the soldier? What did they say? Did they read it?"

"They didn't," says Helena, wiping her tears. "They couldn't."

"Why?"

"Because I ate it."

I sit back on my heels. "You ate Max's note?"

"I'm sorry, Stefi! But I was afraid it said something important, so I tore it up and I ... put it in my mouth, only I was running, and it was so hard to swallow ... I was choking, and then they caught me, and the boy hit me, and it ... it went right down!"

I look at her another second before I hug her again. Harder.

"And then the soldier with the black cap came ..."

I lean back to look at her again.

"And he was going to take me away, and ... and ..."

I hold her face in my hands.

"And so I kicked him, and he made me fall down, and then I bit him!"

"You bit him?"

"In the leg! Are you mad?" she asks, and then she asks again. "Are you mad?" Only this time her voice is muffled by my hair.

I shake my head.

"But it might have said something important ..."

"Which is exactly why you ate it, you clever, clever girl. And you're braver than the whole Polish army, because I bet not one of them has ever bitten a Nazi on the leg. Not once."

"Really?"

"Really."

I kiss her forehead and both her cheeks and then her forehead again, and before I'm done, Helena's tears are drying and a smile is starting to sneak around her split lip. I'm so proud of her I could burst.

And I'm also determined that she will never, ever have to be that smart or that brave again.

Which means that tomorrow, I am going to sneak into the ghetto.

I decide to go early in the morning, after work. The time Max always prefers, because he says the night guards are sleeping on their feet. The easiest way, I've decided, might be through the basement window. If it's unlocked. And if I don't have a Polish policeman watching my every move.

I'm not sure what I'll do if that happens.

I take the back way around the fence, circling in a zigzag pattern through the alleys and behind buildings, until I reach the recessed doorway of the deserted shop. Where I watch, like I did before, looking through the empty glass display windows. I stand there a long time. No patrol goes by, which either means there isn't any or they're going to come any second. I wait more, then walk to the edge of the alley and bend down like I'm tying a shoe. I look up and down the length of the fence. No one is there.

I dart forward and crawl beneath the barbed wire. The window is so close I have to pull it open while I'm only halfway through the fence. But it opens, and I crawl in, turning awkwardly to get my feet in front of me, sliding down into the basement with a bump and a hard landing that leaves the soles of my feet stinging. I hadn't known it was so far to the floor. The window shuts harder than it should, and now there's a crack jagging down the pane, a pane so dirty it lets in almost no light at all.

I'm in the dark.

And then something moves. A shadow that is bigger than a rat and suddenly standing upright. It takes everything I've got to stifle a scream, until I hear, "Fusia?"

"Max!" I whisper. "Is that you?"

"Here, prop the window open a little ..."

He has a stick of some kind to keep the window open, and when he uses it, I can see where his eyes should be, and the shape of him in the dim, but not much else.

"What are you doing in here?" I ask.

"Waiting to see if you'd come to the fence so I could tell you not to. I thought you'd throw a rock. What happened to the note?"

"Hela ate it while she ran, but she didn't know what it said. How is Henek? And Dr. Schillinger?"

"They're going to live. There's a lot of typhus. You need to be careful coming in here. Schillinger was so weak the Gestapo nearly shot him."

"What do you mean they nearly shot him?"

"They were shooting anyone too sick to get out of bed. We put Henek in the bunker in the cellar, but I had to roll Schillinger under the bed. Dziusia sat on top, with her feet hanging down ..."

I think I know where he got this idea. And then it occurs to me how casually we're discussing the cold-blooded murder of the sick.

"You really shouldn't have come," he says. "The ghetto is dangerous right now. Going in and out."

Though I notice he seemed to know I would.

"I have a plan for getting us out, but it will take some days to get the right clothes, the things we need. Siunek Hirsch and I will come first. One week from today. Meet us at the station, on the platform, so if you're late, we can pretend to wait for the train. Then you'll go first, and we'll follow, and if there are police, you will distract them, and I will lead Siunek to Tatarska."

"What time?"

"Six in the morning, the end of the night shift."

"If I'm on the night shift, I can't get there until six thirty. If I'm on the day shift, I will have to meet you at five."

"Walk by the fence gate the day before, and hold up six or five fingers so I'll know."

"I'll do that."

And then Max's arms are around me, and he pulls me into a hug. He's warm and gritty from the floor of the cellar. And very thin.

"Thank you, Fusia," he says.

He lets me go.

"You need to hurry," he says. "Everything is being watched. The cellar window, too. I don't know how you're not caught ..."

I wonder if it's because the window is being watched by my Polish policeman.

"Go out by the old way. It's a block if you take a left out the door and cut right through the next alley. I've loosened the wires again, but I don't think they know. And here. Take this."

Max turns and fumbles in the dark around his feet, then thrusts a bundle into my hands.

"I wish I could go with you, but the two of us together ... If you see the guard change, if you see anything wrong, hide. Or sit on the ground. Lie on the ground. Like you're tired. And if you hear them yell, 'Schwammberger!' you just run. As fast as you can. Promise me."

"Who's Schwammberger?"

"The officer in charge of the ghetto. He likes to shoot people while he walks. If you hear his name, you run. Promise me."

"I promise."

"In five days, walk by the fence. In six days, I'll be at the train station."

And then he will be in Tatarska. For better. Or worse.

Max takes me to the steps leading out of the cellar, up to two slanting doors that go straight onto the street. I'm pushing them open when he hisses, "Fusia!"

I turn.

"Buy me a shovel!"

And I creep out onto the streets of the ghetto like bombs are about to drop.

It's so much worse than the last time. People huddle in little clusters, or by themselves, just sitting in the cold. And then I realize that many of them are dead, or so near to being dead it's almost the same thing. Typhus. And starvation. And who knows what else on top of that. I cut through the alley like Max said, clutching his bundle to my chest, trying not to see.

And then I hear the bark of an order.

"Stop!"

The voice is behind me. I look over my shoulder.

"You there. Stop!"

A man is coming fast down the alley, wearing dirty coveralls like a worker, a cap pulled low on his head. His boots are loud on the pavement.

"What are you doing here?" he demands. "What have you got?"

He's too clean to be a worker. Just like I'm too clean for the ghetto.

Something slows inside me, and my mind speeds up. I look down and discover I'm holding a bundle of two shirts and what appear to be curtains. "Buying curtains," I say. "That's all."

"You know you're not to buy in here. Or sell."

I try smiling. "But I have a sister to feed, and I need—"

"Come with me," he says, grabbing my arm. "Now!" he adds when I resist. "Or should I call the SS?"

He marches me down the alley and then down the street, past the living and the dead, into a building that seems to be offices, though people are sleeping here as well. Cots are lined up along one wall. I pull my arm away and step back.

"Who are you?"

"*Judenrat*," the man says.

"The Jewish police? Where's your uniform?"

He doesn't answer, just leads me to a room with a desk and sits me down. Another two men come in, Ordners, wearing uniforms this time, and there is a long and whispered conversation that I cannot hear. Then they take away my bundle and examine it, shaking out the two shirts and the two sets of curtains. I don't know where Max got those curtains, but the material is dark and thick with white lilies printed on it, and I know immediately what they're for. Blocking hidden Jews from eyes that might be looking through the windows of Tatarska 3.

They leave the cloth in a pile on the desk. The man who arrested me leaves, replaced by another man, also not in uniform. This one sits down behind the desk, the other two Ordners standing at attention behind him. The man looks well fed but weary. And determined.

"Papers, please," he says.

I hand him my papers and decide not to mention that the address is wrong.

"Podgórska," he says, eyes running over my picture. He looks up. "We know who you are."

"My name is on my papers."

He smiles. "Perhaps I should say that we know what you are. And that we know what you are doing."

"You know I'm buying curtains in the ghetto?"

He smiles without humor. "We know, Miss Podgórska, that you want to hide Jews."

If I had looked up and found Hitler sitting at that desk, I couldn't have been more surprised. How could I be caught? Now? When I haven't even done it yet? I sit back in my chair.

"I am not hiding Jews. I've only bought cheap curtains from people who don't need them anymore."

The man sets down my papers and opens a yellow folder. "You have been observed, Miss Podgórska, going back and forth from the ghetto. We have seen you passing goods at the fence. We have seen your sister at the fence ..."

That sends a jolt through me. He shuffles through the file, reading.

"... and we know you plan to hide a ... Dr. Schillinger and his daughter. Siunek Hirsch and his father, Dr. Leon Hirsch. Henek Diamant and Danuta Karfiol."

You forgot Max, I think.

"You see, Miss Podgórska, you cannot lie. We know."

I don't have anything to say about what this man knows. All I want to know is, how can he know it? And can I possibly get out of this? I give him a small smile.

"There's one problem with your information. It's incorrect."

"You are hiding Jews, Miss Podgórska. Or you will be very soon."

One of the Ordners grins, smug. They seem to think their business with me is done up and tied like a parcel from the shops. The man straightens his papers neatly inside the file and places it on the desk.

"As required by law, you will be taken to the Gestapo office, where you can explain yourself and answer for your activities. My officer here will—"

"Whose law?" I ask.

He looks up, surprised. "The German law, of course."

"You are Jews," I say, "and you are going to turn me over to the Germans ... for saving Jews."

A grimace twists the man's face. "We are trying to save Jews, too, Miss Podgórska. You must understand. If everyone follows the rules, then there will be no reprisals. But if even one Jew is caught in a crime, then the SS have promised that hundreds will be punished. You have enabled the criminal activity of seven Jews, Miss Podgórska. That could cost a thousand lives. If anyone is to survive this, we must have order. We must protect the innocent—"

"But the Nazis are killing the innocent! Your own people! And in the meantime, you keep 'order' so those monsters can have a whole ghetto of victims who are easier to kill!"

The man blinks at me.

"You know I'm speaking the truth." I glare at the other two men in the room. They aren't smiling now. "Don't you? Don't you? Or has no one ever dared to say it to your face?"

"We will save as many as we can," says the man at the desk.

"By sitting back while they're murdered and starved? By loading them on trains to be ..." I look at these men, staring at me like I've lost my mind. "I hope you do take me to the Gestapo," I say. "Then I can tell them what I'm going to tell you. That you are cowards. And idiots. Of course I want to hide Jews. I admit it. It's the truth. I want to hide them and save them until somebody decides to end this war. And until that happens, I will fight for the ones I can, even if you won't, and I won't make excuses about it, either."

I stand up. Like I'm ready to go.

My legs are two pieces of soft, wiggly rubber.

"So take me to the Gestapo. Go on. And when they kill me, and all the ones I could have saved, I hope God will forgive you. Though I really don't see how He can."

"Leave us," says the man behind the desk. But he's talking to the Ordners. They shuffle out, and the door closes with a click.

"Sit down."

I stand there.

"I said sit!"

I sit.

"Do you think I like my position, Miss Podgórska? I wonder what kind of choices you think I have. Perhaps you think I chose to be here? That the SS can't walk into my house and shoot my family whenever they please?"

He pulls open a drawer and starts scribbling on a small piece of paper he tears away from a pad.

"We do try to save them," he says. "By giving the wrong lists, delaying the deportations. Limiting the reprisals caused by people like yourself, so that someone, somewhere, might be saved. If you have other suggestions of what I can do to protect my people, please give them." He sets down his pen, waiting for my reply. "No? Then gather your belongings and come with me."

I do as I'm told and fold the curtains and the shirts, my bravado leaking out like water through a sieve. When they kill me, what will happen to Max? To all of them?

What is going to happen to Helena?

I should have done something more for Helena.

I pick up my papers, clutch the folded fabric to my chest, and the man opens the door. I follow him down a long, dim hallway, away from the front, where I entered, threading our way past more rows of cots, some with men asleep on them.

I try to think what to do.

Fight? I don't have anything to fight with but a curtain and some fingernails.

Cry? I might do that anyway.

Push this man down, kick him as hard as I can, and run for my life?

I wouldn't get out of the ghetto.

We come to a little room at the end of the corridor, a makeshift kitchen that is warm with cabbage steam. The man pushes open the back door.

"Take this," he says, handing me the paper he tore from the pad. "Go to the front gate and give it to the guard."

I look up from the paper. "And then what?"

"Go home, Miss Podgórska."

I look at the paper again. I don't understand.

"Go home," he says, "and don't come back. And ..." I have to strain to catch his next words. "And if something is to be done, it would be better to have it done soon. Do you understand me?"

I nod, and nod again, and step quickly through the door. "Wait," I say, turning around. "How did you know?"

"Talk," he replies.

"Whose talk?"

"People like to talk."

"And who else likes to listen?"

He raises a shoulder and a brow. "I don't know the answer to that. Be careful, Miss Podgórska. And God forgive us all."

He steps back and shuts the door, and I stand there, staring, too stunned to feel my own relief, listening to the misery of the ghetto.

I think about what he said about his family. About Izio, dying in the camp because the *Judenrat* made a list. About the Ordner

SHARON CAMERON

who threatened to throw a grenade into Max's hiding place and gave them away.

They should have been organizing an army, not Nazi death trains. They should have fought.

Men like Max would have fought.

That's what I should have told him. That's how he should have protected his people.

Or maybe, like the rest of us, he didn't know what was coming. Maybe they didn't know what was coming until it was too late.

He never even told me his name.

I hurry to the gate, show my note to the guard, and to my surprise, he lets me out. And when my door on Tatarska Street is shut and locked and the lamp is lit and Helena is making my tea, all I can think about is talk, and how long it will be until the Gestapo hears it.

17.

April 1943

I SPEND THE NEXT DAYS SWEATING AT THE FACTORY AND SWEATING AT Tatarska 3. Someone has talked, and I don't know who, or why, or who they've talked to. Maybe we've already been denounced. Maybe the Gestapo will come in the middle of the night and pull me away from my machines. Maybe they'll come in the middle of the day and break down my door. Or maybe they're waiting.

For Max and Siunek to come.

And I have no way to warn them.

I can't sleep. I can barely eat. I tell myself that if the Gestapo knows, then they would know the names of the Jews already. They'd take them from the ghetto, not look for them among the people in the streets. That the SS have never been worried about little things like evidence and proof, so why wait to get it?

If they knew, I tell myself, they would have been here already.

It's easier to tell yourself things like this than to actually believe them.

I can't always expect to be arrested and let go.

In five days, I walk past the fence on my way home from work. I see Max there, sitting on a stoop beyond the patrolling guard. I'm so relieved to see him not arrested that I smile. Like it's Easter and my birthday.

He smiles back.

I hold up six fingers as I walk.

He nods.

I go home and hang the curtains.

And at twenty minutes after six in the morning, I wander past the railroad station on my way home from work. Two men sit on the platform bench. They have caps pulled low on their heads, grease on their faces, lumpy bags that could be full of tools on their backs, and one holds a thermos with a handle. The one with the thermos is Max, and the other must be Siunek, and I'm not sure what kind of workers they're supposed to be. But whatever they are, they get off the bench and start moving in my direction.

I hold my coat closed tight to keep my hands from shaking, even though it isn't that cold, and walk at a leisurely pace toward Tatarska 3. And then I quicken my steps. There's a policeman coming down a side street, turning my way around the corner.

I don't dare look back. I'm supposed to distract a policeman. That's why I'm here. To keep the policeman's attention on me, and not the workers who aren't workers just a few steps behind.

But my brain is not coming up with the first way to do it.

And then I hear a voice say, "Stefania?"

I stop in my tracks. It's him. Officer Berdecki. Officer Markus Berdecki of the Polish police, with his blue eyes, his dimple, and a square chin. The man who is everywhere I never want him to be.

Distraction managed.

He takes off his hat.

"I've been looking for you, Stefania. Are you coming from your work?"

"Yes," I say, telling my feet to get moving again. "And I need to hurry home. My sister is by herself, and ..."

Officer Berdecki falls into step beside me. "That would be your new home, then?"

I glance up at his dimple. Two workers with grease on their faces pass us, moving on up the street.

"You see, I've been keeping up with you," he says. "I knew you had moved, but none of your neighbors seemed to know where. Where is your new apartment? Can I walk you home now?"

"No, thank you," I say.

"Stefania," he says, tugging me to a stop. His voice has lost some of its too-sweet syrup. "Why do you treat me so badly when all I've ever wanted is to be your friend?"

I open my mouth and can't think of a thing to say. What has this man ever actually done to me? Let me go instead of arresting me, asked me to a café, and been a little too aware that he's handsome. It's not his fault that I've always got Jews under my bed or following me down the street, or that I'm always afraid and too full of cares to enjoy one second of my life. And he hasn't mentioned finding me at the ghetto fence. Again.

"I'm sorry," I say. He looks surprised. "Really. I'm just worried about my sister."

"Helena?"

He remembers her name.

"Then let me call you a car and get you home quickly ..."

"No!" He looks surprised again. I glance up the road, and Max and Siunek are barely a shadow. "I mean, no thank you. It would just make it worse. You see, my sister, she's afraid of men in uniforms. Very afraid. She was so upset after you left last time, it took a long time to calm her. I'm sure she'll grow out of it, but ..."

"I'm glad you told me. Then I won't walk you all the way, and you can tell me when to stop, yes?"

I can't think of why he shouldn't. So we walk.

"There is a reason, you know, Stefania, that I looked for you at your old apartment."

"Really?"

"Yes."

I can't see Max and Siunek at all now. They're on their own. My stomach wrenches. We've crossed the market square and started up the hill. But not the hill that leads to Tatarska.

"There's something very serious I want to discuss with you. Though it's not something I want to bring up on the street ..."

I'm hoping Max remembers the way. That Helena remembers to unlock the door.

What if Helena doesn't remember to unlock the door?

What if Mrs. Krajewska is looking out her window, like she always does, and sees the man who was supposed to be my brother sneaking like a thief into my house? She might call the police. She might call the Gestapo.

"You see, I know a secret about you, Stefania Podgórska."

Now I stop my stride, and look up into his blue, blue eyes. He stops beside me. "I don't have any secrets," I whisper.

He smiles. "You know that isn't true. You have a very special secret, don't you, Stefania?"

I stare at Officer Berdecki. He knows.

He knows. He knows. He knows.

"But like I said," he whispers, looking around at the empty street. "This is not the place to talk about serious things. Come to my house on Sunday, when you don't have work. We can talk there. Here is my address ..."

He pulls paper and pencil out of his pocket, using the low stone wall of the Orthodox church to write.

I look back across the hills toward Tatarska. If there was shooting, would I hear it from here? Or will I be taken on Sunday instead?

I feel sick.

"Four o'clock?" he asks.

I take the piece of paper with the address and nod.

"You remember that I said I wanted to help you? In any way I could?"

I nod again.

"That is what I plan to do now. Do you believe me?"

I nod for a third time. He's like an actor in a film. Perfection that no human should be able to reach.

"You are such a serious girl, Stefania." He reaches out and straightens the lapel of my coat. "We will talk more on Sunday. At four."

He backs away down the street, his dimples showing in both cheeks, and tips his hat. It takes him a long time to get down the hill. He keeps looking back and waving. I lift my hand. And finally, he rounds the corner toward the market.

Maybe he's not going to turn me in, I think. Maybe he's just going to blackmail me first. Take everything I have, then give me and Helena, Max and Siunek to the SS.

Unless Max and Siunek never got there.

Unless the Gestapo is there now, waiting for them.

I turn and look across the cathedral steeples and up the hilly lane toward Tatarska. And then I run.

And by the time I come careening around the curve of the lane and see the house, sitting by itself near the top of the hill, the sun is fully up. And Mrs. Krajewska will be awake and making her coffee. Peeking out her windows.

What has she already seen?

At least the Gestapo isn't here.

Unless they've already gone. And taken Max and Siunek.

Helena.

I can't get enough breath. My legs and arms tingle, I have a sharp pain behind my left eye, and my chest feels like it might explode. I want to scream. But I slow down, make myself trudge past the well and into the courtyard, shoulders hunched, like I've had a long night at work. I go slowly around the back, and as soon as I'm out of sight of Mrs. Krajewska's window, I run for the door and bang my fist on it.

The lock clicks, and the door opens so fast I nearly fall through, stumbling into the kitchen. I straighten up, panting.

A thickset young man with heavy dark eyebrows and grease on his face is wearing my apron and slicing bread at the table while Helena kicks her heels in a chair with a glass of milk. She has her ball in her lap. The one we left rolling beside the fence. I don't know how Max got that ball. I can't believe he's hauled it all the way across Przemyśl. The three of them are looking at me in surprise, and then the door shuts behind me.

"Is there trouble?" Max says as he turns the lock. "Fusia?"

I burst into tears.

He puts his arms around me and lets me cry on his neck. "What's wrong? Did something happen with that policeman?"

The policeman. Officer Berdecki with his lovely dimples. Who knows our secret.

Because someone has been talking.

If I don't pull myself together, we're all going to get killed.

"Max." I step back, brushing the tears from my face. "Can I talk to you?"

He nods. "Siunek, would you watch the window?"

The young man wipes his hands on my apron and goes to the curtained window of my bedroom, where there's a full view of the street and anyone who might approach the courtyard. Max pulls out a chair for me, like we're in a restaurant or the club.

"Hela," he says. "Would you get some water? I think your sister might want tea." He looks at me. "Do you have tea?"

I nod, still drying my face, and Helena grabs the bucket and goes out the door without an argument or the smallest noise. She's happy, I think, to have Max here.

And then I tell Max everything. What happened with the *Judenrat*, and what they said, and how they let me go. About Officer Berdecki. When I'm done, I'm calmer, but Max is rubbing his head so hard I'm afraid he's going to lose hair.

"I can't believe it," he says. "I don't believe it. We stood together, Schillinger, the Hirsches, Henek and Danuta, and we swore an oath to God to never speak of this to anyone who wasn't in that room. They knew what it meant, to talk ..."

"What about Dziusia?"

Max shakes his head. "She wasn't there."

"Where, then?" I ask. "Where were you meeting?"

"In the bunker. The one from before. There was no one ... anyone else who knew the place ... they're all gone now. And it's belowground."

I lower my voice. "Are you sure about Siunek?"

"I'd stake my life on it."

He already has.

"But what about you and me?" he says. "In the basement? Could there have been someone else down there?"

I shake my head. That wouldn't explain how they knew the names. The names were already written down in the file.

Helena comes in slowly with the heavy bucket of water and locks the door without being asked.

"Here's what I think," Max says. "The *Judenrat* have people all over the ghetto, just like the one who arrested you. Maybe some of our people talked, but only to each other, and they were overheard. But if the Gestapo knew, I don't think they would have let it go this far ..."

I thought this, too.

"They would have stopped us. Shot us in our beds. And you would have been arrested already. We didn't see anything out of the ordinary on the way here, other than your policeman. No one gave us a second look. And we came around the back, over the wall, so we didn't pass any of the windows ..."

That is a relief.

"And what about the policeman?" I ask. "He knows something."

Max shakes his head. "Fusia. He doesn't know anything. Don't you know when a man is flirting with you?"

That stings coming from him. Like I'm a little girl. "You didn't hear him talk ..."

"I heard him talk last time, and that was enough. He's not going to ask you for money. He knows you don't have any. And if he wasn't going to ask you for something, why talk to you at all? We'd all already be shot or with the Gestapo. They pay pretty quick, I hear, and the word of your policeman is all they'd need."

I noted the emphasis on "your." "So don't you think that's more of a reason for me to go and find out what he knows?"

Max's big eyes narrow just a bit. "Do you want to go over there and find out what he knows?"

"No." And if a tiny part of me disagrees with this, I'm not telling Max. "If I don't, we're leaving a lot to chance. It's a matter of life and ..."

Helena puts a cup of tea in front of me.

"It's life or ... not." I don't want to talk like this in front of her.

"Dziusia is supposed to come in two days," Max says.

I didn't know that.

"And Schillinger and Old Hirsch a few days after that. I can't stop them now. Not without one of us going back to the ghetto, and I do not want that to be you."

It's dangerous for us both. I sip my tea, which is perfect.

"Fusia, you need to say right now. Do you want us to go back? You can end it, if that's what you want."

I think of living without the fear I just experienced, and for one awful second, I am tempted.

"No, Max!" says Helena. We'd both forgotten she was there.

And then I look at Max and remember the alternatives. "No, Max," I say, like Helena did.

He smiles, but it's sad. And then he says, "Does that policeman know where you live now?"

I shake my head.

"Good. Because if he comes here, I might have to kill him." His one pointed eyebrow quirks, like he's joking.

Maybe his eyebrow is lying.

I don't think Max Diamant is seeing very clearly where Officer Berdecki is concerned.

The last thing in this world I want to do is talk about Officer Berdecki with Max.

"I'm tired," I murmur. And it's true. My eyes are closing on their own.

"Go to bed," Max says.

"Drink my tea," I tell him.

"I'll wake you up before work."

I push myself to my feet, make it to the next room, and practically fall onto the bed in my clothes.

I've forgotten there's a man sitting at the window, watching the street and the yard through the crack in the curtains.

"I'm Siunek," he says. He's still wearing my apron.

"Stefania," I murmur. "But you can call me Fusia."

"I already do. Did your sister really bite an SS officer's leg?"

I'm asleep before I can answer.

And then Max is shaking me. The sun has gone away like someone blew out a candle.

"Fusia," Max whispers. "Fusia!"

I pry open my eyes.

"Did you buy that shovel?"

I give him the shovel before I go to work, and every time the blades of my machine cut the groove of a screw, I wonder what Max is doing. And what Helena is doing. And Siunek. If they're safe. Or if they're caught and I'll come home to find them dead. I make my quota, and by the time I put my key to the lock at Tatarska 3, my stomach is cramping with dread. There's no one in the kitchen.

"Hello?" I call.

No answer.

I burst through the door to the bedroom, and Siunek is at the window again, finger to his lips, while Max is up to his knees in a hole where my bed used to be, shirtless and sweaty and covered with dirt. The floorboards are stacked neatly against the wall. Max sticks the shovel in the ground and hops light as a cat from the hole.

"What are you doing?" I ask. "Where's Helena?" I look to the other door, the one that leads to the empty second bedroom.

"I wouldn't go in there," Max says, eyeing the door. "We've been using it for a toilet. There's a bucket!" he says, responding to what must have been a look of disgust on my face. "And not the water bucket. What do you take me for?"

"Shhh!" Siunek warns. Max leads me back into the kitchen.

"We've realized we can hear your neighbor in there," Max says, his voice still low. "The one I met the night we looked at the apartment. Her second floor is right above us, and that means she can hear us, too. I thought it would be better if she didn't hear men in your apartment all day." He starts wiping the sweat and dirt from his chest with the bath towel, watching me think all this over. Watching me make sure the water bucket is in place. "Well, what did you think we were going to do, Fusia? Hold it until the war ends? We can't take a stroll out to the toilets."

I'm not sure why this thought has never occurred to me, but it hasn't.

"Where's Hela?" I ask again.

"I told her she could go play. That's all right, isn't it?"

"And what are you doing?"

"Building a bunker. So we can hide when someone comes to your door. Right now there's only the attic, and if someone climbs the ladder, we're caught."

I haven't thought of this yet, either.

"You're sleepy, Fusia," he comments.

I am. To the bone. And he's full of energy, like a bird building its nest. "But ... what are you doing with all the dirt?"

Max grins. "Come and see."

He opens the door to the little hallway, where the ladder goes up to the attic. This room never had a wooden floor, just soil packed hard and smooth. Only now the soil is several inches higher than it was, sloping upward behind the ladder.

And who, I wonder, told him he could do that? If Mrs. Krajewska sees this floor, she'll know something is wrong. She could make a complaint. Get me kicked out of my apartment.

"Hela's been tramping it down all day to pack it tight," Max says, still watching me closely. "And I thought maybe you could get some garbage or old junk to cover up the back, so it won't show ..."

So now, I think, they need me to run out and collect some garbage. Or some junk. And while I'm doing that, I can go to the market and spend half my pay and the rest of my day hauling food up the hill. Then I can sweep the floor, wipe that layer of dust from Max's digging off the stove, cook the dinner, and wash it all up again, then catch a few hours of sleep that are less than I need in a house that smells like sweaty men and an open grave—a house where it's too dangerous to open a window—before I get up to do it all over again and spend another twelve hours making screws.

And that bucket in the second bedroom probably needs emptying, too.

"You're mad," Max says, brows coming down.

"I'm not mad," I lie.

I'm scared.

I do most of the things on my list. Only when I get back from the market, out of breath from the heavy bags, the floor has already been swept and the stove is wiped clean, and Siunek takes the bags and says he will make something for dinner.

I still have to empty the bucket.

When I lie down, I'm so tired that I ache. I sleep with my bed on the wrong side of the room, though always with either Max or Siunek at the window, and when I dream, it's of Izio, and everything the guard told me they did to him. When my eyes open, I'm sick to my stomach and sweating, the afternoon sun streaming around the edges of the curtains and Siunek's heavy frame.

And the first thought in my head is that I don't know where Helena is, and if I don't know where she is, then she might be dead. My next thought is that Max and Siunek have a bunker, but I don't know where I will run if the Gestapo comes. When the Gestapo comes.

Death to Jews. I hear the man's voice in my head. I count the shots. One, two, three ...

Stop it, Fusia.

Just stop it.

I sit up in bed, and Siunek waves like we just bumped into each other at the park.

Then I remember that it's Sunday. I swing my feet to the floor.

Max is wrong about Officer Berdecki. Even if he's right, he's wrong, because I can't live with the uncertainty.

I get out of bed, tell Siunek to give me a few minutes to myself, and shut the door behind him. I strip off my crumpled dress, dip a cloth in the chipped bowl we use for wash water, and scrub everything I can reach until it tingles. Then I brush my hair and braid it—no time for curls—pulling it back smooth from my face, the way it suits me, and when I'm done, I tiptoe to the bed, slide my hand beneath the blanket, and pull out a carefully folded blouse. Soft, pale blue, with a fraying edge around the bottom that will never show, bought yesterday in the market with what should have been the egg money.

I can always sell it later.

I tuck the blouse into the only other decent thing I own, my brown wool skirt, and from the bottom of my brush bag, I fish out the tiny little compact of lip rouge that had once been Marysia's. There's only a bit left around the edges, and I hesitate, wondering if I should. But when I step out the bedroom door, my lips are blushing red.

Siunek is at the table, watching the yard as best he can from the window, while Max has Helena in his lap. Telling her a story that I think must be about the ocean since I hear him say the word "shark." He looks up. And stares.

"Fusia! You look pretty!" says Helena. "You got a new shirt."

"No, I didn't," I say. "This is my old one. The one I never wear."

My sister is smart enough not to say anything else.

"Where are you going?" asks Max. His voice is quiet.

"Some of the girls at work are having a party."

It sounds ridiculous when I say it. Dangerous and irresponsible. Especially since it's a lie.

"Have a good time," he says. But his eyes don't leave mine.

Helena puts her arms around his neck.

And then I walk out the front door and listen to it lock behind me.

Guilty. I am so, so guilty. But I have to know what the policeman knows.

I walk down the lane and turn the corner from Tatarska Street.

18.

April 1943

OFFICER BERDECKI'S HOUSE IS ON THE OTHER SIDE OF THE SAN, WHERE
Przemyśl was German while we were still Russian. I don't have to
actually find the address, because he's there, waiting for me near
the bridge. In case I got lost, maybe, or changed my mind.

"Stefania," he says, coming up quickly to kiss my hand. "You
are very beautiful."

And so is he. I've never seen him out of uniform. He looks
strong and healthy and freshly shaved. I realize I'm staring.

"Come," he says, "and we will talk." He puts my arm in his,
taking me down the street and around the corner to a row of stone
apartments that are more like cottages, like Tatarska, but with
new roofs, new paint, and new windows. He watches me look them
up and down. "This place was hit by Russian artillery when the
war started," he says, "but they're as good as new now. Many of
the Polish police live here."

He smiles, unlocking the door, and I'm wondering if I've been
tricked and he's arresting me after all, but there are no other
policemen inside. The house is simple. Comfortable. It smells
nice. And it's very quiet.

"Do you live alone?" I ask, surprised.

"Of course."

I don't know why I'd imagined him with a mother, a sister, four or five brothers. What would someone do with a whole house to themselves?

Maybe he's lonely.

"Let me take your coat," he says. "I hope you don't mind, but I made you a meal. This is my usual time to eat, so ..."

"Officer Berdecki ..."

"Please. It's Markus."

"You said yesterday that you knew something about me."

"Yes," he says. And now his handsome face is serious. "We do need to talk. Please, sit down."

I'm standing beside a table laid out with a cloth and cut glass and matching china. Officer Berdecki is holding out a chair for me. It feels rude to say no.

"You are right to get straight to our business," he says. He strikes a match and lights a candle, even though the sun is still up. "But as I said, this is my usual time to eat, and the plates are warm. Do you mind?"

"But you said you knew a—"

"Dinner first." He dimples, his hair shining in the light of the candles.

I fold my hands in my lap, feeling out of place and five years old.

He brings out two plates with slices of sugared ham—real slices, from a farm—potatoes fried in oil and salt, cheese with little crackers, a salad made with pickled carrots, and of all things, a dish of tinned pears. Where did he get tinned pears? Wine sparkles purple into my glass, and it is sweet and delicious. This can't be his normal dinner. He must have made all this for me.

It feels like Christmas. Before the war.

Markus talks about little things, nothing things, and he makes jokes that aren't all that funny, but I laugh anyway. I laugh, and then I wonder why. My cheeks are flushed.

He pours more wine. I eat all my ham. I eat everything, and when he sees how much I like them, he gives me his tinned pears. He's really very sweet.

Markus never takes his eyes off me. He compliments me. And he doesn't ask me to do anything difficult or dangerous or unpleasant. I feel warm, happy. Special. And a little dizzy. I remember there's something I want to know from him.

"We've eaten dinner," I say. It's a little hard to get the words out. "And you said ... you said you knew a secret ..."

Somewhere in my mind, I know this is important.

He dimples. "I do know something about you. More wine?"

I shake my head. He pours me a little anyway, tipping up the bottle.

Yes, that's right. I have been keeping a secret.

"Come sit on the sofa," he says.

Does Markus know my secret? That's what I'm supposed to find out.

"Come sit with me," Markus says again, "and we can talk about what I know." He takes me by the hand, picking up my glass for me with the other.

The sun has gone down, and the room is dim from the candles on the table. The sofa is soft. Cozy. I lean my head back. "Tell me what you know."

I think I'm supposed to be afraid, but I can't seem to feel it.

"One kiss," Markus whispers, "and I will tell you."

He kisses me, and once he does, I think he might as well do it again. I feel beautiful. He is beautiful. His weight pins me to the sofa, but I don't want to move. My braids are coming down. And that same little corner of my mind remembers.

"What about ... our business," I manage while his lips are on my neck. "What secret ... do you know?"

"Secret?" he murmurs. His face hovers over mine. "The secret I know about you, my Stefania, is that you need to be kissed."

He kisses me again. And I am thinking, thinking, remembering through the purple haze of the wine. He thinks I need to be kissed. That is my secret.

He doesn't know about Max. Or the others. He never knew about them at all.

He made me think he knew something. He wanted me to be afraid.

He just wanted me on this sofa.

All at once I bring up a leg and push to one side as hard as I can. Officer Berdecki rolls off the sofa and hits the floor with a thud.

"Hey. Hey!" He scrambles to his feet while I get to mine. "What was that for?"

"You ask me what that was for? You dare to ask me that? I ought to cut you up into a thousand pieces, you snake. You ... skunk!" I tuck in my blouse, looking frantically for my shoes. "Skunk!" I say again.

"What's wrong with you? Are you crazy?" These words are harsh, made harsher by the fact that his soft, flattering voice is gone. "Stop acting like a little girl, Stefania. You're more grown up than that."

Am I?

"You and your cousin ..."

My cousin? He means Danuta. My corrupt cousin from Bircza. What did Mrs. Wojcik tell him?

"Don't play innocent. You knew why you were here!"

Only I didn't. I probably should have. Max even told me. Almost. I'm the stupidest girl in Przemyśl, but I didn't know.

"I came because you said you knew something about me. But you were lying!"

"That was a game!"

"Not to me!"

I grab the empty wine bottle and throw it, and it misses his head by the width of a hair. The bottle explodes into little green chunks, leaving a small splash of purple on the wall.

"You're crazy," he says, and he's not even handsome anymore. His hair is mussed, his clothes all tangled, and there's lip rouge on his face. But that isn't what's making him ugly. The ugliness is in the cold blue of his eyes. "I could make life hard for you. And for your little sister. I could still arrest you. Is that what you want?"

We look at each other, and he smiles. It's not pretty.

"I didn't think so," he says. "Now come back over here, and you and your sister can sleep safe in your own bed." His dimples get deeper. "It's not as if you won't enjoy yourself."

I'm so angry the room spins like my head.

I take two steps forward and snatch my coat from the chair. "I think you'd better arrest me, Officer. Do it, and while I'm being arrested, I'll tell your commander that you like to let criminals go when you think there's a possibility of getting them over to your house for ... dinner."

The threat hits its mark.

"Don't you ever come near me again," I say. And this time I'm not yelling. My voice is low and smooth. "Don't speak to me. If you see me on the street, you're going to turn and walk the other way. Disappear. Or I will go to your commanding officer. Maybe I will anyway."

I cross the room while he stands there and wrench open the door. "And if you even look at my sister, I will cut you into ten thousand pieces, you lying, stinking, filthy little pig."

And I slam the man's door.

I walk as fast as I can down the street. The air is chilly, but I don't stop to put on my coat. I do stop to tie my shoes, and I'm wobbly while I do it because my head is still dizzy. A woman passing by with shopping on her arm gives me and my half-braided hair a long look.

I wonder if I have lip rouge on my face. Like him.

No. I just have tears pouring down my cheeks.

Why did I go over there? Was it really because I was afraid?

It was. Mostly.

But it had also been nice, hadn't it? To imagine that a good-looking policeman would seek me out. To imagine that there were possibilities after Izio and this war, even if they were possibilities I wouldn't really want. It had been ... nice.

And I hate how stupid that makes me feel.

I stop well before Tatarska Street and rebraid my hair in the dim, mirrored glass of a shop window beneath a streetlight. I can't see any lip rouge. I make sure I'm neat and buttoned before walking up the hill. One of them, I know, will be watching me come. And then I feel the familiar little flutter of fear that there's no one left to watch me come at all, and I'm afraid I'm going to lose all that wine I just drank.

I don't lose it. I walk into the courtyard.

I will save them, I think. For as long as I can.

When I open the door to Tatarska Street, I can hear the scrape of the shovel from the bedroom. Someone is shoveling hard. There's a lamp lit in the kitchen. I don't often see the kitchen by lamplight, and it looks softer, prettier than in the day. I should buy some furniture, I think. When I'm trading and reselling. Something cheap that could be painted or repaired. Maybe a shelf for food and dishes, an armoire for the bedroom. A whole table and a sofa.

Maybe not a sofa. I'll get a soft chair.

Or a bench.

The sound of the shovel stops, and Max comes through from the bedroom. He's shirtless again, streaked with sweat and black soil, carrying two buckets of dirt.

"You're back," he says. "How was your party?"

I'm fairly sure Max knows I wasn't at a party. "Fine," I reply.

"You didn't stay very long."

"It wasn't that good of a party."

"Oh." I see something cross his face, but I don't know what it is.

"Is Hela asleep?"

"Yes."

"And you all ate?"

"Siunek cooked."

"And how is the bunker?"

"Done. Except for the floorboards."

He must have shoveled every second I was gone. I open up the door to the attic, and the floor in the back of the little hall is at least two feet higher than it should be. I really will have to find a way to cover that up.

"Hela took out the last few loads and dumped them behind the toilets," Max says. "It was dark. Nobody saw her."

He's being careful of me. I can't blame him.

"Go clean up and give me your clothes," I tell him. "I'll wash them."

"You don't have to do that."

"I don't mind. I can't sleep. I'm on the wrong schedule."

I set the biggest pot I have on the stove and start pouring in the contents of the water bucket.

"Really, you don't have to," he says.

"Your clothes are dirty."

"Fusia, I don't have anything else to put on."

He's still standing in the doorway of the bedroom beside his buckets, dirty, unshaven, and in need of a haircut.

"There are blankets in there. Or are you afraid of me seeing your skin?"

I think he might laugh, since he doesn't have a shirt on anyway. And because we've lived in the same house, and none of the Diamant boys were ever very modest. I was always the little sister. Except with Izio. But Max doesn't laugh.

"I like your shirt," he says.

"I'm going to sell it."

"You shouldn't sell it. It's a nice color on you."

I'm not sure why this makes me want to cry.

I throw another piece of coal on the fire, give Max some of the warm water to clean up with, heat more, and wash his clothes. He falls asleep on the floor, wrapped in a blanket, while I hang his clothes up to dry and start on Siunek's. It couldn't hurt to look for some men's clothes, either, I think, so I won't have naked boys shivering all over the house every time I wash. And we need another bed, too. And more soap. And I think Helena might have eaten the butter.

Maybe I won't mind. Never having a life.

I stay up while the house is quiet, drying clothes by the fire and sewing a rip in Helena's skirt where I didn't sew it very well in the first place. Siunek is at the window, but he's lost in thought. Like I am.

I wonder what he's lost because of this war.

Probably more than me.

I wake Max before I go to work so he can watch the window and let Siunek get some sleep. He's been asleep most of the day. He rubs his eyes and sits up in the blanket, then he rubs his arms. Between the floor and shoveling, I know he must be sore.

"Don't forget," he says. "Dziusia comes tomorrow."

I hadn't. "How are they getting her out?"

"They're going to push her through a hole Schillinger made in the bricks, on the back side of the ghetto where there's no fence, where it's just the buildings with the windows filled in. They're going to do it at five, and you're supposed to meet her at the bridge over the train tracks before you go to work. Once she's safe, walk past the ghetto fence until you see Dr. Schillinger and sneeze. That will mean we have her."

Little Dziusia, with her mass of curly hair.

I can't believe they're sending her alone.

"They won't pay attention to a child," Max says, like I've spoken out loud.

That's what we thought about Helena.

I can feel Max's eyes on me all the way down Tatarska Street.

I work a full shift during which I just make my quota, and I'm feeling the sleep I missed during the day. At a quarter until six in the morning, when my feet are aching and my shoulders are stiff from the laundry and screws, Herr Braun comes to the factory floor and informs me that I have been switched to the day shift.

Right now.

I can work. Or lose my job.

This man really doesn't like me.

I go back to my machines and start the brisk trot required to keep them fed with metal. To keep the water pumps working. In two hours, I'm dead on my feet and once again in danger of losing a hand. The blades whine, and the engines chug in a rhythm.

Dziusia. Dziusia. Dziusia.

They're pushing her out of the wall at five. I can't leave here until six. Herr Braun strolls by, watching me work. Maybe I should just lose my job.

Maybe we'll starve.

Herr Braun watches me all day. On our break, I go stand outside on the iron bridge, slapping my own face to wake up. I'm nauseated with worry, so tired I can't think, and no one on Tatarska Street knows where I am. Januka brings me a cup of strong coffee.

"From the mechanic," she says, and hands over a bite of her sandwich. The blond boy joins us, lighting up a cigarette. Except for the cigarette, the air out here smells new. Like spring.

"Braun doesn't like you," comments the blond boy.

"What gave you that impression?" Januka laughs.

I rub my eyes. "What time does he leave now? Herr Braun?"

"Five o'clock. Usually," says Januka.

Five. It might be just enough.

"I need a favor. Do you think between the two of you, you could finish my shift?"

Januka wrinkles her forehead.

"I've got an appointment," I say.

Januka says, "Can't you just miss it and do it another day?"

The blond boy blows out a puff of smoke. "What's so important?"

"It's ..." My sluggish brain jumps into gear. "It's with the police. The Germans. I'm supposed to be there, and ... you know they don't care anything about my job."

"Are you in trouble?" asks Januka. She looks concerned.

"A problem with my papers. I can fix it. But I can't miss the appointment."

"I'm not sure ..."

"We can do it," says the blond boy. "As long as Herr Braun is gone. The inspector won't care. He knows you worked two shifts."

"Really?" I ask. "Do you think so?"

He shrugs, and my stomach uncramps just a little. I drain the coffee.

"Thanks. I'll do you a favor back, when I can."

"It's Lubek, by the way," the blond boy says. "That's the name, if you were wondering."

"I know!" I say. Though I had forgotten.

Januka laughs again. She always laughs. And then she kisses Lubek on the mouth and goes back in to her bolt cutter.

I didn't know Lubek is her boyfriend.

Lubek throws the stub of his cigarette over the bridge and holds out an arm, inviting me to go through the door first. His hair isn't bright like Officer Berdecki's, more like dried wheat instead of gold. And that smile he's giving me is friendlier than I want it to be.

I'm feeling cautious about smiles.

I go back to the drone of my machinery. If I leave at five, and if I run, maybe I can get to the footbridge before Dziusia does.

But I cannot go at five. Because Herr Braun is walking the floor. And at fifteen minutes after five, he's still doing it.

I think I hate him.

He doesn't leave until twenty minutes after. Lubek takes over my machines, and I run like German dogs are snapping at my heels.

I get to the bridge at five thirty, and there are German dogs. With SS men, at both ends of the bridge. The bridge is guarded now. They're not letting anyone cross into or out of the ghetto.

Oh no.

No. No. No.

I lean on the post of a streetlight, like I'm waiting for a bus, and watch the bridge. Ten minutes later, there comes Dziusia Schillinger. I can see her hair. They've dressed her like a Ukrainian, and she's kicking a can down the street.

She stops when she sees the guards, picks up her can, and goes the other way.

I wait, chest squeezing the air from my lungs.

She comes back.

And goes away again.

She comes back. And this time, slowly, reluctantly, she climbs up the steps to the bridge.

And there's nothing I can do to help her.

She kicks the can past the first guard. I think the dog turns his head. But the guard doesn't. She kicks the can all the way to the second guard, and a train passes underneath her in a billow of steam. When I can see her again, she's left her can behind and is coming down the stairs, looking this way and that in the roaring noise of the train. I step out toward the bridge and walk past it, hoping she'll follow.

She doesn't recognize me.

She wanders toward the little market close to the tracks, the Fish Place, and I try to follow without looking like I'm following. Pretending to shop while I keep an eye on her. But she's always surrounded by people. There's the lady I buy used clothes from. And one of the village women passing through, the one who gives me a good price on milk. I see Dziusia tug on a stranger's sleeve and ask a question. They ignore her. She looks like she's going to cry. But I can't catch her eye. I can't get her attention.

Careful, Dziusia. Careful.

Now she's in front of the cathedral, the one I usually pray in, near Na Bramie. There's a pair of women with scarves tied around their heads coming up the steps from the sunken front doors. She shuffles up to them.

Yes, Dziusia. That's a better choice.

I watch her stop them, and I can almost see her mouth say the word "Tatarska." One of the women bends down. She points in the right direction, and I follow Dziusia through the booths and stalls of the big market square. Up the hill. The higher we get, the fewer people there are, and when the street is empty, I speed up and pass her.

"Dziusia," I whisper. "Follow me."

I hear her give a little sob.

The sun is getting low, but not so low that Mrs. Krajewska won't be looking out her window. I hope she'll think this is a friend of Helena's, come to play. When we get through the courtyard and around the back, the door jerks open. I push Dziusia in, and Max locks it behind us.

"What happened?" Max says. "We thought you were shot!"

"They made me work a double shift."

"Twenty-four hours?"

Dziusia has run to Siunek and put her arms around him. Her eyes are dry. But her breath comes in gasps like she's crying. Siunek pats her hair.

"She's wet," he whispers, pointing. I look down, and it's true. Dziusia's shoes and skirt are soaked.

"There were dogs," she whispers.

"The bridge is guarded now," I say. "SS with dogs. Both ends." Then I see Helena in the corner, watching. "Hela. This is Dziusia."

Did anyone even tell Helena another child was coming? I hope Max did.

"Could you show her where the washing water is and let her borrow your other dress while I get her clothes clean?"

Helena nods, unsure. Dziusia is two, maybe three years older. But Helena takes her hand and leads her to the bedroom.

"I'll get some wash water," I start to say, but Max shakes his head. "I'll wash. You've got to go back to the ghetto. Please. Her father. Dr. Schillinger will be waiting."

I look at his big, brown eyes. His pale face. Then I pull my coat on and go right back out the door again.

He was so worried.

And I am so tired.

There's no good way across the train tracks now other than to get out of sight of the SS and choose your moment well. I do that, then circle the entire ghetto, walking toward the gate like I'm coming from the other direction, from the Minerwa building. On the other side of the fence, at the corner of an apartment block, a man is standing in the shadows. Where the guard can't see him. Rigid. Upright.

I think it's Dr. Schillinger. If it is, he's much thinner. Probably from the typhus. Or because since Max and Siunek came, I haven't brought food.

I walk a little closer to the gate and look up suddenly, like I've lost my way. The guard gives me a sidelong glare. I turn to go the other way, back toward Dr. Schillinger, and ten feet away from me, standing as stiff and still as an Egyptian mummy, is Officer Berdecki.

We stare at each other. I am frazzled. Exhausted. I haven't slept since I saw him last. I've also scrubbed the laundry and the house, been to the market, worked two shifts, and helped extract a little girl from the ghetto. And if he doesn't get out of my way right now, I'm going to walk up and kick him.

He seems to know it. He turns and does exactly what I said in his living room. He disappears. I give myself exactly two seconds to feel satisfied. Then I bend down and sneeze. Loudly.

And the shadow of a man behind the ghetto fence sits down in the doorway and cries.

19.

May 1943

IT TAKES A WEEK TO GET MY SLEEPING AND WAKING STRAIGHT SO THAT I'M not struggling through the day shift. And when I come home on Saturday evening, looking forward to a day off, I discover a house full of chickens.

Max looks guilty.

I turn on him, and he explains that Mrs. Krajewska asked Helena if we had a cat, because she could hear noise in the apartment while Helena was out. Helena told her we did have a cat, all smiles, but Max decided it was going to be impossible to be quiet enough. That the walls were just too thin. Then, at this opportune moment, Helena mentioned a farmer's wife who was selling off her entire lot of chickens in the market, and Siunek still had a little money, and so, following the natural order of things, I now live with chickens.

Again.

I go to sleep to the sound of *cluck, cluck, cluck*ing. When I wake, the chickens are still *cluck, cluck, cluck*ing. It's annoying and makes me irritable. At least Helena had the sense to buy only hens.

The chickens are distracting me from the fact that we all might die today. It's Sunday again, and we are waiting for Old Hirsch and Dr. Schillinger to come.

I bought a sofa after all. And an armoire. Traded earlier in the week for the blue silk blouse. It's a terrible sofa. I'm afraid of whatever substance is on it, even more so after a night of chickens. The armoire looks like a military shell went through it. But Max screws the hinges back on tight, and the shattered hole is in the back, against the wall, where it doesn't show when the doors are shut.

We have to keep the doors shut so the chickens won't roost.

I put Helena and Dziusia to work, laying down hay and making a nesting place in the little hallway with the ladder, which will also help cover up the height of the floor. Max and I take apart the sofa, stripping off its upholstery, washing the dark green cloth in three soapings of hot water. It comes out the color of an artificial lime. It also shrinks, and we laugh while Max and I hold one end, Dziusia and Helena pulling as hard as they can on the other, all of us staggering as we try to stretch it back out. Max even stands on a chair and hangs Helena over one end while she squeals, a technique that works better than I would have thought.

This is also distracting us from the fact that we all might die today.

We haven't told Dziusia her father is coming. In case he doesn't. And I haven't told Helena, either, in case she tells Dziusia. But Siunek is beside himself with worry and won't leave the window, biting his nails until they bleed. The plan before Max left was made by Dr. Schillinger and involves paying off the mailman, a man Dr. Schillinger knew before the war. Old Hirsch will shave his beard, and they will both dress as workers, like Max did. Then they will ride out of the ghetto with the mailbags and get dropped off during the route, somewhere close to the market, then make their way to Tatarska Street from there.

Max assures me that the mailman does not know my name or my address. That he's just being paid to let two Jews ride out on his cart. I tell Max the mail doesn't run on Sunday. He says it does from the ghetto, when all the mail has to go to the Nazis for inspection. I tell him the factories aren't open on Sunday, so dressing as workers doesn't make sense. He says the men who work in the German cafeterias and hotels and boarding houses work every day, and that's what Hirsch and Schillinger will look like.

I don't like the plan. There have been too many loose tongues as it is.

There's nothing I can do about it.

They should be here sometime after three o'clock. At twenty minutes after two, Siunek comes running into the kitchen.

"Police!" he whispers. We stare at him. "The police are here!"

Max drops his hammer and nails. I'm still holding the upholstery he was tacking down. "Get in the bunker," Max says. "Quick!"

We scramble, but we do it in silence. Max moves the floorboards to one side, slides on his stomach beneath the bed and into the hole, Siunek going after, though it takes him longer. I hand him Dziusia, whom I've snatched straight out of a game of hopscotch she and Helena have chalked on the second bedroom floor. I hand Max the floorboards to set back in place, and look around. There's a man's shaving brush and razor on the windowsill. I stuff them beneath my pillow. Helena hands me Siunek's shoes without a word, and I set them in the armoire and close the door.

"Wash the dishes," I whisper to her. She nods. There are too many cups lying about. Then I go to the window and peek beyond the edge of the curtain.

My heart slides straight down to my heels. There are two police-men standing in front of Tatarska 3, clubs in hand, looking the street up and down while they rock on their heels. Why come here? Now? Of all times?

Because they know.

Because someone has been talking. Someone has been talking this whole time.

And any minute now, Schillinger and Hirsch will come walking up the hill.

We really are going to die today.

And I've remembered just how much I don't want this to be true. I want so much for this not to be true it's making me mad.

Someone should find out what those policemen want.

I sit on the bed to tie up my shoes.

"What's happening?" Max whispers from underneath.

"Nothing right now."

He must be able to see my shoes. "Stay inside, Fusia."

"No," I reply. And then I call, "Be right back, Hela!" as I grab the water bucket and walk out the door.

Okay, God, I think. Here's where I know if you're on my side or not.

Maybe I should have brought my rosary.

Maybe I should stop challenging God.

I stop beside the well.

"Hello!" I call. The policemen turn around. "We're not about to be kidnapped by the Russians, are we?"

They both laugh, and my smile is as bright and false as yellow paint.

"The Americans, then?"

"We can take care of them," says one.

"Okay, then who's been robbed? Murdered?" I come closer with my bucket. "Come on, I'm all out of guesses. What are you doing here?"

They glance at each other. They're both young but not that young. Polish.

At least they're not Officer Berdecki.

"Do you live here, miss?" asks one.

"Yes. Around back. Why?"

"Because we have information that someone is hiding Jews."

I leave open curiosity on my face. Inside I am mad at God.

"Jews? Where?"

"Tatarska Street, somewhere between 1 and 5."

And so they're standing in front of 3. Hitting the nail on the head.

"Two rich Jews are supposed to come up here this afternoon, but maybe our information isn't right. It might just be talk."

"I would think so," I say quickly. "I've lived here for a while now, and I've never seen any Jews. I go in all my neighbors' houses. Where would they put them?"

I've never been in any of my neighbors' houses, but I pack my smile with cheerful innocence, and the policeman grins back.

"Don't worry," he says. "If we find them, it's good for us and nothing to do with you."

Or, I think, it might have everything to do with me. Because there is Dr. Schillinger, walking up the road.

And then Mrs. Krajewska comes out her door. "What's happening?"

"It's the police," I say. "They're looking for Jews."

"Jews?" says Mrs. Krajewska.

"Hey!" says a voice behind me. "You! Miss Podgórska!"

I turn slowly on my heel. It's Dr. Schillinger, still trudging up the hill.

I think my heart has stopped.

"Why weren't you at work yesterday?" he yells.

My mouth is open.

"I said, why weren't you at work? We had to cover your shift!"

"Should have gone to work," mutters one of the policemen. They laugh.

"Now, you stop that!" says Mrs. Krajewska, coming out to the street to point at Dr. Schillinger. "Miss Podgórska is a good girl!"

"If she's so good, she should have come to work!" says Dr. Schillinger. He's walking fast, red in the face, swinging his arms. He really does look like he could have come from the Minerwa building. I pull myself together.

"I'm sorry. My sister was sick."

"See! She said her sister was sick!" Mrs. Krajewska's finger waggles. "She can't leave when her sister is sick!"

"Then she should have sent a note!" shouts Dr. Schillinger.

"Now, you be civil ..." starts Mrs. Krajewska.

The other policeman mutters, "Let's walk up the street."

"But I did send a note!" I whine. "I paid the boy in the market. Didn't you get it?"

Mrs. Krajewska is gathering her breath to defend me.

"Come and have some tea," I say quickly, "and let me explain ..."

Dr. Schillinger stops in front of us as the policemen stroll away up the street. There is no sign of Old Hirsch. "I want to hear what you have to say, of course," says Schillinger. "I want to be fair. But you've caused a problem ..."

I take him by the arm and lead him toward our door, and when I look back and mouth the words "thank you," at Mrs. Krajewska, she blows me a kiss. We round the corner, Dr. Schillinger still berating me, and then we're through the front door of Tatarska 3.

I turn the lock, and Max must have already been out of the bunker, watching from the window, because he comes straight out and kisses my cheek. Then he's pumping Dr. Schillinger's hand. He should. Dr. Schillinger just saved us. I slide down the wall and sit on the floor, and a chicken comes and stands on my lap. And then Dziusia is squealing in her father's arms while everyone tries to shush her.

I thought I was about to die. I really, really thought I was about to die.

"Be calm, Dziusia," says Dr. Schillinger, sitting her next to him on the torn-apart sofa. She looks disappointed. He looks like he needs to get over his fright.

And then Siunek says, "Where is my father?"

Dr. Schillinger takes off his cap and looks at it, then shakes his head.

"It was the mailman," he says. "The cart was searched, and he said we were helping with the mail, that we had permission, and an Ordner who must have been in his pay came and told the Gestapo it was true, and so they let us go. Only after that, he lost his head. He drove the horse and cart all around the city, like he was being chased, and then he put us off at the wrong place. We didn't know where we were, especially Hirsch ..."

Hirsch isn't from Przemyśl, I remember. He's from Dobromil.

"He was supposed to stay a few paces behind me so it wouldn't look like we were together," says Schillinger, crossing his legs, which looks strange with coveralls. Dziusia holds him by the arm. "But when I looked back, he was gone." He glances up at Siunek. "Would he go back to the ghetto?"

Siunek shakes his head.

"Does he know this address?" Max asks.

Schillinger nods. And Max looks at me. We look at each other. That could be good, because he could find his way safely here. It could be bad, because he could give us away. I see the question on Max's face.

"The police knew someone was hiding Jews on Tatarska," I tell him. "Somewhere between numbers 1 and 5. They'd heard 'talk,' but they weren't sure it was true."

Max nods, and he is angry. He looks at Siunek and Schillinger, and I know he's going to ask them if they told. And then Helena comes running in.

"There's an old man coming into the courtyard!"

Helena, evidently, is the only one who remembered to keep watch at the window.

We go into another scramble. Schillinger doesn't even know where the bunker is. But there's no time to hide. I'm still getting to my feet when Siunek looks out the window and yells, "My father! My father!"

He throws open the door, and I can only think it's good that there's no one walking to the toilets who could look back and see this crowd of Jews in my house.

Old Hirsch stumbles in, beardless, and Siunek tries to hug him.

"We are killed. We are killed," mumbles Old Hirsch. "We are all killed!"

I get the door shut and locked, and Hirsch starts running from one end of the room to the other. "We are discovered! They are coming! We are killed! We are all killed!"

And then he throws up on the floor.

It's a long time before we can get Old Hirsch calm enough to speak and the room quiet enough for safety. I have to send Helena for two buckets of water to clean the floor, and I can only hope Mrs. Krajewska thinks my supervisor and I are drinking cup after cup of tea. When the floor is clean, I let Helena and Dziusia each take a chicken and go play their new favorite game in the back bedroom. Silent chicken hopscotch.

Or at least, it's their favorite game until someone needs to go to the toilet in the bucket.

I wash my hands and settle the rest of the chickens in the little hallway while the men gather around Hirsch. He did not get lost. He did not get separated from Schillinger. He got robbed.

"The thief pulled me into the alley, and he says, 'Ha! I know you are a rich Jew out of the ghetto, and now I will have your money.' And I say, 'What money?' And he puts a hand on my neck and feels in my pockets until he finds ten thousand *zloty*."

"Ten thousand?" says Siunek. "Why would you carry so much?"

"Because ten thousand is the amount I was prepared for."

Siunek frowns. "Prepared for what?"

"To be robbed!"

"You knew you would be robbed?" asks Max.

"I didn't know. I was prepared! Because ... this is the world."

I shake my head while I dry my hands. If he hadn't just vomited from fright, I would think Old Hirsch might be enjoying himself. And wouldn't any thief have been happy with even a thousand *zloty*? I think how much bread nine thousand extra *zloty* would buy.

"So he finds the money I was prepared to give, but he does not find what I was not prepared to give, and then I think I am dead, because why not now collect what the Gestapo will give him, too? But he says, I am a thief, Mr. Jew, but I am a thief with honor. I am not a killer. Now come with me, and I will watch and tell you when the police have gone."

"So the thief knew where you were going?" says Max.

"Yes! That is why I say we are all killed!"

Max shakes his head, and his anger is back. Someone might as well have printed a poster and put it up in the ghetto. Room for Jews on Tatarska Street.

"When I met with you all in the bunker on Kopernika," Max says quietly, "we made a pact and an oath to God. That no one would mention Stefania's name, her address, or that we were being hidden. It was the deepest secret we could ever have. The most solemn promise I could have asked for, because the promise meant our lives. Ours, and hers, and her sister's. If anyone here has broken that oath, I'm asking that you say so. Whether it was an accident or on purpose. So we can know what to do and save ourselves if we can. If we can't, then we need to give Stefania and her sister the chance to escape. Right now."

Max looks at me. The other three men look at me. Then they all look at each other. Silence falls on the kitchen of Tatarska 3. And then there is a knock at the door that scares me out of my wits.

Why are we forgetting to watch the window?

Old Hirsch lifts his hands, ready to shout, and Siunek covers his mouth. Max stands up slowly, without a noise, and beckons for the rest of them to follow him into the bedroom. When they've tiptoed out and shut the door, the knock comes again, and I peek out the smaller window beside the door.

It's not the police or the Gestapo. It's two little boys.

I open the door a crack.

"Yes?"

"A lady gave me a note for you," a boy says. He can't be more than ten.

"What lady?"

"Some lady," says the smaller one. "She said we have to come back for an answer in an hour."

"Bye," says the older one, and they scamper off.

I shut and lock the door, then open the bedroom. "You can come out," I whisper. The men file into the living room, not even having had time to get the floorboards away from the bunker. I think Dziusia and Helena are still playing hopscotch. I open the note and read it. And read it again. And read it again.

"What is it?" asks Max.

"We're being blackmailed. That's all." I sit down in a chair.

"Blackmailed?"

"This woman says if I will not hide her and her two children, that in three days she will denounce us to the Nazis."

"What?" Max snatches up the note. "Who is Mrs. Bessermann?"

"I don't know! I've never even heard of—"

"Bessermann?" says Siunek. "Malwina Bessermann?" He spins his big body around the small room, finally catching sight of Old Hirsch, settling back down on the partly-put-together sofa. He looks shocked. "Father, isn't that your girlfriend?"

"Your girlfriend?" says Max.

Schillinger shakes his head.

Old Hirsch looks cornered.

Your girlfriend.

Many, many things, I think, have just been explained.

"Send me away," says Old Hirsch. "I am sorry! It was the folly of an old man!"

But he doesn't look that sorry to me, now that he's calmed down. He sits back on the sofa and lights up a cigarette. I don't think he thinks we'll really send him away.

Old Dr. Hirsch, I am beginning to learn, usually has a trick up his sleeve.

He points at me with the cigarette. "If the men are going to talk," he says, "then the girl should leave."

Oh, nice. Very nice.

"You are sitting in her house," says Max. He looks close to hitting Old Hirsch. But I can see the old man is trying to distract. To turn the conversation from the real problem.

"Father," Siunek is saying, "you realize you got this girl arrested."

"She doesn't look arrested."

"You should have said!"

"What should I have said?"

"That you broke your oath and told Malwina Bessermann where you were going to hide!"

"And who was I supposed to tell this to?"

"Your son!" yells Siunek.

"Hirsch," says Schillinger. His voice carries more authority than Siunek's. "Stop toying with us. There are seven lives at stake. Who else have you told?"

Old Hirsch sighs and blows smoke. He looks older, somehow, without the beard. "I swear an oath to you now that I have told no one else. Only Malwina, for the sake of her children. But I cannot say who she has told."

Anyone could know what I'm doing in this house. Absolutely anyone.

I read the note from Malwina Bessermann again, the open note she sent with strangers through the streets. I'm to send a response showing that her note was received, and then I have two days to decide. If she doesn't hear a yes from me by the third, the Gestapo will know about all of us. By name.

It's a horrible way to ask someone to risk their life for you. Low. Selfish. Disgusting. The whole situation makes me angry. And certain. We are not going to live through this. Not all of us. I remember when Izio said that to me, the last night before he went to the camp.

And yet, if I were a mother in the ghetto, if I had lost a husband, parents, siblings to the trains—and that's what Siunek said happened to Mrs. Bessermann—what would I do to get my children out? To save them from that same fate? What would I do for Helena?

Anything. That's what I'd do.

I'd cheat and lie and be as low and selfish as I had to.

I tear off a piece of butcher paper, get my pen, and when I'm done writing, I fold the paper twice and walk outside. Like I'm going to the toilets. Really I'm waiting in the courtyard, looking for those boys. When they come, I slip them my note and go back inside, where the men are still arguing.

Later, when the girls are asleep, packed in my bed, and Old Hirsch is doing penance by taking first watch at the window, I go into the kitchen for water, past figures wrapped in blankets and soft breathing from the floor, to Old Hirsch's jacket, left hanging by the window. I go through his pockets until I find his armband.

I really thought I was done sneaking into the ghetto.

And then I jump when Max whispers behind me, "Fusia, what are you doing?"

20.

May 1943

THE RULES OF THE GHETTO ALWAYS SEEM TO BE CHANGING. BIGGER.
Smaller. No doing business at the fence. This section for workers.
This section for nonworkers. Go wherever you want. Go the wrong
way and we'll kill you. And today, we'll look the other way while
you do business at the fence. It can be hard to know where you are.
Right now it seems to be heavy guard on the gate, no more crossing of the bridge. But once you get inside, we're not going to pay
much attention to you.

I'm careful anyway. I've mussed my hair, dirtied up my face,
hidden my purse, and I have a real armband on my coat instead of
one that will only bear a glance. Max begged me not to go last
night, and I understand why. If something happens to me, they're
all dead. But I think I have to look Mrs. Bessermann over.

It could be a trap. But I don't know why it would be.

I go to our spot, the one we've always gone to, where Max kept
loosening the barbed wire. It's still loose. And from there, it's
just a short walk to Kopernika Street. I slip inside number 5
without attracting attention, then move to the back of the hall,
where there's a brick chimney going up from the basement, heat-
ing the different rooms, and beside that, a door to a closet
beneath the stairs. Only it isn't really a closet. There's a false

wall. And when you move a plank and step inside, there is the door to the cellar.

Max was clever, the way he built this. He's always clever.

I go down the steps, and there's a lantern already lit, Henek and a woman with sleek, dark hair sitting on crates on either side of it. Exactly as my note asked them to. I hadn't realized how much I would hate this place. It's dark and dank, and I don't like the way it smells.

Or maybe it's just because I remember Max, tears running down the scabbed skin on his face, telling me what happened here.

Henek stands, and he kisses my cheek, but he doesn't smile. I sit down, he sits down, and we face Mrs. Bessermann.

She's a lovely woman, in her late thirties, maybe early forties. Much too young for Old Hirsch. I wonder what Old Hirsch promised her. I wonder what she promised him. She sits composed. Perfectly straight.

"Why, Mrs. Bessermann, instead of asking me to help you, did you decide to threaten my life, the lives of five other people, and my seven-year-old sister?"

"And if a stranger had asked politely, Miss Podgórska, of course you would have helped." Her sarcasm could peel the jacket off a potato.

"That's what the others did, Mrs. Bessermann."

Her lips press together. I wait. She folds and unfolds her hands. The water drips. Then she sits up even straighter, elegant on a crate in a dirty basement where people lost their lives. "Then I am asking you, Miss Podgórska. I am begging for your help. For me and my two children."

Henek's brows go up. I look down at my hands.

"I have seven people to feed already in a very small space. Nine when Henek and Danuta come." I can hear her breathe in the dark. "So at this point, three more can't make that much difference."

She sits completely still, taking in my words. Then her smooth face crumples, and she begins to cry.

We sit silent, listening to her sobs.

Who else is there, I think, if not me?

Henek pulls me aside before I leave the basement, glancing back at Mrs. Bessermann. "Are you sure, Fusia?"

"Sadness can become cruelty," I whisper, thinking of my *babcia*. Henek shakes his head.

"This is a mistake," he says.

"I don't think it's a mistake."

"But are you sure? Because a mistake will kill you. And my brother."

I look at Henek closely. It's the first time I've heard him admit he's in danger. He's thin, of course, like everyone. But he looks strong enough, even after the typhus. He's trimmed his mustache.

"When are you and Danuta coming?"

"We're not ready yet. We're both working. We're okay."

That's the Henek I know.

"You should come soon. The *Judenrat* told me that it needs to be soon." I see his confusion, but there's no time for stories, and he knows it.

"We've got plenty of time to sit in your bunker, Fusia. If there's danger, the people in the ghetto will be the first to know."

"But you'll come soon?" I ask again.

"Soon," he replies.

*

"This is a mistake," whispers Max when I tell him. "I don't think she can be trusted."

"She says she was the one who made the mistake. She didn't know what else to do. I think she's desperate. She has two children."

"Oh, Fusia." He sighs.

I hand him a slice of bread, and when he thinks I'm not looking, he breaks off a corner and crumbles it on the floor for the chickens. I smack his arm, and Old Hirsch sits back on the sofa, watching while he smokes.

The next day after work, I go to the little market not far from the tracks, the Fish Place, where Cesia Bessermann, fifteen, and her brother, Janek, who is ten, are waiting for a young lady with a bright red scarf buying potatoes. They follow me to Tatarska 3.

And I'm sure it's not a mistake.

Two days after that, Max calls me to the window curtain, and I cover my mouth to stop my gasp of horror. Mrs. Bessermann is in the courtyard, nicely dressed with a bag over one arm, having a friendly conversation with Mrs. Krajewska.

"She wasn't supposed to come until next week!" I whisper.

Max shakes his head as Mrs. Krajewska waves goodbye, and Mrs. Bessermann steps gingerly through the dirt to my door.

He doesn't have to say it. I think this was a mistake.

Two weeks after that, I'm dumping a bucket of water in the pot, warming it up to wash the dishes, when Dr. Schillinger comes from his watch at the window and whispers, "People in the courtyard."

Not one person speaks. They move in perfect silence to the bunker, because no one is allowed to wear shoes and because Max has made them practice a hundred times. Each person is responsible for their own belongings. No cigarette stubs, no jackets or combs—especially male ones—can be left behind. If you're eating, you take the food with you. Max removes the boards, and the children—Cesia, Janek, and Dziusia—along with Schillinger, and Old Hirsch, and Max, according to today's rotation, go inside the bunker. Once the boards are back in place, Mrs. Bessermann slides under that bed, while Siunek crawls beneath the new one I bought off a junk cart five days ago. It's a tight fit. I make sure the food is put away, Helena checks the house for mistakes, and my people have disappeared in less than a minute.

I haven't even seen who's coming to the door. There's a knock, and a deep voice from the other side.

"Miss Podgórska!"

It's a fake deep voice.

"Have you got a man in there?"

I open the door a crack.

"Surprise!" says Januka. "We found you! And it's your day off!" She's holding up a bottle of vodka and a case of cigarettes. The extra ration we get for working in the factory.

"Stefi! Aren't you going to let us in?" she says.

I open the door, and there's Lubek, three girls I don't know but recognize from the factory floor, and two more couples I've never seen in my life. They pour into my little living room and kitchen.

"What ... what are you doing here?" I ask.

"We always get together the Sunday after rations, you know that!"

Someone is cranking up a phonograph on my half of a kitchen table, next to a plate of cookies.

"But how did you ..."

"We were going up to Anna's ..." says Lubek.

I don't know which one Anna is.

"... and Januka spotted you at the well."

"Isn't this sweet?" says Januka, peeking her head into the bedroom. "Such pretty curtains!"

I know my people are hidden, but I want to run and slam the door shut anyway.

Januka is in high spirits. A little flushed. I think the vodka must be open.

"Ahhh!" she squeals. "Look, everybody! Chickens!"

Much is made over my little hall full of chickens. As if I like to keep chickens for pets. Helena thinks we do. I look around and find her in the corner, wide-eyed and shaky.

"Is this your sister?" asks a stranger. Her lips are ruby red.

"Hela," I say, and hold out my hand. She comes to me, and I bend down to whisper. Then the record starts playing, and I have to talk louder.

"Why don't you go out and play? You don't have to be close by ..." In case something goes wrong. "Just until I can get rid of them."

"Will you make them go?" she whispers, glancing at the bedroom.

"Yes. But it may take a few minutes. Okay?"

She nods as I straighten, running for the door like she's popped from a spring.

"She is shy?"

I look up, and there's Lubek with his cigarette.

"Very," I say, and leave it at that. But I don't like the way he was watching us.

The couples change the record and start dancing in front of the sofa. Januka hands me one of my own glasses, full to the top with vodka.

"Isn't this a wonderful surprise?" she says. "It must be so nice to live on your own. No parents!"

So nice, I think. To have every responsibility land on your shoulders.

She has no idea.

But if I were Januka, with a job and some money, no sister, and a place of my own, I might think this was a nice surprise. I'd sip vodka and bake cookies, pass out the cigarettes and dance if a boy asked me to.

I am not Januka.

I have to think of a way to get everyone out of here.

I find the vodka bottle and go to the sink to pour the contents of my glass back into it. I hate to waste anyone's rations. I always sell mine.

"So you don't drink the vodka, either?" says Lubek.

You need to go find Januka, I think. I start to wash the empty glass.

"So how long have you lived here?" he asks.

"A few weeks."

"It's a good place. But you could have better neighbors."

I look up. Lubek is very tall. "What do you mean?"

"The SS man I saw going in the front. I wouldn't want him for a neighbor."

An SS man. In Mrs. Krajewska's house. What is he doing there?

"Is he there right now?"

"Yes."

I have such a sharp pain behind my left eye, I wince.

"I've been to the ghetto," says Lubek. "With my uncle. He wanted to get married, and there was a goldsmith he knew. He thought maybe he could still make him a ring. You wouldn't believe what the SS do in there."

I would believe it.

There's an SS man next door. An SS man is next door ...

"I've heard the ghetto is about to be gone."

"Where did you hear that?"

"The police were saying it. At the fence."

"Completely gone?"

"Not one left. *Judenfrei.* They say they're moving the Jews somewhere else, but I don't think that's true."

"What do you think they're going to do?"

"Lock the gates and burn it down. Because that's what kind of bastards they are."

I shake my head. "No. They won't use fire. They'll shoot them. Every single one."

Henek. Danuta. You've got to come out.

"They'll kill them, either way," agrees Lubek. "And then they'll start on us." His brows are knitted together. Thoughtful. And then he says, "I think that glass is clean."

I look down. I'm still washing the glass.

"Why don't you show me the rest of the house?" he says.

"There's nothing more to see. Just bedrooms."

"Then you could show me that."

I almost smile. No, Lubek, you don't need to see my bedroom or what's hidden there. And the other one we use for a toilet.

It's a shame I can't say anything I'm thinking.

I settle for, "I don't show boys my bedroom."

"Really?" Now he's grinning. "What about them?"

I turn around, and one of the couples is dancing themselves into the next room, carrying their phonograph with them.

"Wait," I say. "Wait. You need to stay out ..."

I run to the bedroom. The record is so loud it hurts my ears. One couple is dancing across the floor, the other sitting on the bed above the bunker, kissing. And there's a noise coming from under the bed, a sort of spitting sound, muffled, and then a thud. The sound of wood dropping.

What could be happening under there?

My chest compresses into a tiny, pulsing ball.

"Stefi!" says the kissing girl, breaking away from her boy. I have no idea who she is. The thudding wood sound comes again. "What is that? Do you have a cat under the bed? I love cats."

She wiggles out of her boyfriend's arms and drops to her knees. "Here, kitty ..."

"Stop!" I yell. "Don't look under there!"

The dancing couple pauses, the girl on the floor and her boyfriend stare. I don't know where Januka or the other girls are, but I can feel Lubek's presence somewhere behind me. I drop to my knees beside the kneeling girl so I can tackle her if I have to. I can feel the room waiting.

"It's a mean cat," I say. "He'll scratch your face."

"Oh!" The girl raises her hand to her cheek.

"Let me look ..."

I peek under the bed and catch a glimpse of Mrs. Bessermann's mussed hair and frightened eyes. And I think someone is coughing beneath the floorboards.

"Yes, it's just the cat. But he's hissing. We'd better leave him alone ..."

"Miss Podgórska! What is going on in here?"

I straighten up, and now Mrs. Krajewska is in the bedroom, Januka right behind her, mouthing "sorry." She must have let her in.

Why is everyone I know in this room?

"Do you know how loud it is in here?" shouts Mrs. Krajewska over the music. "And it's a Sunday afternoon!" She's holding her rosary, draping from a clenched fist over one hip of her printed dress, and that seems to carry some weight with my partygoers. The needle is ripped from the spinning record, and I wish it hadn't been. Silence falls, and someone is coughing softly beneath the floor.

"I'm sorry, Mrs. Krajewska," I say loudly, helping the girl next to me to her feet. "I won't let it happen again. Time to go, everyone!"

"Well, I ..."

I think Mrs. Krajewska was only going to ask my friends to be quieter, not leave. But I can't let her get away with that.

"No, really, Mrs. Krajewska. I know it was against the rules. I'm sorry."

Mrs. Krajewska looks satisfied and a little confused and relieved that people are gathering up their drinks and their music. I steer them out and shut the door to the bedroom, and in a few minutes, the plates and bottles and purses are collected and the group files one by one out the door.

"Bye, Stefi!" says Januka sadly, giving me a little wave. Lubek grins at me once and shuts the door behind him. Mrs. Krajewska looks around.

"You've been fixing up this place very nicely, Miss Podgórska. Now you know there aren't any rules about having friends over, but ..."

"They invited themselves this time. And I was more than ready for them to go."

Mrs. Krajewska smiles. "You're such a sensible girl. Do you have any tea?"

And then Mrs. Krajewska pulls out a chair from my half table and sits in it. I put the pot of warm water back on the heat and find two clean cups. That pain is pulsing behind my eye again.

"You know I've been worried about you," says Mrs. Krajewska. "A young girl with a sister. All on her own. And not going to work that day ..."

"We only had our shifts confused," I say. "It was all straightened out."

"I thought your supervisor was very rude. What was his name?"

"He doesn't have that position anymore," I reply instead of answering. "Temper."

Mrs. Krajewska nods. "I'm not surprised, coming to your house like that. How is your mother?"

"What?" I say.

"The letter from your mother. How is she?"

Mrs. Bessermann told Mrs. Krajewska she was a friend of my mother's, delivering a letter from her, because she didn't know my new address.

"She says she's well. She's still in Salzburg, but she saw one of my sisters there."

I'm getting good at lying.

Then again, maybe I was always good at it?

I pour the steaming water into the teapot. There's a loud bump from the bedroom, like one of the floorboards fell or was dropped back into place, and Mrs. Krajewska's eyes dart to the door.

"The cat is in there," I say.

She turns her attention to the tea, lifting the lid of the teapot to check its color. My eye hurts so badly, I have to rub it. And then I say, "Do you have a houseguest right now, Mrs. Krajewska?"

"Yes, I forgot to say! My nephew is here, my first husband's sister's boy. He's military, as I'm sure you saw."

"German military."

"Yes, but he's a good boy!" says Mrs. Krajewska, with the exact same tone she used to defend me to Dr. Schillinger. "Not like those other SS, I'm sure."

"Of course not," I say. I pour her tea.

We have the SS living next door. We have the SS living next door ...

"How long will he be staying with you?"

"He hasn't said." She pauses. "He's very handsome."

"I'm sure he is."

"In fact, if you would like me to arrange a little introduction, I could do that. A husband would be a great help to you."

"Thank you. But I think wartime is a little too unsure for husbands. Or boyfriends. I'm going to wait until everything is settled."

"So sensible. But don't wait too long! You don't want to get too old and miss all your chances."

I'll keep that in mind, Mrs. Krajewska. Don't you need to say your rosary?

I have to bite my tongue to keep those words from coming out of my mouth.

She sips her tea. I gulp mine. I think I can hear coughing beneath the floor, but Mrs. Krajewska is too busy talking.

"There is something, though, Miss Podgórska, that I wanted to talk to you about. Something I've noticed about you. Something that's been bothering me for a while now."

The pain behind my left eye spreads across my forehead.

Maybe today is the day after all. If it's not Januka, the SS, or Mrs. Krajewska, it will be because my brain is going to explode.

"I've been very worried about what I've been seeing, because it means you haven't been going to Mass."

I finish my tea. Mrs. Krajewska drinks hers slowly, listening while I explain that I do go to the cathedral on Na Bramie to pray twice a week. If she knew exactly how often I prayed—how often I've prayed in the last five minutes—she'd be surprised.

Then she says she worries about my cat, because of the chickens. And Helena, because she's spending a lot of time alone and doesn't seem to want to play with her boys. Who could blame Helena for that, since Mrs. Krajewska's boys are five- and seven-year-old terrors, and Helena is not alone near as much as Mrs. Krajewska thinks. The last half of her cup is spent telling me what I should and should not do with my house, my money, my religion, my future husband, and other things that I eventually stop listening to.

When she's talking, I can't hear the noise from beneath the floor at all, so I let her talk.

Mrs. Krajewska finally runs out of advice and walks out the door. I lock it and hurry to the window to make sure she's safely home before I whisper, "She's gone."

Siunek and Mrs. Bessermann slide out from under the beds. Mrs. Bessermann is upset. She flings away the boards as Max pushes them up.

"Cesia! Janek!"

But it's Old Hirsch who comes out of the hole first. He's dirty and wringing wet—soaked like he's fallen into a lake—and his face is ashen. He spits out a handkerchief onto the floor—stuffed there, I assume, to keep him quiet—and then he coughs and coughs like he might never breathe again, still on his belly. I bring him water, and now Max is putting back the floorboards, Mrs. Bessermann stroking the pieces of dirt from Cesia's hair. Dziusia and Janek are near to hitting each other, while Dr. Schillinger and Siunek are on their knees, trying to help Hirsch.

"Bring him into the other room," I whisper. "Quick!" Mrs. Krajewska and her SS nephew will not think that cough is mine. "And who's watching the window?"

They start moving, but slowly. I need Max. But he isn't in here. "Listen to me!" I point and barely say the words. "There is an SS man on the other side of that wall!"

That gets their attention. Old Hirsch is whisked to the other room. Cesia goes to the window. Mrs. Bessermann breaks up the fuss between Janek and Dziusia. And when I go into the kitchen, there are chickens everywhere. Someone has opened the door to the hallway, and since the hallway is empty, they must have gone up the ladder.

I climb, and Max is standing in the dusty light from the window, staring at the attic with his arms crossed. We have to be very quiet up here. Mrs. Krajewska has second-floor rooms, and the walls are thinner than downstairs. I stand beside him.

"This isn't working," he whispers.

I know.

"There are too many for the bunker already, and I don't think I can make it any bigger, not without undermining the house or falling into the cellar."

Which is Mrs. Krajewska's.

"And what will we do when Henek and Danuta come?"

"More beds?" I suggest.

He smiles. Then his eyebrow quirks, and he says, "Oh, Fusia. The cat."

"It'll scratch your face."

We both laugh now, as quietly as we can. Even though it really isn't funny. I think we're both just relieved to be alive.

We were so nearly not alive.

"You heard about the SS man?" I ask.

"Mostly. Around the coughing. You don't want to go on a date with him, too, do you?"

I shake my head. I can tell from his eyebrow that he's teasing. But I don't like his use of the word "too." I think he's still upset about Officer Berdecki.

"You need to be careful. With Lubek."

"How do you know his name?"

"You'd be amazed at what I can pick up from under a floor. He asked you a lot of questions."

But I can't tell if Max thinks Lubek is curious about me or my illegal activities. He's pacing the attic now. In his sock feet. Then he comes back close. So we can talk.

"I've been thinking about a wall. Right here." He walks forward a few steps, arms waving, showing me a line that would cut the long, narrow attic short.

"If we could get wood," Max whispers. "Old wood, nothing new, I could build a false wall right here and make a space for us behind it. It would be tight, especially with two more, but better than being cramped underground. You can't imagine how much it hurts to stay in the right position, how cold it is. It's scary for the children and hard for Old Hirsch and even Dr. Schillinger to get under the bed quickly. They all might do better with a ladder."

I tilt my chin, trying to imagine what he's showing me. "You can do it," I say.

He turns his head. "You think so?"

"The one you made on Kopernika was really good."

Now he frowns. "What were you doing down there?"

"It's where I met Henek and Mrs. Bessermann."

"I wish you hadn't gone in there," he says.

"I know. I'm sorry."

We both look at the wall. Or the wall that Max wants to build.

"It won't happen here," I say to him. He knows I'm talking about the basement of Kopernika. "We won't let it happen here."

He nods. "I'll find a way to make this work."

I knock some of the dirt from his shaggy hair.

I think he will.

21.

July 1943

I SEARCH THE MARKETS FOR MORE THAN THREE WEEKS WITHOUT SEEING any kind of wood that looks as if it could belong in our attic. Then, in the early sun, on my way to work, I spot a man pushing a cart toward the market square, a load of old planks piled almost as high as his chin. He's demolished a house, he says, ruined when the Russians were fighting the Germans, but this wood is still okay, and what would I want with a lot of old wood, anyway? Firewood, I lie, and run back home to Tatarska for my money, and to warn everyone in the house that a man will be delivering wood to the back.

I leave Helena in charge of this, explain to Mrs. Krajewska that someone has given me a load of old wood for the fire, so she won't think I bought it, and by the time I fly back down the hill and cross the iron bridge to Minerwa, I'm late. But Herr Braun hasn't noticed yet, because Lubek has started my machines.

Januka and Lubek and I almost always spend our breaks together now, and I can't tell exactly what the arrangement between the two of them is. But there have been no more parties. They seem to have gotten the idea that I didn't appreciate unin-vited guests, and neither did the custodian of my apartment.

Mrs. Krajewska's nephew's name is Ernst. He's SS, on some kind of leave from his post, and I think he's foul. He mostly stays inside the house, drinking, I assume, because when I do see him, he's drunk. But he makes my eight hidden Jews have to whisper and tiptoe, even with the chickens, and that makes them testy. Especially the children. Helena escapes when she can. I don't even know where she goes. And the window watch is changed every three hours. Night and day.

When I come home that night, Max has several planks of the wood in the living room, because he's talked Helena into dragging them through the door for him. He's been pulling the rusty nails to use again, picking up the planks, and putting them down like pieces of glass, quietly planning his wall. He smiles when I come in, running his hand over the rough, weathered wood.

"It's just right," he whispers. "Exactly what we need!"

And because he can't say much else, he grabs my face and kisses both my cheeks. Like his father would have. Or maybe not. Mrs. Bessermann huffs, but Max doesn't notice. He's just happy.

Three days after that, on my day off, I go to Mrs. Krajewska and ask if she has a hammer. I tell her I'm washing all my blankets and linens and I want to nail up some rope to hang them in the attic so they won't get dirty again or wet in the rain. She not only gives me a hammer and nails, she brings out some extra rope, too, in case I don't have enough. Then I have to haul the water and actually wash all the linen. Helena takes the chickens out to the yard, one of the Krajewska boys comes to chase them, and Max creates a chain of hands to pass the wood up the ladder.

He's careful, doing as little hammering as possible, and when he's done, I can't tell that his wall is not the wall of our attic. Not until he moves two of the vertical planks, showing me the space behind. He's even hung a laundry rope.

"I'll move up some of the odds and ends from the second bedroom," I tell him. "To make it look like a storage space."

"We'll need a bucket," he says, "in case, you know ..."

I look at the space behind the wall. The roof slopes down to two low windows on one side, letting in some light. Most of them won't be able to stand up, there's going to be no privacy, and beneath the summer sun and the tin roof, it's hot as the devil's stove up here. But what does that matter when your life is at stake?

"We also need something over the windows," Max says. "Did you know the Krajewska boys climb on the roof?"

No. But I bet Helena did. "Did they see you?"

"Nearly."

"I'll get curtains." But I don't know with what. I'll have to start checking the rubbish piles again. We're feeding ten people on two ration cards, my income, and Hirsch's contributions, and it's not quite enough. Mrs. Bessermann doesn't understand why I don't buy better bread. Old Hirsch wants to know where his cigarettes are.

I don't dare tell him I'm selling my cigarette ration.

"Have you heard from Henek or Danuta?" Max asks.

I shake my head. They were supposed to leave a blank piece of paper under a rock outside our weak place in the fence, showing they were ready to come. I was supposed to leave a hairpin beneath the rock to show I got the paper and was ready to have them.

"He's going to wait too long," Max says. "He's the only brother I have left. And he's going to wait too long."

I check the spot at the fence every day in August. And beginning in August, Lubek starts dropping by. Often.

"Fusia's lover!" whispers whoever is on duty at the window, which I do not appreciate. Then eight people have to disappear to the well-curtained attic and lie on the floor unmoving, in complete silence, miserable and sweating, while Lubek talks and smokes cigarettes at my half kitchen table.

This is not bringing harmony to my home.

But Lubek is interesting. His cousin delivers fish wrapped in foreign newspapers, and he hears the Germans aren't doing well in their war against Russia. That the British are putting up a fight with the help of the Americans, even though the Americans are also fighting Japan. Germany has two huge fronts.

They might lose, Lubek says. Maybe they'll lose before they can kill everyone, and Przemyśl will be in Poland again.

Lubek is thoughtful. He's nice-looking. Less of a boy than I thought. I've never seen him lose his temper. He's never been unkind. Except maybe to Januka, because I don't think she knows he's coming here.

Lubek makes Max mad, which amuses Mrs. Bessermann. I offer to meet Lubek somewhere else so everyone doesn't have to sit in the attic. But Max doesn't like this idea, either. Which also amuses Mrs. Bessermann.

Mrs. Bessermann is irritated because Siunek pays too much attention to Cesia. Cesia is fifteen, but she doesn't look it, and we are in a small space. Dziusia fights with Janek on a regular basis, because he torments her, and Dr. Schillinger stares into space instead of defending his daughter, which means Max or I have to do it. Old Hirsch sits and broods as well, sniffing the residual smoke of Lubek's cigarettes.

I don't blame Helena for disappearing every day. It might be safer for her. It might be saner for her.

But it makes me worry.

So after a day when Dziusia had to go in the bucket in the attic, and then fight Janek because he said he'd looked, which caused me to explain to Lubek that the cat was upstairs chasing rats, I get into bed beside Helena. The moon is bright, shining silver around the cracks of the lily curtains. I pull the covers over our heads, and Helena puts her head on my chest. She smells like the outdoors and a little girl. I whisper, "Hela, what do you do when I'm at work?"

"Feed the chickens and get the water and take out the dirty bucket. You know that."

"Yes. But what else?"

She thinks. "Fight the Krajewska boys. When they won't give me the water."

Now I wish I could see her. "What do you mean?"

"They always say the well belongs to their mama. But if I don't take in water, then our people will be thirsty, because they can't go outside. And then I have to hit them. The boys. And sometimes they try to come in, and I have to hit them then, too."

"I see." I'll be talking to Mrs. Krajewska about this. "And when you're done with those things, where do you go?"

"Different places."

"Like where?"

She thinks again. "There's a broken stone house up on the hill. Like a castle. I play there sometimes. Like it's a real house. And I go to the convent, because sometimes the nuns have cookies, and I go to the cathedral ..."

"You do?"

She nods. "It smells nice."

"Do you ever play with anyone else? Other boys or girls?"

"Of course I don't!"

It would be hard to have a secret like hers and be around other children. It's not a secret for just one or two nights anymore. Not like Mickiewicza 7.

"Sometimes," Helena says, "I play a game in my head where Mama comes back and she sews me a dress, and the fieldmen bring lots of food to the house ..."

I'm surprised Helena remembers the men who used to work our fields.

"... and during the day while Mama works, I go to school so I can know all the words on the shop signs. I know a lot of them, but not all of them."

"I could teach you to read, Hela."

Only this is a voice outside the covers. I pull the blanket down, messing up our hair, and Max is on duty at the window, the chair leaning back on two legs.

"Would you like me to?" he asks.

Helena smiles, then smiles bigger, and when I come home from work the next evening, her brown head is next to Max's dark one, poring over a dental textbook. Helena doesn't care about the subject. She is just thirsty for the words.

I didn't realize she was so lonely.

And then Cesia runs in and says, "Fusia's lover!"

They move with precision and silence, grabbing every belonging and disappearing up the ladder without disturbing the chickens. I check for dishes, and Helena sighs when Max takes away the textbook. But I see Max hesitate. And at the last second, instead of going up, he slips into the bedroom.

To the other bunker. Where he can hear me talk to Lubek.

I'm annoyed.

Lubek knocks and tries to walk straight in, which he can't do because the lock is turned.

It's really not good that he feels so comfortable here.

I open the door, and Lubek grins, pushes a pecking chicken away from his feet, and goes straight to the pot to make himself a cup of tea.

He talks about the fire we had at the factory, a small one that shut down everyone's machines, but not for long, and how bad the smoke was. I tell him this is funny, considering how much smoke he breathes all the time. He says that's different.

I can almost feel Max's ears stretching out in our direction.

So I say in a clear voice, "How do you feel about eavesdropping?"

His brows go up. "Same as anyone, I guess. No one wants to think their private conversations are being listened to. Who's been ... Wait. Where's your sugar?"

"What? Oh. Sorry. I'm out."

"But you weren't out the day before yesterday. You had a half-kilo sack."

And Mrs. Bessermann and Cesia baked, which made Max angry, because what were we supposed to tell Mrs. Krajewska or the foul SS man, Ernst, when they saw the smoke coming from the chimney? When they smelled the smell? That Helena was whipping up a batch of *babka*?

"I don't think I did," I say.

"Yes," he insists. "You did."

"I ate it," says Helena from the sofa. I turn to look at her. I'd forgotten she was there.

"You ate a half kilo of sugar?" asks Lubek. "Do you know how much that costs?" My sister looks stubborn while he shakes his wheat-gold head. "You're going to have to punish her, Stefi."

And don't tell me how to deal with my sister, I think. Especially since she's wonderful.

"Why don't you take that chicken outside?" I say sternly to Helena. "And we'll discuss this later."

When she's picking up the chicken, I turn my back to Lubek and blow her a kiss. She grins and blows one back, which probably looks impertinent from Lubek's point of view, and runs out the door.

"I wouldn't want to raise a little sister," he says. "What else do you think she's eating?"

Other than the occasional bite of butter, I don't know what he means.

"You're going through a lot of food. I see the *kasha* sack going down every time I come here. You can't be eating that much. What are you doing with it all?"

Lubek is much too observant.

"Selling," I say. "I'm reselling for a profit. Sending money to my mother."

He nods and lights a cigarette. "That sounds like you." He doesn't say anything more for a few minutes, and I hope Max is having leg cramps.

"I wonder what you're thinking," Lubek says suddenly. "About what you might want to do after this war. Do you have any ideas?"

Find my family. But other than that, I really don't know. I shrug.

"I want you to think about it," he says.

"Why?"

"Because I want you to think about doing it with me. I want to make plans. Loose ones. But I want to make them. With you."

And that's all he has to say about it. He finishes his tea, tells me to be firm with Helena, and leaves me to my thoughts.

I really, really wish Max hadn't heard that.

I think Max agrees. When he comes out of the bunker with dirt in his hair, he doesn't meet my eyes. He only says, "If he keeps coming here, we're going to be found."

I know it. But that night, snuggled next to Helena, part of me wonders if Lubek would keep my secret. Maybe even help me. Then I remember what Emilika said about German spies. What Lubek is doing would be an excellent way to flush out Jews.

I avoid him the next day at work, talking with Januka until he leaves for home. She walks me over the iron bridge, and I keep my steps slow so that if Lubek comes to the house, I won't be there to let him in.

I know Helena won't let him in.

I don't mention any of this to Januka. But I do tell her I have to stop by the coal merchant's to buy a few kilos for the stove. She says their box is low, too. She might as well go with me. The coal yard isn't that far out of her way.

We buy five kilos each, in drawstring bags. And then Januka starts flirting with the coal merchant. Actually, she's playing the coal merchant like a cheap violin. I'm impressed. And I don't feel quite so bad about Lubek. And then I notice that the coal merchant has a watch on.

"Is it twenty after eight?"

Januka tilts her head to look at the man's sooty wrist and says, "Oh!"

Curfew isn't until nine, but I have nearly half an hour of walking, and Januka has more. We need to hurry.

We dart out of the coal yard with barely a word and walk fast down the sidewalk. The sun has dipped behind the hills, the twilight coming down, and the streets are clearing. The safe feeling of a crowd is gone. We walk faster, and the coal is getting heavier, and then we reach the corner where Januka needs to turn and I need to go straight on to Tatarska. We pause, say a quick goodbye, and then two German soldiers are crossing the street, one of them waving a hand. At us.

"Halt! Wer ist da?"

Januka and I look at each other. It's not nine o'clock yet.

The first soldier is young. Maybe not older than me, with a machine gun strapped on his back and a pistol at his side. He holds out a hand, asking for Januka's papers. She sets down her coal and starts searching through her purse. The second soldier comes to me. His hair is dark brown, and he has a tiny little mustache. Like Hitler. I hand him my papers.

They give our information the quickest glance, then start talking to each other. They don't seem to speak any Polish. They don't hand our papers back.

The watch on the wrist of the first soldier says forty-seven minutes after eight. I wait, tapping my foot, staring at the hole where the synagogue used to be. The two soldiers laugh, a joke for only themselves. But I catch one word I know. *"Neun."*

Nine. They're going to hold us here until nine. So they can arrest us.

I look at Januka, and her eyes slide over to mine.

We are in trouble.

The German soldiers keep talking, and now it's obviously about us. The younger one runs his fingers through Januka's hair, and when I tell them it's almost nine o'clock, goodbye, and try to walk away without my papers, the one with the mustache yells at me, pulling me back by an arm. Januka is frozen, petrified. And then the cathedral bells ring.

The young soldier laughs, and they hand us our papers. I think they're going to let us go. We pick up our coal. But then they take us each by an arm and walk us down the street. Back the way we came.

We are in big trouble.

And my senses sharpen like knives.

I know the street we're on. They're walking us right down the middle of it, because the sidewalk here is pockmarked from bombs. There's a German boarding house at the end, where soldiers stay, mostly the ones who are with the police. But before the boarding house, there are apartment buildings. On the right and the left side of the street.

My soldier isn't joking anymore. He's ignoring me, lips pressed together, his eyes straight ahead. His grip on my arm is hard, bruising. Purposeful. Januka's is touching her hair again, putting his face in her neck and smelling her while they walk. She cringes, and my soldier barks something sharp that must be telling him to stop.

Or to wait.

"I don't think they speak Polish," I say quietly to Januka. We both look for a reaction, but other than watching us, there is none.

"Smile," I say. And we do. "Laugh," I tell her, and we do.

Surely even a Nazi couldn't think that had been real. But the grip on my arm relaxes just a little.

"There are buildings coming up," I say in a pleasant tone. "Apartments, with front and back doors, a hall going straight through. Do you understand? Laugh now, Januka."

She laughs and shakes her head no at the same time.

"When I count to three, we're going to hit them in the face with our coal. I'll run right, you run left, into the front door of the building and out the back. Run like the devil. Can you do it? Laugh now."

She laughs. Loudly. And nods. I laugh with her. My soldier looks smug.

Januka has to give this all she's got, or it will never work.

"As hard as you can?"

She nods, but she doesn't laugh. Her eyes are big and frightened.

I look ahead to the buildings, choosing. And I think I see two that will do. Our feet tap together on an empty, silent street. The buildings I want are coming.

"One," I say, smiling at Januka. Then I look ahead. "Two. And three ..."

I grab my coal bag suddenly with two hands and use my whole body to swing it upward. The bag smacks my soldier straight in the mustache, and he goes over backward onto the paving stones. I pause for a heartbeat, stunned that he actually fell, and then I hear Januka squealing, "Run!"

Her man was down before mine.

I run. Like a rabbit. Like the wind. Like I've never run before. And my heightened brain shows me the door latch just before I need to turn it. I slam the door shut without breaking my stride.

Down the dark hall and to the next latch. The door opens and shuts, and I haven't lost a second. Down the steps into an alley. I turn right, and quickly left. I hope I'm not going to hit a dead end. And there are shots in the street. Pistol shots. Words yelled in German.

Oh, Januka, I think. Please be all right.

But I cannot stop. I stay in the back alleys, twisting and turning until I have to climb the hill to Tatarska. Now I just stay in the shadows. I don't know if there's anyone behind me. I can't hear them.

I think if there was someone chasing me, I'd be shot.

I fly into the courtyard and around the back in the dark, and if Mrs. Krajewska sees me, it's probably only a blur. I bang on the door, and Max flings it open, pulls me inside, and turns the lock. He must have been on watch at the window.

"What's wrong? What's happened to you?"

I lean on the door and gasp. And gasp. I don't have any breath.

But I do have a bag of coal. I drop it on the floor.

"Your young man came," says Mrs. Bessermann.

"Get her some water," orders Schillinger, and Dziusia goes to get the glass. Siunek and Cesia are coming from the other room, Old Hirsch looking frankly curious on the sofa. I see Helena sitting in the corner, shrinking her body down to fit the space. I hold out my hand, and she comes to me, throwing her arms around my waist.

They must have been terrified when I didn't come before curfew.

When my breath comes back, I tell Max about the soldiers and about Januka, who might be dead. The thought leaves me shaky. A little teary.

Max grits his teeth while I talk. He rubs his head. Then he bangs the front door behind him with a fist. Helena jumps in my arms.

"Okay," he says. "That's enough. I'm teaching you how to box. Right now."

It's interesting to me that Max has become the leader of the hidden. Dr. Schillinger is older, and in the dental practice, he was Max's boss. Hirsch is older than Schillinger. Mrs. Bessermann is a mother, used to ordering people around, and Siunek is twice Max's size. But when a decision needs to be made, they all look to Max. If Max says I need to learn how to hit a Nazi—or anyone else who might deserve hitting—then they clear a space and assume I'm about to learn how to hit a Nazi.

Max and I are left standing inside a circle of eager people, and even Helena sits to watch, shoulders hunched in anticipation. Other than the daily danger of being found by Ernst the SS man, this is probably the most interesting thing that's happened since two of the chickens got chased by a dog.

Helena may be hoping for some pointers for the Krajewska boys.

I feel silly. And tired. And jumpy with adrenaline. It's an unpleasant combination. Then I imagine what would have happened if I hadn't had a bag of coal and decide this might not be such a waste of time after all. It might actually feel good to hit something. I raise my fists.

"The first thing to remember," Max whispers, so the neighbors can't hear, "is to be on the defensive before you are on the offensive."

"Where did you learn to box?" I ask.

"Gymnasium," he says. "You might have missed all my black eyes. Now be light on your feet, ready to dodge ..."

"You can't hit if you've already been hit, girl!" says Old Hirsch. He's enjoying himself.

"Go on, Fusia," says Max. "Bounce."

I bounce. Just a little. I'm back to feeling silly.

"No, get on this part of your feet. Like this. Ready to move."

I get balanced on the correct part of my feet, and Max makes me practice dodging his blows. I'm pretty good at that. Helena claps. I think Janek would prefer it if Max hit me, but I don't think Max is really trying. Then he shows me how to punch.

"Thumb here"—he adjusts my fist—"and bring your body into it. Keep your mouth closed. Use your weight ..."

I know what he means. Like I did with the coal sack. I pull back, use my weight, and hit Max hard in the nose.

I hadn't meant to do that. I was thinking of the coal sack.

I see the shock on his face. I feel the shock on mine. Helena has her hands over her mouth. Then Mrs. Bessermann says, "Good for you!" Janek claps, and Old Hirsch bursts out laughing without a thought for noise while Max bleeds all over his shirt.

I stand behind Max, one hand on his tilted neck while the other holds a wet cloth to his nose. I'm waiting for the bleeding to stop. And for Siunek to show mercy and stop teasing Max. Max takes it with good humor. Mostly. When Siunek has had his fill, I finish cleaning up Max's face and sit beside him at the table. He pokes gingerly at his nose. It's a little swollen. His eyebrow quirks.

"I think I've decided you don't need lessons."

"I'm sorry. I lost my head."

"It's my punishment for eavesdropping. I accept it."

The mention of Lubek stops the conversation.

"Do you like him, Fusia?"

"I do."

Max frowns.

"As a friend," I add.

"You didn't tell him that when he was asking you to marry him."

"I don't think that's exactly what he was—"

"Yes, that's what he was doing."

I don't want to admit that.

"If you're serious, you'll have to make a choice. If he keeps coming, you'll have to trust him with our secret. Do you think you can trust him?"

I don't know.

"What do you want, Max?"

"Oh, Fusia," he says, feeling his nose. "This is not a good time to ask me what I want. I don't think you'd like it. Just ... remember what's at stake."

I don't need Max to remind me what's at stake. But I lie awake in the bed next to Helena, thinking about it anyway. And I'm still awake when Schillinger takes over for Mrs. Bessermann at the window.

And the next morning, on the way to work, I see a man hanged. In the market square, with a guard of SS and German soldiers, and half of Przemyśl there to watch him die.

He was hanged for hiding Jews.

I run to the factory. And there is Januka, coming across the iron bridge to hug me. They shot at her, and she ran so fast she slammed right into the back wall of the building instead of through the door. But she got away.

She says she doesn't know what we'll do if we ever see those soldiers again.

I keep seeing the dead man's legs swinging in the breeze.

And I know I can never share my secret with Lubek.

I can barely concentrate. I let the water pump go dry on one of my machines. I miss my quota almost every day that week.

Lubek takes his breaks with me on the iron bridge, and nothing seems to have changed. Except that he watches me even more closely. On Friday, when Januka goes inside, he says, "Have you thought about what you want to do after the war?"

I bite my lip. "It's not a good time for me to be making plans."

"There's never a bad time for making plans. Unless you don't want to."

"Lubek," I say. "I don't want to. Not right now. Not with you."

He nods and lights a cigarette. "Take your time," he says. "I've made up my mind. And I won't change it."

And then we hear a volley of shots in the distance. It's coming from the ghetto. We stare in that direction. There's screaming, rising up and echoing between the buildings, between the chugging trains. And three minutes later there's another volley. And then another.

"You were right," says Lubek. He makes the stub of his cigarette glow. "They're shooting them."

We listen to volley after volley, about three minutes apart.

Oh, Henek, I think. I don't care if you're a *Dummkopf* or a *yutz*. I don't want you to be dead. Danuta, why did you let him wait so long? Why didn't you make him come? Why didn't you come?

The shots are still going, volley after volley, when our break is over and we go back inside the factory. The noise of the machines drowns out the dying.

And I don't let Lubek see my tears.

22.

September 1943

FOR TWO DAYS AFTER THE SHOOTINGS, SMOKE BLACKS THE SKY. THE
Germans are burning bodies. Heaps of them. The smell is horrible. And it leaves a film of greasy soot all over the train station.
But there's still a guard at the gate of the ghetto, so someone must
be alive. I check the spot at the fence, just in case, but there's nothing under the rock.

Max is dark. Silent. His eyes are red.

He's the only Diamant left.

Lubek comes to the house two nights in a row. I try not letting
him in. I try to tell him I have to go to the market. But he just
turns and falls into step beside me, and then I can't buy what I
need, because he notices the amounts. The third day I ask the
inspector to come to my station first and get my count of screws,
and then I slip out the door quick, before Lubek and Januka are
done. I tie a scarf around my head against a chilly rain and run
through the damp streets until I see the door I want. I hesitate,
take a deep breath, and go inside the photography shop.

Emilika is at the counter, helping a man in a wet hat. Her eyes
widen when she sees me, but she goes on with the man's order. I
wait. Feeling nervous. Dirty and dowdy among all the smiling
portraits and canisters of film. The man turns up his collar

against the rain, the door shuts, and Emilika leans her elbows on the counter.

"Well. Stefania Podgórska. I thought you'd run off to Russia or something."

I shake my head. "Just a new apartment. It was ... an opportunity."

"You didn't say goodbye."

I was going to give her an excuse, an apology I worked on all afternoon at the machines, but I tell her the truth instead. "I am so sorry. I shouldn't have done it. It's just ... I thought you were mad at me, because of our ... conversation."

"What conversation?" she says lightly. "I don't remember."

I smile.

"How's Hela?" she asks. "How's your new apartment? Where is it?"

"Hela's fine." I avoid the question about the apartment. "But I do have a little problem."

"Oh?"

"I have a boy."

"Really?" She's all interest. I knew she would be.

"I have a boy ... that I don't want. And he is very ... umm ..."

"Persistent?"

"Unrelenting."

"Hints don't work?"

I shake my head.

"How about saying no?"

"Not so far."

"So how can I help?"

"I was wondering if maybe you could give me an extra print. Of an SS man."

Mischief blooms all over her face. Despite all her faults, I've still missed Emilika.

"I have the perfect thing!" She slips behind the curtain covering the back of the shop. "I just finished these this morning," she calls. "He's such a dream! And you're so lucky, because Mr. Markowski isn't here today ..."

Her voice gets louder again on my side of the curtain.

"... and I have a batch with a spot. Bad paper. It's hard to get good paper now. Everyone thinks bullets are more necessary. But I think this might do the job! What do you think?" She lays a photograph on the counter and spins it in my direction.

This is a beautiful man. With light hair and light eyes and a profile that any Norseman would be proud of. Even his teeth are perfect. He doesn't have his cap on, but there are two lightning bolts on his collar. I pick up the photograph.

"Oh, yes," I tell Emilika. "That will do."

I tilt my head at the picture. I think I might prefer dark hair.

And Lubek is going to hate me. So much.

I've still got the picture in my hand when the door of the shop opens. I don't see Emilika's expression. Not until it's too late.

"Guten Abend, Fräulein," says a voice.

And when I look back, it's the handsome SS man. The one in the photograph. And he sees me. Holding his photograph.

His mouth falls open.

He may be handsome, but in person, he looks a little stupid.

There are two more officers behind him, crowding into the shop. They chuckle and point when they see what I'm holding, elbowing their friend in the ribs. He frowns and turns to Emilika, says something in German, then switches to a very broken Polish.

"You are ... selling the ... *Fotografieren?*"

"Oh no!" says Emilika. "Just looking." She smiles brightly at him. "Handsome." She sneaks a hand across the counter to my arm and pinches.

"Handsome," I say.

"*Gut aussehend,*" one of the others translates, elbowing him again, and the officer's face lights up.

"You ... like?" he asks.

I nod, because I don't know what else to do.

Some things are the same everywhere, I suppose, because even in German, it's easy to see that the handsome SS man is now being teased by his friends. They're laughing and looking at me and jostling each other. Emilika pinches my arm again. Her lips barely move. "Run," she mouths. "Run away!"

I set the photograph on the counter. "Good day," I say, and start to move, but the SS man holds out an arm.

"*Nein, nein, Fräulein!*" Then he thinks about the word and says, "Wait," holding up a finger. There's a lot of talk from his friends. Then he gets shoved forward a little. He picks up the photograph, pushes it to my chest, and sticks out his cheek.

A kiss. I can keep the photograph for a kiss.

I kiss his cheek, because I need the photograph.

I wonder if he shot Henek. Or Danuta.

And then I kiss the other cheek he presents, because what would happen if I didn't? And while I do, I wonder if this man is responsible for the horrible smoke.

The other two SS men cheer and clap, slapping their friend on the back. Emilika reaches under the counter.

"Here," she says, handing me a large yellow envelope. I tuck the photograph inside it and under my coat.

"Thanks," I tell her quietly.

"Auf Wiedersehen, Fräulein!" calls the handsome one, waving.

I shut the shop door and stand between the display windows, catching my breath before I step out into the rain. That's the second time I've had to kiss a German soldier. I liked it even less than the first.

And I don't think I'll be telling Max about this.

When I come up the hill to Tatarska Street in the wet and soggy dark, I feel the familiar little flutter of fear. Like a bird has taken flight in my chest. I'm going to find the door kicked open. I'm going to find the house and bunkers empty. I'm going to see everyone shot. And tonight, when I turn the knob, the door is unlocked.

I think I'm going to be shot as soon as I open it.

I stand in the rain, the photograph safe under my coat.

The flutter becomes a painful squeeze.

I push open the door, slowly, and see Helena sitting in a chair, kicking her heels. Her eyes are big. And on the sofa sits a straight-backed woman with a fur hat and a dark brown coat. A woman I've never seen. I'm so glad she isn't Gestapo, I step inside and shut the door. It's silent but for my dripping.

Everyone must be in the attic.

I hope they're in the attic.

The woman stands up. "Miss Podgórska?"

"Yes?"

"My name is Mrs. Krawiecka."

I take out the envelope with the photograph, set it safely on the sugar tin, and hang my sopping coat beside the door. "Can I help you with something, Mrs. Krawiecka?"

"Yes, you can. I want you to hide a Jew for me."

I stare at the woman, scarf half off my head.

"What did you say?"

"I want you to hide a Jew for me. I can't be more frank than that."

I hang the scarf, pull up a kitchen chair, and sit on it. The woman settles back down on the sofa. Helena looks back and forth between the two of us.

"Why would you ask me something like that?" I say.

"Please. I am being honest with you. Have the courtesy to be honest with me. I have a Jew, Jan Dorlich, who would like to be hidden here."

"I don't know any Jan Dorlich."

"Really? You play the naive girl so well. Because he knows you. Mr. Dorlich escaped the ghetto before the trains came yesterday. Did you know the trains came again yesterday? The fences are being taken down. The ghetto is empty."

No, I hadn't heard this. My chest squeezes again. Hard.

"Mr. Dorlich got as far as my house, but I cannot let him stay. It isn't safe. He knows you are hiding Jews. The Hirsches, the Diamants, and the Bessermanns. So I really do think it would be best for everyone if you took one more."

Best. Best for who? For all of us? So she doesn't tell? And I suppose she won't be back, wanting money, either. This woman is nothing more than a blackmailer. Again.

I may kill Old Hirsch.

"Mrs. Krawiecka, I think you've come to the wrong house. I don't know you. I don't know a Jan Dorlich. And I am not hiding Jews. I work, take care of this house, and feed my little sister. How would I have time for taking care of all those other people? I've never even heard of those people."

"Stop playing games, my girl. You are in no position to refuse me."

"Or what? You're going to turn me and my little sister in to the Gestapo and let them torture a confession out of us? Is that what you want?"

Having just kissed a member of the Gestapo, my temper is boiling. This blackmailer has chosen the wrong day.

"You need to be sure of your facts before you come traipsing into someone's house, accusing them of something like hiding Jews. Why would I hide Jews? I hate Jews!"

I see Helena wince.

"But ..." The woman's hand goes to her throat.

"Maybe I should go to the Gestapo and tell them that you have a Jew."

"No! I mean, he was so certain ..."

"Do you see any Jews around here, Mrs. Krawiecka? Please, inspect the house. Look in every corner!"

She decides to do it. She walks the length of the sitting room and kitchen. Looking at everything. She goes into my bedroom and peeks behind the curtains and under the bed. She goes into the second bedroom. And comes right back out again. She comes back into the kitchen, opens the little door, and pokes around at the roosting chickens. She puts her foot on the ladder.

"Yes," I say loudly. "Look in the attic. Please!"

She climbs up far enough to stick her head through the attic floor and see the junk I have stored there. She climbs gingerly back down, stepping over the chickens, marches to the sugar tin, and picks up my envelope.

And finds a photograph of an SS officer.

Helena is covering her mouth. She seems to think Mrs. Krawiecka's frustration is funny. Or my temper.

"Well," the woman says, dropping the photograph on the table. "I have been given false information. I will know what to do. I apologize for taking your time."

I lock the door behind her and sit at the table. Helena goes to the window, and after a minute or so, calls, "She's gone!" I reach out without getting up and open the door to the attic.

The chickens get out. And then here come my Jews, one by one down the ladder. They heard most of it. And they are shaken.

"I'm sorry! I am sorry!" says Old Hirsch. His beard is growing back. "A thousand times I say that I am sorry!"

Max drops into the chair next to mine, rubbing his head. "Fusia, you do know Jan Dorlich."

I look up. I've had my face in my hands. "What?"

"He was our mailman. On Mickiewicza."

Mr. Dorlich. I'd forgotten. I can't believe I forgot, though I'm not sure I ever knew his first name. And no wonder he knows. He probably knew the other mailman who Schillinger and Hirsch paid to get them out of the ghetto. I look at Max. "What should we do?"

"I don't know. I hope he's all right, that's all."

Now I have guilt on top of my fright.

Then Max picks up the photograph of the SS man. "Oh," he says. "Yes, I think that will work. I think that will be very good."

He knows what it's for. And he's happy about it. I'm annoyed.

"Lubek's coming!" calls Helena.

And eight people have to scramble back up to the attic. Except Max. He looks at the ladder. He meets my eyes. And he goes into the bedroom. To listen. Helena follows and shuts the door. She has the dental textbook hidden beneath our pillow.

I didn't want to do this tonight.

Lubek tries to come in, but the door is locked.

"Wait a minute!" I check the house for belongings, shut the door to the attic, and set the photograph upright beside the sugar tin. And open the door.

"You left work quick today," Lubek says, stepping in out of the rain. Not even a greeting.

"I had somewhere I needed to be."

"You always seem to have somewhere to be." He shakes off his coat just outside the door, then hangs it up and shuts out the rain. "You're not avoiding me, are you?"

"No." I go and sit at the half table. Any minute now, he'll make tea and reach for the sugar.

I know I'm doing the right thing. I've chosen the seven lives above my head and the one below the floor. But I am dreading the moment he sees that photograph.

Lubek grins. "I think you don't want to talk about what I want to talk about."

One thing I do like about Lubek is that he gets straight to the point, without games. And right now, he's sitting where he can look me in the face. With his back to the picture. I decide to be direct.

"Lubek, you've been a good friend to me. But I'm not the girl for you."

"Why?"

Because I lie to everyone, all the time. Even to you. Because I could be shot any day. Because I loved a boy once, and he was murdered, and I'm afraid that will happen to me again.

I hadn't realized that last one.

"Because I like you," I say aloud. "But I don't love you."

There, Max. I hope you enjoyed that.

Lubek frowns. I'm surprised he hasn't pulled out a cigarette. "That could change."

Maybe it could. But it can't.

I shake my head at him. Lubek pushes back his chair, stands, and turns. To make the tea.

And he sees the photograph.

He goes as still as stone.

I cross my arms over my stomach. I know what I have to do.

"Who is that?" he asks.

"Just a boy I've been seeing."

"You've been seeing ... one of them?"

"He's very nice," I say, thinking how stupid he seemed in the photography shop. "He's ... from Salzburg."

Lubek stares at the handsome SS man, paralyzed. "Is that where you've been going after work?"

"Sometimes."

"And then you sit with me at this table."

To be fair, I have never invited Lubek to have tea with me at this table. But I haven't minded.

Lubek finally looks at me. And he is so angry. "I suppose he has money."

"Some," I whisper.

"I never knew you were so cheap."

I blink, but I don't let him see me flinch.

"I thought there was more to you. That you were better than Januka and those other girls. I thought you had a brain in your head. And now I find out you're just up for sale like the rest of them."

SHARON CAMERON

He goes to the door and grabs his coat.

"I told you I don't change my mind. I was wrong. It's changed." He pulls open the door and looks back. "You disgust me."

And the door slams so hard it rattles the walls.

I get up from the table, walk to the door, and turn the lock. Then I lean against it.

That had hurt. A lot.

It's been a horrible day.

When I open my eyes, Max is coming back into the room with an untucked shirt and bare feet. I'm sure he heard Lubek leave. I haven't given the signal to the others in the attic yet, and he doesn't, either. He just comes and puts his arms around me. I cry into his neck.

"I'm sorry," he says. "I'm sorry."

"He called me cheap," I whisper.

"I know." He strokes my hair. "You're not cheap. You're the best person I know."

It feels so good to be held. Max puts his hands on either side of my head and kisses my forehead. Like his father used to.

Only it's not like his father at all.

The feel of his mouth on my skin makes my breath stop.

And everything has changed.

We pause, his hands in my hair. I think Max is going to kiss me. Really kiss me.

But he can't. Because I've crossed the room to wipe my face and put away the teapot. He stands by the door where I left him.

And my heart is beating like I've run a race.

"I'll let them know they can come down," Max says.

"Wait," I say.

He stops. Frozen.

"You've got some dirt in your hair."

He runs a hand through his hair while I do something unnecessary with the teapot. And soon there are people down the ladder and the room is full and he's reminding everyone to be quiet for the millionth time, because we have an SS man living next door.

I take the photograph and shove it under my mattress.

Lying in bed that night, I think over every conversation, every minute of time I can remember spending with Max. Had he really wanted to kiss me, or was I just upset? Maybe I made it up in my head. Had I wanted to kiss him? What would Izio think if Max had kissed me?

I don't want to love anyone. Not during a war.

Love will make me hurt.

Then Siunek is startling me from a deep sleep I didn't know I was in. My neck aches. I've been sleeping on the textbook. And the fear wakes up, flutters in my chest, jumps into my throat. I sit straight up in bed.

"What's wrong?"

"They're coming to the door," Siunek says. "Henek and Danuta!"

"Get Max," I say, and throw the covers off the bed.

I've kissed Henek's cheek and hugged Danuta, and now they're with Max, their three heads together, talking softly. Max is holding both his brother's hands.

And he's crying.

I want to stroke that dirt from his hair.

Henek waited too long. Nearly. Hiding until the last trains were gone. And then the SS started clearing the buildings. Shooting whoever might be left. But Danuta had been ready. She'd saved a little food. Clothes that would pass in the busy streets.

And then they'd decided to sneak through the city after curfew, giving the Germans all the best chances to spot them in places where they shouldn't be.

I'm just glad they're alive. Especially for Max.

But there are twelve of us now. And there are people who know we are here.

I wonder how long we'll last.

The pain behind my eyes aches all day, and at work, Lubek treats me like I'm already dead.

I go straight to the market after the factory and buy what's left, which is a ten-pound sack of small potatoes, some carrots, and four onions. I haul it wearily up the hill to Tatarska, dealing with my usual flutter of fear. Maybe today is the day Mrs. Krawiecka has sent the Gestapo. Or that the officers of the *Judenrat* told what they knew, if they're even still alive. Or maybe Ernst the SS man has stopped drinking long enough to figure out what's on the other side of his wall.

I wonder if today is the day I should make soup.

When I lock the door behind me, tired, aching, worried, and frightened, Max and Siunek are milling around the table. Moving the dishes in the sink. Eyeing me. Eyeing each other. Shuffling their feet.

Guilty.

I drop my potato sack. "Okay. Who ate the butter? Because I've been blaming Helena."

They don't answer.

"Was it the sugar, then?" I drop into a chair.

"Would you like a cup of tea?" asks Siunek.

I decide to accept. My head is splitting open. He's already got the water hot.

"Is something wrong with Henek?" I ask. "Or Danuta?"

Max sits down opposite me and shakes his head.

"Dziusia?"

"No, its ..."

"Hela?" I nearly leap from my chair.

"No, no." Max rubs his head. "I need to ask you a question."

I wish he would.

"I want to know how you would feel about ... hiding one more."

"One more who?"

"Jan Dorlich."

I sit back in my chair. Siunek is making my tea, but he's watching me carefully. I push on my aching temple and sigh. "If he needs help ... then he needs help. And I don't think that woman is going to give it to him. Not for long."

"So ..." Siunek says. "You would take him?"

"I'll hang just as easily for eleven as for ten, I guess." I look to Max. "Should I go to that woman?"

"No need," he says.

"What do you mean, no need?"

"I mean," says Max, "he's in the attic."

I look at Max and then at Siunek.

"The mailman is in the attic?"

They nod. Siunek puts the tea in front of me. I blow on it and take a grateful sip.

"Then tell him we'll have something to eat as soon as I drink my tea."

Max sits back in his chair. "You were right," Siunek says, like Max has won a bet.

Max glances up. Meets my eyes. Smiles. It's almost shy. Then he goes into the bedroom with Siunek.

I think he's trying not to be alone with me.

The next day after work, I go to the market, because we are again out of food. I use the last of Hirsch's money for the week and buy what I can find. Turnips and some *kasha*. I trudge up the hill to Tatarska Street, wondering if today is the day. If I'll open the door and the house will be a grave.

Maybe I'll put the turnips in the rest of the soup. To make more soup.

And when I lock the door behind me, and my back is tired and I have a cut on my hand from one of the screw machines, Max and Siunek are standing in the kitchen. Shifting their feet. They look like Mrs. Krajewska's boys caught with a pack of cigarettes.

I take off my coat and sit down at the table. Max sits down opposite. Siunek sets down a cup of tea.

"Who is in the attic?" I ask.

"Monek and Sala," Max replies.

It's like the clouds are raining Jews.

"They've been hiding in a cellar without anything to eat since the ghetto was closed," Siunek says. "They had nowhere to go ..."

"But how did they know to come here?"

More guilt.

"Wait. What's their last name?"

Max hesitates. "Hirsch."

"I am sorry!" calls Old Hirsch from the ladder.
I blow on my tea and sip it.
Thirteen, I think. Thirteen Jews in the attic.
It's not like the Nazis could kill me more.

23.

December 1943

TATARSKA 3 IS FULL. WE HAVE TO START USING THE SECOND BEDROOM, creating a private corner with a sheet. But one bucket is not really enough, and Helena has to empty it several times a day, just to deal with the smell. And it takes longer to get to the attic from there, and longer to get up the ladder. I have to tell Mrs. Krajewska or occasionally one of the girls at work to wait after they knock, that I'm getting dressed, while thirteen people snatch their belongings, line up, and go one by one up the ladder. And if my visitor is someone I've already seen that day, I really do have to change, so I'm wearing something different than the last time they saw me. Mrs. Krajewska, I think, has decided I am vain. But the worst difficulty is maintaining silence when thirteen people are arguing all the time.

Monek Hirsch is Old Hirsch's nephew, Siunek's cousin, but that doesn't mean that any of them get along. I'm not sure they got along before the war. Sala is Monek's wife, and she and Danuta work together against Mrs. Bessermann, and Mrs. Bessermann sides with Janek against Dziusia. Jan Dorlich always agrees with Schillinger, whose mail he used to deliver, and Cesia just stays with Siunek. And Max defends Henek to the skies, even when Henek's being unreasonable. Unless he's having heated arguments with Siunek, Ernst or no Ernst, about the proper way to slice carrots for soup.

Helena runs away when she can.

And then there's the laundry. Each person's clothes and blankets must be washed once a week, or we have more arguments over smell than from the bucket. But it's difficult to bring enough water without alerting Mrs. Krajewska, since the well sits directly outside her window. If two washings get done each day, I suggest, including mine and Helena's, then everyone's will get done in a week, and then the cycle can start all over again. Eight days into this, Max comes to me after work.

"So Old Hirsch tried to pay Mrs. Bessermann to do his laundry with the food money, and now Mrs. Bessermann's mad because she didn't get paid, even though she made Cesia do her share. And now Cesia won't go again, and Siunek says she shouldn't, and it's Danuta's turn, too, but Henek says she's too delicate and won't do it himself."

I set down the bags I've just carried up the hill. "Max," I say, "I have just made thirty-one thousand screws in twelve hours and walked five miles to find us dinner. This one is your problem."

And the shopping is mine. The farmer's wife who sells me milk asks how two girls could possibly drink so much, and I get almost the same question from the grocer who sells me the eggs. And these comments are for only half a week's supplies, because on other days I shop at different markets to avoid this very problem. Mrs. Krajewska mentions that she sees me coming with bags every day, and even Lubek noticed the *kasha* sack.

So I create a business. A fake one. I am now buying food from farmers and having Helena resell it in the market while I'm at work. Because our mother needs money in Germany. Just like I told Lubek. Almost.

This means Helena trudges up the hill in the evenings with two heavy bags of supplies from the list I've given her, and every morning leaves down the hill with two bags that look like they're full when they aren't, because Max has rigged them that way. He tacked two pieces of wood inside to keep them open, a board across the top where a loaf of bread or other things can balance. Full bags. Helena practices walking hunched over, as if she's carrying a weight, and if Mrs. Krajewska asks why her bags are still full, she says she didn't sell much that day and will take it back out tomorrow.

The evening bags really are too heavy for her to carry up the hill, and the wind is bitter, even without the snow. We're low on coal. And then Old Hirsch hides the food money because I refuse to bring home cigarettes.

For two days, we eat cabbage and potatoes, and on the second day, there's not much of that. The chickens are in danger. And then, Ernst or no Ernst, there's a fight. Max, Schillinger, Henek, and Danuta against Old Hirsch, Monek, Sala, and Mrs. Bessermann. But Siunek finds the money. In a little hollow on top of one of the roof beams in the attic. Max takes over the accounts, making a careful tally on the wall where Old Hirsch can see it, and when I bring home dried fish and dried apples, and the chickens save themselves by producing four eggs, our little war is over.

We need more grocery money.

So the next time I get paid, I come home from the market with an investment. Four old sweaters, ugly and full of holes, and five pairs of knitting needles. The children carefully unravel the sweaters; Danuta saves the water from the boiled beets and re-dyes the yarn. And when the yarn is dry, everyone learns how to knit. The women who know teach the men who don't, my thirteen are occupied, and Siunek is a surprise prodigy, able to finish a sleeve in just a couple of hours. I sell the first sweater to one of the girls at work, and within a few days, I've got orders for five more.

Even Old Hirsch can't think about cigarettes when he's counting stitches.

I use a quarter of the sweater money to buy more old sweaters. The next quarter of the sweater money I turn into something good, like chicken or cheese or, one memorable day, five jars of pickles. But the rest of the sweater money I hoard. Secretly. Because it's nearly Christmas. And because Christmas Day is on a Saturday, I will have Friday, Saturday, and Sunday away from the factory. And Jewish or not, my thirteen need a break.

We need a celebration.

I am full of secrets.

On the Sunday before, I get up early. Cesia is doing her watch at the window, though I'm not sure she wasn't asleep because she starts when I swing my legs from the bed. I tuck the blankets back around Helena, slip on my shoes and coat, and act like I'm going out to the toilet. But I lock the door quietly, wrap a scarf around my head, and take off down Tatarska Street while the cathedral bells ring. Curfew is over, and I have the sweater money already tucked inside my coat.

One of the older ladies at the factory told me about a man. Eight kilometers outside Przemyśl and far off the road in an old house in the forest. A man who has things for sale. All sorts of things. Things you can't get in the city markets. Things it's probably best not to ask where they came from. And if you're lucky, he'll bargain with you.

I'm going to try my luck.

I keep a fast pace in the semidarkness, my breath coming out in a cloud, and when I find the turn off the main road, the sun is only just beginning to thaw the air. My body is warm from the exercise. Sweating even. But my fingers are numb, nose and toes tingling. There's a house coming into sight through the trees. Not much more than a shack. Dark. No lights. But there's a barn to one side with a lantern in the window. The barn door creaks open, and a man sticks his head out.

"What do you want?"

I stop short. "To make ... some purchases?" Maybe I've got the wrong house.

He looks me over, a black knit cap pulled down over his ears, and pushes the door open a little wider.

"Quick, girl," he says. "You're letting the heat out."

I dart inside, and the barn is a warehouse. Bottles, cans, and boxes line shelves along one wall, and the horse stalls are like market booths with goods piled inside them. There are cows in the barn, too, helping with the heat. Maybe they're part of what's for sale.

I have a long look at what's on offer. Five dozen socks, army-issue. A crate of canned beans. Stockings. Perfume. One tube of lipstick. Vodka. Aspirin. Toilet paper, army-issue. And stack after stack of tinned pears. I wonder if Officer Berdecki shops here.

In fifteen minutes, I've gathered what I want. I know what I can pay. I don't know if he'll give it all to me at that price.

And then I see a box tucked in the corner. Odds and ends, from someone's house, maybe. And to one side, there is a doll.

Not a baby doll. A girl, with blonde braids and blue painted eyes and red lips. She has sawdust leaking out of one leg and stains on her clothes. I hesitate, then put the doll with the other items in the crate and bring it all up to the man in the knit cap.

He looks at the items, does some addition in his head, and names a price. I shake my head and offer him what I have. He shakes his head.

"I'm not giving things away, angel."

"If I was someone's angel," I reply, "I'd have more money than I do."

He grins and names another price. Still too high. I offer to halve the sugar. It's cheaper here, but I can get it in the city. He shrugs. I take out two cans of pears. He shrugs again. I hesitate and take away one of the kilo sacks of fine flour—the kind I haven't seen outside a bakery since 1941—and a bottle of aspirin. Then I hesitate again, take out the doll, and put back the aspirin. I paid half my wages for aspirin when Henek got typhus. The man watches me set the doll aside.

"St. Nicholas Day has come and gone," he says.

"I know." I'd told Helena that St. Nicholas would have a hard time getting to Przemyśl this year. He'd have to come right through the middle of a war. Which didn't mean much when he managed to find the Krajewska boys.

"Okay," the man says. "I'll find you a sack."

I don't know why I'm so disappointed about the doll. It isn't practical. And it could cause problems with Dziusia and Janek. Not that they would be expecting to celebrate St. Nicholas Day. Though I'm sure they remember treats at Hanukkah well enough.

I pay him, and he packs up the items in a sack that can be tied on my back. It's heavy. Very heavy, and the eight kilometers back to the city leave me sore and aching. But I am pleased. My thirteen are going to be so surprised. I go to the market on the way home, even though there are only a few booths selling on a Sunday, and get some cabbages and more potatoes to give some excuse for my absence. Then I haul everything up to Tatarska at once, so Helena won't have to.

I don't know who's at the window, watching me come, but I try to hold the crate in front of me as I come up the hill so they can't see the sack on my back. And then Mrs. Krajewska is coming out her door to wave at me.

"Miss Podgórska! There you are. You've been selling for your sister today, I see. You shouldn't do that on a Sunday."

I stop in front of the well.

"But I do understand about your mother. I knocked on your door, but no one answered . . ."

My eyes dart to my curtained bedroom window, where I know someone is watching. Helena must be out.

". . . and I wanted to tell you that you need to be careful with that cat."

"What? Oh, the cat. Yes. Why?"

"Because it's after your chickens! I could hear it thumping around in there while they squawked . . ."

That sounds like Siunek falling down the ladder in his sock feet. Mrs. Krajewska might be surprised to know that my cat is six feet tall, knits, and needs a shave.

". . . and I also wanted to tell you that we'll be leaving over Christmas, going to my sister's. So could you watch over the house?"

"And what about your nephew?"

"Ernst? He's going with us, then rejoining his unit in Berlin. It's a shame you never spent any proper time together ..."

She goes on for a while, and when I tell her my arms are aching, she finally gives me dates and times. I sneak around back to the toilets, leave the sack with my illegal items behind the building, and that night, when everyone is asleep, bring it back inside, covered in a blanket, and while Mrs. Bessermann is staring out the window, I shove it under my bed beneath a sleeping Helena.

"What are you doing?" whispers Mrs. Bessermann, turning around at the noise.

"I thought I heard a mouse."

I push the sack farther under the bed, but something falls out. It's the doll.

I smile.

I fly through my work that week, singing while I do it, and make my quota every day. During my breaks, I work on the doll. I sew up her leaks, wash her clothes, Januka rebraids her hair, and even brings me some tiny ribbon snips to tie at the ends. I use an inky pen to repair some spots on her eyebrows and lashes where the paint has come off, and when we're done, she looks nearly new. Or new enough. She looks pretty.

"Your sister will be so excited!" says Januka. "I wish I had a little sister."

Lubek watches us work in silence, smoking, waiting for Januka to be done. He leaves the factory with her these days.

I wrap the doll in butcher paper and hide it in the rafters of the storage room next to the toilet block. That night, I can't sleep. I'm tossing under the covers. Max turns in his chair beside the window.

"What are you up to?" he whispers.

It's the first time he's started a conversation just for us since that night he kissed my forehead. He's been avoiding me, and I've been afraid of what that means. I don't know what I want it to mean. Tonight, I don't care. I tiptoe through the cold in my nightgown and sit on the floor.

"So, Fusia," he says. "Back at the window."

He's staring out through the curtain crack to the little pool of light on Tatarska Street, arms crossed, pushing the chair onto its back legs. He gives me a glance.

"Are you going to tell me what's happening?"

I shake my head. Hiding my smile. "There's nothing to tell."

"You're a terrible liar."

"Actually, I'm a very good liar. Just only to the right people."

"So I'm not the right people?"

"If you want to be lied to, no."

He seems to take offense to this, though I can't imagine why. "I thought maybe you were so happy because you were in love."

"With who?"

"How can I keep up with your loves?"

There is anger in those words, and it hurts. I feel sure I made up that feeling with the kiss on the forehead.

Then he whispers, "I'm sorry."

I watch his dark head, his dark eyes, staring at the little bit of light outside. He used to risk getting shot just to leave the cage of the ghetto. Now he can't leave these three rooms and an attic.

He must be going out of his mind.

"I was thinking of *Mame*," he says. "And lighting the candles. And challah. And how she was always cooking and cooking and used to send me out at the last minute for the little things she forgot. I'd run fast down the sidewalk, because she said if I didn't get the jam, there wouldn't be any jelly doughnuts. But really, I just liked the wind in my hair."

I can imagine that. Small Max darting like a fish through the current of Mickiewicza. "What day of Hanukkah is it?" I ask.

"Two."

I only spent one night of Hanukkah with the Diamants, since usually I'd gone back to the farm for Advent and Christmas by then. But I remember the doughnuts. And the candles.

"I've been thinking about gingerbread," I say. "This whole week, Mama would have been making gingerbread, and all the desserts for Christmas Eve."

"More than one dessert?"

"There were twelve courses, for the twelve apostles, so half of them were usually desserts. But I loved the gingerbread. Mama would always make one into the shape of a star for each of us."

Max stares out the window.

"We'll never get them back," he says. "Even if the war ends. I didn't know I was living in days that I could never get back."

I wish I could give them to him. Wrapped in paper and tied with a ribbon.

"We're always living days we can never get back," I say. "So we make new ones. That's all."

"Are we talking?" mumbles Dziusia from her blanket. In an effort to get her to sleep quietly, her father has told her that people don't talk at night. Max smiles at Dziusia's curled-up form, and then he smiles at me.

305

I don't know who reaches out first. Maybe it's both of us. But suddenly, Max has my hand in both of his.

"Will you stay with me, Fusia? While I watch?"

I do. I stay with him until the moon has set and my eyes are drooping and Schillinger takes over at the window.

And in the morning, when Schillinger is still at the window and everyone else is asleep, I very gently wake Helena. It takes a few seconds for her eyes to focus. Then I whisper in her ear, covering it with my hands. She nods and creeps out of bed. Sleepily. Like she's going out to the toilet. But I see when Schillinger sees her, darting across the courtyard in the frost. His back stiffens.

"What's she doing?" he mutters. I creep up behind him and watch through the curtain. I had meant for her to put on her coat. And her shoes. She knocks on Mrs. Krajewska's door. She looks through the windows. Then she comes running back into our side of Tatarska.

"She's gone!" Helena yells. At the top of her lungs.

Siunek, Janek, and Jan Dorlich are up from the sitting room floor, Old Hirsch, who has the sofa, still struggling to get free of the cushions. Mrs. Bessermann appears in the doorway, Cesia and Dziusia with her, and I even see Monek and Sala, and Danuta's sleepy face following Henek, coming out of the second bedroom. Max has been on his feet since Helena ran out of the house. His mouth is tight. He's afraid.

"Do you want to tell them?" I ask.

Helena nods. She's bouncing on her feet. About to burst.

"Mrs. Krajewska," she announces, "has gone on a trip!"

I see blank faces all around. Old Hirsch waves a hand and lies back down on the sofa.

"And she took her husband, and her boys, and her ugly SS man with her! And her ugly SS man isn't coming back!"

Old Hirsch sits back up again.

"So for one week," Helena says, "we can make noise. Like this!" And she jumps up and down, waving her arms and squealing.

There's a moment when my thirteen don't know what to do.

Then Janek says, "I want to make noise!" He runs into the room, fast, in case anyone might try and stop him, whooping and jumping with Helena. Mrs. Bessermann laughs. Jan Dorlich laughs, loudly, then Danuta takes Dziusia by the hand and skips her in circles, singing an old marching song.

> *Hey! Whoever is a Pole, to your bayonets!*
> *Either we win, or we are ready*
> *To build a barrier with our corpses,*
> *To slow down the giant that brings chains to the*
> *world.*
> *Hey! Whoever is a Pole, to your bayonets!*

Which is maybe a little violent for Christmas, but the children are enjoying it. Monek and Sala, who only got married the week before they left the ghetto, dance a waltz to it, and Siunek gets Cesia to join in, stepping over Helena and Janek, who are now rolling across the floor. And Max is laughing.

It's like a cloudy day in the mountains, when the water is flat as the metal of a tank. And then the sun comes out and makes everything sparkle.

We're in danger of breaking our furniture.

I dodge my way through the chaos to the bedroom and drag my sack from beneath the bed, bringing it out to the kitchen while everyone is occupied. I poke up the fire. I've got the water ready to heat, and then I fish a tin out of my sack.

Mrs. Bessermann, who always watches everything, comes straight across the room. "That's not ..." She takes the tin from me. "Coffee!"

"Surprise!" I say.

This brings Old Hirsch from the sofa, to supervise its making, and the smell is such a relaxation, such a memory of home that the room settles into a happy buzz of conversation. I slice the rest of the bread with a scraping of butter for the children and call the women to the kitchen. Max comes, too, because he's curious, and I empty my sack with a flourish. A warrior with her trophies. Sala reaches out and touches the flour like she can't believe it's there. Max quirks his brow.

"Now," I say, "who knows how to make challah?"

The cooking and baking become a group effort, with Siunek and Max and even Schillinger sometimes lending a hand, since he had always been the one to peel the potatoes for his wife. Mrs. Bessermann will let no one help with the challah. I leave Max chopping beets and take Helena out to the storage shed, where we can't be seen by whoever is on watch at the window. And I unwrap the doll.

"Oh," says Helena. "Oh, oh."

"St. Nicholas was a little late."

"That's okay," she whispers.

"I thought maybe when I'm at work, she could keep you company."

Helena nods. She touches the braids, the red lips, and moves the doll's arms. Then she looks up at me. Worried. "But what about Dziusia and Janek?"

"They don't celebrate St. Nicholas the same way," I say, feeling guilty. "But maybe we should keep her hidden, just for now."

Helena nods, kisses the doll, and wraps her back up. We go inside, and while I'm rolling out the dough for the cookies and Monek Hirsch is telling a loud story about a fish he once caught—with heavy corrections from his uncle—I hear a whoop from the bedroom. Helena has presented Dziusia and Janek with her ball, the one Mr. Szymczak patched, that Max brought on his back to Tatarska while trying not to be shot. The three of them devise a game that involves kicking the ball through one doorway or the other, and we're lucky it never lands in the slop bucket or the soup.

Tatarska 3 smells like Christmas all day.

When the sun is setting, I bring all three of our lamps to the table for the third day of Hanukkah, Old Hirsch sprinkles salt on the challah, and we eat borscht and latkes and tinned pears and one of the chickens, sacrificed while Helena was safely playing ball. Then there are the cookies, cut into rather awkward stars because I don't have a cookie cutter. And after we've eaten our fill and the dishes are stacked up and the children are sleepy, I have everyone gather in the living room and bring out my last surprise.

Vodka. And a whole case of cigarettes. My unsold ration. Old Hirsch kisses both my cheeks, Monek hurries for glasses, and half the room lights up.

We play Guess What I Am. And Jan Dorlich, we discover, is a dark horse as an actor. But after the vodka has gone around, the whole thing devolves into Max with a soup pot on his head, talking when he's supposed to be silent, taunting Hitler in what I think is supposed to be a British accent, only it isn't. He's obviously being Churchill, but no one will guess it, just to make him keep on. I laugh so hard I cry, and when Henek, who has no sense of humor, finally yells, "Churchill, Churchill! God save us all!" I laugh even harder, and Siunek actually ends up on the floor.

Max takes off his soup pot and sits next to me on the sofa. "I was good, yes?"

"You were good, no!" I giggle. He grins and puts his arm around me.

And the sofa feels warm and cozy, and I love everyone.

The good feeling lasts for a long time. While the children play ball in the bedroom and Helena sleeps with her doll and I sit with Max on his nights at the window. Even when Mrs. Krajewska returns and we have to go back to being quiet again. When the cigarettes are gone, and the sweaters need knitting, the laundry is dirty, and we're back to eating cabbages. When the weather turns bitter and I go to work in the snow and Helena struggles up the hill with the food bags and there's just not money to buy enough coal.

Until a day when Sala Hirsch calls the warning from the window and my thirteen disappear into the attic. When I answer the door and find the Gestapo.

When the SS man looks at his list and says, "*Fräulein*, we require your house."

24.

January 1944

I STARE AT THE SS MAN. HE HAS TWO MORE GESTAPO WITH HIM. THEY LOOK irritated. Bored. And I can only say, "What?"

The man's brows come down below his cap. "We require your house," he says again, in very distinct, German-accented Polish. As if I might be stupid. And then he pushes his way inside, the other two officers following after.

They walk through the empty rooms. They look in all the corners, and the first officer makes notes on his list. And my nerves are tingling, ready to burst through my skin.

They want my house. The Nazis want my house.

Please, Helena. Don't come home.

Then the officer opens the door to the ladder, stepping back and making a noise of disgust at the chickens. He looks at me. "Where does this ladder go?"

My throat is dry. Closed up.

"Where does the ladder go?" he barks.

"Attic," I whisper. And I watch his shiny boots step one rung at a time up the ladder. He goes all the way up. His boots disappear. The other two officers watch me closely, the picture of Mary and the Christ just behind them, while the boots make the ceiling creak over my head.

Please, God. Please, God. Please, God.

The attic is quiet. The sky is quiet. The man comes down the ladder and makes a note on his clipboard. He says. "The empty building across the street will now be a German hospital ..."

I'd seen workmen going into the old college last week, doing repairs. I hadn't guessed what it meant.

"... and the staff must have housing. The new tenants will arrive in two hours. Take your personal belongings and leave the furniture."

Two hours. The Nazis want my house in two hours.

"But ... I can't pack ..."

I can't leave here at all.

"Leave or be shot," the man says.

I stare at him.

"If you are here, we will shoot you. Do you understand, *Fräulein*?"

I understand. Too well.

"We will be back in two hours," says the SS man. He ticks his list, and the other Gestapo follow him out the door.

I lean on a chair and suck in one long, gasping breath. And then I jump over the chickens and scurry up the ladder, pushing aside the loose planks and crawling through the little door.

Danuta lets out a tiny scream, but other than that, it's silent. Even the ones who are crying. I can't imagine how they felt when they knew the Gestapo was coming up the ladder.

Or maybe I can.

Max is on his knees, a thick plank of wood in his hand. I think it was to bash my head in.

312

"Fusia!" he hisses. "Tell us next time! What—"

"They're taking the house," I say. "The Nazis are taking the house in two hours. Stay where you are. I'm going to find a place for us to go."

But where am I going to take thirteen Jews? Right now?

I don't know.

Max grabs my arm. "When they come, we're going to fight. That's already decided."

"I'm going to find something."

"Take Hela," Max says. "And don't come back."

"If she comes, tell her to hide at her castle ruins ..."

"Fusia, take Helena and do not come back!"

"Tell her I'll find her there," I say, and go down the ladder like he hasn't spoken.

I run down Tatarska Street in the bitter wind, and my eyes are roaming, roaming. Where can I take them? A cellar. A garage. How will I get them there in the daylight? They're dingy. Shaggy. Unshaven. Pale. They look like they've been sitting in an attic. Where can we go?

I fly through the door of the housing department, causing outrage when I push aside the men and women in line. The woman who helped me get Tatarska is sitting at the desk.

"I need an apartment," I say. "Right now. The Germans are taking the house, and my sister and I have nowhere to—"

"Five days at least to get an apartment," the lady says. She doesn't call me her butterfly or mouse or anything else this time. Probably because I'm being rude.

"More like two weeks!" yells a man from the back.

"You don't have anything right now?" I ask her.

"Of course not!"

After that I run aimlessly up and down the streets, because I don't know what else to do. Looking for anything that might be empty, where I could put thirteen people for a day, for two days. Two weeks until I get a new apartment. But would that apartment even have a place I could hide them? I knock on two doors where there are signs in the window, but no one is willing to let me move in before I do my paperwork. I run into the cathedral, wet my cold fingers, kneel, and cross myself so fast it makes two women stop their praying and turn their heads.

I ask. I beg. The arches of the ceiling feel empty above me.

The bells ring.

I have half an hour.

I have a decision to make.

I run from the cathedral, letting the heavy oak doors thud shut, and don't stop running until I'm at the door of Tatarska 3.

Helena is there. And Max. And all of my thirteen, just standing in the living room. Max has his board. Mrs. Bessermann a kitchen knife. Siunek has a hammer.

We have fifteen minutes.

The door isn't even locked.

Max sets down his board and walks up to me. He takes my face in his hands and looks me in the eyes. "You listen to me," he says. "You have done enough. You take Helena, and you run. Do you understand me?"

His eyes are dark and angry and desperate.

"Go, Fusia," says Siunek.

"Run," says Jan Dorlich, and Sala, and Mrs. Bessermann. They each put a hand on me where they can.

"Go now, girl," says Old Hirsch.

"Run," says Dr. Schillinger.

Dziusia puts her arms around my waist. And I am looking at Max, and I am crying.

Because I cannot run.

"Helena," I whisper. "Go to Emilika. Until Mama comes home."

My little sister shakes her head. She puts her arms around me with Dziusia.

We have ten minutes.

"Stefania," Max says. He's still holding my head while I cry. He's crying, too. "You take Hela, and you go. Right now!"

Except I can't live with that. I want to live, but I can't live with that.

I shake my head.

"I'll make you go!" Max says.

"Fusia," says Henek. "You run! Now."

Danuta is still crying. She puts a hand on my shoulder.

I don't know what to do. What can we do? Helena has to go. My heart beats and beats, hard against my chest. I can't watch Max cry. I close my wet eyes.

And a calm steals over me. Warm. Soft. Like the night I found the furs. Like the night I found Tatarska Street. And like that night, I have a conversation with some other part of myself.

Send them to the attic. Open the windows. Act like you're not afraid. Get the second bedroom clean.

That's ridiculous. Why should I do that when I'm about to be shot?

Because they're not going to shoot you.

But the Gestapo said they would shoot me. And then they'll find the others.

They won't shoot anyone. They just want a room. You can give them a room.

They'll shoot Helena.

No, they just need the room. Act like you're not afraid. Give it to them.

But . . .

Give it to them. Do it now. They're coming.

I open my eyes. And Max is shaking me. He might have just slapped my face a little.

They're going to think I'm crazy. I'm risking Helena's life. It might not work. My head says it won't work.

But inside, I know. It's quiet there. And I am not alone.

"Go up to the attic," I say. "All of you!"

"Please," Max whispers to me. "Don't."

"Go!" And I walk away from his hands, from all their hands, and turn the lock on the door.

"Go," Max says, his voice low. "And don't make a sound."

And they go. Like ghosts up the ladder, taking their weapons with them. They'll fight, when the time comes. Only the time won't come. Max grabs his piece of wood, looks at me one more time, and goes up the ladder. Now his eyes are only sad. More than sad. He looks lost.

He thinks he won't see me again.

"Hela," I say. "Quick. Empty the bucket from the bedroom and leave it outside. Then chase out the chickens and stay with them. I'm going to lock the door behind you."

She doesn't say a word. Just pulls on her coat and does it while I take down the curtain where the bucket was and throw it under my bed. I pull back the window curtains and push up the sash. Breathing the clean air. I'd forgotten how this room looked with the light streaming in. And then I sweep. Singing. The hidden space in the attic is directly over my head.

I know Max thinks I've lost my mind.

I might have lost my mind.

If I have, I prefer it.

The bells ring in the steeples. And there's a fist on the door.

I don't hurry to answer it. I don't go slowly, either. I go carrying my broom. I'll open the door when I get there.

I'm going to find out whether I live.

Or whether I die.

I open the door.

It's an SS man. A different SS man. Stern-looking. With a nose red from cold and a pistol. He's alone.

"Miss ... Podgórska?" he says, checking his list. "I am here about the housing?"

More decent Polish. I take a deep breath.

"Yes, they said you would come. I was just sweeping out the room for you."

"I will look, please?"

I didn't know the Gestapo knew how to ask permission. I open the door wider and smile at Helena, who is shivering in her coat, peeking around one side of the toilets. The SS officer thinks I'm smiling at him.

He walks through to the back bedroom, makes some notes, and when he passes my bed, he stops and picks up an envelope. It's the letter from my mother. Helena had been reading it again last night. Suddenly his face is much less stern.

"Salzburg?" he says. "I am from Salzburg!"

"My mother and brother are in a labor camp there. That's why I'm raising my little sister."

"The one outside? She is very pretty. Very shy." He smiles.

He doesn't seem like he's about to shoot me.

He sits with me at the table. He says they have only two nurses left to house, and he doesn't see why they would each need a bedroom. They can share, while my sister and I stay in our current room. Would that be acceptable? It's so good that we didn't move too quickly, because it works quite well for us to stay. Soldiers will be coming in a few minutes to deliver two beds. And could he take a letter to my mother for me when he goes back to Salzburg?

I thank him and shut the door.

He had a gun, but he didn't use it.

I am alive. Helena is alive. We are all alive.

Then I have to open the door again because the soldiers are here, carrying painted iron bed frames. They set them up in the back bedroom, and the German conversation and the banging are loud. I wonder what my thirteen can be thinking. And in the middle of it all, the two nurses arrive. Karin and Ilse. Young. In their twenties, with painted nails and freshly curled hair. And they do not seem so pleased with their situation. They had not intended to share a room. They cannot live without electricity. Or a proper kitchen. And the toilets are where?

I get all this from the reactions of the soldiers setting up their beds, because the two women do not speak Polish at all.

Maybe they'll want to go away so much that they'll find a way to make it happen.

While they're settling themselves in, I say that I'll be moving a few things out of their way. I do this by pointing in several different directions and leaving them looking confused. They seem to be just as repelled by me as by their new surroundings. Helena sits at the table, ready to whistle if there's trouble—like if the nurses try to climb the ladder, or more Nazis come to live with us—while I creep up to the attic with the dirty bucket and the clean one full of water. I don't think these women will be leaving anytime soon.

Max is already opening the false wall. He's half in, half out the little door when I go to my knees. He grabs my forehead and puts it to his, and says in barely a whisper, "You are such an idiot."

I nod, my forehead rubbing against his. I know.

I leave the buckets and crawl back down.

And later that afternoon, Ilse comes to me and says, *"Ratte. Ratten!"* She's pointing upward. At the ceiling. I realize she's telling me that we have rats.

I think she's telling me she can hear something in the attic.

"Oh," I say, letting understanding blossom on my face. "Rats, yes. Sorry."

I shrug. She looks disgusted.

I need to warn Max, but I can't.

The nurses help themselves to our supplies. As if my food is German Army issue. They eat all the bread. And the butter for the week and half the eggs. There's nothing left that I can slip up to the attic. Not without cooking. Then they sit on the sofa for a while, talking to each other. They seem in better spirits. Ilse helps Karin with her lipstick. Then she answers the door when someone knocks on it. Like I'm not even there.

It's two German soldiers. One of them SS. They all greet and kiss each other.

Then they all go to the back bedroom.

They don't seem concerned that there's a child in the house.

Helena and I sleep on the sofa that night. Or, at least, she does. I lie still with my eyes open, waiting for the best moment to crawl up to the attic. When I do, Max barely moves the planks, in case of noise. He's made a tiny peephole in the boards, to see who's coming.

"They can hear you," I whisper.

"We can hear them," says Max.

I know. "You have to keep everyone quiet."

"The children are hungry."

"Helena will come as soon as they go to work. But all of you, you have to be silent."

Max nods yes, but I don't think he's sure he can keep them still enough.

I'm not, either. Some of our thirteen are a handful. Some of them are just too young.

When I lie down on the sofa beside Helena, and the house is finally quiet, the old fear comes back. It's never gone away. Just stewed and simmered, lurking beneath the lid of false security I'd dropped on top of it. But my security is gone now. It's hard to breathe, hard to think, and there's such a sharp pain behind my eyes it makes me see lights. I want to grab Helena and run. Like they told me to.

I was such a fool not to run. I've only delayed the day. Made them all suffer.

And then I remember my certainty.

There has to be a reason.

There has to be a chance that we will survive this. I cling to that thought like my belief in God.

There are four Nazis sleeping in the bedroom.

There are thirteen Jews in the attic above their heads.

Helena and I are standing in between.

I think we are all about to reinvent our notions of hell.

25.

February 1944

IT IS IMPOSSIBLE TO FEED THEM.

I go to work earlier than the nurses. I come home at about the same time. Their boyfriends come not long after that. Since the hospital is directly across Tatarska, it's no trouble for them to run home for a change of shoes. A forgotten sweater. For warming up beans and frying sausages for lunch while my people lie in the attic and smell it. Their days off rotate during the week, and when they don't go to work, they sleep late. Some days, they never go out at all.

I lie awake at night. Jumping at every tiny sound.

Helena is doing her best. She sneaks the dirty bucket down and the water bucket up every morning, as soon as Karin and Ilse are gone. Then she goes to the market for the next day, hauling the fake bags back and forth, while two of my thirteen sneak downstairs to wash, stretch their legs, and prepare food for the others. On Danuta's day for doing this, she puts on thirteen eggs to boil, only to get just enough warning to slip up the ladder with Henek before Karin comes waltzing back through the door, home to fetch her boyfriend's SS hat. When Helena trudges back to Tatarska, exhausted from hauling the food bags up the hill, she gets a slap in the face from Karin for starting a fire in the stove and leaving it.

We have words over that, Karin and I. Very broken words in German and Polish. But I think I make my meaning clear. Hit my sister again and you will be hit yourself, and I don't care who your boyfriend is.

I go to work the next day and beg Herr Braun to switch me to the night shift. I flatter him. Grovel. And he says he won't do it. And I am nauseated at work, sick with fear about what might be happening at home. And Karin watches us both like a Nazi eagle. Especially when we eat.

I always have to hide the food now. If the nurses see it, they eat it.

Two weeks into my new life running a Nazi boarding house, I come home from work with a basket of beets. I peel them, slice them, put them in the soup pot, and Ilse starts to sniff the air, polishing her nails on my sofa. She's waiting for her boyfriend. Karin joins her, and they watch me stir, talking among themselves. But I hear them say, "borscht." And when Karin finally gets impatient, she strides over with a spoon and lifts the lid of the pot. Only to recoil, drop the lid down again, and complain loudly to Ilse.

And after the boyfriends have come and everyone is locked away in the back bedroom, I lift the pot lid and fish out the ball of yarn from the borscht, which is not that different from yarn dye anyway, and then sneak the whole pot up the stairs. The yarn was clean, and Max says the tiny fibers left behind just made it more filling.

If I really thought they could eat yarn, I would feed it to them. Max is very thin. And when it's Sunday, and the nurses are both on duty, and it's his day of the week to come downstairs, I discover he has fleas. There really are rats, he says, because of the food in the attic. And the rats brought the fleas. Everyone is bitten.

Everywhere. I let him wash in the bedroom while Siunek is on duty at the window, and I think about our time at Christmas, when Max had his arm around me on the sofa. And the night before that, beside the window, when I thought he must have felt so caged.

Now his cage has shrunk again.

I want Max to live. I think I've decided I want Max to live more than I want not to be shot.

I sacrifice another chicken and use the rest of the potatoes to make a stew they can take upstairs, and while it's boiling, I try to comb the fleas from Max's hair. I'm not sure I'm doing any good, but the combing makes him relax. His hair is so long. And his beard, too. I should cut his hair, but I know I'd ruin it. It runs black through my fingers.

"We're a mess, aren't we, Fusia?" he says with his eyes closed.

We're alive, I think.

I give him the baking soda while Siunek takes the soup. "Scatter some on the floor. Use the rest of it on their skin," I say. He nods.

I want to cry when he climbs so slowly up the ladder.

But he's left me a present beside the sugar tin, where the picture of an SS officer once sat. It's a piece of paper with a simple pen drawing. Of me. "Fusia," it says, my hair tumbling on either side of my face, and Helena is labeled, too, smiling by my side. But instead of arms, Max has drawn Helena and me with angel wings, spreading from one end of the paper to the other, and under our wings are thirteen faces. Max, Dr. Schillinger, Dziusia. Siunek and Old Hirsch. Malwina Bessermann with Cesia and Janek. Monek and Sala, Henek and Danuta, and Jan Dorlich.

I touch the one labeled Max, and when I hear Ilse's voice outside the door, I hurry to my bedroom, and tuck it safe underneath the mattress. With everything else.

The next day, on my break, Januka tells a story about a woman on the other side of Przemyśl, across the San, who was hiding Jews in an attic. Her husband had rigged up a system, an extra pipe that ran down the side of the house, where the people in the attic could take care of . . . you know, only the pipe leaked, and the lady downstairs kept having horrible dirty windows. So the husband of the lady downstairs looked at the pipe, realized it shouldn't be there and what it meant, and called the Gestapo. And they found four Jews and shot them, right there in the yard, and then they shot the woman who was hiding them, her husband, and her two children. The man downstairs felt so bad he went inside and shot himself, too, and now his wife has gone crazy with the grief of it.

Januka tells this like a horror story, the kind you scare your friends with in the middle of the night.

But it's too real for me. Much too real. I feel the pain behind my eyes.

Lubek watches me while he smokes.

I hurry home to Tatarska, thinking about what Januka said. Thinking that today could be the day the nurses climbed the ladder. Broke through the false wall, looking for rats. And then I'm stopped on the street by Mrs. Krajewska.

"How did you do it?" she says, her shopping over one arm. "I've been trying for the longest time, but those German girls just snapped their fingers and poof!"

"What are you talking about, Mrs. Krajewska?" I want to get home. I want to know who's alive.

"Electricity!" she says. "They were getting ready to run the wires when I left a few minutes ago. I suppose you'll enjoy having electric—"

"Run wires?" I say. "Run wires where?"

"Through the attic, I imagine ..."

I sprint. Dash. Race down the street. Even if it's to get there just in time to be shot.

And when I get to the top of the hill, I'm so out of breath, I can't speak and I have a stitch in my side that makes me hobble. It's just like Mrs. Krajewska said. There are two workers on my roof, right over the bunker in the attic, and a little crowd of neighbors in the yard, watching the spectacle. Including my two nurses, smiling with satisfaction. Including Mr. Krajewska, who I never see come out of the house for much of anything. I run up beside him.

"What's going on?" I pant.

"They're going to put a post through the attic to attach the wires," he says. "Cutting a hole right through the roof. They're going to ruin the walls, I say. This stonework is old ..."

"Put a post through?" I ask.

"Yes. Into the attic ..."

No. No. No. They can't do that.

"... then they'll go in and screw it down from the inside ..."

No. No. No. They can't go in.

"... and run the wires through from there."

They're going to cut that hole and look down into the faces of thirteen Jews.

The man is pulling out an auger, ready to drill.

No. He can't. He can't ...

"Wait!" I shout at the roof. "You shouldn't do that!"

The man on the roof pauses. My little crowd of nurses and neighbors waits to see what I'll do next.

"We only need electricity in one room," I yell. "And it's freezing, and the light will be gone soon. Wouldn't it be easier to just go through the window?"

"She's right," says Mr. Krajewska. "You're going to tear up the walls."

The man on the roof considers, then sets down his auger. "Coming down," he says.

I feel one second of relief before I think what must be going on in the attic. They must have been hearing all the neighbors outside and that man getting ready to drill right above their heads. But they had to stay quiet.

I hurry into the house. Helena is in the corner of the living room, making herself small on the far side of the sofa.

"I've stopped them," I tell her. "Go outside and let me tell them what's going on in the attic."

I fly up the ladder—the chickens are outside—and dart into the storage space and through the hidden door, moving the planks back into place just in case someone comes up after me. And when I turn around, my thirteen are huddled together in the corner, like Helena was. Only they are half-dressed and wild, with hay in their hair and baking soda on their skin, and Schillinger has his hand over Dziusia's mouth, holding in the noise of her sobs. Max crouches in front of them with his hand out, telling them to be quiet.

I know what fear feels like. Now I know what it looks like.

"They're not coming through the roof," I whisper. "And not into the attic. They're going through the wall downstairs right below you. No noise!"

I check through the peephole, and then slide out the false door, replace the planks, and hurry back down the ladder.

And when I open the door, Ilse is there, watching me come. We stare at each other and I smile, even while my stomach threatens to toss my one bite of Januka's sandwich onto the floor.

"The roof is fine," I say, pointing upward. "They didn't hurt it."

I don't know if she can understand any of my Polish. But later I see her opening the door and looking at the ladder. The pain behind my eyes shoots from one side to the other.

And when the boyfriends come, I discover what was so important about the electricity. They have a radio. I sit on the bed and brush Helena's hair while she plays with her doll, trying to listen while they find a station.

Isn't it funny, I think, how worried we were about Ernst the SS man on the other side of the wall. Now there are four Nazis in the next bedroom, and I'm brushing Helena's hair, hoping for the news.

I can't hear it. Whatever they're listening to, it's a static blur beneath conversations I can't understand. But I know it's Ilse talking, with a little help from Karin, every now and then with a response from the men. And I hear one word I recognize. "*Ratten.*"

I lie down with the pain behind my eyes. I don't like the way Ilse was looking at the ladder. I don't like the feeling in my stomach.

And the next day, I stay home sick from work.

I'm not sick.

I'm afraid.

As soon as Karin and Ilse are gone, Helena goes to the well. And fights the Krajewska boys. I thought I'd put a stop to that.

Their mother was supposed to have stopped it. I wish Helena would have said something. But she does win. And she brings in the water. And takes it up the ladder. And brings down the dirty bucket. Rung by rung. Over roosting chickens. Without a mess, and with a smell in her nose that would turn anyone's stomach.

I ask a lot of Helena.

I stay in my nightgown so if one of the nurses comes, I can play sick, and I start porridge. A huge pot of porridge. And then Max comes down.

"Hela said you were staying home from work. Are you sick?"

I don't know how to explain all the tiny things that are worrying me about the nurses. Worrying me enough to justify losing a day of pay. "Just pretending," I say.

"Good," he says. "I want to tell you something."

He makes me smile. He's got more energy than the last time I saw him. His bites are healed, his face bright like the Hanukkah lanterns we set on the table. Helena comes in to return the rinsed-out bucket, and Max bends down automatically, letting her ruffle his long hair and then scratch all through his beard and he makes noises like a well-petted dog. Helena giggles and says, "Good morning."

"Good morning."

This must be some sort of attic ritual I didn't know about.

"What are you doing down here, Max?" Helena asks.

"Being bad."

"Okay." She giggles again and chases out the chickens.

"It's Monek and Sala's turn, so I only have a minute, but I wanted to show you. Look." He holds up a stethoscope.

"You've had a heart attack?"

"Not yet. But I can"—he pauses for drama—"listen through the floor." He waggles the stethoscope.

Listen through the floor. To the radio. "What did you hear?"

"Bits and pieces. They only left the Polish translation on every now and then. But I can put pieces together. It's not going well for them. Anywhere. The Russians are retaking the Ukraine. The Germans are retreating."

"That's close."

"If they push west ..."

"They might come here."

"And if they do, we're free," says Max.

Hope is a beautiful thing to see on his face.

And then there are voices outside. In the courtyard.

No one has been watching the window.

Max vanishes up the ladder. But the door to the little hallway is still open when both Karin and Ilse walk in. With Karin's boyfriend.

The SS officer.

My hand creeps up to the neckline of my nightgown, holding it closed, making me hunch over a little. Which must, inadvertently, make me look a little sick.

Or maybe that's the fear.

"You are not well, *Fräulein*?" says the SS man.

So he speaks Polish. That's good to know.

I shake my head in answer, clutching at my nightgown, a spoon held over the porridge. Karin says something, pointing, telling him to ask me.

He says, "Where is your sister?"

My fear spikes so hard I can barely hold the spoon. Helena didn't come back after she took out the chickens. She probably ran off to play.

Run, Hela. Run.

"My sister is gone to the market," I say. "Why?"

"These ladies say there is something wrong in your house."

I look at my two nurses. "What do you mean?"

"They want me to look in your attic."

The man has his shoulders back, head up, standing ramrod straight. No expression. And yet he looks uncomfortable. They've talked him into this.

They're trying to get me killed. And Helena. A little child.

And maybe that's good, because it pushes my fear away. Far, far away into some deep place where I've put Izio and my *babcia*, and all those people I used to know, the faces in the ghetto that got on a train and didn't come back again. A deep place where I don't have to think about it right now. Where I can deal with it later.

Now I'm just mad.

"Fine," I say. "Go look in my attic." And I turn and stir the porridge.

The porridge I've made for fifteen people.

I can't see their reactions. But I can hear them muttering.

Oh, please, Max. Please have the boards in place. Please God, help the children be quiet.

I hear boots walk across the kitchen. And start climbing the ladder. I put the lid on the porridge and walk over to watch him climb.

"Careful!" I tell him. Loudly. So Max can hear. "I think there might be rats."

He steps up the rungs quickly when I say that. Probably to get his head through the hole and away from the floor level.

This member of the Gestapo, I realize, is afraid of rats.

"Do you see any?" I call. "I've been putting out traps."

His boots have stopped on the second rung from the top. I see his body twisting to look around.

"It is a very small attic," he says.

"The rest belongs to the house next door," I tell him.

Karin calls up something in German, and he answers, looks for another few seconds, and then he says, "*Was ist das?*"

He's asking a question. Like he's seen something he doesn't expect. My heart pounds so hard, I think the nurses must see it through my nightgown. I cross my arms and look past them as if I don't care. But I am staring at my picture of Christ and the Virgin.

Please, God. Please.

Then the SS man comes down the ladder again, fast, brushing off his jacket and shaking his head. "*Ratten,*" he says.

I think he might have actually seen a rat.

Karin looks surprised. Ilse disappointed.

"You've seen enough?" I ask.

"*Ja.* Yes. Thank you, *Fräulein.*"

"Could I ask a favor of you, while you're here? Since you speak Polish?"

The SS man nods, still straightening his jacket. He looks a little angry.

Not as angry as I am.

"Could you tell them that my father is dead, my mother and my brother are in a labor camp in Germany, and that it is up to me to care for my little sister?"

He does, his brows down.

"And could you tell them that my pay is barely enough?"

He does it. And he's losing patience.

"And so when they take my food away and eat without asking, they are leaving my little sister hungry."

He pauses, and then he translates. Karin starts to say something, but I cut her off.

"And also tell them that I think it's very rude to bring guests into the house without asking. Through my bedroom. And to keep them there, with my little sister present."

He looks uncomfortable again, but he says it.

"And Karin may understand this already, but if she hits my sister again, I will call the Gestapo myself."

Now he doesn't translate, he just yells at Karin, and Karin yells back, and so does Ilse. I wait. And eventually, they take their argument out the door.

I move the porridge off the heat. The huge pot of porridge for fifteen that none of them even noticed. And I know I'll pay for this later. Even if Karin and Ilse never come back.

Because I know the fear will be back.

Przemyśl taught me long ago not to divide people by their country, their religion, or even their preferences in politics. The city taught me how to put people in their proper places on the map.

And I know exactly where to place my nurses.

26.

March 1944

SOMEONE IS FOLLOWING ME TO WORK.

I notice for the first time in the morning, with the spring mists rising up from the hills around Przemyśl, the sun coming up earlier and earlier in a watery sky. There's a man looking at a newspaper near the market stalls being set up in the square. He has a thin face and heavy brows that have nearly grown into one. And later, when I'm getting ready to cross the iron bridge to the factory, there's a man standing near the tracks below with a long heavy brow and a newspaper underneath his arm. When I change shifts with the evening workers, he's leaning against a wooden pole for a telephone wire.

I don't look back. I don't do anything different. But I do wander by the market as it's closing. I pause, looking at the wares, turning to hold them up in the fading light. And every time, somewhere in the thinning crowd, he's there.

And it's the same the next day. And the next.

I'm scared to leave the house.

I'm scared not to.

Even though the nurses are nicer to me now. Not long after the incident with the SS boyfriend, Ilse manages to ask me how old I am. I show her eighteen fingers. I might be nineteen, I can't remember. She seems surprised, and it occurs to me that maybe they thought Helena was not my sister. Or maybe they're just afraid of the SS, too. But they say thank you, and they don't eat our food. They still bring their boyfriends home, though Karin's is a different one now. But at least they're more polite about it.

Or maybe they're more polite because they still suspect me, and they're just having me followed instead.

Hoping the man with one eyebrow will forget me, or lose interest, I stay home from work for two days and help Danuta, Siunek, and Sala knit sweaters to make up for the lost pay. We lock the door and let everyone down from the attic before they lose their minds.

Some of my thirteen are unrecognizable. Wild hair. No color. Frown lines where they shouldn't be. Schillinger is weak. Jan Dorlich is a fence post on legs. And Dziusia has learned to go away into her own head. She just sits. And sits. Janek is having trouble walking. They are on top of one another up there. They can't move, or the floor creaks above the nurses. They can't speak, or someone will hear. They are hungry and cannot groan. They are angry and cannot react. They can't cough. They can't sneeze. Or snore. They let the rats crawl over them.

I think some of them blame me.

I think some of them blame Max.

I think they need someone to blame.

It feels like this might go on forever.

It must have been Karin's previous SS man who wanted to listen to the news broadcasts, because now the only thing coming through the stethoscope is dance tunes. We've heard nothing about Russia. We know nothing about the war. Mrs. Krajewska took her boys to visit her sister again, and at some point, I realize that she never came back. But we can still hear Mr. Krajewska. Max says his footsteps go back and forth on the other side of the wall. There isn't as much food coming into the market, and what does come is expensive. The hope that was so lovely on Max's face has dried up and gone.

Maybe the Nazis have taken over the world after all.

And when I go to work the next day, my single-browed friend trailing faithfully behind me, I discover that I am being deported. To Germany.

The whole Minerwa factory is being moved to Berlin, along with its staff. We are to leave at the end of April.

I go straight to Herr Braun, who tells me to go and talk to the director and leave him alone.

I go to the director, who is sitting behind his desk wearing the inevitable wire-rimmed glasses. And he tells me that yes, my name is on the list. I know my name is on the list, I say, that's why I am here. Because I have a little sister who cannot be left without support. And he says that is no problem, because Berlin contains many nice boarding schools, to which he will be glad to recommend her.

But I am not qualified to go because I don't understand my work, I tell him.

He says I am practically a mechanic because I fix all the water pumps.

I sigh. The real reason I can't go, I say, is because I've been sick.

He looks at my days away from work, for which I have written the excuse "woman's problems." He shuffles the papers away. This is not sickness.

Yes, it is sickness.

It is not sickness. Not unless a doctor says it is. So I am going. If I go to Germany, my thirteen are dead.

The one-brow man follows me to the doctor. After a long wait, the doctor pushes around on my stomach, and I tell him all sorts of lies about my symptoms. But I don't know the right things to say.

"Girls your age often have little difficulties like this," he says, writing in his notebook. "It's very normal, and everything will regulate as you get older."

"But I'm in pain," I lie. "It's hard to work."

"Yes. I'm sure it feels very hard. But you will need to learn to bear up, if you want to be a mother."

What I want is to kick him. But I smile instead, like I'd really like for him to buy me some chocolate. His face goes sympathetic. And then I look worried.

"I have another problem. You see, I have charge of my little sister. She's eight years old, and my factory is being transferred to Germany. They're going to take her away and put her in a school, and my work really is very tiring, and I don't feel well enough for the journey. It would be better if I could get a medical card saying I am too ill to travel, so I can keep my sister in Poland and work here. Don't you agree that would be better?"

Now the doctor frowns, clearing his throat. "I will not sign a card for someone who is not ill. To do so would be treason against the *Führer.* Leave my office. And next time, go to another doctor."

I leave, biting my lip, and let the one-brow man follow me to the bottom of Tatarska Street. He never bothers climbing the hill.

I wonder how many spies the Germans have sent into that doctor's office, trying to catch him at doing something wrong.

I wonder how sick I'm going to have to make myself.

When I go to work the next day, I don't have to fake being tired and pale, because I can't sleep. I don't have to fake my headache. My dress is hanging loose. At break time, everyone runs out to the iron bridge, because lying in the ditch below is a dead woman. Frozen. Shot, Herr Braun tells us all, for hiding a Jew. Some of my coworkers say it's awful. Some of them say she deserved it. Lubek just smokes.

The rest of the day, I'm so distracted I don't make my quota. The inspector presses his lips into a line. And then, while the one-brow man follows me home, I hear a hiss. And a *pssst*. And then, *"Fräulein. Fräulein!"*

I look around, and there's an SS officer with his cap pulled low, standing by himself across the street, collar turned up around his ears. He's waving for me to come over. I feel the familiar flutter of fear, but I pay no attention to it. I am a bottle that can only hold so much. I cross the street, and then I realize.

It's him. The SS man from the picture beside the sugar tin.

He gestures and waves and thinks, and then points to himself and says, "Handsome?"

He's asking if I remember him. I nod, and he seems relieved. He's still just as handsome. But he's not any better at Polish.

I wonder what my shadow thinks of me talking with the SS. Maybe he'll go away.

The handsome SS man is thinking again, trying to come up with words. He rubs his hands together because the wind is cold. "Do not ..." he says, and then the word "walk."

"Don't walk?"

"Ja," he says. "Do not walk. Go ..." And he turns me around and gives me a symbolic push in the other direction. His brows are down. He looks concerned.

I am just confused.

So he takes me by the arm, gently, and guides me down the street. The way I was walking in the first place. We stop at the corner, he peeks around, and he points.

A group of German soldiers is standing around a fire built in a trash bin. They're raucous. Loud. Like soldiers. The SS man points at them and at me. "Do not walk," he says.

I step back from the corner. Is he trying to say those soldiers are waiting for me? It happened to another girl at the factory. Walking alone and picked up off the street. She was replaced. Because she had to be. And I don't have a sack of coal this time. And there are too many of them to punch.

I thought I was filled up with fear. I was wrong.

The handsome SS man sees when I understand. He walks with me back down the sidewalk until I am safely at the next corner, then he shoves me again, just a little, moving me the other way. Telling me to hurry up.

"Thank you," I say. He nods and waves his hand, and I run away.

He really does deserve a kiss this time, but I don't give it to him.

He's still SS.

I lock the doors of Tatarska 3 and check every window. I shiver and think in my bed all night. And when the sun comes up the next morning, I don't go to work.

And I don't go the next day, either. Or the next. I pay a boy on the street to take a note to Minerwa saying that I am sick. Very sick. I stay in my bed while the nurses are there, and Ilse comes and feels my forehead and asks me what's wrong. Or I think that's what she asks. I clutch my abdomen.

When I've been out from work for seven days and the nurses are on their shift, I sneak out to the secondhand shops, looking for some sweaters to reknit or clothes to resell, to make up for the loss of my pay. The weather is warming just a little, and I don't see the one-brow man, and I don't go farther than the square. I tell myself it's because that wouldn't be wise, when I'm supposed to be sick at home. The truth is I'm shaking in my shoes just being out alone on the street.

I hate being afraid.

When I come home, Helena is on the sofa, reading the dental textbook, and Januka is standing in the living room, holding her purse and tapping her foot.

"There you are!" she says. "You idiot, Stefi! The police have been here." I look at Helena. She's only pretending to read. Her lip is trembling. She is so frightened of the police.

"Why were the police here?" I ask.

"Because you quit coming to work! And it's a government job, Stefi!"

"But I told them I was sick."

"They don't believe you! And so they sent a supervisor to check on you. Lubek heard them talking about it. Only you weren't here, and then they sent the police, and you weren't here, and now they're coming back any minute to arrest you!"

She ties her scarf and tosses her purse over her shoulder.

"I have to go. I can't lose this job, or my brothers don't eat."

I hadn't known that.

"You might want to disappear tonight, Stefi, and then go back tomorrow and grovel about being sick to Herr Braun. I know they'd rather not replace you, because you can fix those water pumps. So you might get away with it."

"Thanks, Januka," I say, and kiss her cheek. She looks annoyed and rushes out the door.

I turn the lock. I cannot be arrested any more than I can go to Germany. My thirteen will be caught. Shot. Or they'll starve.

"Hela, are you okay?"

She nods, still pretending to read. I'm not sure she's okay.

"What did you tell the other people that came?"

"That you were sick, but we had to have food and I'm too little to take money to the market, so you got a farmer to give you a ride in his cart."

Oh. She's so good.

"That is perfect. If they knock on the door, do you think you can say it again?"

She nods. But I'm worried she doesn't mean it.

"Can you tell them that my stomach hurts, all the time, and that I stay in bed? And that you've been having to do all the work?"

"But we have to eat, so you went to the market," she whispers.

"That's right. We—"

Someone bangs on the door. Hard.

If I'm arrested, they're dead.

"Can you do it, Hela?" I whisper.

She nods.

I turn like one of my ghosts and run up the ladder.

Max is waiting for me at the top. He's heard. We both crawl through the hole into the attic, and he resets the boards.

It's chilly in here. And it smells. Henek holds Danuta, who is shivering, and Dziusia and Janek are surrounded by a circle of backs, to keep them warm. The rest crouch in little groups, or on their own. They are dirty and weak, feral and hungry-looking, like I've wandered into the den of some wild, desperate pack with Max as their leader.

The only thing standing between them and death right now is my eight-year-old sister.

Max watches from the peephole.

I hadn't realized how much you can hear up here. Not words, exactly. Not from the living room. But I can hear the hinges of the door, and I can hear Helena's voice, and a man's, asking her questions. Short things, I think, like "Where is your sister?"

I hear Helena giving a response. And then the man's voice comes clear to the attic.

"Little liar!" he shouts. I jump. His next words are unintelligible, except for "seen in the market."

Someone must have seen me in the market. Maybe that nasty man who follows me.

Helena is denying it, or saying I rode on a cart, and then comes the clear sound of a *smack*. Skin on skin. Helena squeals once and says, "I don't know!"

He just hit her. He hit Helena.

I move toward the little door, but Max holds out a hand and shakes his head. I try to push him aside, and he shakes his head hard and puts a hand over my mouth. I freeze. If we scuffle, we'll be heard.

The man yells clearly, "Where is your sister?"

"I don't know!"

Smack. Smack. Helena cries.

I lunge for the door and Max tackles me, hand back over my mouth. He gets on top of me, holds me down, and shakes his head no.

Smack. Helena is screaming. Smack. A piece of furniture topples over.

"Are you going to tell me where she is?" the policeman yells.

She could tell him where I am. But she doesn't.

Smack. "Are you going to tell me?"

Now Helena is crying too hard to answer. She's stuttering words that don't make sense. I struggle again, and Max holds me down.

Smack.

Smack.

Smack. My sister screams with every blow. And I am crying.

Smack. Smack. Max bites his lip so hard it bleeds. He puts his face in my hair.

Smack.

That man is going to kill her.

I struggle again, hard, and Max pushes me tight against the floor, muffling my noise with his neck. Mrs. Bessermann lies down beside us, staring, watching without a sound.

I think we're all going to lose our minds.

And then I listen.

The door has slammed. Helena is crying, but everything else has gone quiet.

Max lets me push him away, and I knock down the planks that make the little door, nearly falling down the ladder to get to the bottom. The chickens we have left are running all over the house, and Helena is in a heap on the ugly rug in the living room, one of the kitchen chairs turned over on top of her. I move the chair and fall to my knees, pulling her gently into my lap.

Her lip is split, mouth and teeth full of blood, her eye swelling, and she's got a knot on her forehead that must be from hitting the floor. She's not crying anymore.

She's shaking like a mouse in a snowstorm.

I rock her. Like I did when she was a baby.

Max is in the room now, too. He turns the lock on the door and says for God's sake will someone come down and watch the window and bring Hirsch. Old Hirsch had been a doctor, not just a dentist.

Max finds a cloth, wets it in the water bucket, and starts cleaning Helena up while I hold her. Very gently. She doesn't stop shaking. Old Hirsch hobbles down the ladder and looks her over. He looks translucent. A pale shadow. I'm not sure how well he can see. But he says there's nothing broken. Nothing permanent.

Except that Helena has not stopped shaking. And I can't unglue her arms from around my neck.

After the first time, I don't try anymore. I just stagger to my feet while she clings, Max supporting some of her weight, and he helps me get her to the bedroom.

She's so much bigger than when I first brought her to Przemyśl. Her legs dangle down past my knees.

We lie down on the bed together, her arms still around me, and Max covers us up with the blanket. She shakes and she shakes. She hasn't said a word. Max sits beside us, a hand on her head while Monek watches at the window, his fingers turning over and over and over themselves, and the rest of my thirteen take the opportunity to stretch their legs.

Little by little, Helena stops shaking. Because she's fallen asleep.

SHARON CAMERON

And then I cry. I cry and I cry, and Max lies down beside me, covering us both with his arm.

I cry because it's so wrong. Everything is so wrong.

I cry because I have never felt so powerless.

And I cry because I have never, ever wanted so much to give up.

27.

April 1944

WHEN I WAKE UP, ILSE IS SHAKING ME. I START. GASP. AND SIT UP. BUT MAX is gone. There's no one at the window. They must have left when the nurses came home. And then I start again, because there's no Helena, and there's a stranger beside the bed, too. A woman I've never seen.

Ilse says something in German, and the woman nods and speaks to me in Polish. "I'm Edith," she says. "I'm a nurse across the street, and my Polish is ... mostly good." She smiles. "Your sister is in the next bed. Karin has given her ..." She struggles with a word. "... something ... to make her sleep."

I look at Helena, peaceful and black and blue in the next bed. Her eye is swollen shut.

Ilse speaks again, and Edith translates. "They want to know what happened to your sister?"

I can't think why they shouldn't know. "I've been too sick to work, and the factory sent the police, and when Helena didn't know where I was, they beat her."

Edith frowns and tells Ilse this, and then Ilse frowns and shakes her head. She acts like she's sorry, when a few weeks ago, she nearly got my sister killed.

We all hear a creak and scrape across the floorboards above our heads. Edith looks up, and Ilse says, *"Ratten."* They have a quick conversation, and then Edith turns to me.

"She wants to know have you been to a doctor?"

I nod. "He didn't believe me."

Another, longer conversation happens between Edith and Ilse.

Then Edith says, "Ilse wants to say she is sorry about what happened before. Karin is ... she is ... the word, the word ..." She thinks of another way to say it. "She is worried about Jews."

Poor Karin, then. Living with thirteen of them over her head. I nod. As if I understand.

"She says they caused you trouble, and if you would like to see a German doctor, there is one across the street who could see you right now, so you won't have problems with work."

"Could he write me a note for a medical card, excusing me from work?"

Edith translates, and Ilse shrugs and says, *"Ja."*

"But what about ..." I look at Helena.

"She will sleep for a long time," says Edith. "Karin will stay. She's a very good nurse."

I don't know what to do. I don't want to leave Helena. I don't want to leave Karin on her own with the run of the house. But if I don't get that card, I'm going to Germany or I'm going to be arrested, and if that happens, my thirteen are dead. And maybe me. And Helena, too.

I suppose I'm not giving up.

Because I'm swinging my legs out from beneath the covers.

We cross the street slowly in the dark, and I wonder when the sun went down. Edith helps me on one side and Ilse on the other, because I'm supposed to be sick. And then we step up and enter the hospital.

346

I've crossed the front lines now. Into enemy territory.

They take me down a long hallway painted blinding white. And there are nurses walking by and doctors with their coats. It all looks very clean. Sterile. Precise. As different as it could be from rat-infested Tatarska 3. Then we turn into an office with a desk and portrait of Hitler and a waiting area with chairs, and Edith says *auf Wiedersehen*, which is not good, because now I don't know what anyone is saying. Ilse sits with me, and then the doctor comes and takes me to an examining room.

The doctor speaks a tiny bit of Polish, and I think he basically understands the same set of lies I told the first doctor. He listens to my heart. Takes my blood pressure. Has me lie back and presses on different places on my abdomen. I ask him if he can sign a medical card excusing me from work. He says he thinks he can, but he needs to be sure. He gives me a hospital gown and tells me to go behind the screen and undress.

Then he lays me back on the table, puts on gloves, and examines me. Thoroughly. Much more thoroughly than the other doctor. And while he's doing this, which is humiliating, four more doctors enter the room, and he starts talking. Lecturing in German. I think he's teaching them, and he's using me to do it. They listen carefully, crane their necks to see, take notes while I blush. And the doctor is not being gentle. He presses hard with his other hand, pushing into my abdomen. I grimace. I start to sweat. Their cold, clinical stares make me want to run and never stop. He really is hurting me.

And I am trapped. A specimen on the table.

The first doctor is still telling the others something about me. And one of them objects. To something. I can't tell what. The doctor argues with him. They all argue. They have a fight that sounds

like it belongs on the factory floor. Then the doctor finally takes
his hand away, I breathe a sigh of relief, and Ilse is there, with
her hair covered and a mask on. She's holding a tray with a
syringe. A needle about an inch long. They're all still arguing, and
my forehead breaks out in a sweat again.

What would I do for that medical card?

If I get it, then maybe I can keep Max and the others alive until
something happens. Until the war ends. Until the Russians come.
If I don't get it, then they will be left on their own with Ilse and
with Karin the Jew hater.

I think of Izio. And Mrs. Diamant. What would I have done to
keep them alive if I could?

What would I do for Izio's brothers? For my *babcia*'s sons?

What would I do for Max?

There's only me between him and the Germans. Just like
Helena stood between us and the police.

If Helena can stand it, then so can I.

Ilse comes and holds my hands, or maybe she's just holding me
still, and the doctor puts that needle right into me. Deep. It stings,
and then it burns. Horribly. I cry out because I can't help it. Then
it's over, and the other four doctors finish their notes and argue
among themselves while I'm sent behind the screen to dress with
shaking legs.

He never even said what he thought was wrong with me. And
the awful part is, there wasn't anything.

I leave much more slowly than I came, because now I really do
hurt, and I can barely shuffle across the street.

But I have that doctor's note clutched tight in my fist.

*

Helena and I wake up together in the morning. She is stiff and sore, can only see out of one eye, and never knew I was gone. She doesn't speak; she only clings to me, like the day before. She wants to be carried. And I can't. I have a strange, swollen place in my lower belly. Like I've swallowed an orange whole. I can't straighten. It's hard to walk. I can't go to the toilet. So we stay in bed, and I let her hold her doll, and I stroke her head, but she always has one hand out, clinging. A fistful of my hair. A fistful of my nightgown.

Ilse comes by at some point and checks Helena's eye and then pulls back the covers to press on my belly. I yell, and she *tut-tut*s and brings us both some aspirin and some water.

The good news is, I really am sick.

The bad news is, I can't get my note to the labor department to tell them.

The other bad news is, no one has taken food or water to the attic, and we haven't fed the chickens.

I don't have anything to give the chickens.

I don't have much to give the people.

When Ilse and Karin are gone and Helena is asleep, I creep out of the bed and go painfully up the ladder. Max is watching, as always, and a plank moves, and his shaggy head pops out. "What's happening?" he says. "How's Helena?"

"We're both sick."

"What's wrong with you?"

"Nothing."

I can't tell him. I may never tell him.

"Come down while you can and do what you need to," I say.

There's not much to do, because there's hardly any food. But they take what there is.

I wonder how soon it will be before they actually start starving.

The next day isn't any better, and I make sure Helena has her hand on me before she wakes up. She still hasn't spoken.

I don't have any wages. I haven't sold anything. And there's nothing to eat.

I do have Old Hirsch's money.

"Hela," I whisper. "We have to get some food, don't we?"

She nods, her hand in my hair.

"Would it be better to leave you here, tucked in bed, to wait for me to come back, or would it be better if you came with me?"

She shrugs, which isn't an answer.

"Can you tell me which is better?"

She shakes her head no. Okay, so the questions need to be yes or no.

"Do you want to stay here?"

She shakes her head.

"Do you want to come to the labor department and the market?"

She shakes her head no. And then yes.

We bundle up, because even though it's April, it looks like snow, and the wind is an icy sharp knife that cuts right through clothes. I wrap Helena's head in my scarf to keep her warm and to cover some of her bruises, and she holds my hand, and we move down the street like I'm one hundred and three years old.

I get cold. I can't move my body fast enough to warm my blood. And when we finally reach the bottom of the hill, I see the man with one brow, sheltering in the covered entrance of the cathedral. Only today he has a fur hat on.

Oh, just follow me, then, if you don't have anything else better to do. It will be funny to see you figure out how to do it when I'm moving this slowly.

We shuffle our way across Przemyśl to the labor department building. Avoiding soldiers. And SS. And policemen. Anything in a uniform. And my shadow spends a lot of time walking in circles and staring into shop windows, pretending to look inside. When we get up the stairs and into the correct office, we have to wait. Of course. For the German at the desk. With his stack of papers. He's not wearing the glasses, but I can see them lying to one side. Ready.

I explain my situation. I hand him my paper from the doctor.

The man *tut-tut*s. He sighs. He puts on the glasses.

And says he cannot accept my note.

Because this note is from a military doctor. From an army hospital. That will not be acceptable. And why will it not be acceptable? Because the note has to come from the city hospital. Those are the rules, and no, he doesn't know why they are the rules, but his job is to obey the rules, so *auf Wiedersehen*, and enjoy Germany.

We leave the office, and I am hurting so much, I want to sit on the paving stones and cry.

Only we have no time for that. Everyone needs to eat.

Because it looks like sleet or snow, the market is set up in the covered building just behind, which isn't exactly indoors but is warmer than the outside. I look and look for what will feed us while the one-brow man slips in and out of the crowd. What I find is porridge and *kasha* for a quarter of our money. Helena carries the kasha sack, and we start our slow ascent to Tatarska 3.

I stand at the bottom of the final hill, looking up. Helena holds my hand, silent, waiting for me to move, bent beneath the sack.

I feel tired. Cold. Broken and defeated.

And when I look down, I'm bleeding all over the newly falling snow.

Now I have to do the laundry.

And then a voice says, "Can I help you, miss?"

I think it's going to be the man with the eyebrow. But it's not. It's a policeman standing on the street corner. A Polish policeman.

Helena shrinks into my side. She nearly knocks me down. But it's not the man who hit her. I can tell from the voice. And it's not a policeman I ever saw in the ghetto, either.

"Are you Miss Podgórska?" he asks.

There's no point in denying it.

"Then you are who I'm looking for. Let me help you carry those."

I don't know what my thirteen think when the police come to Tatarska 3. Again. But this policeman's name is Officer Antoni. He brings in our groceries and lets me shut the door, change, and get into bed. Helena doesn't take her hand off my arm, even when I take off my dress. She gets into bed with me. And then Officer Antoni knocks, brings in a chair, and sits beside us.

He's come because the Minerwa factory has contacted their office again to see why I'm not coming to work. I explain that I need a medical card, but no one will give it to me. He asks about my parents. He asks about what happened to Helena, and he is angry about that. He asks to see the letter from the hospital. He thinks it's all ridiculous. The doctor says I'm ill. It's obvious that

I'm ill. They should be helping girls like me, not shipping them off to another country.

Let him take care of it, he says. He will go back to the labor department. Or his superiors.

"And poor little lamb," he says, trying to touch Helena's knee. She doesn't let him. "Not all policemen are bad. Remember that."

"But how will I know whether I've gotten a medical card?" I ask.

"You'll receive a letter."

I sigh. In my experience, letters like that can take a long time to come.

A week later, when the food is nearly gone, Helena again makes the slow trip with me to the market. I spend a quarter of what's left of Old Hirsch's money.

We eat tiny portions, and sometimes I go without. Ilse checks my belly, *tut-tut*s, and shuts herself in her room to eat cake with a Nazi SS officer named Rolf while my thirteen starve in silence above her head.

Two weeks after that, we make the trip again, this time a little faster. I haven't had a letter. But no police have come, and no smoke rises from the stacks at Minerwa. My one-brow friend joins us in the market, and I spend half of what is left of Old Hirsch's money. I make a new hole in the belt for my dress.

A week after that, we spend Old Hirsch's money, and a week after that, we can't go to the market at all, because Old Hirsch's money is gone.

But I am better. The swelling in my abdomen is down, and sometimes I can even carry Helena when she wants it. Other times I cannot, and she clings, to my arms, my waist. My clothes. She still doesn't speak, cringing every time Rolf stomps through the house in his shiny boots. The weather has gone warm and soft. I still wonder, every time a uniform comes, if it will be to take me to Germany.

There is not a moment I relax. At night, when it's quiet, I sleep on the edge of fear.

My body has healed, but I am tired.

And then Max comes careening down the ladder.

"Mrs. Bessermann has typhus."

28.

June 1944

HELENA AND I ARE NOT ALLOWED NEAR THE ATTIC. BECAUSE WE CANNOT BE sick. At least not with typhus, though I can't help but wonder if typhus might have gotten me that medical card. Max comes down when he can, though he stays far away, and he tells me this is worse than Schillinger and Henek. Her fever is high. Very high. She's covered in spots. Maybe she will die.

If Mrs. Bessermann dies, what will we do with the body?

We don't think we'll have to worry about it. Because Mrs. Bessermann is delirious.

She can't be still.

She can't be quiet.

And that means we're all going to die.

The first night Mrs. Bessermann's fever runs high, they put Siunek on her legs to pin them down, Henek on one arm and Jan Dorlich on the other while Max, Schillinger, and Cesia take turns covering her mouth with cold wet cloths every time she makes a sound. I don't know how they aren't smothering her. Or drowning her.

The second time I hear a noise from the ceiling, I knock on Karin's door and ask with vivid sign language if she would please switch the radio on to some music to help Helena sleep. Karin is embarrassed. Rolf is in there. And Ilse. And a brand-new SS man I've never seen. She thinks I want to mask the noise. What I really want is to mask the noise above her head.

I go to bed and think that tonight is the night. It seems a sad way to end our struggle.

But somehow the sun rises, the Nazis go to work, and we are all alive.

I'm not sure how that can be.

As soon as they're gone, Max comes down the ladder with a slip of paper. He sets it on the table and backs away from me. So he won't infect me. Or Helena, who is hanging on my skirt. The paper is from a prescription pad, and it has a fake signature. Of the German doctor who signed my letter.

"You're very talented," I say.

"Is there any way we can get that?"

He's not in the mood for joking. He hasn't slept. He doesn't have a shirt on. None of them are wearing much of their clothes, because it's hot now and they can't open a window—and what can it matter when you're all doing your business in the same bucket, anyway? He's covered in sweat. He could have typhus. He's close to starving.

He's going insane from being stuck in that attic.

"I sold three shirts in the market," I say. "And that's what we have to eat this week."

"If we don't get something to keep her quiet, we won't need to eat," he snaps. And then he blinks and smiles at Helena. Like he's just dropped in from the attic for a chat. "Did you dream about the beach last night, Hela?"

She shakes her head no.

"You should dream about the beach," he says. "Before you go to sleep, imagine warm sun and sand and salty water and sharks ..." He makes a little snapping noise with his fingers, like the snap of teeth. She smiles and leans into me, and when I meet Max's eyes, he looks away. Embarrassed.

And I want to tell him to hold up his head. He said once that I was the best person he'd ever known. But it's not true. He is the best person I have ever known. I am nothing compared to him. Not the other way around. I want to tell him not to be ashamed. Because he is a survivor.

But I don't know how to tell him that. So I look at the forged prescription. Getting this is going to be dangerous. I will be questioned. And I've never even told Max about the man with one eyebrow. Sometimes I am so ready for the idea that I might die, I barely notice the feeling.

"Max," I begin. But I can't say anything that I want to.

They're not going to give me this medicine. And if they do, we can't eat. We are living on borrowed time, because at any moment, one of the Nazis is going to hear something. Or see something. Mrs. Bessermann is going to give us away.

But maybe Max knows somehow. Just a little of all the things I don't say.

"So we'll just fight on, Fusia," he says. "To the end."

I nod. A fight to the end.

I think it might be coming soon.

I take the forged prescription, put on my coat, and for the first time, Helena decides to stay home without me. She gets into bed with her doll and huddles in the corner. I tell her I'll lock the door. That she doesn't have to answer it, even for Karin or Ilse. I leave her the dental textbook and go out to see if I will survive the day.

It's been raining, and the streets are messy. Flooded in places. Though this hasn't helped at all with the heat. I decide to cross the bridge to the other side of the city, to go to a pharmacy where I'm not known. The San runs fast beneath my feet, white froth on top of its waves, and the air smells like hot truck exhaust and steaming rain. And the mood is tense. I can feel it. There aren't soldiers on the street corners, standing around with nothing to do. The ones I can see have their heads down, walking fast. Going somewhere. It reminds me of the day the blue-eyed Jewish girl was shot. A day when no one wants to look at one another.

I quicken my steps. And there, reflected in the glass of a long-closed butcher shop, is the man with one eyebrow, hands in his pockets, pretending to look at an ugly poster about Jews.

I am sick of the man with one eyebrow.

I pick up my pace a little more, let a delivery truck rumble by, and make a quick dash to the opposite sidewalk, walking back the way I came. The man has to stop in his tracks, act like he's going into a shop. Act like he's changing his mind so he can turn and walk in the same direction as I am. I do it again. And again. And then I lead the one-eyebrow man on a wild-goose chase through Przemyśl.

We go up hills fast and down them slow. I stand in one place in a grocery and look at maggoty cabbages for fifteen minutes while he tries to decide what to do. I go into the cathedral. And walk back out again. I go into a different cathedral. And walk back out again, just as he's catching up. Then I put my hands in my pockets and walk in one big circle, weaving in and out of traffic, switching sidewalks, until we're standing in the exact same spot we started from.

And when he's moving at a trot to catch up, I make an unexpected dart through the front door of an apartment building. And straight out the back of it, turning right down the alley, and stepping into the back door of the next one.

I stand in the hallway of the building next door, watching through the side glass as the one-eyebrow man runs out the door I first darted through, turning circles in the street, looking for where I might have gone.

All this time in Przemyśl, and he doesn't even know that apartment buildings have front and back doors. What a *Dummkopf*.

He settles on a bus bench to wait, and I turn to go out the back door. And then I turn back. And I go out the front instead, down the steps, and down the sidewalk toward the bench. My heels click on the stones. I don't know who this man is. If he's German police. Secret police. If he's some sort of private investigator for Minerwa. I don't know if he's a Nazi, or hunting Jews, or maybe the man just wants a date. Whatever he is, he's been following me for months, and I'm done with him.

I walk up to the bench. The man has his back to me. He's just pulling out a newspaper.

"Excuse me," I say.

He jumps up, turns, opens his mouth in surprise. And I hit him in the nose. Just like Max taught me.

His hat falls off, and he sits hard on the ground, while I turn and walk into the nearest apartment building, then out the back door and down an alley. I smile as I go, shaking out my fist, and hurry off to find a pharmacy that will sell me an illegal prescription.

I find one in a part of Przemyśl I've hardly seen, and when I step inside, I know I've made a mistake. The store is empty.

And the pharmacist has nothing to do but ask me questions. What is the illness? Who is the medicine for? Why do I have a prescription for such a strong pain medication from a German Army doctor? I pretend to look at bandages before I go somewhere else, and then a whole group of soldiers walks into the pharmacy, talking loudly in German. I move quickly to the counter.

"Could I pick this up now, please?"

The pharmacist glances at the prescription. He barely looks at me. He's worried about the soldiers, because sometimes soldiers like to forget to pay. He gets the bottle from the back, counts the pills right on the counter, writes it down in his book, and asks me for my *zloty* with an eye on the men sifting through the items on his shelves.

He didn't ask for enough. It's not near enough. But I'm not going to be the one who corrects him. I give him the money, stick the bottle in my pocket with the change, and make a dash for it before he can notice.

And I feel good. Better than I have in weeks. I buy the cheapest sack of porridge meal I can find at the market, and a little hope pierces my soul like sun through clouds. It starts to rain again. And when I get back to Tatarska 3, I can hear Mrs. Bessermann from the courtyard. Almost from the street.

She's demanding cheese.

Today is the day, then. Because Mrs. Bessermann wants cheese. I put the key to the door and lock it behind me.

Danuta practically slides down the ladder. "Have you got it?"

I give her the pills, and she runs back up again. I hurry through the bedroom, where Helena has stayed huddled, and peek into the nurses' room. Their beds are unmade, underclothes on the floor, clean stockings left draped and hanging to dry from the electrical wires dangling through the window.

I knew they couldn't be here. Because the Gestapo isn't.

That doesn't mean the Gestapo isn't coming.

And then I step all the way into their room. Because there's a green piece of paper sticking out from beneath the radio. I look behind me once and slide it out. Feeling guilty. And then I don't feel guilty, because the paper has my name on it.

It's my medical card. Excusing me from work. The envelope it was mailed in sitting just underneath. The postmark is more than a month ago.

The policeman must have done what he said. No wonder they didn't take me to Germany.

I wonder if those nurses picked up my mail by accident.

I wonder if they hid this from me. But why? Did they think if I was taken to Germany, they'd have the house to themselves?

Then Mrs. Bessermann screams for scrambled eggs, and I wonder if Mr. Krajewska is sitting on the other side of the wall.

I hide the medical card deep under my mattress, with the SS man and the picture Max drew for me, and the attic goes quiet. Mrs. Bessermann must have gotten her medicine.

We wait all day for the Gestapo.

Max can't come down, so Cesia brings me the dirty bucket, crying because she thinks her mother is going to die. Helena watches the window while I wipe Cesia's face and her eyes, and carefully comb the bugs from her hair. So much for keeping me away from my thirteen.

I send up two buckets of clean water, make a tasteless pot of porridge that will at least keep someone alive, and then Helena and I clean. I scrub while she sweeps, from one end to the other, and she does a good job with the broom. The rain comes down, and I'm grateful. One of the nurses will probably end her shift soon, and rain on a tin roof is loud.

I sit with Helena on the bed, and we play the string game, though I'm the only one who sings. And then there's a commotion above us. A big one. Yelling. A thud. A scuffle. Helena's eyes go big, watching the ceiling. I think Max has finally lost control up there. Then it sounds like someone is falling down the ladder. I get up from the bed. Our last two chickens squawk. The front door opens, and I yank back the window curtain.

Mrs. Bessermann is outside. In the courtyard. In the rain. Screaming for the Gestapo.

Time slows.

Some things are foggy. The sky. The shed with the toilets. The Krajewskas' front door. The drips of water trickling down the pane. But some things are so clear, so sharp, they hurt my eyes. The car driving slowly up Tatarska. The electric lights in the windows of the hospital, men and women running in and out the front doors in a hurry. Max in the courtyard with his hands out. Mrs. Bessermann with straggling hair and dirt running with the rain off her cheeks, a faded, filthy blouse hanging off one shoulder. She has red spots on her face, neck, chest, and hands.

"I want bread!" she screams at Max. "And cheese, and scrambled eggs with horseradish! Do not put your hands on me!"

She staggers in the mud.

"You bring it to me, or I'm calling the police! I'm calling the Gestapo!"

"Stefi," says a voice behind me. "You need to go out there."

The voice is small. Creaking and dry. And it's Helena's. She's still sitting on her bed with her doll. She looks at me. I look at her.

And I move. Like lightning through the house. The rest of my thirteen are huddled around the sofa. Danuta is crying. Monek is crying. Old Hirsch is wringing his hands. "We are killed, we are killed, we are killed ..."

"Cesia! Janek! Come with me!"

I take them by the hand and pull them into the rain, into the enormous outside where people have ears and eyes and there's nowhere to hide.

Max still has his hands out, his long hair slicked close to his head, trying to reason with Mrs. Bessermann.

"We can get those things," he says. "Just not yet, not—"

"I want it now! And I don't want to share! I won't share! I won't share anything with Hirsch!"

"You're going to kill us!" Max pleads. "Is that what you want?"

Some people in the hospital yard are staring through the rain across the street.

"Yes!" says Mrs. Bessermann. "The Gestapo can come, and we can be done, and it can be over! Police!" she croaks. "Jews! There are Jews! Police!"

And then Cesia says, "Mama?"

Mrs. Bessermann pauses, swaying as she wipes the water away, her eyes focusing on Cesia.

"Mama, I'm not ready to die. And if you don't come inside, you're going to kill us ..."

"But you are going to die, my sweet," she says. "You're going to die ... so slow ... Gestapo!" she yells. "I want my eggs now!"

"Please, Mama!" shouts Janek. "Please don't call them! Don't kill us!" He runs to his mother and throws his arms around her. His pants are at least four inches too short for him. "The trains haven't come. Don't kill us, Mama, please!"

"Come inside," Cesia says, taking her arm. "It's not like him. Not like *Tata*. The trains aren't here. Please, Mama, come inside and get well."

Mrs. Bessermann looks confused, but she lets Cesia lead her, Janek crying and hanging on to her waist.

"Max, get inside," I say, and rush to get behind Mrs. Bessermann, to shield her from the eyes at the hospital. Because she looks exactly like what she is. A sick, crazy woman who's been shut up in an attic. When we're in, I turn the lock.

Someone has called the police by now. I just don't know how long it will take them to come.

I can't believe today is the day.

"Max, get them up the ladder," I say. "I'll clean up the mud ..."

"You don't have to do what she says!" yells Mrs. Bessermann, her huge pupils roving around the room until they land on Old Hirsch. "And I don't have to do what he says! I don't have to marry you ... just because you say ... just because I said ..."

The old man's brows are down, but his face doesn't even register a reaction. Did Mrs. Bessermann promise to marry Old Hirsch? Was that their trade? A marriage for a hiding place?

"And I don't have to do ... what I said," mumbles Mrs. Bessermann. "And you ..." She swings her head toward Max. "You don't ... have to do what she says ... just because you love her! You don't ... have to ..."

"Mama, come with me," says Cesia, looking away from my startled face.

"When you love them, it ... doesn't ... mean you have to!" screams Mrs. Bessermann. "Max! You remember that ..."

"Help me, Janek," Cesia says. "Quick, before the police come ..."

"You don't have to, Max!" Mrs. Bessermann yells, and Siunek helps push her up the ladder.

Max doesn't meet my eyes. "I'd tell you to run, but you're not going to, are you?"

I shake my head.

"Okay. We'll be ready when they come. Send them up if you want to." He smiles, even though he knows it's not funny, and he goes up the ladder. And he still doesn't look at me.

The others file up slowly after him. Danuta is still crying on the sofa. Henek has his arm around her.

"Mrs. Bessermann was always muttering about bread and cheese," he says. "The kind you could get before the war. Even when we weren't supposed to talk. Putting us at risk, to lie there and tell the maid over and over again to bring her bread and cheese. I can't believe it drove her crazy before it did me."

"She's just sick," I say.

"Maybe," whispers Danuta, wiping her eyes. "But it's no different than what she always says. That she won't marry Hirsch. That she's going to give us away so we can all die and stop trying. She just really tried to do it this time."

"She did more than try," says Henek. They get up together and walk hand in hand to the ladder. They look delicate. Frail. Danuta tilts her chin to the hole in the ceiling and stares. She doesn't want to go up.

"What did she mean?" I ask her quickly. "What Mrs. Bessermann said about Max?"

"She's always going on to Max about doing whatever you say, as if it's just because of that and not Max trying to save us. It's not fair ..."

"But what do you mean, 'just because of that'?"

Danuta looks back, one foot on the ladder. "Oh, Fusia. Please."

"Don't be such a *Dummkopf*," Henek says, and follows Danuta to the attic.

Do Henek and Danuta, Mrs. Bessermann, everyone in the attic, do they all think Max is in love with me?

When I look around, Helena is standing in the doorway of the bedroom. "Don't you think we should clean up the mud?" she says.

I kiss her because I'm so happy to hear her speak. Even though we're about to die.

She helps me clean, and when the floor is tidy, the cloths rinsed out, and I'm dry from the rain, we lie down on the bed and wait for the Gestapo to come. Mrs. Bessermann has gone quiet. I don't know if they gave her more pills or none, but it's working. And then I think about Max.

I know Max loves me. I love him. We've been like brother and sister. We have lost the same people and cried for the same grief. We've been through the best and the very worst times of our lives together. He's my best friend. But that is different from what Mrs. Bessermann meant. In love with me is different.

"Everybody knows Max loves you, Stefi," says Helena, stroking the hair of her doll. "But nobody knows if you love him."

"Why do you say that?"

"Because he looks at you funny, like Mr. Szymczak used to look at his wife. And because I heard Henek say so."

I prop my head on an elbow. "What did Henek say?"

"That Max should let it go, because you were never going to forget the other one, Izio, and that Max can't fight a ghost." Helena looks up. "I don't know what that part means. About fighting a ghost. How would you fight a ghost?"

"I don't know, Hela," I whisper.

I think of that kiss on the forehead. The one that wasn't fatherly. Or brotherly. And didn't make me think of Izio.

I told myself I wouldn't love anyone. Not again. Not during a war. It's too hard.

But maybe there's no way to help it.

And then there's a knock on the door.

I kiss the top of Helena's head, a long kiss that says how much I will always love her, no matter what. And I get to my feet and go to the door.

But it's not the police. Or the Gestapo. It's Karin and Ilse. Mad because they were locked out in the rain.

They tromp into their room, dripping and without speaking to me, not even one look that might mean "I saw a crazed Jewish woman yelling in your courtyard." And for once, no boyfriends come. The radio switches on, and not to music. It's the news. All in German. I can hear the words "Hitler." And "Americans." And "Berlin." They listen to the news low for half the night.

Something must be happening with the war.

I slip my nightgown over my head and wonder if they'll notice that I found my medical card. I wonder if Max is trying to listen to the broadcasts with his stethoscope. If maybe he was listening to my conversation with Helena with the stethoscope. And then I wonder why the Gestapo hasn't come for us.

Maybe they are busy.

I spread the blanket over Helena and let her snuggle in next to me. There are two beds, but right now, we sleep in the one. The radio hums low from the next room. It's silent above us.

But I know that silence is full of breath and heartbeats. Thought and feelings that can't be voiced. The silence above us is full of life, even if death comes in the next few minutes.

Quiet does not mean emptiness. Not always.

Not for me.

And in the morning, when the rain is gone and the summer sun shines in warm yellow streamers through the crack in the window curtains, the teeming silence is still there, and I wonder why we're still alive.

I don't know why.

But we are.

And then I wonder if Max took Henek's advice and decided to let me go.

29.

July 1944

THEY KEEP MRS. BESSERMANN ASLEEP UNTIL HER FEVER IS NEARLY GONE.
She wakes up weak, half her size, but alive. Like the rest of us.
Like a miracle. Because no one else has come down with typhus.

And something is happening in Przemyśl. Soldiers move in
and out, knapsacks on their backs, tanks are driving through, and
there are bare shelves in the shops. Nothing for sale in the market
except from the farmers, and it's too early in the season for there
to be much of that. What there is for sale, the prices are expensive.
More than expensive. They're outrageous. We eat the rest of the
chickens. I try to sell the sofa. The half table. The broken armoire.
I offer to trade them with a farmer and even offer the shoes off my
feet. But no one has any need for my shabby furniture or my
shabby shoes. No one has money for anything but food.

Then the day finally comes. The one I've been trying to fend
off since the beginning of the war. And it's not the coming of the
Gestapo.

It's the day we have nothing to eat. Nothing at all. And no way
of getting it.

I think we've survived only to starve.

When the nurses go to the hospital, I call down my thirteen
from the attic. Max sits us all in a circle in the living

room—except for Siunek, who is on duty at the window—and I'm reminded of a pack of snarling dogs.

I should have planned better.

Max should have planned better.

Max should have never listened to me.

I should go to the market and see what I can steal.

I should go in the nurses' room and see if I can find their money.

There's probably food across the street in the hospital, if I just had the courage to walk in and get it.

No one is at their best when they're starving.

And then Sala Hirsch says, "We should go to Mrs. Krawiecka."

They stop arguing. Max says, "How well do you know her?"

"I knew her well," says Jan Dorlich. "My sister worked for her. She was all right until she thought I'd lied to her ..."

Sorry, Jan.

"I think she would have helped me if she could."

"She knows me, too," says Sala. "Her husband did business with my father. She's known me since I was a little girl."

"But do you think she would go to the Gestapo?" Schillinger asks. Dziusia lies curled up, silent at his feet, smiling a little. She's gone away in her head.

Sala shrugs. "She didn't before."

"But that was because Fusia scared the hell out of her," says Max. He glances sideways, meeting my eyes for maybe the first time since Mrs. Bessermann, and the brow quirks. He smiles. I smile back. Losing my temper with Mrs. Krawiecka must be a fond memory for him. Danuta raises a brow at me, like, "See?"

I look away from her. "I'm not sure she'll open the door," I say. "Not the way we left things."

"Then take Sala with you," says Max.

"No," says Monek.

"Stop being selfish," says Mrs. Bessermann.

Sala puts a hand on Monek's arm. "I think I have to, if we want to convince her to help us."

"Are there any other ideas?" Max asks.

"Other than we eat each other?" says Old Hirsch. "Starting with you? Now, that is an idea!"

It's nice to hear the old man being himself.

We decide to go that evening, in the twilight before dark, when most people will be hurrying to their homes and the nurses are in their bedroom. It means risking coming back after curfew and coming back while Ilse and Karin are home, but Sala doesn't have decent clothes, and we are desperate.

Sala creeps down the ladder while the nurses listen to the news broadcasts on the radio. We're lucky, because once again, there are no boyfriends tonight. Unless they're at the door. Now. Sala seems to have imagined the same possibility, because she's shaking just from being in the kitchen.

"Shhh," I say. "Clean your face."

We clean her up. Comb her hair. She hasn't worn her shoes in so long they're awkward on her feet. I put my coat over her fraying blouse, even though the summer air is too hot for it, and wave to Helena. Helena waves back and locks the door behind us without a sound.

We still have to get past the nurses' window. Electric light glows from the radio behind the curtain. But we slip past and down Tatarska Street.

"You know the address?" I ask Sala. She nods. "You know the way?" I ask. She nods again.

"Smile," I say. "It's fun to go for a stroll, remember?"

We're supposed to be friends, out for a walk. That was the plan. But Sala is cringing, clutching my arm like a vise. If I were her, I'd face any danger for the opportunity to walk down the street and get out of that attic. But maybe I don't know what it feels like to think that every person you meet wants to kill you.

A woman passes by with her packages, and Sala's breath comes fast. She jumps at the train whistle. She jumps at the honk of a car. I think she's going to faint.

"Sala, there's not a sign on your back," I hiss. "They don't know."

"But it feels like they know!"

"Okay. Let's just walk faster then."

It's a long way to Mrs. Krawiecka's. Almost to the opposite side of Przemyśl. Jan Dorlich must have been thinking about riding in a mail cart when he said we could get there in half an hour. I don't think we're going to get there without being questioned, not with Sala turning her face from every soldier or policeman on the street. But everyone seems busy tonight. Preoccupied. No time to bother with two young girls.

We reach the address. Finally. We walk up the steps. And I realize we're not at an apartment building. This is a house.

Somehow I missed the information that Mrs. Krawiecka is incredibly rich. And anyone who has stayed incredibly rich during this war must be working with the Germans.

Mrs. Krawiecka may have a lot to lose.

Now I feel as nervous as Sala.

I raise my hand to knock, but Sala points at a button. An electric bell. I push it, hear a ring, and when the door opens, it's a girl not much younger than us. Sala turns away, shrinking behind me.

I smile. "Could I see Mrs. Krawiecka, please?"

"Wait here," she says, and shuts the door again. "Mother!" I hear her call.

I tap my foot. We need to get off the street. But what if there are Germans in this house? Right now?

The door opens.

"Well," says Mrs. Krawiecka. The lines on her forehead go deep. "It's Miss Podgórska, isn't it? And ... oh!"

Sala has turned around.

"Oh! Sala!"

Mrs. Krawiecka whisks us to a room in the back of the house and turns the lock. "To make sure we're not disturbed!" she says. "You're not being kidnapped, Miss Podgórska. I know you already think I'm a blackmailer."

"I'm sorry, I ..."

But Mrs. Krawiecka is busy hugging Sala. "I thought you were dead," she says. "And your dear papa. Is he?"

Sala nods.

"Sit here and tell me what's been happening."

She does, while I sit on a sofa so soft I sink down inside it. Mrs. Krawiecka says things like, "Great God," and "Mother Mary!" and without being irreverent. I not only don't have to apologize, I don't have to speak. Or even ask for help.

"Thirteen above, the Nazis below, and you in between," says Mrs. Krawiecka. "Well, well, Miss Podgórska. You are quite the little manipulator after all."

I think I'm being complimented.

She goes to a desk, gets out a piece of paper, and starts to write. Quickly.

"Take this note to the back door and give it to the girl there. She'll know what to do. Hurry now. I've kept a business partner waiting for a very long time, but it was worth it, and we're going to get you safe inside before curfew. Can't have you being seen, can we?"

She kisses Sala's cheeks.

"You were right to come. You've barely got flesh on your bones. I'll take care of everything. Goodbye, Miss Podgórska. I'm glad we have such a good understanding."

And before I know it, we're practically running down the hall, giving our note to the girl in a white cap who waits there. She reads it and ushers us straight out the back door and into the rear seat of a car. Then the girl says, "Wait here!" and disappears into the fading light. It's nearly dark.

"Do you think she's doing business with the Germans?" I ask Sala.

"Probably. And taking them for all they've got."

"Do you think she's doing business with the Germans right now? As in, in the house?"

Sala looks up at the house, all four floors, and her mouth opens.

And then a man opens the car door, puts some heavy sacks in our laps, gets in the driver's seat, starts up the engine, and we're off in a blast of exhaust.

I've ridden the bus a few times, and the train, of course. But I've never experienced the smooth speed of a car when you need to get somewhere.

I want one.

We take the hill up Tatarska like it's nothing, and I ask the man to pass the house and stop around the corner, near the convent. I don't want the nurses seeing us dropped off by a car. We take the sacks he gave us, slide off the seat, and hurry back down the street while he drives away. It's just a few minutes until curfew.

"Do you think there's food in here?" whispers Sala.

I nod.

"Do you think we can cook it now?" she asks. And then we're in the courtyard, passing the radio glow in the window, and I unlock the door of Tatarska 3.

There are two German officers sitting on my sofa.

Sala bumps into my back.

I smile. Like I'm going to sell them everything I've got.

I probably am.

"Hello," I say. One of the Germans stands up.

"Miss Podgórska? Do you remember me?"

I pull Sala through the door with me and shut it.

"No, I don't remember. I'm sorry ..."

"I am one of the doctors you saw at the hospital. I observed your procedure."

One part of my mind shoots straight back to that moment on the table, and I blush. Another part thinks this man speaks good Polish and he never told me what was happening to me. The other part of my mind wants to stuff Sala under the sofa.

My only hope is that it will never occur to these German doctors that I might walk through the door of my house right before curfew with a Jew carrying my shopping.

"This is my friend Sala," I say. Sweat beads up on my neck. "Here." I thrust the rest of the sacks into her arms. "Would you put these things away for me?"

She nods her head, mute, and takes the sacks to the table.

Please don't fall apart, Sala. Please.

I bring a kitchen chair near the sofa and sit on it.

I want to know where my sister is.

The German doctor sits back down, and then Karin comes rushing in. Her gaze roves right over Sala and straight to the food. Then she turns back to the doctors and says something in German.

The doctor says, "Karin has been keeping up with your progress ..."

I glance at Karin. Has she, now?

"... and we think your case should have more study."

"I'm not interested in having more study."

"But we insist that you need it. For your future healing."

"The injection you gave me didn't heal anything. It caused me pain for a long time."

"Ah," he says. "Such a reaction means you should be under observation, Miss Podgórska." He goes on, like the matter is settled. "The hospital is being shut down and moved back to Berlin. We are catching the last train from the station this evening. Karin will help you pack."

Karin is watching me. They all watch me.

I study the face of the doctor and remember it as eager. Curious. While my insides burned like fire. What have these people done to me?

And when I glance toward the kitchen, I see that the sacks are unpacked and Sala has disappeared. The silly girl has gone up the ladder.

I focus again on the doctor, smile, and swipe a bead of sweat from my temple when I adjust my hair. "It's not possible for me to leave tonight. I'm sorry."

"It must be tonight," he says. "It is very important for your health."

Somehow, I think the opposite is true.

"You will bring your sister, of course," he adds.

The other doctor has not spoken all this time. He lights a cigarette and watches, head tilted, as if I am interesting. He has a gun on his hip.

My options are limited.

I keep my face pleasant. "I'll just need a few minutes to pack," I say.

The first doctor looks relieved. "Most of your needs will be taken care of at the hospital," he says. "We will wait and escort you and your sister to the station."

I smile again and walk toward the bedroom. Karin follows, and the doctor looks around.

"Where is your friend?"

I turn. "Oh, Sala? She left a few minutes ago, didn't you see? It's after curfew. She was afraid of getting into trouble."

I step into the bedroom, and as soon as I shut the door, Karin makes hurry motions with her hands. The door to the second bedroom is open, and there are clothes everywhere, Ilse throwing shoes haphazardly into a suitcase.

"All right, all right!" I say to Karin, and wave for her to go hurry herself. I shut the door to the other bedroom. Like I'm going to change. Like I have something to change into.

"Hela!" I whisper. I look under the bed. I look under the second bed, and one of the floorboards pushes up just a little. She's in the bunker.

"Come out," I say, grabbing the floorboard. "Quick! Before the nurses see you. We've got to pack."

"But where are we going?" she whispers.

"Nowhere," I say.

I get one of the bags we used to move from Mickiewicza, which is really an old potato sack, and stuff a blanket inside it, along with my hairbrush and Helena's doll. So we look like we're ready to go somewhere. In two minutes, Ilse and Karin come out with their hats and gloves on, suitcases in their hands. Karin seems pleased when she sees Helena and my bag. Ilse looks worried.

We walk into the living room, and the smoking doctor is examining the hallway with the ladder. But he turns away when he sees that we're ready. I take Helena's hand.

"Good," says the other doctor. "There is a car waiting across the street."

He opens the door and lets Karin and Ilse go out first, and then I shuffle around while holding on to Helena's hand so that the smoking doctor leaves next.

"Oh!" I say. "Helena, you forgot your hat!"

Helena's eyes meet mine. She nods and scurries off to the bedroom to get her hat.

Helena doesn't have a hat.

She doesn't come back.

"She can't find it," I tell the doctor. "I'll help her."

I walk back toward the bedroom, bag still in my hand, and someone—the smoking doctor, I think—shouts words that include "*schnell*." The doctor lets go of the knob and steps through the door to answer him, yelling German that probably means we're hurrying, or the girl is getting her hat, or something like that. And when he does, I take three quick strides across the room, grab the knob, shut the door, and turn the lock.

Two seconds, and the doorknob rattles. The whole door shakes. And there's a fist banging. Shouts. The doctor bangs harder. Whatever these people did to me, they're not going to do it again. I walk calmly through the room and check the locks on the windows. And then Max is coming fast down the ladder with that heavy plank of wood.

"Move!" he whispers. "He's got a gun!" He pulls me away from the flimsy walls toward the stone of the bedroom, shuts the door, grabs Helena, and pushes us both down on the floor to one side of the bedroom window. Where a bullet can't reach us.

The doctor is still shouting, hammering his fist on the door, and there are other voices in the courtyard, too. And even though I don't understand the words, the tone is easy enough. They're annoyed. Or afraid. They have to go. They want the doctor to leave me behind. And after a few minutes, he does, and we hear brakes squealing their way down Tatarska.

I turn to Max in the silence. The wonderful silence. He's still bare-chested and sweaty from the summer heat of the attic.

"How did you know he had a gun?"

"Sala said one of them did."

"And you came down here to defend me with a piece of wood."

"It's what I had."

"I think if there was a fight," says Helena, "Max would win."

"Always my girl," says Max.

I lean my head against the wall and smile. And then I laugh.

No more boyfriends. No more pilfered food. No more dreading every creak from the ceiling.

The nurses are gone.

I jump up from the floor, climb the ladder, and stick my head through the little door of the attic.

"Come down!" I whisper. "The nurses are gone!"

They appear one by one, like ghosts coming to life, and I'm scared to see how much trouble Old Hirsch and Schillinger have just getting down the rungs.

But it feels so good not to have any Nazis in the house.

I investigate the sacks from Mrs. Krawiecka, and there are four kilos of beans, four kilos of flour, *kasha*, butter, salt, a sack of potatoes, and two cabbages. Riches. We boil potatoes with their skins, so we won't waste a thing, and eat them with butter and salt. I watch Monek stretch to his full height and Cesia walk from room to room with her arms out, feeling the space. Janek finds a corner and lies on the floor. As if he's still in the attic.

It's so easy to believe the nurses might come back.

Max watches the window. Just in case. But he does it standing up.

I go to sleep. The Gestapo could still come. We could all be killed. But not having the enemy in the same house with us feels peaceful in comparison. I relax into my bed.

And in the late night, as the early summer sun is just beginning its rise behind the hills, I hear a rumble. A boom in the distance.

I sit up, listening. To a whistle and a whine. Max steps back from the window, and the boom hurts my ears. The light hurts my eyes. Tatarska 3 trembles underneath us. Dziusia screams, and another yellow-orange light flares beyond the curtains.

And I know what this means. If Przemyśl has taught me anything, it has taught me to know this.

We are being bombed.

I can only hope we are being bombed by the Russians.

30.

July 1944

MOST OF THE BOMBS FALL ON THE LOWER CITY AND THE TRAIN TRACKS, but a few make the dust crumble from our ceiling. We huddle together against the far wall of the bedroom, and it reminds me of the cellar of the apartment building, when Izio held my hand where his mother couldn't see. So I wouldn't be scared.

Now Max is the one sitting beside me. He's not scared of the bombs. Not as much as who might win this fight. If the Germans keep Przemyśl, then there's no hope for him. For any of them. I look at our little mass of people. At the remnants they have left. Dziusia with Dr. Schillinger, Old Hirsch with Siunek, and Monek and Sala. Mrs. Bessermann, with an arm each for Janek and Cesia, Henek beside Max but holding Danuta, and Jan Dorlich, who has no one left at all. But they have survived. Against the odds, and for reasons I don't even understand. They have outlived everything. And if the Russians come ...

They will be free.

And so we sit. And we wait. And Max just thinks, fingering his plank of wood. He's so skinny and dirty. And brave. Determined.

I don't want to love him.

But I think I do.

I think he might love me.

But I don't know if he wants to.

The bombs stop falling. Smoke drifts over the city. Quiet. And Przemyśl has taught me what this means now, too.

The soldiers are coming.

We hear the machine guns in the streets. Jeeps. The deeper blasts of tanks. We move together, staying in a group, to the safer wall, out of reach of bullets that might come through the window.

We wait.

We pray.

For days.

And I am hoping. Hoping.

The city goes quiet again. For a long time.

Max watches carefully from the edges of the curtains. And then he says someone is coming. A soldier. Right down the middle of Tatarska Street. He doesn't even have his gun out.

And he is German.

The Germans have won.

No one wants to look at each other. No one speaks. We close our eyes. Or stare at the floor. Helena lays her head in my lap.

I had thought, for a little while, when the bombs fell, that maybe we might come out on top. That this nightmare life of hunger and fear that we've been living might be over. That I might win this game I've been playing against hate. And now, family by family, I watch my thirteen decide to go back to the attic.

I hold Helena's hand while they climb, slowly, rung by rung, up the ladder.

Except for Max. He stands with me, and he says, "I won't go back."

SHARON CAMERON

I nod. I can't make myself speak. But I understand.

"I've asked you for so many things, Fusia. And I'm going to ask one more time. Take Helena and go back to your farm. Find your mother and your brothers and sisters. Will you give me that?"

I don't want to leave him.

"Please give me that ..."

I don't think he's learned that I cannot leave him.

A man yells in the courtyard. Right outside the window.

Max grabs his plank of wood, steps toward the curtain, and I'm turning Helena, ready to run to the bedroom, when the door is kicked open, a little explosion of splinters flying from the lock. I scream, Helena screams, and the room is suddenly full of men and machine guns.

And I stare at them.

They aren't German guns.

"Russians," Max says. "You're Russian!"

"Drop away ... weapons!" says the leader. He's got soot and sweat on his face, and his Polish is terrible. I take a step to put Helena behind me, and two guns swing my way.

Max drops his piece of wood. "Where are the Germans?"

"Who has the city?" I ask. "Does Russia have the city?"

"Przemyśl belongs to Russia," the man says, straightening a little over his gun. "We are ... looking for Germans ..."

I turn to Max. "The Russians have won. The Russians have won!"

"Where are the Germans?" Max insists. "Are they coming back?"

The Russian officer shakes his head. "Germany is ..." He looks for the word and settles on "... finish in Poland."

Max looks at me. "It's over," he says.

"It's over," I tell him. And Max rushes across the room, grabs me by the waist, and picks me up. "Russia has won!"

"Russia has won!" Helena shouts.

The officer smiles, motioning for his men to stand down, but then the guns jump back up again because people are pouring down the ladder from the attic.

"Stop! Who is—"

"They're Jews!" I shout from the air. Max is turning me in circles.

The Russian soldier lowers his gun again. "Jews? I am a Jew." He looks around at Old Hirsch, clapping his hands, at Henek swinging Danuta, at Janek and Dziusia, jumping and jumping and jumping up and down. "You were hiding?" He looks at me. "You were . . . hiding Jews?"

And now the Russian soldier takes me from Max, picks me up around the waist, and bounces me up and down. "Hero!" he shouts. "Hero, hero!" And the rest of his men shout with him.

Max laughs, and Jan Dorlich laughs, and I laugh, and when the soldier puts me down again, I throw my arms around Max.

It's over.

And then we run outdoors. All of us, into the sunshine. And we don't care that the air is hazy with smoke and stinks of burning and war. We don't care that the German soldier walking down the street is now being searched by the Russians, his hands on his head. Or that Mr. Krajewska is poking his head out his door, frightened of what's going on. We are shouting for the fun of shouting, running for the fun of running. Old Hirsch lies on the ground, staring at the sun, Sala sings, and Max hugs and hugs his brother. And then Siunek finds a full bucket and tosses water into the air, making it splash and rain, and everyone is wet as they scream and squeal. He throws a bucket on Cesia. He throws a bucket on me, and we drip and cry while Helena dances because the war is over.

The sky is so full and bright above us, shining down in all the hidden places.

Because somehow, in some way, we are alive.

We feast on the rest of Mrs. Krawiecka's bounty that night and laugh when Dziusia yells, "Max! Put a pot on your head!" We listen to Karin and Ilse's radio, getting the Polish broadcasts on the news of the war, which is still going on in other places but not for us. The next day, a man comes to the house, delivering more food sacks, with Mrs. Krawiecka's blessings. Sala and Danuta make bread, hot from the oven, and Max and Siunek find an unbroken tub in a bombed-out house and drag it all the way up Tatarska Street, joking while they stop every few feet to rest. Then we all take turns having baths. Real baths, warm and luxurious. And slowly, as the Russians begin to reorganize Przemyśl, and we get used to living again, the talk turns to what might happen next. And one thing is certain.

The pieces of so many shattered lives are not going to fit back together again. Not all of them.

Mrs. Bessermann leaves first with Janek, early in the morning, without saying goodbye, and so does Jan Dorlich. Cesia tells us that they've gone, wiping her tears. She will stay with Siunek and his father. It hurts, after all we've been through, to have them turn their backs in this way. But I decide it isn't me they've turned their backs on. Just the very worst moments of their lives.

No one wants to remember the attic.

Then Dr. Schillinger takes Dziusia, hoping to restart his dental practice. Dziusia clings to my neck and kisses me goodbye.

I worry what will happen to her in the dark. When the fear comes back.

Sometimes I dream that the nurses are in the room with me, crawling up, up the walls, to listen at the ceiling.

I dream of my *babcia*, crying out as they take her from the ghetto.

I dream of Izio, hanging upside down.

I dream that I am trying to catch Max as he drops from the window of a moving train.

But when I wake, Helena is there, sleeping beside me, and I remember that life has started over again.

Max doesn't need me to save him anymore.

I wander into the kitchen in my nightgown, wishing there was tea, and find Monek and Sala fixing their breakfast. Henek and Danuta aren't awake yet, and Old Hirsch is snoring on the sofa. But Max's blanket is empty, left heaped in his spot on the floor.

"Where's Max?" I ask, stifling a yawn.

"He left," says Sala. "Early this morning."

I stiffen. "What do you mean?"

"She means he walked out the door," says Monek.

"When is he coming back?"

"I don't know," replies Sala.

Max left.

Something squeezes inside my chest.

He left. He left. He left.

I turn on my heel to go to the bedroom, to yank on my dress, to do I don't know what, and Monek laughs a little.

"Max doesn't need his little *goyka* anymore ..."

I stop in my tracks. *Goyka*. Non-Jew. Me. But the way he said it was ugly. Demeaning. Like I am a piece of gum to be spit out once the flavor is gone. I run into the bedroom, button my dress, and barely tie my shoes before I hurry out the door again.

"Fusia!" Sala calls, but I don't listen to her.

Max has left. He can't have done that. He shouldn't have done that.

I think he let me go.

"Fusia, wait!"

I let the front door slam, round the corner in the courtyard, and Mr. Krajewska is at the well.

"You," he says. "I should have known there was something strange about you. The wife always thought there was something strange ..."

I move on, ready to ignore him. He might be a little drunk. And then he says, "They killed a Jew this morning. Down in the market."

I freeze. And the fear rises inside me like a bird. Flapping. Fluttering.

Squeezing.

I look at Mr. Krajewska. "Who did they kill?"

"Some boy. Stayed hidden the whole war."

Max.

"And now somebody decided he should be punished for not getting killed in the first place ..."

He left this morning. Max walked out the door.

"... someone thinks they should be doing what the Germans left undone ..."

No. No. No.

"And you, I knew there was something. I saw those men coming out of your apartment. You weren't reading novels with them, were you? I don't suppose you could ..."

All this time, and Mr. Krajewska still doesn't realize that I have been hiding Jews. He thinks I'm a prostitute. I stop listening. I don't even care. I leave him talking and go flying down Tatarska Street.

My feet hit the pavement so hard the soles of my feet sting.

I didn't want to love him. Love leads to hurt.

But I do love him. And being without him is going to hurt so much worse.

Why did you leave, Max?

Why, why, why?

There's a man coming up the opposite sidewalk with a package in his hand. He stops to stare at me.

"Fusia?"

And when I look at him, I see the big brown eyes, the quirking eyebrow. The boy who used to make me laugh at the windowsill. The man who can survive anything.

I run across Tatarska and throw myself at him, and his package goes rolling down the paving stones.

"What's wrong with you?" Max says.

I smack him in the chest. "You left!" I smack him again. "You left! You left!"

"I went to get my hair cut!"

No wonder I didn't recognize him.

"And then I bought some butter, and you made me drop it."

And now I start to cry. Not because he's gone, but because he's not. I am such a *Dummkopf*. He pulls me into his arms.

389

"You're supposed to be with me," I tell him. "You belong with me!"

"I know," he says. "And you belong with me."

"I know."

"Do you?"

I nod.

He takes my face in his hands.

"You gave me my life," he says. "Now let me give it back to you."

I nod again. I let him kiss my lips and my tears.

We belong together.

And we will survive everything.

Stefania and Helena Podgórska, during the war.

Author's Note

**"He came for one night, and
he stayed for fifty years."**

STEFANIA PODGÓRSKA MARRIED MAX DIAMANT ON NOVEMBER 23, 1944.
All the Podgórskis survived the war, including Stefania's mother
and brother in the labor camp in Salzburg. However, they disap-
proved of Stefania's marriage and disowned both sisters for saving

Jews during the occupa-
tion of Przemyśl. Anti-
Semitism was prevalent
in Poland at the time,
with vigilante groups
bent on finishing what
the Nazis had begun. To
keep his new family safe,
Max changed his name
to a very Polish one,
Josef Burzminski, and
together Joe and Stefania
raised Helena until her
entrance into university
and medical school.

*Max and Stefania in 1944, perhaps
on their wedding day.*

Max Diamant's ID card, which is stamped with "Jude" to identify him as a Jew.

Henek Diamant married Danuta, became a dentist, and moved to Belgium in the 1970s. He died in 2004. Danuta passed away in 2011. Henek and Danuta have one daughter and seven grandchildren.

After the war, Dr. Wilhelm Schillinger married for a second time and went to Wroclaw, Poland, to become an oral surgeon. His daughter, Dziusia, remained close with the Burzminskis, even living with them for a time, and always considered Stefania to be her second mother. She married and moved to Brussels, Belgium, in the 1950s, where she now has a son, a daughter, and four grandchildren.

Malwina never married Dr. Hirsch. She and Janek immigrated to the United States in 1949, where Janek eventually became an electrical engineer for IBM. He has two sons and a grandson. After a short time with the Hirsches, Cesia joined her mother and brother and also immigrated to the USA. She traveled to Argentina in 1988 to testify against Josef Schwammberger, the officer responsible for many of the atrocities in the Przemyśl ghetto. She has a son, a daughter, and four grandchildren.

After leaving Tatarska Street, Dr. Leon Hirsch and Siunek found themselves living in Russia after the restructuring of the Ukrainian border. Siunek Hirsch died of cancer in 1947. Monek and Sala Hirsch changed their surname to Jalenski and, along with Jan Dorlich, immigrated to Israel. Monek did eventually apologize to Stefania for calling her a *goyka*.

Stefania Podgórska and Max Diamant in the 1950s.
Max changed his name to Josef Burzminski in 1944.

Josef and Stefania Burzminski moved to Israel in 1958. Joe ran a dental practice there, assisted by Stefania (or Stefi, as she became known), and testified at the trial of Nazi war criminal Adolf Eichmann. Due to the medical procedure—or experiment—that Stefania endured in the German hospital, she was told she would never have children. But eventually, after more than a decade of marriage, Stefi and Joe welcomed a daughter and a son. In 1961, they immigrated to the United States, where Joe discovered that his Polish medical degree would not be recognized. So despite nearly twenty years as a dentist and oral surgeon, and while learning to speak English, Joe went to Tufts University in Boston. He earned his second degree in dentistry in 1966. Helena remained in Poland, where she became a doctor of radiology. She lives in Wroclaw with her daughter.

In 1979, Stefania and Helena Podgórska were named Righteous Among the Nations by Yad Vashem, the World Holocaust Remembrance Center, which is the leading institution for Holocaust education, documentation, commemoration, and research. Stefania and Helena's heroism during the Holocaust has been recognized with numerous other awards, articles, film documentaries, television interviews, and a 1996 television movie called *Hidden in Silence*. Stefania gave a speech at the 1993 dedication of the United States Holocaust Memorial Museum in Washington, DC, where she shared the stage with then Israeli president Chaim Herzog, then president Bill Clinton, and First Lady Hillary Clinton, and where she was famously snuggled by Vice President Al Gore. (It was cold.) She and Joe appeared on *The Oprah Winfrey Show* in 1994, where Stefi, also famously, pointed one finger and firmly told an ever-questioning Oprah to "Vait a minute."

Stefania, Max, and Helena visit the beach after the war (from left to right).

I became aware of Stefania Podgórska in the early 1990s, long before I had ever thought of becoming a writer. Not from an article or a movie or Oprah, but when a portion of her oral history interview was aired on my local PBS station. I stopped everything to watch, and I never forgot her story. For more than twenty-five years. In 2017, I discovered her full interview on the website of the United States Holocaust Memorial Museum. I watched it three times, and when I was done, I knew three things. This was a story that needed to be told. This was a story that should be a novel. And for better or worse, I was the one who was supposed to write it.

Stefania, Max, Helena, Henek, and Danuta after the war
(from left to right).

After some shameless internet stalking, I contacted Joe and
Stefania's son, Ed Burzminski, and he shared with me a writer's
chest of gold: Stefania's unpublished memoir. This became the
backbone of *The Light in Hidden Places*, fleshed out with hours
of filmed interviews with Stefi and Joe, the oral histories of Cesia
and Janek, other memoirs, and scholarly works documenting the
city of Przemyśl before and after the Second World War. The
family Stefania sees murdered by the SS is based on the killing of
Renia Spiegel, the "Polish Anne Frank," a young Jewish girl from
Przemyśl whose diary has only recently come to the public eye. I
believe this is the same murder of hidden Jews referred to in

Stefania's memoir. The man hanged in the market square of Przemyśl while Stefania was on her way to work was Michal Kruk, executed for hiding Jews.

In 2018, Ed and I went together to Belgium, where we interviewed Dziusia Schillinger, one of the loveliest ladies I've ever met, and then to Poland, where we interviewed Helena, a beautiful soul who makes a potent homemade wine. Both of these ladies treated me with such generosity and kindness, when I was there to dredge up memories that were horrible. Then Ed and I walked the streets of Przemyśl, finding the apartment where his mother hid his father, the site of the tool factory, the basement window where Max had a hidden bunker in the ghetto. And oh, how we searched for the site of the Diamants' store! We stood in the attic of Tatarska 3 and looked out to a beautiful run-down building that had once been a German hospital. We drove to the village of Lipa and sat in the kitchen of an elderly lady who could name all nine Podgórska siblings. We went to Bełżec, where Ed's grandparents and uncle, and countless others were murdered. We climbed an embankment and stood at the curve of the railroad tracks where a young Max Diamant jumped from a moving train.

I came home and wrote nonstop.

The difference between *The Light in Hidden Places* and Stefania's memoir is that I couldn't tell it all. Not without writing a one-thousand-page book. And since real life is not a novel, time and order of events got some tweaking to suit a narrative structure. Peripheral characters were sometimes combined into one. Gaps were filled, particularly where Stefi's emotions were concerned. But with the exceptions of Stefania getting her papers (we know she fudged the truth), getting her job (we know she slipped someone a bribe), and a punch to the nose of the one-eyebrow man

Ed, Joe, and Stefania Burzminski.

(which I'm convinced she would have done if given the chance), every incident in this novel is how Stefania and Joe described it. It is a reimagining of what was.

I met Stefania Podgórska once, in 2017, though she didn't know she met me. She had dementia, and after our visit, I went with Ed to help pick out some new pajamas for her. Which is a long way from sitting in my living room, watching PBS on a weekday. Both Stefania and Helena suffered psychologically after the war. Dziusia told me that in one part of her mind, Stefania had never left Tatarska Street. Today we'd call it PTSD. But ironically, dementia freed Stefania from all that. She sang and danced and reverted back to the happy child she was before the war.

Joe told an interviewer in Boston that he wished they could have known on Tatarska Street that one day he and Stefi would be sitting in the United States, celebrating their fiftieth wedding anniversary with their children. "It was a dream," he said. "But it came true." Josef Burzminski passed away on July 17, 2003, in Los Angeles, California, where he and Stefi had moved to be closer to their children. They had been married for fifty-eight years. His first grandchild was born after Joe had already passed away.

Stefania Podgórska Burzminski died on September 29, 2018, during the writing of this book. I wish she could have known it was being written. I helped edit her obituary, which was an honor. How many people have the privilege of summing up the life of a person they admire so much? And how much more of a privilege to write an entire book about such a person? In a 1988 interview, Stefi was asked if she felt her life had a special importance because of what she did in the war years. "Oh, I don't know," she replied, waving a hand. Then she pointed that finger. "But I know my story will be published."

She was right, wasn't she?

The legacy of World War II has dark tentacles that keep stretching forward, deep into the present day. For many whom I talked to, it is an ongoing war. The scars are not healed, and the repercussions still ripple. Loss of family. Loss of friends. Loss of histories and futures. Fear that cannot be forgotten. But for all that was suffered, never in any written word or a single interview did Stefania ever say she regretted doing what she did. Only that she would do it again. "One death or thirteen Jews," she said. "It was a good trade." Even though the death she referred to was her own.

That is my definition of a heroine.

• • •

Stefania and Helena in the late 1940s.

Acknowledgements

I'VE ALWAYS FOUND ACKNOWLEDGMENTS TO BE AN IMPOSSIBLE TASK. There is no way to properly thank the countless wonderful people who make a book come to life in just a few short sentences. With *The Light in Hidden Places*, this is doubly true, because this story was never mine. I am only the temporary custodian of it. This story came to be because extraordinary people lived it. The words came to be because some extraordinary people helped me. And I will do my best to thank them.

Ed Burzminski. Thank you a million times for the unbelievable amount of time and care you gave to me and this project, like you give to all who seek you out, wanting to know more about your remarkable parents. Because of you, their story will live on. And, Lori and Mia, thank you for sharing him while we ran around Europe!

Helena Podgórska- Rudziak and her beautiful daughter, Małgorzata Rudziak. I can honestly say that your kindness and generosity will never be forgotten. And, Helena, thank you for giving me what was most difficult to give: your memories.

Krystyna Nawara (formerly Dziusia Schillinger) and her family. What a beautiful joy you all are. Thank you for making me so welcome in Belgium and in your home.

Maciej Piórkowski and Bożena and Wiesiek Skibiński. Thank you for the incredible tour of Tatarska 3. And for the cathedral, and the crypts, and allowing me to crawl through the floor of those crypts and run my hands over eleventh century stonework, and the candlelit cemeteries, and especially for letting me open that casket! Best Halloween ever.

Monika Lach. Thank you for teaching Stefania's story to the children of Przemyśl and for helping me understand the Przemyśl that was.

Piotr Michalski. Thank you for sharing your extensive knowledge and for all the calories I burned trying to keep up with you on the streets of Przemyśl!

Ewa Koper of the Bełżec Concentration Camp Memorial and Museum. Thank you again and again for the kind and gentle way you explained the horrific experiences of the Bełżec camp and for your project to name every victim. I know my people when I meet them, and you are one.

The United States Holocaust Memorial Museum. I cannot thank you enough for making the personal histories of those who experienced the Holocaust available and at my fingertips. This is history that should never, ever be lost.

Many thanks to Dr. Agi Legutko, Lecturer in Yiddish and Director of the Yiddish Language Program, Department of Germanic Languages at Columbia University in the City of New York, who reviewed the Yiddish and offered many wise corrections, and to Tami Rich, Historian & Cultural Heritage Advisor, for her careful and insightful review of the manuscript. Any mistakes that remain are my own.

Kelly Sonnack, my agent. You have my back. Always. It is such a privilege to call you agent and friend.

Lisa Sandell, my editor. We make good books together, don't we? It is such a privilege to call you editor and friend.

Really, I don't know what I did to deserve the pair of you! But I know when I am blessed. Love to you both.

Scholastic Press. For six books now, you have felt like my team and my family. David Levithan, Olivia Valcarce, Josh Berlowitz, Ellie Berger, Rachel Feld, Shannon Pender, Erin Berger, Lauren Donovan, Amy Goppert, Lizette Serrano, Emily Heddleson, Jasmine Miranda, Danielle Yadao, Matt Poulter, Lori Benton, John Pels, the sales team, and everyone in Book Fairs and Book Clubs.

My critique group of more than a dozen years now. Ruta Sepetys, Howard Shirley, Amy Eytchison, and Angelika Stegmann. There is no one like you. How dear you all are to me!

And last but never least, my family. Philip, Chris and Siobhan, Stephen, and Elizabeth. I love you more than can be said in the back of a book. And, Philip, you win the good egg award yet again. You are the love of my life and my very best friend. Thank you for all of it.